*Coming soon from DAW Books
And don't miss THE VALDEMAR COMPANION
edited by John Helfers and Denise Little

THE HILLS HAVE SPIES

FAMILY SPIES
BOOK ONE

MERCEDES LACKEY

DAW BOOKS, INC.
DONALD A. WOLLHEIM, FOUNDER
375 Hudson Street, New York, NY 10014

ELIZABETH R. WOLLHEIM
SHEILA E. GILBERT
PUBLISHERS
www.dawbooks.com

First Printing, June 2018

1 2 3 4 5 6 7 8 9

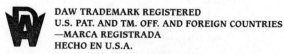

Dedication:
Paul Fisher, Keeper of the Book of Face

*W*_{*ham!*}

Perry's captor slammed the door behind him, and the entire building quivered for several long moments with the force of the door crashing into place. Of course, Perry couldn't actually *see* this; he had a bag over his head. He hadn't expected the noise, and it made him jump and his heart pound frantically.

It wasn't a very well-maintained or constructed building, given how much it shook, and Perry coughed a little as debris sifted down onto him from what was probably the disintegrating— or at least old—thatch roof above him. Fortunately, the bag over his head protected him from most of it. *Calm down,* he told his heart, sternly. He wasn't going to be able to think with his heart pounding like a horse at the gallop . . .

He shut his eyes to clear his mind of distractions and concentrated on his surroundings.

He knew the roof was thatch despite the bag, because he heard and sensed mice and sparrows up there and got brief glimpses through their eyes, though he hadn't yet put his mind to contacting them directly. And there were a couple pigeons as well, but they were on the rooftree, rather than in the thatch or on the rafters. While he slowly counted to a hundred, to make sure the man who had captured him was not coming back soon, he eased his way into one tiny mind after another, getting acquainted with them, getting them used to his presence in their heads.

He didn't bother with the pigeons for now. Anything on the outside of the building wasn't much use to him at the moment.

One by one, he coaxed the mice out of the thatch and had them line up on the central rafter, where the sparrows already were. He soon figured out that the mice were too nearsighted to do him much good, but the sparrows' sharper vision gave him a clear view of the room where he was being held.

There he was, flour sack over his head, sitting on a simple wooden chair in the middle of an otherwise barren room with a rough plank floor. He'd been trussed up expertly, feet tied to the chair legs, hands tied behind the chair back. The chair was a pretty stout one: solid seat and back, thick legs. Heavy, or at least it looked like it. That was very smart of his captors; if they'd just left him tied up on the floor, he'd have been out of his bonds within a candlemark. The chair made things much more difficult. If he tried to tip it over backward, he'd probably break his wrists or hands, and if he tried to tip it over sideways, he'd surely break his wrist or forearm.

A very careful survey, as the sparrows peered around at his request, told him there was nothing in the otherwise bare room for him to use in any way.

Or so his captor probably thought.

The walls were also rough planks, but since there wasn't any light coming through the cracks between the planks, they might be cob or plaster outside, or both. The windows were shuttered, and the shutters were barred in place on the inside, light leaking into the room from cracks between the boards of the shutters. *Huh.* This place looked stouter than he'd thought. Maybe the reason it had shaken when the door slammed was because of the strength of his kidnapper, not because the building was in bad repair.

There were two windows in the right-hand wall, two in the left, and a door at either end of the room. The one behind him was nailed shut with rough boards. The one in front of him was the one his captor had left by.

So, this is probably a one-room house with only one floor, unless that door leads to a staircase. It can't be inside the Old Wall of Haven or the roof would be shingle or tile, not thatch. And he didn't carry me far enough for this to be completely outside Haven.

Now Perry transferred his attention to the pigeons strutting up and down the roof outside. There was an advantage to using such stupid birds; they scarcely noticed he was in their heads, and it was easy to get them to do what he wanted. And what he wanted right now was a view of the entire building and the neighborhood it was in.

The first time he had entered the mind of a bird and made it fly, he'd thrown up afterward. It had been worse than when he'd taken that dare to spin around while Trey counted to five hundred. Now, though, he was used to it; his gut was finally convinced that it wasn't *his* body jerking up and down and making those crazy gyrations. The pigeon he picked was perfectly happy to launch itself into the air and sail in a circle around the building while he looked things over.

It took him a while to identify the neighborhood; it was outside the old wall, but the building he was in was a very small one and quite old; it probably had been a storage building or a laborer's cottage for a big farm back when this had been farmland. Cob walls much the worse for years but still weatherproof, shutters closed and barred from the inside, and a very thick thatch roof gray with age and green with moss; it was unusual only in that it was built on a slightly raised wooden platform so that you had to go up three rickety steps to the door. The street began practically at the bottom step, and it was closely surrounded by other one- and two-room buildings in a similar state of repair. They were all weather-proof and sound, but not one single thing had been done to them to take them beyond that point. It was as if a single landlord owned everything on this street and adhered to the absolute letter of a contract requiring his cottages to be "stout and livable."

The street seemed oddly deserted . . .

And then the pigeon turned its head and looked beyond the immediate street, and Perry knew exactly where he was and why it looked deserted. Everyone here was at work in the bigger building, three floors tall, that squatted two streets over, like an enormous sow among her piglets. This was the neighborhood of the Bannerites.

The Bannerites were an odd but harmless sect comprised entirely of bachelors—unmarried men and widowers disin-clined to wed again. The Bannerites gave men a trade, a place to live in one of the tiny houses surrounding their central building, and enough wages to keep them decently clothed and fed. In return, they made a heavy twilled sailcloth that was highly prized for its strength and durability; as well as sails, virtually any sort of clothing that needed to take rough wear could be made from it. Raw flax came in at one end of that building, and finished sailcloth exited out of the other. Everything that needed to be done to turn fiber into cloth was done within those four walls, from the retting of the flax, to the spinning of the fiber, to the weaving and finishing of the cloth, the finish depending on who ordered it. Three times a day all work stopped so that the men could pray to the "Ban-ner Bearer," though that was the only information anyone outside the group had about the being they worshiped. Every eight days, the Bannerites took half a day off for worship and instruction in the faith, and there were evening instruction and prayer sessions for those who wanted more. Work began at first light and ended at sunset, so the workdays were shorter in winter than in summer. If this was an untenanted Bannerite cottage—and it probably was—he could make all the noise he wanted to and no one would hear him until the sun went down. And by then—

It wouldn't matter. *By then I won't be here.*

He let go of the pigeon's mind and turned his attention back to the mice. This was going to be tricky. He was going to have to convince them that *he* was no threat and that the rope around his wrists was edible. It was a logical solution to getting free; mice could gnaw their way through rope in almost no time. *Come on down, my little friends,* he coaxed—but with feelings, not with words.

But no matter how hard he tried, he could not persuade them to come down out of the thatch. Evidently the Bannerites were pretty vigilant about chasing them off, and he couldn't overcome their fear of human beings. Every time he got one to creep as far on the rafters as the wall with the door in it, the others panicked and scuttled back up into the thatch, and the one he had been coaxing panicked with them and retreated.

Dammit.

There weren't any rats close by either, not even in the crawlspace under the building. A sharp, curious mind brushing briefly against his told him why. A cat.

And as he cast his mind farther afield, he sensed more and more cats, all of them sleek, semi-feral, but not starving. Clearly the Bannerites encouraged cats in the same way that farmers did, and for the same reasons. Which made sense—a little food and shelter bought you a great deal of pest control.

Well . . . all right. He brought his focus back into the building and hunted for one of the sparrows, eventually choosing a saucy little male. *He* wasn't afraid of humans; probably the Bannerites put up with their occasional droppings because they hunted insects in the thatch and the buildings while the tenants were away. Perry had no trouble encouraging the little fellow to fly down and perch on his bound hands.

He couldn't actually take over the bird's body. All he *could* do was show it what he wanted it to do and encourage it to do so. That little beak wasn't as sharp as mouse teeth, but it might be able to saw through the rope fibers, if he could get the bird to peck at the same place over and over.

He concentrated so hard on his task that sweat ran down his face inside the bag, his jaw muscles clenched until they ached, and then—

Peck. Tentative at first. Then *peck,* a little harder.

Wordlessly he flooded it with encouragement, and the bird exploded with energy, pecking and pulling at the fibers of the knot, scissoring its way through the first strand, then the second. The little fellow didn't need any guidance at all now, and he could not have been more enthusiastic.

Even better, as soon as his fellows noticed him working away at the rope, after some puzzlement, they decided this was something that needed doing, so with some dim idea that they were going to get a reward out of it, three more crowded onto his wrists and hands to peck away alongside the first one.

Now he had another problem entirely. They didn't always hit the rope, and those sharp little biting stabs *hurt.* He had to bite his lip to keep from wincing and crying out and frightening them up into the rafters again.

He kept up the tension on the rope by pulling his wrists apart, or rather trying to, and after what was probably a candlemark or two, but felt like a lot longer, he sensed the rope giving.

And when it finally parted and his hands came free, sparrows fluttering off to the ceiling, he nearly shouted for joy.

His first action was to pull the bag off his head, and the dust-laden air smelled impossibly sweet. His second was to untie his legs; he ignored the twinges and cramps as he was finally able to move. His wrists were raw from the rope, speckled with blood from dozens of badly aimed pecks, but it didn't matter. He was free! And he was going to get out of there!

But before he did, there was one more thing he needed to do.

He unraveled the rope that had been around his wrists into hundreds of fiber bits and left them in a pile on the floor by the chair. *That* was what the sparrows had been after: good strong bits of material for their nests. The sparrows descended on the pile as if it had been grain and carried strands up to the thatch to add to their nests.

They deserved their reward.

And he couldn't wait to get out of there.

Up or down? He looked up at the exposed thatch of the roof and saw what he had been hoping for: a trap door set into the roof to make it easy to get up there to repair the thatch.

Up.

Mags glanced at the time-candle as the light from his window was interrupted by something perching on the sill. He raised one eyebrow, smiled slightly, and turned to greet his eldest son.

"I expected you to take at least a candlemark longer," he said, offering Perry a hand inside and noting the abrasions and tiny marks on the lad's wrist. "Mice?"

"Sparrows," said Perry, with a grin that also betrayed a touch of pain. "The mice were too scared." Mags fished some soft bandages and a pot of ointment out of his desk and passed them wordlessly over; the boy deftly soothed and bandaged his wrists himself and handed the pot back.

As he wrapped his wrists, Mags regarded his son thoughtfully. Peregrine would be thirteen in two weeks, and he looked like a larger, better-nourished version of his father at that age, at least, as far as Mags could determine. He hadn't looked at himself in the mirror that often back then, but Perry looked like what he remembered: dark hair that never stayed tidy, dark eyes with more than a hint of mischief in them, narrow face, and wiry body. "I think we can call the exercise a complete success," he said, allowing his pride in his son to show in his words. "What did you do to the men I had watching for your escape?"

"Left 'em trying to catch me. I made a pass up in the attic of the Bannerite workhouse; they didn't dare follow me in, and I left in a shipment of sailcloth." Perry grinned, very proud of himself. "If I hadn't been able to do that, I figured to drop down among the boys hauling the flax around and leave at sunset."

Mags grinned and reached out to hug his son. "Good lad. Your mama was going to hold dinner for you, but now she won't have to. Go tell her yourself."

With a whoop of joy, Perry dashed across Mags' workroom and out the door into the large central room of the suite. Mags smiled and went back to work constructing a series of delicate little telltales of a single hair with a sliver of wood knotted to each end. When fastened in place with a bit of wax, it would be easy to tell in an instant if a door or a container had been opened.

He and Amily no longer lived in the Heralds' quarters attached to the Palace nor in the suite off the greenhouse at Healers' Collegium. With three children, they needed more room than the two rooms off the greenhouse or any of the three-room suites could have provided. Not to mention the fact that the presence of three active children would not have made them very popular with whoever was living next to them. So they had been moved into a suite of rooms right next to the King's quarters, which had been convenient for Amily as King's Own and convenient for all the children—their three and the King's four—as they all played and studied together until they were old enough to attend Collegium classes. There just were not that many small children here on the Hill. Most of the courtiers with children who were in residence at the

Palace left them on their estates until they were old enough to make marriage alliances. Those who had manor houses on the Hill and had small children had their own nurses and tutors and kept the children in their own nurseries and away from the Palace. Sedric's children and Mags' just naturally ended up together. Fortunately, they all liked each other.

Mags finished the last of his little telltales and closed them carefully into a small box built like a tiny drawer that he could easily slip into a pouch or one of the many pockets hidden in his clothing. He flexed his fingers carefully and listened to the cheerful noise in what served as the gathering room for everyone. It sounded as if at least two of the four Royals had joined his brood, and Perry was relating his training exercise. Once again, Mags was happy to be reassured that he and Amily were not raising potential hostages. He'd had quite enough of that for his family already.

As for King Sedric's four, well, they were getting a modified version of that same training, mostly steered toward evading potential captors and knowing where to run to and all the hiding places in the Palace. There had been a lot of those before. Thanks to Mags and Lord Jorthun, there were a lot *more* now.

Maybe it's time for them to learn how to deal with being tied up. There were plenty of tricks to use to make sure that bonds were not tied as tightly as a captor thought they were. And young joints were more agile than old ones when it came to getting wrists within reach of a pair of strong teeth. Perry, Abi, and Tory had learned these tricks at a very young age indeed; that was why Perry had been tied up by an expert in all those tricks this time. The King's littles shouldn't need anything but some simple escapist ploys.

He took a deep breath and consciously relaxed all the muscles that had tightened up while he worked. *That's better.* It was still a little strange to think of Sedric as King, but shortly after the birth of Sedric's fourth child, King Kyril had announced he was stepping down in favor of his son. Of course he had warned everyone close to him that he was planning this a good year before he did so, but it still came as something of a shock to the highborn and his lower-ranking subjects, who probably had thought he wouldn't go through with it. A King? Stepping down? Unheard of! Surely he was ill! Surely there was something wrong!

It had taken nearly another year before everyone was convinced that no, there was nothing wrong. It was still a source of wonder that a King of Valdemar had *chosen* to leave the throne.

And at the same time, Amily's father, Herald Nikolas, had quietly retired from the most public parts of his duty. He and Amily had been working for years to ease her into prominence as the "real" King's Own; she was a fixture as the Crown Prince's attending Herald long before the King abdicated, and when he did, that was the final push it took for people to see Amily as King's Own.

We've been incredibly lucky, Mags thought, as he put his tools and supplies away in his worn wooden work desk and stood up. *This has been the easiest, most successful transfer of power in the history of Valdemar.* The Crown Prince and Princess had had *long* years of training at the King's side, and Amily had had her father to teach her everything the King's Own ought to know. *And me being me, it makes me wonder what horrors the universe has lying in wait for us. Well, a pessimist is never unpleasantly surprised.*

The suite that had been given to Mags' family was arranged in a rectangle, nine smaller rooms and an entryway out into a hall, arranged around a central larger one. That gave each of the children the unheard-of luxury of having their own small rooms, with the other six devoted to Mags' and Amily's bedroom, their very own private bathing room and indoor privy, Mags' workroom, their own library, a pantry and tiny kitchen if they didn't want to eat at the Collegium or with the Court, and a storage room. The storage room was part armory . . . if anything went wrong in the Palace, neither Mags nor Amily intended to have to run to the actual armory to ensure that all *five* of the family members were equipped for mayhem. At this point, all three of the children could hit their targets every time with slings, knives, or hand-crossbows.

Sure enough, Perry was holding court among his sibs and the Royals. They were all clustered at the far end of the big room, where the fireplace was. Light came in through all the open doors on the two sets of the rooms that were on outer walls. He had unwound the bandages on his left wrist to display his rope burns.

The children all leaned close to examine them, the three dark heads of Mags' offspring clustered with the four of varying shades of light brown of Sedric's. "Ouch!" said Sedric's eldest, Prince Trey. "Did he have to tie you *that* tight?"

"It wouldn't have been a proper test if he hadn't. It's not bad," Perry shrugged. "I think all the sparrow pecking hurt worse."

"And now they have a taste for *human bloooooood!*" said Abi, making her brown eyes big and round and wriggling her fingers in the air. "You've unleashed *killer sparrows* on Haven!"

Sedric's youngest, Prince Kyril—called "Kee" to differentiate him from his grandfather—looked seriously alarmed. He was the only one of the four who had blue eyes, and they grew enormous with apprehension. "Really?" he said, in an uncertain voice. He sounded as though he was valiantly trying not to cry.

"No, Kee, not really. Abi is just making things up." Princess Katiana—predictably, "Kat" for short—elbowed Abi, making her giggle. "You've got to stop that, Abi. Kee doesn't know things like that can't happen. Tell him, Abi."

"I *am* just making it up, Kee," Abi said, patting him on the head. "You know I like to make up stories."

Kee looked relieved. "I don't *like* that story!" he replied. "I like your stories where *nice* things happen."

"Well, this story has something nice in it," Perry put in, wrapping his wrist again. "I took the rope to bits, and the sparrows all carried it up to their nests. So tonight they'll be weaving walls up there in the thatch with all that stuff, and their eggs will be safe as houses from now on!"

Kee beamed. It occurred to Mags, not for the first time, that Kee was an extraordinarily sensitive child. *Wonder if I ought to have the Healers check him over for Empathy.*

:Good idea,: his Companion Dallen said. *:You should definitely do that. If he's Empathic now, even a little, the sooner someone trains him to ground, center, and wall out unwanted emotions, the better.:*

All of the children were dressed fundamentally identically, in sturdy brown or gray canvas tunics and breeches and lightweight matching linen shirts. Except for the fact that their clothing was free of mends and patches, they probably couldn't have been told from any ordinary craftsman's children. Trey and his younger brother Niko were the ones in Gray—Trainee Grays, to be precise.

They had always dressed like this—no finery for the Royals. This was deliberate, for several reasons; the practical one was that neither family felt it was worthwhile putting active children into expensive clothing. Why either force them to be careful about their clothing or scold them when the inevitable happened? But another was that if anyone got this far into the Palace looking for the Royals, he wouldn't find children that *looked* Royal. And the longer an intruder stayed confused, the better the chance for the children to escape or get into hiding.

This must have been the sort of thing that Nikolas had to consider all the time, Mags thought, as he watched them. *Nikolas probably would have suggested the common play clothing, but we thought of it before he got a chance to.*

Amily would not have been able to play with King Kyril's children, not with her leg healed all wrong and twisted. From what Amily had told Mags, Sedric and his sibs had been extremely active children, so she had fallen in with Lydia and her friends instead, who didn't spend every waking moment they could escape from their tutors out of doors.

"Enough of Perry's test for now," Amily called from the other end of the room. "I need you all to come set the table while I light the candles."

This was the disadvantage of this suite; the big common room in the center didn't get a lot of light, and the rooms on the two inner sides didn't get *any*. Once again he found himself wondering what it could have been intended for. It was right next to the Royal Suite; could it have been a big nursery, with rooms for the Royal Children and their servants and nurses and storage? It was certainly convenient to have windowless bedrooms for the children; with no windows, they didn't wake up at the crack of dawn. . . .

Thank the gods. He'd had more than enough of active toddlers crawling into the bed he shared with Amily at unholy hours, demanding rides on Dallen *right now, Daddy!*

For once, there were no objections, not even from Perry. All of them trotted over to the long trestle table and picked up a stack of dishes or handful of tableware and began setting them out. *Looks like we have all the littles tonight.* It really was too much to ask the youngest of the lot to sit through a Court Dinner more than once a week, so both broods ended up eating with Mags and Amily or in the Royal Suite depending on where they ended up by supper time. Mags got the distinct feeling they'd have been happier *never* dining with the Court, but that was one of the things that the Royals had to learn to do. And out of sympathy, Mags' three always joined them. And out of sympathy for *them*, Mags and Amily made the gathering complete.

Just as the children finished laying the table, the servants arrived with platters and baskets of food, and pitchers of water and tea. As usual, they left those on a sideboard and exited. Getting waited on was only for eating with the Court. With only a little fuss, the children took their seats on the two benches. Mags and Amily had the chairs on either end. Tonight it was Amily's turn to hand the dishes around; as compensation for having to do that, the one that handed round got to fill his or her plate first. In a very short period of time, they were all eating.

"So, I didn't ask you, Perry, but did any of the Bannerites spot you in their workhouse?" Mags asked.

Perry shook his head. "I came in at the attic and hid in one of the carts when no one was watching it."

Mags nodded in satisfaction.

"When do *I* get kidnapped?" Abi demanded.

"When you are better at escaping your bonds," her mother told her.

Abi frowned rebelliously. "Perry *cheats,*" she protested. "Perry gets animals to help him."

"You cheat," Perry retorted. "You keep escape tools in your underwear."

"I—!" Abi began, furious with indignation, her face growing red.

"You both cheat," her mother said firmly. "And so you should. You don't play fair with kidnappers, you play dirty. You take every advantage you can get, and you make some more up if you can. Perry can use his Animal Mindspeech, and that's why you have weapons and tools, Abi, because you don't have that Gift. As soon as we figure out what Gift you *do* have, we'll teach you how to use it to save yourself and others. Eat your greens, Trey, don't push them around on the plate to make me think you've eaten them, or you won't get any seedcake."

Trey made a face, but he pushed the scattered stewed greens together into a heap on his plate and, with a sigh, doggedly started shoving them into his mouth.

"So, Trey, do you think your Mindspeech is good enough to be kidnapped yet?" Mags asked the eldest Prince.

Trey looked eager for a moment, then crestfallen. "Not really," he admitted. "No. Lyspeth still isn't big enough to come to my rescue. She'd get hurt. So unless you let me use it to call a Herald—"

Mags shook his head. "What if no Herald is in your range? What if you get taken outside the city? Either you're going to have to learn to escape your bonds as well as Abi can, or no kidnapping for you yet."

Trey sighed with disappointment.

Prince Trey had been Chosen, but in a startlingly rare occurrence, his Companion was little more than a foal. He'd been on Foal Watch—his uncle's Companion, Darly, had specifically asked for him even though he wasn't a Trainee, and the King had thought it would be good practice. They should have guessed that something was up, but none of them had. The newborn Lyspeth had Chosen him as soon as she was able to stand, much to the astonishment of his parents and everyone else. So a good part of Trey's Collegium education was being postponed until she could take his weight.

It wasn't as if he hadn't been taking the academic classes and weapons training for years now, so he wasn't behind on those things. In fact, Mags had been concerned for Trey in the last year or so. At the time Lyspeth Chose him, he had been fifteen and still hadn't been Chosen, and he looked as if he had been feeling the strain.

But now he was relaxed again. There was now an official Crown Prince, and it helped him even more that his younger brother Niko had been Chosen four moons later. The Royals took their duty seriously, even as young as they were.

Still, actually putting on Grays and becoming an official Trainee had meant that he was something apart from his little brothers and sister and his three friends. Mags suspected that Trey was looking at his relatively carefree childhood, and now that the stress of *not being Chosen* was over, he had grown apprehensive about what was coming next. As Crown Prince, he was well aware there were a lot of expectations about him, and a great deal he had to live up to. Did he wish now he wasn't having to grow up so fast? Very likely. *Poor lad. That's a lot for young shoulders.*

Trey's next brother, the almost-silent Niko, had been Chosen by a Companion that was a young adult, and Niko—named for Amily's father, Nikolas—was already well into his first year at the Collegium. From his general demeanor, which was a steadfast contentment, Mags judged he was doing well and still considered himself to be one of the "children" without thinking about it too much. He had Lydia's temperament: calm, and difficult to ruffle. He still lived in the Royal Suite and, like his older brother, did not seem to be in a hurry to leave.

Not that anyone is going to ask them to move into the Collegium rooms, not when they are infinitely safer where they are.

Perry, on the other hand, seemed impatient to "grow up." He was always eager to try whatever training Mags suggested; he couldn't wait to be allowed to go down to work in the pawn shop, where Mags bought as much information as he did goods. He'd even had a stint or two as one of Mags' runners and had done well at it.

And . . . he was, at least according to Lord Jorthun, one of the best students that worthy man had ever had, excelling at whatever was taught him and plunging into learning with the dogged determination of someone whose mind was set on mastery. And when he *did* master something, he was as good as an adult. For instance, when Perry didn't want to be found, not even Mags could find him. And that was saying something.

At that moment, as he watched his eldest son dig cheerfully into his portion of rabbit pie, Mags realized that Perry had gone far beyond his father's simple determination that none of his children would *ever* find themselves helpless in the grip of an enemy determined to use them against their parents—or against their Kingdom. Perry had a real aptitude for spycraft.

I never intended—

But it had happened without Mags intending anything.

He dropped his eyes to his own plate and considered this. The first thing he needed to do, as soon as they were alone, was discuss this with Amily.

Perry was pleased with himself on the whole. Of course, the escape might have been easier if he'd been Chosen—but then again, it might not have been. Companions were giant white signals that there was a Herald about. Even though Dallen was *spookily* good at keeping himself hidden, even he couldn't have managed it well enough to have been close enough to get Perry out of trouble. This wasn't the first time he'd had this ambivalence about whether or not it would have been useful to have a Companion.

. . . but he'd seen how his father was with Dallen and his mother with Rolan. And now, how Trey was with Lyspeth . . . and he wondered. What was it like, to have a friend like that? Someone who would always stick with you, would always *be* with you? Sure he could Mindspeak with animals, but that wasn't even close to being the same thing.

And so, the arguments went back and forth in his mind.

That wasn't all. Sometimes it felt . . . uncomfortable, as if people—not his parents, but other people—were eying him as they'd eyed Trey, wondering if there was something wrong with him, that he hadn't been Chosen yet. And he found *himself* wondering that.

And other times . . . all he could think of, especially when Lord Jorthun was teaching him something, was that having a Companion around wasn't at all necessary for what he needed to do. In fact, a Companion might just get in the way . . .

Sometimes when he thought that, he felt sort of guilty. And yet, it was undeniably the truth.

He was just as glad that everyone seemed to be too busy with dessert—strawberry pie!—to ask him any more questions about his escapades this afternoon. Truth to tell, he was tired; he'd done a lot of climbing and a lot of roof-running, it had all been planning-on-the-fly, and he wanted to sit quietly and think over what he'd done to see if he could have done anything differently.

So he was pretty pleased when the Royal Nurse popped her head in just as they were finishing to remind his friends that their parents were expecting them this evening. That meant Trey, Kat and Niko—baby Kee would probably only manage to stay half-awake for a goodnight kiss before he was taken off to bed.

The servants came in to clear away the dinner things, and his father raised an eyebrow at him in that wordless language he and Papa seemed to have had for as long as he could remember. He shook his head slightly and looked at the door to his room. His father gave the slightest of nods, and the faintest of smiles, and took Mama's arm.

Abi picked up a book from the shelf where she had left it and went to her own room. She was always perfectly happy to settle in a window seat or on her bed with a book until Mama came to remind her about bedtime, and Tory, like Kee, was ready for bed as soon as he finished his pie. That meant Perry could retreat to his own quiet bedroom, lie back on his bed, and watch the moving shadows on the ceiling as the candle flame wavered while he thought.

After he was satisfied in his own mind with what he had done, he glanced over at the marked candle. A whole candle-mark had passed. He listened—hard—to the murmurings in the other rooms. Then he cast around the area for an eavesdropper. By pure luck there was a sleepy bird just outside the room where the voices were—Papa's workroom. Concentrating on what the bird could hear, he could make out not only the words, but that one of the three voices was that of his father's good friend Teo, from down in Haven. Teo had been Perry's kidnapper.

". . . cleaner'n a rat's whisker," Teo was saying, with admiration. "Prettier piece'a work I niver saw."

Perry smiled in satisfaction. If he'd left *Teo* in the dust, likely the only person who'd have been able to track him would have been someone else trained the same way he and his father had been. He stopped listening through the bird. It tickled him no end to hear Teo praise him, but his pride wasn't so great that he needed to hear more.

Despite his bandaged wrists—trivial, really—it had been an altogether excellent day. *And no lessons tomorrow.* There had been a big box of new books delivered to the Palace library a few days ago, and he and Abi had been given leave to take whatever they wanted from there to read. In fact, that was probably where Abi had gotten the book she was reading now. He got up and trotted over to his father's workroom, which was where Teo, Papa, and Mama were talking. He made sure to make enough sound so they noticed him.

All three heads swiveled toward him as if they had been pulled by the same invisible string. Perry choked back a giggle.

"Library?" he said.

His father made a shooing motion. "Go. Stay up reading as long as you like. Sleep as late as you like. You've got no lessons tomorrow and you've earned it."

"Aye, that!" Teo agreed heartily.

Perry grinned and trotted for the door. This was turning out to be one of the best days of his life.

2

As of this year, when he had turned thirteen, Perry had followed in Trey and Niko's footsteps; he had left the little schoolroom in the Royal Suite where all the youngsters had studied together under the auspices of a pair of tutors and began taking classes at the Collegia—mostly at Heralds' although the history class he was taking was taught at Bardic. But since he wasn't a Trainee and didn't have the classes with a Companion—combat riding and agility training—his afternoons alternated between private lessons with Lord Jorthun's own Armsmaster and spycraft lessons with Lord Jorthun himself. The private lessons were devoted to the sort of fighting that never took place on a battlefield—dirty tricks stuff, real street combat, and the sort of thing you'd get into scrumming with criminals. He knew how to ride, of course, and Armsmaster Leandro combined his arms training with riding—but there were specific things that the Trainees learned with their Companions that required that mind-to-mind bond. Whenever he watched them, particularly the Grays about a year away from going into Whites, it always made him drop his jaw in amazement. And he felt more than a mere twinge of envy when he watched his father and Dallen practice; they were at one in a way that simply was not possible, and would be life-risking to try, with a mere horse. Or would it? Could he master Animal Mindspeech well enough so that he *could* do that sort of thing with a horse? He wondered sometimes. It would have to be a remarkable horse . . . and he'd have to be awfully good at Mindspeech. And it would never be the same as being Chosen . . . but . . .

He didn't miss the schoolroom itself, though he missed the competition with Abi. It didn't seem right to make lessons into a competition with his classmates. He couldn't put a finger on *why,* exactly, just that it didn't. Maybe it was that the competition with Abi was always friendly, and he wasn't sure how the other students would take it? Or just that now that it wasn't among family, it didn't feel right to compete? Or maybe it was just because he could see some of the others were struggling, and it felt as if he shouldn't be making them feel worse.

At any rate, morning was lessons in the classrooms of the Collegia. Afternoons were spent with Lord Jorthun.

His Lordship had warned Perry a long time ago that "spycraft is mostly boring." What Lord Jorthun had actually meant, Perry suspected now, was that "spycraft is mostly *watching.* " Which, of course, it was, and watching could be boring if you had to do it for days and days and days. But also, in order to make yourself invisible so you could do that watching, you had to learn to do a lot of potentially boring things.

Today, for instance. Lord Jorthun and some of the Queen's Handmaidens were staging a Court Feast—an abbreviated one, of course—with himself and Lady Dia standing in for the King and Queen. Ostensibly this was a rehearsal to train the Handmaidens in the etiquette of such an affair. Actually this was a test for Perry. He was among the highly trained servants, and he was supposed to pass for one. He'd been preparing for this for a good moon; now they'd all find out if he could not only pass for one of the servants to those supervising the servants, but also pick out which of the Handmaidens were passing information to each other.

He had to rush to the kitchen, select the platter someone of his training would be allowed to handle, and rush out, serve properly, and rush back to the kitchen with the platter. He wasn't allowed to wait on the Lord or Lady—that was the privilege of the highest-ranked servants. He also wasn't to take platters to those—here, imaginary—guests "below the salt." They were only "waited on" by the lowest-ranked servers, who left platters of food at intervals along the table and, at a real dinner or feast, took them away only when empty. He was serving the Handmaidens on the left side of the table; offering the platter to each, describing what was on it, and then serving some of the purely imaginary food to her if she indicated she wanted it. He was not to drip any sauces or spill anything—Lord Jorthun and the Head Steward were both keeping a sharp eye on all the boys to make sure platters stayed perfectly level and imaginary serving was deft. He was not to skip any of the girls he was assigned to. He was not to make conversation with them nor dally too long with any of them. He was not to laugh or be flirtatious. Above all, he was not to stand out from among the other serving boys. And all the while, he looked for the tiny signs of messages being passed.

About halfway through the "meal"—thank goodness, no one was actually being served or eating anything, because that would have made this torturously long—he knew which of the girls were his targets. And he was fairly confident none of the servants had any idea he wasn't one of them. He'd managed to fetch and carry and pretend to serve and clear away without a single fumble.

It was all over in about two candlemarks. Lord Jorthun thanked the servants (borrowed from the Palace) and his steward sent them back; Perry thought the steward was giving them little gifts of money for their extra service, which would be just like Lord Jorthun. The steward had been the only one besides those at the table who had known he wasn't what he seemed. The other servants probably assumed he was one of Lord Jorthun's household.

Perry went off to a storage room where he changed from his borrowed livery into his regular clothing and joined his mentor and the Handmaidens. The Queen's Handmaidens were Dia's own clever spy corps.

How the group had come to exist was a little story in itself. The Palace simply could not support all of the attendants most of the highborn ladies would prefer to have brought with them. And those maidservants that they *did* bring were often at odds with one another and the cause of a great deal of disturbance and even outright fighting among themselves and between the ladies they served. In the middle of one such outbreak, Dia and Mags had had the brilliant idea of creating the Queen's Handmaidens to tend to the ladies' needs, instead. These were young women of highborn status but no wealth, who might otherwise have been little better than unpaid servants to their better-off relatives. Trained by Dia, they got regular pay that they could save for their own purposes, a certain cachet and status, were housed in the Palace itself, and were not under the control of any single lady, but rather reported to the Queen's steward. They served as the personal handmaidens to the ladies of the Queen's Court—and kept their clever eyes and ears open at all times. There wasn't a breath of gossip that stirred that one or more of them didn't hear. And they reported it all back to Amily and Dia.

"All right, Perry, I can tell you that not one of the servants suspected you were anything but what you seemed, so you've passed the first half of your trial," Jorthun said, as he entered the library where they were all sitting. "My steward is satisfied with your serving abilities. So now, for the second half, can you tell me which of these young ladies was a naughty minx?"

"Alyson and Seris," he said, promptly. "They were passing notes under the dish of salt. Alyson sent Seris two, and Seris sent Alyson three."

The other Handmaidens giggled, as a red-faced Alyson held up the three, tiny folded pieces of paper she had gotten, and Seris held up her two.

"Girls, if you have to pass a note, pass only one," Dia chided gently. "The more notes you pass, the more likely it is you will be caught. And do so by dropping it in your folded napkin to the floor, if there is no tablecovering, or simply exchanging napkins under the table covering if there *is* one."

"Yes, Lady Dia," they chorused.

"Now to be fair, *I* did not see the exchanges," Dia continued. "So at least you were not obvious to a simple participant in the meal. And also, to be fair, with actual food on the table, probably the only person who would have had a chance of catching you would be a real spy among the servants, as Perry was, or a spy among the guests."

"And if there is a spy among the servants, it had better be one of Mags'," Jorthun growled, with a fierce glower. Which only made the Handmaidens giggle again.

"All right, then, young ladies. Back you go to the Palace, before your ladies miss you," Dia told them, making a dismissive motion with her hands. "And thank you for helping."

When they had gone, Perry took the seat that Jorthun indicated, facing him and Lady Dia.

This was an extremely comfortable room, and it was the one in which his mentor met him the most often. But that was not because of the comfort—it was because it was the room in which they were the least likely to be spied upon themselves. Thanks to the muffling qualities of the walls of books, anyone speaking quietly could not be heard at either the door or the windows, and there were fire screens specifically designed to prevent voices from traveling up the chimney in front of the hearth.

The furniture was also comfortable, wooden settles softened with stuffed cushions on the seats and backs. Lord Jorthun sat at ease, looking his usual dignified self: long, silver-white hair, imposing eyebrows, and neatly trimmed beard making a frame for his piercing blue eyes. It was hard to say just *how* old he was; certainly he had been a spymaster long enough to have trained Herald Nikolas, Perry's grandpapa. He was staggeringly rich as well as highborn; how he had turned his hand to spycraft was probably a fascinating story, but it was one he hadn't shared with Perry.

More's the pity.

As for his wife, Perry thought Lady Dia was probably the most beautiful woman he knew, bar the Queen. He loved his mama, but Lady Dia was something very special. He couldn't have articulated why she was so beautiful, only that she was, and everyone in the Court would probably agree with him. Today her knee-length dark hair had been braided and wound into an elaborate crown held in place with a couple of silver ornaments. Beneath that crown of silken hair was a face everyone called stunning.

"Well, you've mastered being a table servant, Perry," Jorthun said, when they were all settled. "What would you like to learn next?"

"Dog boy," he said promptly. Lady Dia was known for her special dogs; there were waiting lists among the highborn for her protection mastiffs and her muff-dogs. "Pretty much any highborn living in the country has a pack of hunting hounds and probably other dogs, too. Nobody ever pays attention to the hound boy."

"Good choice," Jorthun said, as Dia nodded. "Your gift of Animal Mindspeech should make this an easy task to master, so why don't we add stable boy and falconer to the list for you to tackle this summer? That will get all three out of the way at once, and all three put you in a good position to hear most of the household business."

"Turn up tomorrow morning in old clothing that you won't need to worry about, because hound boy is a dirty job," Dia added. "I'll tell my kennel chief to expect you."

He grinned. He was going to enjoy this, dirty job or not. And it would give him a lot more exercise in his Gift. He enjoyed the bright, sharp minds of the birds of prey—simple, deadly, unambiguous. And of course, there was nothing better to be among than the affectionate minds of dogs and horses. Actually, he was rather glad his Gift was *Animal* Mindspeech. He did not envy his father having to delve into the murky, tangled, and devious minds of human beings.

Lord Jorthun craned his neck a little to look out the window. "Well, Perry, we seem to have finished the test much sooner than I anticipated. Run along to the armory and tell Master Leandro I think he should give you a little workout before you go back to the Palace for supper."

Perry sprang to his feet. "Aye, m'lord!" he said with enthusiasm, sketched a suggestion of a bow, and, as ordered, ran.

Master Leandro was indeed in the Armory, doing an inspection. Lord Jorthun rarely allowed anyone into his armory, and if he had, they would surely have been surprised, even shocked, at the number of weapons stockpiled there. The room was easily big enough to hold eight farm carts, and it was *full* of weapons: weapons on racks bolted to the stone floor, weapons on racks bolted to the walls, pole weapons and spears neatly bundled in stands in the corners, and entire chests of crossbow bolts and arrows. It looked as though Lord Jorthun was prepared to outlast quite a long siege.

Part of the reason for that was that Lord Jorthun's manor was one of the oldest on the Hill, at least, the core of it was. Things had been uncertain enough in those days that every highborn with a manor on the Hill had his own private militia to augment the Guard. So some of the weapons in Lord Jorthun's armory were heirlooms, dating all the way back to those long-ago days. Perhaps even as many as half.

But half were certainly not. And only a select few people knew that every one of Lord Jorthun's servants was trained in the use of at least one weapon, even the smallest pages, who were impressive shots with slings. Although not every ruling Lord of Jorthun's line had been a spymaster in the service of the King, they all had fielded a secret force consisting of the members of the household in case of a dire emergency.

Hence, Jorthun's own personal armorer and Weaponsmaster.

But Master Leandro was more than "just" that. He was as much Artificer as weaponsmaster. He had created the weapons that Amily and Mags had had sewn into their formal Whites and their wedding clothes—as well as the garrotes and wire saws that were sewn into the hems of all their children's outfits. He had created a clever little folding hand-crossbow that could fit in a sleeve. And he probably had plenty more inventions of offense and defense that Perry hadn't been shown as yet. He kept all of those in a workshop only Lord Jorthun and Lady Dia were allowed into. Yes, even in Lord Jorthun's own manor, Master Leandro could forbid *anyone* entry into his workshop!

Master Leandro turned at the sound of Perry's running steps and grinned to see his pupil. "Finished early, did you? Excellent! I was just thinking I wanted to give you a refresher in dagger."

"Wood or full metal?" Perry asked promptly, heading for the rack where the practice weapons he had been allotted were kept.

"Wood," Master Leandro replied, in a lazy drawl. "I'd rather not go into armor this afternoon."

Perry perked up at that. When Master Leandro used that tone of voice, and didn't want to go into armor, it meant he was going to teach Perry a new trick or two.

Half a candlemark later, Perry was extremely glad that the grass in the spot in the gardens that Master Leandro used for outdoor practice was thick and soft, because for the tenth time, he was lying on his back with the breath knocked out of him.

The Master had already taught him a clever disarming technique that also left your opponent with his arm immobilized with pain from a rap on the elbow in just the right place. Now Leandro was trying to teach him a feint-feint-leg-sweep pattern that let you catch your opponent off balance. A *very* dirty-tricks move, since Perry could easily see how you could, if you were on the right sort of ground, combine that with a handful of dirt or sand in the eyes and have your opponent completely at your mercy. Assuming he could get the timing right, because when he didn't, Leandro put him in the grass. Which was ten out of twelve tries so far.

Three more grass landings. He was getting bruised all over and was beginning to think this was going to be trickier than he had thought.

Another half a candlemark, and he lay in the grass, panting, and realized he was not going to be able to get up for a while. At least, not on his own. As he stared at darkening blue sky framed by green branches, Master Leandro's narrow face interposed itself between him and his view. His expression harbored a rare hint of sympathy.

"I believe I wore you out," Leandro said conversationally. "I haven't done that for a while. To be fair, I didn't think you'd get the timing of this in one session. And you certainly got the disarming trick fast enough. I'm satisfied." Leandro offered Perry a hand. Perry took it, and Leandro hauled him to his feet as Perry groaned.

"Whoever taught that to you must have been a demon in human form," Perry said, feelingly.

Leandro held out his hand for the practice dagger; Perry gave it to him and brushed himself off. "You didn't do badly," the Master observed, which made Perry feel a *little* better, even if it didn't help the bruises. "Your father certainly didn't do any better when I taught it to him, if I recall. Two or three more sessions and you might have it. Get along with you." And with that, Leandro turned and headed back to the armory or his workshop. The Master generally did not waste time on idle chitchat. When you were done with a session, you were done, and he expected you to get to the next thing on your schedule, since he certainly would.

Perry got, and he plodded wearily by back ways to one of the Palace gates usually used by servants, the Guard, and other underlings; by now, of course, the Guards at that gate knew him by sight and were well accustomed to seeing him turn up with grass-stained clothing, bruised, and much the worse for wear. They let him in with only the challenge of the password of the day—which the previous shift had given him on the way out—and a sympathetic look. After all, they knew all too well something of what he'd just been through. They all had weaponstrainers, too, and by their very nature, trainers were never easy on you, because being easy on you had the potential to get you killed.

Now would be a nice time to have a Companion, he thought wistfully, as he trudged along the path to the Palace, which seemed about a hundred furlongs away. *I'd be in a hot bath already.*

———————

A quick wash-up and a change of clothing restored his spirits, if nothing else. When he returned from the bathing room that the family suite shared with the Royals, he saw that both his parents were waiting in the big central chamber. Amily was in her semiformal Whites, and his father was wearing a Royal Guard uniform instead of Herald Whites. "Oh, good, you're back" his mother said. "Abi's gone to collect the others; an ambassador's turned up a day early, so we adults will all be doing a full Court dinner. You younglings will have to make do at the Collegium."

"It's pocket-pie night," his father added, with a wink, and Perry perked up right away. He and his sibs shared their father's hearty enjoyment of pocket pies. And he didn't think, after this afternoon, he'd have been able to bear a long, tedious Court dinner.

He plopped down on a cushion to wait for the rest, as his parents left for their duties. They didn't take long.

"Come on!" Abi said, poking her head in the door, just as the Collegium bell for dinner rang. "Don't dawdle!"

He snorted, getting as quickly as he could to his feet. As if he'd dawdle on a pocket-pie night!

They all hurried in a group down to the Heralds' Collegium Hall, a big communal room that was mostly used for eating but could serve as an indoor gathering space for almost any function that needed room for a lot of people. On pocket-pie night, instead of platters being brought to the tables, the Trainees were expected to serve themselves from a sort of sideboard, and they were free to take their food anywhere they cared to eat. Most still chose to eat in the hall, but some went outdoors, especially in good weather like tonight, and some ate in their rooms, studying or reading.

As usual, Kee was subdued when surrounded by all the boisterous Trainees and stuck to his sister Kat's side as if he had been sewn to her tunic. Still feeling sore and bruised by his workout, Perry took pity on him—and on Kat, who looked rather tired of him—and took the little boy's hand.

"What do you want?" he asked; he'd have whispered it, but in the din he'd never have been heard.

Kee looked up at him gratefully. "Chicken an' berry," he said. Fortunately his voice was high-pitched enough that Perry heard him clearly.

"Righto," Perry replied. "Kat, what do you want?"

"Are you getting them? The same, please!" Kat turned toward him with relief in her eyes, and he didn't blame her. The scrum around the platters of pies laid out on the sideboard was a bit intense as Trainees descended on the food quite as if they were starving to death. Abi, Trey, Tory, and Niko were already somewhere deep in the scrum, looking for their favorites.

Perry dove in and returned in glory with his prizes; six each of the desired flavors on a wooden platter. He would have preferred beef, but not so much that he was eager to face the mob again.

Of course, he could wait . . . but then the pies would be lukewarm.

He and Kat and Kee took their prizes to the far left corner of the hall, out of the way of most of the others, with little Kee on the bench between him and Kat, and he was pleased to discover that not only had he gotten chicken pies, but he'd managed to snare the coveted chicken and mushroom. Really, only beef and mushroom would have been better, and the pies were so hot inside that they had to nibble their way carefully to avoid burning their tongues.

Abi and Tory joined them, looking flushed but pleased. "Trey and Niko are with their Trainee friends," Abi announced, as she and Tory swung their legs over the bench and sat down across the table from them. "What did you get?"

"Chicken and mushroom," Kat replied before he could answer.

"I got mushroom and squash and cheese," Abi said a little wistfully. "Tory got sausage and cheese, but he won't trade."

"Well, I will!" Kat replied eagerly, and the two swapped their second pies.

"Won't trade for veg, but I will trade for chicken," Tory pointed out, raking his hair out of his eyes. Perry thought he was overdue for a haircut, but Tory had decided he was going to wear it in a long braid down his back . . . and it wasn't even long enough yet for a little pigtail braid. *So he'll just have to keep looking like one of Lady Dia's muff-dogs for a good long while. Well, Mama said he'll get tired of that long before his hair will grow.*

"Done," Perry agreed, and with that, he and Tory swapped *their* second pies. As for the dessert pies, Perry's sibs both had custard and were happy to swap for berry.

All this time, little Kee had been quietly eating, first his first chicken pie, then his first berry pie, his eyes on someone one table over—a little boy about Tory's age, in Trainee Grays that looked too big for him. At first Perry had been too busy eating to pay any attention to the youngster, but as he licked the berry juice off his fingers, he realized the boy had been sitting there, not eating, and with no food in front of him, for as long as they had been greedily inhaling their dinner.

Before he could get up to find out what was wrong, if in fact there was anything wrong, Kee had wriggled out of his seat, seized a pie in either hand, and trotted over to the boy. There was too much chatter in the hall for Perry to make out what Kee was saying, but the little boy brightened up, took the pies, and set to eating immediately. Kee trotted back to them and hopped into his seat between them, a smile of satisfaction on his face.

"That's Willy," he said. "He's new. He didn' know how to get fed. I tol' him what t'do."

Perry and Kat exchanged a startled glance, and Perry broke off a third of his custard pie and gave it to Kee, who thanked him and began carefully licking the creamy custard out of the middle.

By the time they were all finished, the initial mob at the sideboard had thinned, and young Willy had not only gotten seconds, he'd found a friend. They all decided on one last pie each to take back with them; Niko and Trey were hanging on every word of the captain of the Blue Kirball team, so there was absolutely no use trying to get their attention. They'd come back when they came back, and that was that.

Court dinners always went late; and with an ambassador there, Perry knew that it was pretty likely there would be entertainment afterward, so it would be a long time before his mother and father got back to their rooms. And he was comfortably full of pie, still bruised and tired, and wanted sleep, badly. But there was that odd thing Kee had done . . . and he wanted to talk to his parents almost as badly as he wanted sleep.

I know, he decided *I'll leave a note on their bed.*

So he did: a nice long report, actually, of the sort that his father had him write after a stint as a runner or in the pawn shop. He left that right in the middle of their bed where they couldn't miss it, and feeling now that he'd done the right thing, he sat in the open window of his father's workshop and listened to the music coming up from the Palace until he could scarcely keep his eyes open anymore. Then he went to bed—noting, with a chuckle, that there was still a reading candle burning in Abi's room, and there were faint snores coming from Tory's.

He could still hear the music coming from the Palace as he drifted off.

———————

Mags was very glad to strip off the Guard uniform and hang it in his closet among his other disguises. He didn't envy the poor lads their finery, not one bit—it was heavy and hot, and the only thing good about it was that it concealed light plate armor for the torso and upper arms.

"Mags!" he heard Amily exclaim, with a note of amusement in her voice. "Perry's left us a report!"

"He has?" Mags pulled on a pair of light sleeping trews before turning. Amily was already in her shift, with her hair down, standing next to the bed with papers in her hands. "What about?"

"Oddly enough, Kee. Our observant little agent has made the same deduction you did—Kee needs to be tested for Empathy." She looked at him, smiling, with more than a hint of pride in her expression. "I'll read it to you, shall I?"

Mags nodded.

"Mama and Papa, when we were in the dining hall, Kee somehow saw a boy in Grays sitting alone, a boy who was so quiet no one was taking any notice of him. I looked where Kee was staring and had just noticed that the boy hadn't gotten any pies, when Kee picked up two of his pies and took them over. You know, he never goes to strangers, but this time he did, and he stayed there talking to the boy before coming back to us. When he went over to the boy, he looked worried, but when he came back, he looked happy. He told me and Kat that the boy was Willy, he was new, and that he, I mean Kee, had told him what to do. And that was all. But I began to think about how in the last few moons Kee always sticks close to Kat in a crowd, how he doesn't like crowds much, and how he always gets this look like he's having a headache around crowds. So I wondered, if we should ask the King if Kee should be tested for Empathy? Because if he had any other Gift this young, a Companion would probably Choose him to help him with it, but that wouldn't happen if he's going to be a Healer. That's all. Perry." She put the papers down as he sat down on the side of the bed. "Well! What do you think?"

"I think he's right, and I suspect you do too," Mags told her. "Huh. Our lad is an observant little sprog."

Amily sat down on the other side of the bed, and swung her legs up onto it. "He's more than observant; he acts on what he observes. He didn't just keep that to himself, he wrote out a report for us!"

"Well, now," Mags replied, blowing out the candle and reaching for her. "That's only to be expected."

"Why?" she giggled, tweaking his nose in the dark before snuggling into his arms. "Because he takes after you?"

"Of course not. Because he takes after *you.*" And then he stopped her from answering in the best possible manner.

3

Being a dog boy was dead easy.

Perry thought he had never been so contented. Right now he was cleaning out the pens the bitches and their puppies were kept in until the puppies were housebroken. He didn't really mind the smell all that much, and the work was easy enough. Take the bitch to the clean pen. If the puppies were mobile, they'd follow, and if not, once he settled the mother, he could pick up the pups and take them to her. Thanks to his Gift, the mothers didn't fight him, get overprotective of their litters, or get anxious when separated from them. And the puppies—were puppies. Who *wouldn't* be happy with a head full of puppies?

Then he'd clean out the straw and the mess, scrub the bricks down with water and a big, stiff push-broom, then load in new straw and bring the next bitch in.

Once the Houndmaster had given Perry his instructions, the man left him alone to do things at his own pace. Since he knew who Perry was and what his Gift was, he knew his precious dogs were absolutely safe in Perry's hands. So basically, his afternoons were filled with *the best job in the world* except for the parts where Master Leandro pounded him into paste.

And when he was done, he could either play with puppies or go out and take the bigger dogs for a walk. He didn't need leashes; they packed up around him, and he could always call them back mentally if they got distracted by an interesting scent.

Today was not a day when Master Leandro was supposed to drill him on that maddeningly difficult leg-sweep combination.

He brought in armloads of fresh straw for the last pen, and when he was finished, he straightened up and looked around with a deep feeling of satisfaction. Lady Dia's whelping "barn" was, in fact, structured rather like a stable. The pens that the bitches about to whelp and the ones with puppies were kept in were built like the loose-boxes that the Companions used in their stables, with walls just as high. That kept the puppies safely confined, and kept their mothers apart. And right now, it smelled great. Clean straw, fleabane strewn in the straw for the obvious reason, clean dog. And in his head, the background of a building full of contented mothers and playing puppies.

But it was late, and it was time for the last feeding of the day. He wouldn't be doing that alone, of course, but he'd better get moving if he didn't want to earn a frown from the Houndmaster.

Once again, his Gift was perfectly suited to this job; he could keep each dog back while he emptied and refilled water bowls, then brought in the carefully measured bowls of food. Since he'd been working the whelping barn, the Houndmaster kept him at the same spot. About half of the litters were weaning or starting to wean, so the pups in those pens got their own bowls as well.

He found himself grinning as his head filled with the pure

bliss of dogs filling their bellies. *I'm going to feel really sad when I don't get to do this job anymore . . .*

———————

Mags leaned against the wall of the center room with his arms folded over his chest and watched as Amily sat at the desk the whole family shared and scanned through a series of letters of introduction. The Seneschal and the King's personal secretary had already been through them, of course, and so had she when they first arrived, but she needed to refamiliarize herself with the people who would be presented to the King and Queen over the next few days. She had done her hair into a loose knot, and strands of it were coming down a little in what he considered to be a very attractive manner. "Enjoying yourself?" she asked, dryly, without looking up.

"I always enjoy watching someone else work," he drawled lazily. "Best part of my job is that there's damn little paperwork involved."

"Yes, well—" she began, when Mags heard footsteps coming from behind him and turned as quick as a cat, his posture going from "lazy" to "ready for anything" in a heartbeat.

"Amily! I—oh!" He relaxed, recognizing the person who had come through the open door immediately. It was Herald Laurel, the Head of the Heraldic Circle.

She looked every inch the perfect Herald. Laurel's hair, so Mags had been told, had once been a brilliant red; it was now pure silver. Her slim figure hadn't changed much since she first went into Whites though, he suspected, and she was still a striking woman. But looks weren't why she was Head of the Heraldic Circle. It was her knack for diplomacy, her decades of experience, and her Gift, something in the Empathy family. It worked whether she was concentrating on it or not, and it made everyone like her and want to cooperate with her. When you were dealing with potentially explosive interpersonal situations between Heralds, that was an exceedingly useful Gift to have.

"Oh, Mags, good, you're here too. I wanted to talk to Amily about this—" She waved a letter in the air. "—but it's actually better if I can talk to the both of you. This might be something in your . . . well, you know." Laurel flushed a little. She didn't really like acknowledging that there was a Herald who was also a spy. She liked everything to be open and aboveboard. She was a naturally open and honest person, and subterfuge made her uncomfortable. Fortunately these traits also served her well in her current position.

Amily shuffled the letters back into a neat pile and set them aside. "I'm all ears, Laurel. What have you got for us?"

"Well, it's this letter," she said. "It's from Arville."

Quickly, Mags ran over what he knew about Herald Arville; it wasn't much. Laurel, her husband Herald Rod, and their friends Herald Alma and Herald Arville had been absolutely inseparable from long before they were Chosen until the day they finally had to split up to ride their own separate Circuits. In fact, that enduring friendship was something of a legend. They had remained the firmest of friends, no matter the distance between them.

Rod was currently serving down in the City Courts, and Alma taught practical field skills at the Collegium. But Arville was semiretired in a village right at the edge of the Pelagir Hills—and something about that was nagging in the back of Mags' memory but wouldn't come out.

Wasn't there some odd reason he went there? Mags didn't know Arville personally, though his father-in-law, Herald Nicolas, did. And there was something unusual about Arville . . .

But Laurel was not waiting for his memory to unstick itself. "He says there's something not quite right going on where he is," she continued, brows furrowed. "To be honest he's been sending me letters about it for almost a year now, but this one is really insistent. He says there is *something hinky going on,* whatever that means, and that I need to send another Herald out there right away. I've never known him to be so insistent before."

"Has he gotten any more specific than that?" Amily asked, turning to drape one of her arms over the back of her chair so that she could see Laurel better, and tucking one of those unruly strands of dark hair behind her ear.

"That people have been going missing—but it's the *Pelagirs*. People go missing on the roads all the time." Now Laurel sounded a little impatient. Well, Mags could sympathize with that. It would be hard to make any kind of decision based on so little information. "I checked, and the number of missing people from around where Arville lives isn't much different from anywhere else that borders on the Pelagirs."

"And what does Alma say?" Amily asked. "You know she's the most sensible and logical of all of you."

Laurel looked uncertain again. "That Arville's instincts are usually good. And that he wouldn't be plaguing me with letters for a whole year if there wasn't something making him uneasy." She waved the letter again. "I just don't know what to do. The Herald on Circuit there didn't find anything, but he doesn't live there, he only stayed two days, and he might not notice subtle things. But if I'm going to post a Herald out there, I need a really good reason, not just someone feeling that things aren't right. It would be different if Arville were a Foreseer, but he's not."

Amily held up her hand. "It sounds to me as if you are sure Arville is right, even though you have no logical reason to believe him."

Laurel sighed and dropped the hand with the letter in it to her side. "I guess I am. Convinced, that is. But I'm the Head of the Heraldic Circle and I can't just send people out on such a slim reason."

"You leave that to us," Amily assured her. "You just go put out some of the other fires I know you left burning. We'll take care of Arville's problem. And it won't be by sending him a letter saying he'll have to solve it on his own."

Laurel beamed at them. It looked as though she was going to go into a gushing fountain of thanks—which was something she tended to do—but Mags just waved her off. "Shoo," he said, gently. "We'll let you know what we have in mind in a day or two."

Laurel took the hint, and left, closing the outer door behind her. Mags cocked his head at his wife. "Well?" he said. "What *do* we have in mind?"

She hesitated. "I hope you won't think I'm trying to get rid of you—"

"But you think I should go?" He scratched his head. "I'm best in cities. Out there in little villages is not my strong suit."

She actually snorted. "That's like saying an otter can't swim well because it's not a fish. But I wasn't thinking of just you going. I was thinking that you ought to take Perry."

He blinked at her for a moment, considering the idea. "That's . . . not a bad thought. He hasn't actually been outside of Haven. You could ask Nikolas to come take over what I've been doing here—everything pretty much runs itself now, and all that's needed is someone to collect the information and sift through it. It would do Perry a lot of good to go off without his sibs for once."

"And he has learned more than you had at his age about spycraft," she pointed out. "He just hasn't had a chance to put it to practical use yet, at least not on some kind of task. Besides . . . I'd like him to have something to take his mind off the fact that he hasn't been Chosen."

He nodded after thinking about that for a bit. "Does that bother you?" he ventured.

She snorted again. "No. But I worry that *he* thinks it does, and you know Perry. He's twice as responsible as Abi and Tory put together."

"He's also older—"

"Which has absolutely no bearing on the situation. No, I'm not worried about him not being Chosen. And I hope you aren't, either."

"If he is, he is," Mags admitted. "And if he's not, it's not as if he isn't going to make a damn fine agent. And he *likes* the work. And he's good at it."

She raised both hands in a shrug, then reached for one of his. "There, you see? No reason to worry. This sounds like something the three of you can handle—you, Perry, and Arville, that is. And if it isn't, you Heralds can easily call for help."

It was his turn to snort. "I think the one likely to call for help is Perry. You're forgetting his Gift. If we needed help, he could probably call us an army of Pelagiris monsters."

Her eyes got big as she thought about that for a moment, then she smiled. "All the more reason to not worry, then."

He leaned down and kissed her on the forehead. "I don't know about this plan of yours," he teased. "I think you're just trying to get rid of me so you can have an affair with Lord Jorthun."

"Beast." She mock-punched his biceps. "You should know better than that."

"So I should. But why?" He kissed her again, this time on the ear, which generally led to a lot of other things.

And it did this time, too. "Because Dia would murder me," she murmured into his neck, just before nibbling it.

Good thing the younglings won't be back for at least two candlemarks . . .

"Perry," said his father, as he was finishing the last of his berry custard. It was one of those rare nights when the Royals were having their dinner with their parents in their own suite. "Your mother and I want to ask you something."

What? He blinked, ran over the events of the last couple of days in his head, and the only thing he could come up with was that he still hadn't managed to learn Master Leandro's leg-sweep trick. And that wasn't important enough for a *your mother and I want to ask you something.* So . . . he probably wasn't in trouble. Besides, if he was in trouble, they wouldn't be bringing it up in front of Abi and Tory. But maybe this was why his friends weren't here. "All right," he said agreeably; he ate the last bite, putting his spoon down and looking at them expectantly.

"How would you feel about going on a long trip with me?" his father asked. "Just us. Possibly for the whole summer."

A trip? He tried to curb a surge of excitement so he wouldn't shout his answer. "Yes, please!" he said eagerly, as Abi started to pout.

"But—" she protested. Their mother quelled her with a look. She subsided, but she looked rebellious.

"You'll get your turn," their mother promised. "This is Perry's turn."

Tory just blinked thoughtfully, then turned to Perry. "Whatcha gonna bring me?" he demanded.

"I don't know where I'm goin' yet!" he protested. "How can I tell you what I'm gonna bring back for you?"

"We're going to a village near the Pelagiris Forest," Papa told them all, though he was looking at Perry.

Tory scratched his head, perplexed. "Bring me somethin' shiny," he said, finally.

Well, that was easy. Perry nodded agreement, and that was more than enough to satisfy his little brother. He turned back to Papa. "Why are we going?" he asked.

"Because there is a very old Herald living there who thinks there is something not quite right. We're going to go see if he's mistaken, or if there actually *is* something going on." Papa waited for his response, watching him closely. He sucked on his lower lip, thinking.

"I think we should be traders," he said, finally.

"I think that's an excellent plan. I'll make the arrangements." Papa smiled, as though he was really pleased with Perry's answer. "We might as well keep our real names. It will be easier, and no one out there will have ever heard of Herald Mags."

Perry nodded, and grinned. This was going to be fun. He already had a pretty good handle on tradecraft—when he worked at the pawn shop, he was learning how to evaluate all sorts of things, and often as not, when people bought something there, they would rather trade an item for it than pay in cash. "What kind of traders are we goin' to be, Papa?"

"Well, that's what I'll have to go consult with people about. What we'll bring *with* us to trade—that's actually easy. We'll take things they can't make for themselves. Fancy cloth, ribbons, pins and needles, colored thread. What we don't know yet is what we'll be trading *for.* I'll have to check with some people I know to find that out." Papa raised his eyebrow at Perry. "And you should consult with Lord Jorthun about what he knows about the area and what he can find for you in his library. I expect you to study as hard as you would for an examination. This will be a working trip, Perry. And although you might not be taking actual lessons, I'm going to be teaching you and testing you on what you're learning the whole time."

"Oh. . . ." Abi said. Perry glanced at her. She was no longer pouting. "You're going where there aren't any libraries, I guess?"

Papa and Mama laughed. "Abi, in a village this size, there probably aren't more than a dozen books in the entire place, much less a library," Mama pointed out.

"Oh. . . ." Abi sighed. "Then when it's my turn, I don't want to go anywhere that doesn't have a library."

———

Of all the rooms in Lord Jorthun's impressive manor here on the hill, Perry liked this one the best. It wasn't just all the books; it was that the room itself was somehow both quiet and inviting. "I, personally, do not know anything about the area around the village of Whithern," said Lord Jorthun, as he consulted one of the bookshelves in his library. "Except that it is between Forst Reach and Prytheree Ford. I do, however have a book—ah, here it is—that will have some general information about that area. And I know a great deal about Herald Arville, who is the cause of this journey." He took the book down off the shelf and handed it to Perry.

Perry tucked it under his arm, and followed his Lordship to a comfortable corner of the library. His Lordship wasn't concerned about being overheard at the moment, so all the windows were open, and the breeze coming in was delightful. "Herald Arville is possibly the most *interesting* Herald I have ever met," Lord Jorthun continued, with a deep chuckle. "For two reasons. His Gift and—well the other thing takes some explanation."

Jorthun indicated a pair of chairs. Perry waited until his mentor was seated before seating himself. "What's his Gift?" Perry asked, opting for what seemed to be the simplest explanation first.

"It's unique as far as I am aware," Jorthun said, when they had both settled into their seats. "It's Luck . . . or something so identical to Luck that the effect is the same. He can trip and fall and come up not only unhurt, but clutching something useful, important, or occasionally even valuable. He's almost never hit during fighting, not because he's good, but because his opponents always make inexplicable mistakes. If there is something important for him to know, he's in a place where he can see or hear it at exactly the right time. I could go on and on, but I'm certain you have the idea now."

Perry blinked. He thought he knew of all the possible Gifts, but this one was entirely new to him. How had anyone ever figured out Arville's Gift in the first place? "How can you *train* a Gift like that?" he asked, dumbfounded.

"You can't. All you can do is train the wielder how to recognize those golden moments of Luck and take advantage of them." Lord Jorthun shook his head. "Arville was always one of the best people to have out in the Pelagir area, because he was safe from virtually anything out there. And that is where the second remarkable thing about him came from. Arville bonded with a *kyree.*"

Perry looked at his mentor blankly. "I don't know what that is," he admitted, a little embarrassed. Here he had thought he was well educated. There was a lot more out there in the world than he'd encountered inside the bounds of Haven!

"Give me the book," Lord Jorthun replied. Perry handed it to him, and Jorthun thumbed through it until he found the place he wanted and handed it back to Perry.

On the left-hand page was an illustration of something that looked a little like a wolf but clearly wasn't. It had a wolflike head, but the cranium was big, as if it must have a bigger brain in there than a wolf did. And the body was shaped wrong for a wolf; it was more feline than canine. The drawing itself was very good, and Perry riffled through a few pages until he came to something he recognized—which was by the same hand, and accurately drawn.

"The artist drew all his subjects from life," Lord Jorthun told him, confirming his guess that the odd drawing wasn't just a distortion of a wolf, or something from hearsay.

On the right hand page, the text began. *The* kyree *is native to the Pelagirs. It is highly intelligent, fully as intelligent as a human, and both Mindspeaks and attempts human speech as well as it can, given that its mouth is not well suited to the task. They live in packs and have three genders—male, female, and neuter. The neuters serve as teachers to the cubs and are the historians of the pack. When there is an excess of neuters in the pack, some of them leave the pack to explore the world and bring back what they learn. These* kyree *are known to bond to humans in a similar way as Bondbirds bond to Hawkbrothers.*

"Huh!" Perry said as he finished the paragraph. "And Arville's Companion was all right with that?"

"Evidently," Jorthun replied.

Perry considered what he had been told. "I think I need to read this book," he said, finally. Lord Jorthun nodded.

"I will leave you to it, then," the old man replied, got up from his chair, and went about his business, while Perry dived into the book.

What he found there was astonishing. Things he had heard of, yes, but far more things he had not. *Tervardi, dyheli, kyree,* firebirds, ice-drakes, shadow-cats . . . the fellow who had written all this—"Eran Jathon," according to the inscription inside the cover—had been there and seen all these things with his own two eyes. And Perry had not read too much of the little volume before he found out how this had come about.

Herald Arville had been his guide. In fact, it had been Arville's own *kyree* Ryu who had sat as the model for the drawing.

The unusual wildlife of the region was by no means the only subject of the book; there was a whole section on plant life that only grew there and another on some unique geological features of the area. It was pretty obvious that Master Jathon was not in the least interested in the people; a couple of villages barely got a mention, and then only for their proximity to things the author *did* find interesting.

But he was a good writer; Perry certainly wasn't bored. He read on steadily as the sun patterns coming through the windows migrated steadily across the floor. It wasn't a very long book, and he finished it a little before Lord Jorthun came to look in on him.

"I'm afraid I can't let you keep that," his lordship said, apologetically. "There are not many copies in existence, and they were all hand-created. I really should get another copy made . . ."

"That's all right, sir. I think I got what I need up here—" He tapped his head. "About what time is it?"

"About a candlemark and a half until dinner," Jorthun replied promptly. "And you are welcome to dine with Dia and me and the three Handmaidens in training—"

The last time he had done that, it had been a bit embarrassing. The Handmaidens had been rather effusive about what a handsome boy he was and how he was going to break hearts in a few years. And he knew they were just trying out their training on him, gushing over him the way they would be expected to gush over the young sons of the ladies they served . . . but it made him uncomfortable. "I won't impose, m'lord," he said instead, politely, as he got to his feet and handed the book back to his mentor. "And thank you for finding this and for telling me about Arville. It's a big help. I'm just sorry I'm not going to be around to learn hawk and horse tending."

Lord Jorthun waved his hand, indicating it was nothing to worry about. "You'll be back before autumn, I am sure, and you can resume then. The dogs, the hawks, and the horses will all still be there. Master Leandro will see you tomorrow, Perry. Until then, enjoy the rest of your day."

But as Perry walked slowly back to the Palace, he wasn't exactly "enjoying" himself. For the first time in his life he found himself immersed in doubt, and a bit of regret. Of course, he'd said *yes* as soon as his father had asked him if he wanted to go along on this journey. But now he was having some second thoughts.

For one thing, this meant he'd be away from his friends for part of, if not the whole of the summer. Oh, there were lessons during the summer, but they tended to be lighter than the rest of the year, partly because a hot classroom was no place to be stuck in and partly because all three Collegia felt that there was no point in overworking the Trainees during the best season of the year. They'd planned a hundred things to do—and there was the Midsummer Faire in Haven, the biggest Faire in the entire Kingdom, and he was going to miss it just as he was going to be old enough to attend on his own! He'd been hoping to find someone willing to teach him ropewalking, and pole balancing. . . .

But that wouldn't happen at all. If there even was a Midsummer Faire at this little village, he'd be hard put to find a mere juggler there. And he already knew how to juggle.

And then there were the other things he'd been planning to learn. Teo knew someone who knew someone who was willing to teach him how to pick locks! And who knew if the man would still be willing three or four moons from now?

Then there was the fact that he was going to be all alone with Papa for that long. Which meant Papa would be watching him all the time. Instead of getting reports from Lord Jorthun or Teo or Master Leandro about his progress, Papa would be watching him and judging him all day, every day. He tried to reassure himself; Papa was fair. Always fair. But they'd never been completely alone together like this for what would probably be at least a couple of moons.

Then there was probably the most unnerving thought of all.

He wasn't sure which would be more nerve-wracking: that his father would actually be depending on him, or that his father clearly wouldn't need him for anything and would just give him make-work and tests.

And then there was the wagon in the room. That he was thirteen and still hadn't been Chosen. Neither his mother nor his father had actually said anything about that, but it certainly would be *there,* hovering over the whole trip, like a bird of ill-omen.

The more he thought about it . . . the more second thoughts he was having. When he'd said *yes,* all he'd been able to think about was the adventure ahead. The only times he and his sibs had ever actually been out of Haven was when they'd gone to visit Nikolas, who was living with the abdicated King Kyril and his wife on an estate about a day's ride away. The entire property was mostly gardens and farm; Companion's Field was wilder.

His mental mood lightened a bit and took on a more hopeful color. So this would be going out into authentic wilderness, where there would be all sorts of wild animals he could test his Gift on, and whole candlemarks when he wouldn't actually have anything he needed to do or learn—

Then his thoughts darkened again. Except, maybe that wasn't as true as he'd thought. Maybe every bit of this would just be one long test, where his father would be seeing if he could do things on his own initiative.

And what if he couldn't? What if he just wasn't sharp enough to figure out what Papa wanted without Papa having to ask him for it?

What if it turned out he *couldn't* control truly wild animals when Papa needed him to?

What if those strange Pelagiris animals could resist him?

But he couldn't back out now, not even if he really, truly wanted to. He'd already said yes.

When he got back to the family suite, it was empty. Which suited his mood; he didn't really want to talk to anyone, and he didn't really want to think. He wanted to not-think, to not-worry. Instead, he threw himself down on his bed and went looking for an animal.

He found exactly what he wanted: a pampered Palace cat, sunning herself on a cushioned window seat.

For once, he didn't try to control the cat, or even communicate with it. Instead, he remained in her head, a passive passenger, watching her thoughts, and relaxing with her in the warmth.

It would be nice to be a cat, he thought. *Everything is so simple for them. Food or not-food. Thing to play with or thing to ignore. Favored human or not-favored human.*

Now, in particular, this cat's world was perfect. She had just been fed, the sun was exactly the right warmth, on exactly the right place. The cushion was perfectly soft. No one was disturbing her. She was one unit of contentment, from her whiskers to her tail. And it was exactly what he needed right now.

Being a cat, of course, this did not last forever. She heard a suspicious scuttling sound behind her, and she was instantly on alert, and he disengaged from her mind before she could go on the hunt. By that time, he heard Abi and Tory in the main room and went out to join them in setting up the table for dinner. Not long after that, Niko, Kat, and Kee joined them, and they were all too busy chattering to one another for him to get caught up in his gloomy thoughts again.

But when he went to bed, the doubts came back with a vengeance.

They ran around and around in his head until finally he'd had enough of them.

Because all the doubts in the world didn't matter. The fact was, *he was going.* And Papa wouldn't have asked him to go if *Papa* didn't think he was ready.

Think! he reminded himself. *How many times has he asked you to do something scary that you* weren't *ready for? In years and years . . . maybe five or six times at most? And when he figured out you couldn't handle it, he didn't get mad. He just caught things before they got out of hand, helped you through it, and then you tried it again when you were ready. This won't be any different.*

And even as he told himself that, he could feel his insides calming down. Because it was true. If there was one thing that could always be relied on, it was Papa. As long as you did your best and didn't shirk, everything would come out right in the end.

And as soon as he had convinced himself of that . . . like the cat, a wave of contentment overcame him, and at long last he fell asleep.

Lord Jorthun had given Perry the pick of his stable—and what Perry had chosen for this journey was an unassuming little chestnut cob with one white foot and a white nose. But one touch of his mind on this horse's, and Perry knew this was the one for him. Pog was his name, and he was clever, steady, and willing. He liked Perry immediately, and he was not at all skittish about Perry being in his mind. He might not be the fastest horse in the stables, nor the largest or strongest, but he had loyalty and heart.

Now, normally, Pog might have had trouble keeping up with Dallen. But there was an aspect to this trip that Perry hadn't considered. Since they were traveling as traders, not as a Herald and his son, Mags was going all-in on the disguise.

They were driving a trader wagon, a genuine caravan. Not some rough thing, oh, no . . . this was evidently a caravan that the Collegium had in storage and had kept in top condition in case it was needed. Why it had been built and acquired in the first place, Perry had no idea, but it was a truly magnificent piece of coachwork.

It looked to have been painted in several colors over the decades, but now it was a nice, dark brown, with a slightly darker roof. It was big; big enough that it took two stout horses to pull it. Expensive leaf springs sandwiched between wishbone axles peeked from behind carved bentwood coachwork. It was luxuriously appointed within; there were six bunk beds, an actual iron stove for heating and a little light cooking, and storage both underneath the wagon and in every possible nook and cranny inside.

Just now, Pog ambled behind the caravan, tied to the rear by his reins, wearing his tack so if Perry decided to take a break from the hard bench at the front, he could ride without stopping to tack up, Dallen, also tacked up, ambled alongside. Perry gingerly handled the reins of Daisy and Lily, the two good-tempered vanner horses especially bred for this sort of thing. It wasn't that he was worried about being able to control them, it was that he was trying to get the feel for how they sensed the reins and the bit, because if he had his way, he'd direct them with just his voice and the reins and get rid of the bit altogether. He'd managed to teach Pog how to do without the bit in a single day, and he reckoned to be able to do it with these vanners too.

There were a lot of advantages to doing without a bit. It let the horses browse comfortably on the verge if they stopped for a while. It made them much more willing to put on the bridle. And that made one less piece of equipment to clean—potentially the messiest of all.

His father sat beside him on the bench, which was called a box for some reason. It had its own set of springs, which was a good thing on this road—just dirt and pretty rutted from the spring rains. It was also beneath an extension of the caravan roof, which he could tell was going to come in handy when it rained. Well . . . it would come in handy as long as the rain wasn't being driven at them from the front.

They drove through low, rolling hills in farming country, with the next village just barely in sight as they topped the hill. The vanners heaved sighs of relief as they began the easy descent into the next valley. To the right were hayfields, and Perry felt the vanners' vague longing to get off the road and into that juicy, sweet grass. But they knew their duty, and they ignored the impulse, hunching their hind and back muscles a bit to hold the caravan to a steady pace. To the left was an orchard, but Perry didn't know enough about fruit and nut trees to tell what sort of orchard it was. All he knew was that the evenly spaced trees hadn't grown that way naturally.

He and his father had been on the road for three days now, and most of his apprehension had melted away. Mags hadn't been any different than he was at home. At no time had Perry had the feeling that his father was watching and weighing him. What *had* been happening was that he was learning all sorts of new skills. He'd never built a fire in the open before— never built a fire at all, in fact, that he hadn't been able to start from buried coals left from the night before. His father taught him three ways to start one, first with a clever little glass lens he kept in a special pocket. That was the easiest way. Then with flint and steel. And finally with something called a fire-bow, using the friction of a stick spun in a hole made in another piece of very dry wood. That had been the hardest, and it had taken him every bit of a candlemark to get the knack of it. He'd learned how to gather and chop wood and how to find kindling even when the forest was soaked with rain. He'd already learned several edible plants and a few of the mushrooms that were safe to eat. The experience of gathering his very own wild strawberries and eating them in his morning oatmeal had tickled him no end.

Then there was cooking. Perry had never, ever cooked before. And here on the road they didn't cook all the time either; often as not, Mags would buy something in an inn to eat at the time or later. But so far Perry had learned how to make oatmeal porridge, how to fry eggs and bacon, and fry slices of bread in the bacon grease, and bake eggs in a covered pot over coals, how to make pease porridge—which took quite a long time actually, so that wasn't something you wanted to do if you were starving right then. He hadn't known his father could cook. He hadn't known *he* could cook!

And, of course, with Pog, Lily, and Daisy to tend, he wasn't going to have to learn how to be a stablehand or a groom from Lord Jorthun's Stablemaster after all. That had been the easiest thing to learn; he'd gotten it from the horses themselves. They were used to things happening in a certain order, and they pictured those things in their minds in anticipation. All he had to do was follow those pictures.

It had been strange to sleep in the caravan, though. Mags had given Perry first choice of beds, and the first night he'd slept in one of the bunks just under a window, thinking how grand it would be to fall asleep watching the stars. That had been a mistake. He forgot how dulled sound from the outside was in his little room back home. He kept hearing unaccustomed noises all night long and waking up when he did— rustlings in the trees or the bushes, the horses stamping or snorting, strange calls and cries . . .

And then the sun had come up, and he wasn't used to that, either. Back home, his room stayed dark until someone opened his door. The noises of birds and the horses increased exponentially in volume as the first light began, and then the sun had filled the caravan, and . . . ugh. Mags had taken pity on him and let him get a nap during the day, but it had been hard to sleep in the swaying, rattling, jouncing caravan, and he was still dry-mouthed and exhausted when they pulled over to camp for the night. It was still twilight as he wolfed down his dinner; then he'd gone straight for the bed at the head of the caravan, the one under the one that had the hatch that let out onto the driving box. It had curtains across it, and he drew them tight and pinned them in place with a clothes-peg so not even a hint of light could get in. Then he buried his head under a pillow to shut out the night-sounds and finally got a good night's sleep.

"Do you want to stop at an inn tonight for a change?" his father asked, breaking the silence between them. "To sleep, I mean. It would be a change from the caravan. Quieter, maybe."

He thought about that. "Are you going to be a Herald or a trader?" he asked.

"Trader," Mags replied.

"Then just for supper, and we can camp outside the village," he said instantly. "It's not fair to Dallen to make him hang around out of sight all night. And I don't want to share a room with strangers when I have a nice bed without bugs in it here." He made a face. "It won't be quieter if everybody but you is snoring."

His father laughed. "Depending on the inn, us common folk might have to share a *bed* with strangers," he pointed out.

Perry grimaced at that. Oh, he knew that was normal. What wasn't normal was for a youngling his age to sleep alone. Even in the Palace, among the highborn, sisters or brothers shared beds because space was at a premium. Common folk often slept whole families to a single bed, and on the road only Heralds or the rich had rooms to themselves.

"If I have to do that I will," he replied stoutly. "But it'd look wrong, us having this great big caravan, if we didn't sleep in it and left all our trade goods alone. Wouldn't take but a minute for someone to get in and find something he could sell."

"Good reason," his father said easily. "We'll pick up something from the inn for supper, and we'll move straight on again and camp. It's not as if you aren't used to lurking inconspicuously in a tavern or an inn. I very much doubt you need any practice at it." Then he laughed. "For that matter, if we chose to camp just outside the inn, you could listen all we wanted through the ears of a cat or a mouse, and Dallen could hide among the horses when we picket them. If we throw a blanket over him, he won't stand out as much. So why don't we compromise and do that? Eat dinner in the inn and then camp nearby?"

Papa wants me to listen in to inn conversation for some reason. I wonder if he thinks we are close enough to our destination we might start to hear rumors, if there are any? He nodded.

"Good. Now, if you'd like to ride for a while, I can take the reins—"

Perry shook his head. "I'd rather be here. I'm getting the vanners used to the idea of being driven without bits."

To his pleasure, his father chuckled. "One less piece of tack to clean at night, and I'm sure they'd be more comfortable without bits. You know, Perry, that makes me think—if you ever need to hide yourself in plain sight, taking on a more flamboyant role, you could disguise yourself as an entertainer with a troupe of at-liberty horses. Have you ever heard one of those?"

Perry shook his head and listened thoughtfully as his father described an entertainer and his horse troupe that had come to the Midsummer and Harvest Faires one year in Haven. "It was amazing, and he did it all without Animal Mindspeech," Mags concluded. "And then there was the animal show that *was* done with Animal Mindspeech that your mother and I and Bear and Lena saw when we were Trainees. That was a mixed-animal show, which would have been pretty difficult without Animal Mindspeech, I think, since there were as many as thirty or forty creatures performing at the same time."

"I think I could do four or five horses, but I wouldn't want to try more than that at once," Perry replied after thinking about it a while. "At least, not mixed animals. Horses, if you pick the right ones, you can get to follow the leader. Dogs I could probably do that many or more; dogs want to please you."

They talked about how various animals reacted to him for the rest of the afternoon. It was the first time he'd ever talked at length about his Gift with his father; somehow he'd assumed Mags knew all there was about it. After all, he'd inherited his Gift from Amily, he just happened to have it stronger than she did.

Or so he'd thought. Now, after a couple of candlemarks of discussion, he knew differently.

But that gave him an uncomfortable revelation.

Suddenly . . . his father wasn't all-knowing and all-seeing. Suddenly he realized that as smart and observant and clever as his father was, there were still things he didn't know.

And what was more, his father was willing to admit that he didn't know them.

And that unsettling understanding made him feel a little as if he had been struck by lightning.

———————

Mags saw it in his son's eyes—the moment he realized that his father wasn't infallible. The moment he left childhood, and the surety of childhood behind.

But Mags kept on talking, kept on asking questions about Perry's Gift, what it felt like to command the mind of a stupid bird, like a pigeon, as opposed to a clever bird, like a raven. He wanted to ease Perry through this moment, let him get used to the facts before he actually had a chance to think about them in depth. And he watched as the horses remained steady in their pace, Perry's hands still firm, but easy, on the reins. Because this was something else Perry needed to learn—how to keep his Gift under control in the most stressful of circumstances.

In a way, this was as difficult for him as it was for Perry, because he had literally nothing to compare this moment to. He'd had to learn how to believe that other people had his welfare at heart and that he could trust them to be smarter and more knowledgeable than he was, rather than the other way around.

:Of course, you never actually had a childhood. There were no adults in your life you could depend on, none who were worthy of your trust, so of course you never had a moment like this one,: Dallen noted.

:Well, I might *have had, once I trusted you, except that we all know Companions actually are infallible,:* he teased. *:So there was never a question of discovering my guardian had hooves of clay.:*

:I can neither confirm nor deny that statement,: Dallen responded dryly. *:But I'm relieved you managed to arrange for this particular revelation to come painlessly for Perry, rather than in the middle of a screaming emergency.:*

:Aye, that. I've been planning it for a while, actually. It's one thing to teach the younglings to be self-sufficient. It's quite another to get it through their heads that their parents are mere mortals, and I really *didn't want to prove my mortality the hard way.:*

:Proof of mortality all too often comes at the end of sharp, pointed objects,: Dallen agreed. *:Much better to show it during a nice, calm discussion on a beautiful early summer day when there is no one shooting at you.:*

"So what happens when you can't control something?" he asked Perry, who had finished describing how easy it was to control pigeons, since they couldn't tell the difference between your thoughts and their own. He already knew the answer, of course, but he wanted to keep Perry talking and not thinking just now.

He had purposefully *not* done any research on Animal Mindspeech, nor asked anyone who had it (mostly Healers who specialized in treating beasts), because he had been planning for this moment from the time Perry first demonstrated his Gift. And it was nearly a present from the gods that the occasion to spring all this had come now, and as Dallen said, not in the middle of some emergency. Dallen was right; *he* had never been under the illusion that any adult was infallible. If anything, it had been very difficult for him to trust them, and to be honest, it had only been Dallen's influence on him that had allowed him to trust the Heralds at the Collegium *at all.*

He had steeled himself for this situation with Perry, because breaking an illusion can be painful for both parties, even under the best of circumstances. But it had to happen. The only way for Perry to learn to trust his knowledge and instincts was for him to truly understand deep in his gut that not even his parents knew everything.

But maybe Herald Arville's legendary Gift of Luck had extended all the way out here to them, granting him the perfect moment—

:Much as I hesitate to suggest this?: Dallen broke into his thoughts, his Mindvoice more than a bit troubled. *:But if you just happen to be right . . . and Arville's Luck is easing your way just now? It means Arville is right. There* is *something seriously wrong out there. And the Luck is clearing your way to get to him faster.:*

———————

The Weary Traveler Inn was *huge,* even by Haven standards. It sat right at the intersection of two major roads and was something like a small village in its own right.

Mags noticed that it was built for defense, too. It had been constructed in the form of a square, with the stable yard on the inside of the square. It was two stories tall, with walls of solid stone. The small windows on the first floor all had iron bars on them, and he had no doubt that there were solid wooden or even metal shutters that could be closed and locked on the inside. The larger windows on the second floor were barred as well.

Of course, that's also one way to make sure your guests don't escape in the night without paying their bill.

A square opening in the middle of one of the four wings led

into the stable yard; an actual iron portcullis could be lowered down to shut it off, and stout oak doors were behind that, currently folded up against the stone walls. Even the roof had been built with an eye to defense. It was made of slates, not thatch nor wooden shingles. He knew from personal experience that even in good weather it took a skillful roof-runner to keep on his feet on slates. And it would be damned hard to chop through them. Especially if someone was shooting at you from one of the four tiny towers that peeped up above the roofline.

Right now, though, there could not be a more welcoming or more cheerful place. There were people walking or sitting at wooden benches placed about the exterior, and the stable yard seethed with activity. The Weary Traveler had a sterling reputation among Heralds, Bards, and Healers alike.

:Well,: Dallen said cynically, as he trotted off to hide among the trees before anyone at the Inn caught sight of him, *:they have to maintain a good reputation. They're a very big target should they stray from the path of righteousness, and I am sure that every innkeeper in this part of the Kingdom would sell his wife or firstborn child for a chance to take it over.:*

Mags had taken over the reins from Perry and now guided their team through the tunnel into the stable yard under the second story. He noted with a glance upward that there was a murder-hole up there in the ceiling of the tunnel through which oil could be poured and a torch dropped and that there was a second portcullis on the inside. Should anyone be trapped between the portcullises, they could be burned alive without the stone of the walls and ceiling getting much more than warm. But there was rust on the gates and on the chains and a mat of spiderwebs on the murder-hole. So while at some point in its history, these precautions had probably been needed, even used, that hadn't been for a long, long time.

Once inside the yard, they were assaulted with a cheerful uproar. Horses being led to the stable, horses being taken from the stable, a riot of chickens underfoot, servants running everywhere, guests ambling about or walking toward one of the inner doors with a purposeful step.

A boy in good, stout boots, showing he worked in the stable, darted from out of nowhere to come take the vanners by the bridles. "Be ye stayin' or just eatin', Masters?" he shouted over the din.

"Just eating!" Mags shouted back.

"That'll be a copper fer fodder an' another if ye want the van guarded!"

Without bothering to shout back, Mags flipped the boy a copper bit, then a second, and hopped down off the box, followed by Perry. Having caught both coppers out of the air, the boy led the vanners over to the stable wall where a farm cart and a second, smaller caravan were already lined up, maneuvered them expertly into place, and tied them up by the cruppers to a ring in the wall. He ran into the stable and came back a moment later with two full feedbags. Slipping off the bridles and hanging each bridle on the respective horse's shoulder-harness, he pulled the feedbags over the horses' heads, and when they were munching happily away, he hopped up onto the box and settled in, arms crossed over his chest. Mags chuckled. This was clearly a boy who knew his business. The farm cart was empty and unattended, but there was a second boy in attendance on the smaller caravan.

The yard was surprisingly fly-free . . . but there were boys with shovels on the alert for horse droppings, and chickens—not the fat chickens kept for meat but small, very spry little chickens. And they weren't dashing aimlessly about as he had thought—they were in pursuit of fast, airborne prey. So that was the reason for the lack of flies!

With a mental nod to the innkeeper's cleverness, he signaled to his son, and they carefully made their way around the perimeter of the yard, staying out of the traffic, until they reached the wing on the opposite side of the yard from the stable. There were two doors in the wall here—it was pretty obvious from the sounds of shouting and the smells of cooking which one led to the kitchen. They avoided that one and went in through the second door.

As it closed behind them, they found themselves in a small, dark, blessedly cool antechamber. A necessity in a place like this, it would keep the cold of the winter out—and the chickens—and the heat and dust of the yard in summer. He and Perry looked at each other, dusted themselves off, tidied their hair a little, and opened the inner door.

They walked out into an enormous room, easily the size of the dining hall at the Heralds' Collegium. It had a low ceiling with dark beams and plaster in between, pale stone walls as thick as Mags' forearm was long, and a darker stone floor. As he had expected, metal shutters were folded up on either side of the small, barred windows. There were four fireplaces in here, one in each wall, though only one currently had a fire in it, and it was obvious that was going just to keep the giant kettle sitting on the hearth warm. Servers trotted to and from that kettle with trays full of wooden bowls, and even as they stood there, two boys came out of a door to their right with a smaller kettle between them, which they took to the larger one and tipped in. Clouds of steam carrying a meat scent rose from the big kettle as they carried the empty one back to the kitchen.

That would be tonight's stew.

Most inns offered a very basic meal of pease porridge or stew and bread. The stew generally wasn't as meaty as this one smelled, but then, The Weary Traveler was in the middle of nowhere and was big enough to have a hunter and trapper on staff. Mags sniffed again; the scent wasn't gamy enough to be boar, and piglets would be roasted and served whole, so it was probably either rabbit or sow. Most likely sow. Wild pigs could easily outbreed everything in the forest and turn a beautiful wild place into a wasteland if left unchecked, so they were fair game in any season and at any age.

As in the Collegium dining hall—and most inns, for that matter—the space between the four fireplaces was filled with trestle tables and benches. These had been made as sturdily and heavily as possible, of whole and half-logs, black with age and use and polished by thousands of behinds and hands.

About half the tables were full, and servers moved among them with bowls of stew, platters of bread, wooden mugs and pitchers of beer. Most people, being hungry after a long day on the road, would opt for the easy and immediate—stew, bread, and beer, down in front of them in moments. Mags motioned to his son to follow and went to a quieter part of the room. Eventually one of the servers noticed them and hurried over. It was a young lady with very red cheeks, wearing a practical set of trews, a baggy shirt, and a reasonably clean apron tied over it all.

"The stew is pig," she said, before Mags could even open his mouth. "Pig, carrots, onions, peas, beans. The bread is barley today. One bowl, one mug, one slice, five coppers. Butter's a copper extra. Cheese is two coppers extra. Apple pudding with last year's apples and honey is a copper extra."

Mags looked at his son. Perry nodded. The stew sounded better than anything he could put together out of the supplies in the wagon. "Two meals, butter, and apple pudding." Perry didn't get beer very often . . . but inn beer tended to be weak. Especially in an inn this large, you didn't want your customers actually getting intoxicated.

The server held out her hand. Mags counted out coppers into it, and she bustled off and came back quickly with bowls of stew, a plate with two thick slices of bread on it and a decent amount of butter on the side, and two mugs of thick beer. She dashed off again and returned with bowls of apple pudding, golden honey poured over the top.

"Keep your ears open," Mags murmured, as he dug his horn spoon out of his belt pouch and Perry did the same. "We're listening for anything about people going missing."

He honestly did not expect any information this far from Whithern, but you never knew. This was the biggest inn out here, and if rumors were starting to fly, they'd end up here.

Meanwhile, he was going to use his Gift, sifting through the surface thoughts of those around him, allowing information to come to him passively. As he sifted, he discarded. Concern about profit. Irritation at a partner's laziness. Idle speculation about a server. Not so idle speculation about a table full of women at the back of the room—and Mags didn't even have to sift through their thoughts to know why they were there. Although The Weary Traveler did not supply bed partners, the host made no objections to women plying their trade there. Having professionals on hand meant his staff didn't get assaulted, and food and drink and beds were all being paid for regardless.

:And if any of the professionals become a problem, out they go, and they'd better figure out some form of transportation, because it's a long way to the nearest village.

He didn't find anything at all out of the ordinary in his cursory sweep, so he finished his meal—the bread was surprisingly good for cheap barley bread—and since Perry had already finished his, he got up and headed out the door, knowing Perry would follow.

The very last hint of sun vanished as they crossed the stable yard. The yard was considerably quieter now; the last of the free chickens were scrambling into a coop in the corner as one of the staff waited to close the door behind them. Another member of the staff walked around the yard, lighting lamps. The boy watching their wagon sat up as he caught sight of them, jumped down, and untied the horses. They were wearing their bridles again, and there was no sign of the feedbags. Mags nodded with approval. It also looked as if he'd given the vanners and Pog a good brushing.

He tossed the boy another copper. The lad snatched it out

of the air, grinning, and led the horses slowly and carefully out into the yard, making sure the caravan was clear of any obstacles before handing over the reins. "There's a good camping-spot about five furlongs up the road," he offered. "Should be four-five wagons there already. Fresh water, though it's pretty well browsed over. Hay's a copper."

Mags laughed, and flipped over another copper. The lad loaded up the little porch at the rear of the caravan with as much hay as it would hold, tying it all down with a cord also made of hay. Pog, who was tied to the rear, looked at it longingly. Mags moved him to the front. He'd get his hay soon enough.

They drove out into the twilight, and sure enough, before they had gotten too far, they saw the lights of several wagons and a campfire.

But Mags had not gotten where he was by being unsuspicious. He halted the horses for a moment, and opened his mind to surface thoughts. It didn't take long for him to find a few things he didn't like.

"Petty thieves in one of those caravans," he said softly to his son. "I doubt the stableboy knows; he read guileless to me."

"So what do we do?" Perry asked, looking up at his father.

"We turn left instead of right, and after we cross the bridge, not before. Then we follow the stream. I'm sure we'll find a camping spot." Actually he was more than sure. He remembered a note on his map that said there was a Herald's Way-station on a path following the stream to the south.

"And we aren't going to go there to guard the other people because we don't want to look different." Perry made that a statement, rather than a question, and nodded his head. "Papa, I got an idea. I can see if one of those caravaners has a dog and tell it to be alert."

Petty thieves were unlikely to have a dog around themselves. "That's a good plan," he replied, wishing he could *show* Perry which of the caravaners were the thieves. Still, one night of unease with a fool dog barking every time someone went to take a piss was better than losing your goods.

They passed the camp quietly; the caravaners were too busy passing around a bottle and enjoying themselves to notice the wagon moving at a walk passing their campsite. Mags was grateful for the darkness, and the big fire they'd built, which effectively blinded them to everything outside the circle of caravans. As they crossed the bridge—hoofbeats muffled by a layer of mud on it—Mags spotted the path and turned the horses down it. Pog didn't like having brush hitting his right flank, but fortunately he only showed his objection by tossing his head.

Insects sang loudly to their right, and frogs leaped into the stream with alarm to their left. "I'm beginning to wonder if *we* should get a dog. It would be child's play for you to train it."

"I could do that!" Perry agreed eagerly. "That'd mean we wouldn't have to keep a watch at night. Not a puppy. I wish we'd thought of that before we left; we could have gotten one of Lady Dia's mastiffs."

"Damn if I don't wish the same," Mags said with chagrin, thinking of the size of those mastiffs and how it would be worth sharing the caravan with a dog big enough to take up the whole of one of the bunks for the sake of the protection.

:And what am I? An ornamental doorstop?:

Mags laughed aloud, and Perry looked at him with that little smirk that told him his son knew Dallen had made him laugh. And just at that point, the moon rose above the trees, flooding the clearing and the Waystation with light.

Perry bounced on the seat. "This is a Waystation!" he exclaimed.

"Yes, it is, and we won't be using it, or touching the supplies," Mags cautioned him. "Officially, I am not a Herald, and we need to make a habit of acting like traders."

Dallen trotted into the clearing as soon as the caravan had

gotten off the path and pulled up next to the Waystation. "Can I look inside?" Perry begged.

"Be my guest. It's nothing special, though." Mags hopped down off the box and cut the hay-string tying the hay onto the porch, letting it all fall to the ground. He ran the tie-out rope between the porch rail and a tree right at the waterline, then unharnessed Pog and the vanners, slipping on simple hackamores so they could eat, and put them on the tie-out. They could choose between hay and the lush, overgrown grass, and water themselves at their leisure. Perry came out of the Waystation, shutting the door carefully behind himself, in time to take over rubbing down the horses so Mags could attend to Dallen. Dallen, of course, didn't need to be tied out. And Dallen, not having had the benefit of a feedbag at the inn, got a ration of grain poured out for him away from the others.

Mags stripped to his bare skin and gave himself a quick wash in the stream. After hesitating a moment, Perry did the same. The water was quite cold, but Perry didn't complain. *And* he got the water bucket and filled the water barrel on the back of the caravan without being asked.

"So, did they have a dog?" Mags asked, sloshing clean water over himself after giving himself a good scrub.

"Yes, and I don't think the thieves are going to have a good night of it. He really didn't like any of the other people camping, so he'll be barking every time one of them moves." Perry jumped to the bank and toweled himself off vigorously. Mags did the same, and they both hurried back to the caravan. Biting insects had already discovered them, and Mags was not eager to find himself a mass of welts in the morning.

Perry dove straight into his cubby bed; Mags opened all the windows and made sure the fine linen window guards, made of the same material flour sieves were made of, were all fastened securely in place before taking to his own bed.

"Are we gonna watch the people in the inn?" Perry's voice came, muffled, from beneath him.

"As long as you can stay awake, yes, please. Now will be the time, when stronger drink comes out, and people huddle closer together against the darkness, when odd stories will be told. Just tell me in the morning if anything crops up."

"Yessir," came the polite reply, and then attentive silence.

The frogs came back and began to croak. The sounds of equine jaws munching and tearing at grass and the frog and insect calls were all that broke the evening quiet. Mags yawned, wondering if he should be sifting through the thoughts of those people in the campsite, or whether he could just sleep.

Better safe than sorry. Besides, they might know something.

But he discovered that they were already abed. Well, the honest ones were. The thieves—predictably, they only owned what they could carry on their backs—were bedded down next to the fire where the smoke would keep insects away, pretending to sleep, waiting for a chance to go through the storage compartments under the caravans.

Except that the dog—a big, rangy mongrel—was watching them on the other side of the fire. And every time they moved a little, its head came up off its paws, and it stared holes in them.

Mags smothered a chuckle, and he let his mind drift back to the inn. But the stories around the tables tonight were all cheerful ones. No mysterious disappearances. No rumors of kidnappings. So whatever was going on—and the closer they got to Herald Arville, the more certain he became that the old man was not starting at shadows—news of it hadn't made its way here.

But he could think of a very good reason why it might not have.

Traders of the sort that he and Perry were imitating, prosperous ones with a decent equipage, had regular routes, like a Herald's or Healer's Circuit. If they went missing, they'd be missed. But there were plenty more people who were desperate enough to take their chances out there on the fringes who did not have a regular route; instead they made their way like vagabonds, trading what little they had, hoping to kill or find or trade for something worth a *lot* of money back in civilized lands. If someone like that vanished, who would know?

And there were always people who ran off—or were run off—from their villages. Once again, unless you were keeping track of comings and goings, and noticed that the goings did not match up with the comings, there would be no chance you'd realize someone hadn't arrived where they intended to go.

Was that what Arville had been trying to convey in his letters? When pressed, Laurel had admitted that Arville's reports had never been particularly good, and he struggled with the written word. And when he was just reporting on routine matters like village problems on his Circuit, it had never been an issue.

But if there *was* something going on that was beyond his ability to articulate, Mags could only imagine his frustration.

And all this is just speculation, he reminded himself. *We'll see what we'll see. And meanwhile . . . this trip is doing good things for Perry. That is reason enough for it.*

Pog trotted along a road that was barely big enough for the caravan, thick forest on either side, with Perry riding easily in the saddle. He hadn't admitted it to his father, but part of the reason why he'd driven as much as he had was because he had discovered that riding for a long time had made him saddlesore. He'd decided to make a virtue out of necessity by training the vanners while he built up to riding for candlemarks at a time. He had assumed that being able to scamper over rooftops would have used every single muscle in his body . . . but evidently riding used some he hadn't been aware of until an entire morning in the saddle.

At this point, the vanners were trained to work without bits—and he could finally ride for most of the day without needing assistance out of the saddle.

Perry had quite literally never seen forest this old or this impenetrable. Or at least, it seemed impenetrable from the road; his father assured him that the thick undergrowth only persisted for a length or two away from the road and that only the break in the canopy above the roadway allowed such thick bushes and luxuriant weeds to thrive. He wasn't willing to put that to the test.

He was, at this moment, acutely aware of just how much of a city boy he was. This forest, this road, was unnerving. The trees loomed over the road, at times enclosing them in a green tunnel, and when the sky was overcast, it was a gloomy green tunnel. He didn't recognize most of the calls and sounds out there. He couldn't even tell whether some of the sounds came from a bird or a beast. He found himself encountering utterly unfamiliar minds when he used his Gift.

One good thing, though, he had not yet encountered an animal or a bird he couldn't coax into cooperating with him. But the wildness, the fierceness, of some of those minds had taken him aback.

And so far he hadn't even encountered a single one of the famed Pelagir beasts, just ordinary things like wolves and wild boar. Right now, he was very, very glad of that. The wolves weren't that bad, but the wild boar? That thing was vicious . . .

The road was, of course, not paved, not this far away from the capitol. And, in fact, it saw so little traffic that there were weeds and grass growing between the parallel wheel tracks. The vanners' hoofbeats were more muffled than he was used to hearing.

Dallen was somewhere farther ahead, scouting. They should be meeting with Herald Arville soon, according to what his father had said this morning, but so far there had been no sign of him.

And just as he thought that, they rounded a gentle curve in the road, and there he was—or at least, there were two side-by-side bits of white, glowing against the green of the forest in the far distance.

"Ah, there's Arville," Mags said, needlessly, but he did not cluck to the horses to speed them up. "He already knows we're supposed to be traders who are old friends of his family, and he'll have told everyone in Whithern that. So we'll be sleeping in real beds tonight, and we'll be staying in his house as his guests."

"I don't mind the bunks," Perry replied. "It's the sun I don't much like! It's up way too early for me."

His father laughed.

Slowly, the two parties approached each other. And as soon as Herald Arville was near enough to make out clearly—well, Perry had to work very hard not to stare. Because he had never seen a Herald who looked quite like Arville.

To begin with, every piece of his uniform looked as if it had been made for someone else. The fit was . . . well there *was* no fit, it all hung oddly on him. Arville's gray hair looked like an unmade bed, all tousled. His beard and moustache were short and yet, somehow, scraggly. Maybe it was because both were sparse, and looked as if he had grown them more to avoid having to shave than because he wanted them. And he slouched; he carried himself as if he was trying not to be noticed.

And yet, there was a huge grin plastered on his face, a grin of welcome in which there was quite a bit of relief. "When they said Herald Mags was coming, I thought they were spinning me a tale to shut me up, but here you are!" Arville exclaimed gleefully. "Laurel finally took me seriously!"

Perry gave Pog the signal to trot forward, holding out his hand. "Laurel finally came to my father, and Father convinced her, I think. Heyla, I'm Perry."

Arville seized his hand and gave it a slightly overenthusiastic shake. "I'm Arville, but you knew that." He had an odd voice, higher than Perry would have expected from someone as tall as he was, and a little hoarse, with a self-deprecating manner that would have seemed forced on anyone else. "This is Pelas. And thi—"

Something easily the size of one of Dia's biggest mastiffs came trotting stiffly from around the other side of Dallen. *A kyree!* Quickly, before they could react poorly to the strange beast, he put calming thoughts into Pog's, Lily's, and Daisy's minds. Just in time, too. Pog had tossed up his head, and he snorted in alarm before Perry was able to calm him.

It was instantly recognizable from the drawing that Perry had studied. Head very wolflike, body very catlike with an arching back, long, curved, shaggy tail, dark gray fur a little longer than a wolf's. It had a very white muzzle, and between that and the way the *kyree* moved, it was probably as old as Arville.

Perry reached for its mind. *:Hello—:* he said, tentatively.

The *kyree's* jaw fell open, and it sat down right there in the middle of the road in surprise. *:Why—hello youngling! You can speak with me! How absolutely delightful! What a wonderful surprise!:*

:My Gift is Animal Mindspeech,: he explained, then thought, belatedly, that the *kyree* might find being taken for an "animal" a little insulting.

But it didn't. *:Well, this truly is a pleasant surprise indeed! I'm rather glad no one told us you had such a Gift—it makes the surprise even better. I am Ryu, young one. Pleased to meet you, Perry! That would be a nickname for Peregrine, surely, rather than your parents naming you for a pear wine?:*

He had to laugh at that. But neither Arville nor his father noticed; they were already deep in conversation, as the vanners waited patiently for the signal to move on.

While he and Ryu were talking obliviously away, Arville and his father were getting acquainted, so he felt perfectly free to ignore the other Herald and concentrate on the *kyree* without being rude.

:It is Peregrine. My father is Mags. I hope we can either solve Arville's problem for him or put his mind at ease by proving there actually is no problem.: The novelty of having an actual mental *conversation* with another creature was . . . just amazing. He found himself grinning like a right fool over it.

:I hope you can solve it too, my fine youngling,: came the

sober reply. *:Because I would stake my tail on it; my bondmate is not mistaken. There is something out past our village that is very, very wrong. And the fact that we have not been able to trace it to its lair is not a good sign. Of course, part of that is our age.:* The *kyree* uttered a gusty sigh. *:We're no longer fit for much besides a gentle jog down the road to meet with visitors. But most of it, I fear, is more sinister than that.:*

Perry said nothing, just projected an air of waiting for the *kyree* to finish.

:I fear,: it said, after an appropriate pause, *:that whatever is making innocents vanish, it is clever enough to completely overcome Arville's Luck. And that would have to be diabolically clever indeed.:*

"Well," Arville said, as they turned off the road. "Here's my house."

Perry's eyes nearly popped out of his head. He'd expected a neat little cottage, or perhaps even a real house, with an extra bedroom or two that he and his father would use.

He hadn't expected something the size of a highborn city manor!

It was three stories tall. Most inns out here weren't that big. It must have had six or eight bedrooms besides the one Arville used, maybe more. Like The Weary Traveler, it was built of pale stone with a slate roof, and it looked as if someone had basically copied the design of one of its three living wings, with a detached stone stable in the rear.

The *kyree* clearly saw his shock and surprise. *:Arville's parents were quite wealthy,:* the beast told him. *:They were also quite proud of him becoming a Herald and left him a substantial sum on their passing. He invested it in this home, building it here for when he was too old for riding Circuit anymore.:*

:But why not live at the Collegium?: Perry wanted to know.

:Because of me. There are those who would look askance at a kyree *in Haven. Here, they know us, and he's useful. People come to him to solve problems. And we can play host to any Heralds, Healers, or Bards that come along this way, as well as the local Guard patrol on this road. There's generally someone here, most of the time. Journeyman Bards even spend the winter.:*

By this time they had come around the side of the substantial building to the stable, which was just as stoutly constructed as the house itself. There was room for ten ordinary horses and loose boxes suitable for four Companions. Perry put Pog up in the first one, untacked and brushed him down, then got the vanners as soon as his father had backed the caravan into place. Both vanners perked their ears upon seeing where they were being taken, and Lily gave a snort of approval. Meanwhile his father took care of Dallen, who also looked entirely well pleased with his situation.

Arville put Pelas up in the box next to Dallen. "Who's hungry?" he asked brightly, throwing Pelas' saddle over the place for it on the side of the stall. "I know I am!"

Without waiting for an answer, he led the way in through a rear door, which proved to lead to a kitchen. And without a pause, he went to the pantry on the right and emerged with bread, butter, cheese, ham, and pickles. "Help yourselves!" he said, as he proceeded to make himself a plateful, then a second that he placed on the floor for Ryu. The *kyree* lay down to eat it, probably because his neck was stiff.

Perry was always willing to eat, so he filled a plate for himself—his father waited to go last, and buttered a little bread and added some cheese, probably more for politeness sake than anything else. They all sat down on stools around the big table in the center of the kitchen; there was a pitcher of water and pottery mugs next to it in the middle, and Perry poured them all water.

"I don't have a fancy dining room," Arville explained around bites. "Never liked 'em. Anybody that's too fancy to eat in the kitchen's no one I want to be around. Kitchen's warmer in the winter anyway, and food comes hot to the table."

Perry and his father both nodded; there was sense in that.

"I've got a room where everyone can sit around the fire, the kitchen, and a bathing room. Everything else is bedrooms or storerooms. I'm not *quite* a Herald resupply station, but I come close!"

Mags chuckled. "So rather than you going to the Collegium, the Collegium comes to you? That's brilliant, Arville!"

The old man blushed. "I dunno about that, Mags. I just like being useful, even if we can't go racketing all over the countryside anymore. And sometimes when she's got people she doesn't want to leave in their cottages, Healer Ivy brings them to me and I put them up until they're well enough to go home."

When Perry had first heard about this old man, he had felt . . . well, kind of sorry for him. He'd pictured the old Herald living alone except for the *kyree*, in a tiny little cottage, like a hermit. But he could not have been more wrong. Arville was clearly in the heart of Whithern, even though he lived on the edge of it, with friends (and ears) everywhere.

"So, all these people coming and going . . . is that how you began coming to the conclusion there was something wrong out here?" Mags asked.

Arville nodded. "It's hard to explain on paper," he replied, awkwardly. "I'm sorry if I didn't do it so good. But, you know, I'd hear that some 'no-good' girl ran off with a boy, and instead of hearing that they'd turned up to live in Byeless, or Rasneck, and getting to listen to the old hens cluck about how the people there are no better than they should be, and that water finds its own level—there'd be nothing. And people would forget about them. Or one of those pack-peddlers would turn up, leave, and there'd never be another word about him. So about a year ago I started writing down all the people in the last few years that seemed to have fallen down a hole—and started asking about them—and all I got was a lot of nothing. I put all that in my report to Laurel, but all she said was that people go missing all the time out here. But not so *many!*" he finished, the last word sounding like a cry of despair.

"That's because Laurel was looking at the records of people who were reported missing," Mags said thoughtfully. "Not the ones that you think went missing. I'd like to have a look at your list—not now—" he cautioned, when Arville looked as though he was going to leap to his feet. "Nothing we can do in a couple candlemarks is going to make a bit of difference one way or the other. But in the morning, when we can both put our heads together over this."

:I hope your father intends to use Mindspeech to look at Arville's thoughts,: Ryu put in thoughtfully, looking up at Perry. *:Arville's not the most articulate of the Fearsome Foursome.:*

:The who?:

:Arville, Herald Laurel, Herald Alma, and Herald Rod,: Ryu clarified. *:That's what they called themselves. The Fearsome Foursome. It was rather amusing at the time. Anyway, Arville is kind, and clever in his own way, and absolutely dogged when he's got a job in front of him, but not terribly articulate. He's worse on paper.:*

It occurred to Perry that the one thing that had been conspicuously absent in the tally of rooms was a library. *:So he doesn't read either?:*

:That's why we like having Bards here for the winter. Obviously I can't read, or I'd read to him.: The *kyree* uttered a small sigh. *:I tried to help him with his letters to Laurel, but he got muddled anyway.:*

:I'll tell my father to ask if he can use Mindspeech,: Perry promised.

:Thank you.:

Meanwhile, as they talked, Arville had been telling his father about the village and about the Pelagir Hills, which Whithern literally sat on the edge of. There had even been a Hawkbrother enclave not more than two or three candlemarks away when Arville had first gotten the Circuit that included Whithern—but they were long gone. They'd left in the third year he'd been stationed out here.

"Normally Heralds are moved around, so villagers don't get too used to them," Mags observed. "Why did they keep you out here?"

"Well, there's my Luck, for one thing," Arville explained. "There's still plenty of weird stuff out here, and my Luck kept me alive and pretty much unhurt. Then there's the people. They weren't used to Heralds out here. They were really suspicious about strangers. So once they got used to me, they told Haven they didn't want anyone else." He shrugged. "And I like this place. And it's close enough for Ryu to visit his relatives, or for them to visit him."

"Wait—relatives?" Mags said, blinking.

"There's three kinds of *kyree,* Papa," Perry interjected politely, when it looked as though Arville was going to stumble over his explanation. "Male, female, and neuter. The neuter ones are kind of pack historians, and when there are several of them in a pack, some of them go out and collect history and stories from outside the pack territory."

"*Exactly!*" said Arville with relief. "So every so often, one of Ryu's relatives comes here to collect stories, or when we were both younger, he'd go to them. In fact, that's where I got information about some other missing people. Ryu's pack collects things like that."

:Not entirely accurate, but close enough,: Ryu observed to Perry.

Arville finally stopped eating, but only when all the food he had brought out was gone. Perry was amazed. He had never seen anyone eat that much food in one sitting—and Arville was so lanky, it looked as if he hardly ever ate at all!

"All right," Arville said, with a glance out the kitchen window, where the light was definitely taking on a darker gold tinge. "It's almost sunset, and you were traveling all day. Let's get your things and move them into bedrooms. Right next to the bathing room good?"

"Excellent," Mags said with a smile. "We both need a bath."

"Rod built me this terrific system with a cistern and stuff. It's all black on the outside so the sun warms it up!" Arville nattered on as they went back outside to where the wagon had been parked. Long shadows stretched across the fields, and the air was already appreciably cooler and damper.

It took about three trips to get all their personal belongings out of the wagon and to their rooms. The rooms weren't big—just about the size of a room at the Collegium—but the bed was extremely comfortable, and the windows had shutters and linen inserts so you could open them to let the breeze in while still keeping the bugs out. Mags was still talking to Arville when Perry checked the bathing room; he decided that he was going to get a bath while his father was occupied.

There was a big metal tub with a hole in the floor of it and a plug made of a thick disk of wax. It had two hand-pumps, one with a blue handle, and one with a red handle. Perry fitted the wax disk over the hole and molded it in place, then began pumping.

The bathing rooms in the Collegium and the Palace had water heated in big copper boilers that needed special attendants to keep them hot and make sure nothing went wrong with them. Big inns and community bathhouses had the same. Perry could easily see why that wouldn't work here; if Herald Arville had any servants, they didn't seem to be around now, and it would be pretty foolish to keep a servant on just to make sure there was hot water for one man. But if Herald Rod had figured out a way to let the sun heat up bath water, well, that would be easier. All you'd have to do would be keep the cistern topped up, but even if it went dry there wouldn't be a problem.

He stripped down and eased into the tub. He'd really missed hot baths; bathing in cold streams wasn't too bad, but it wasn't all that good, either. The water was comfortably hot; it felt fantastic and made him very sleepy. By the time he slipped on a clean nightshirt and got to his room, he decided to put his things away later, and he got straight into his bed. It was even more comfortable to lie in than to sit on. It was a lovely twilight out there, and the sounds of insects and wild things were comfortably farther away than they were in the caravan.

I'm gonna like it here, he thought contentedly, and he listened to the summer night until everything faded away.

The adults let him wake up on his own, which, he thought, was very nice of them. It wasn't dawn when he finally opened his eyes, but it wasn't midmorning yet either. And he smelled bacon. Probably that was what had woken him.

His stomach, although it had been full when he went to bed, now registered a complaint with him at that savory aroma. He scrambled into clothing and headed for the kitchen.

There were three people there: Arville, his father, and a sturdy-looking woman enveloped in a huge apron, who was using a spatula to transfer flatcakes to their plates.

"Perry!" Arville greeted him. "Missus Weaver was just asking when you were going to wake up!"

"I said, I thought the bacon smell was good enough to wake the dead, so I was surprised he wasn't here already," Mrs. Weaver replied, bending down to add a pair of flatcakes to the bowl Ryu was eating from, under the table. "Only two for you, old man. Flatcakes aren't that healthy for puppies."

"Res ra'am," Ryu replied, and he waited while she put a dollop of honey on his cakes.

Perry scrambled into the chair with an empty plate in front of it and was soon feasting on bacon, flatcakes, and honey, while Mrs. Weaver dished up a second bowl of chopped meat for Ryu and put it down for him. Mrs. Weaver, he soon gathered, lived in Whithern, where her husband was, predictably enough, a weaver. She did almost all of Arville's cooking for him, while her two nieces cleaned his house and a nephew took care of outside work and chopped wood. Whithern boasted a miller, a blacksmith, and a baker, she told Perry proudly. He wasn't sure why that made her proud, but he nodded enthusiastically and kept his mouth full so he didn't have to betray his ignorance.

She and Arville kept up a conversation concerning local people, none of which was terribly interesting—but he listened carefully to all of it, because as he had learned from Lord Jorthun, sometimes the key to a problem lay in the most trivial of details you might overhear. By the time he was stuffed, she had finished cleaning the kitchen and took her leave. She left behind two pies baking slowly in the oven built into the hearth, admonishing Ryu to "keep a nose on them, and tell Arville when they're done," and a pot of soup simmering on the hearth. The pies, he gathered, were for dinner, and the soup for supper. Then she bustled off, passing two giggling girls who slipped by her in the doorway, ogled his father, looked at him and dismissed him with a glance, and gave a respectful greeting to Arville.

"I need to go put my stuff away," he said, not wanting those strange girls to start poking through his things. Without waiting for an answer, he made an awkward little bow to Arville and his father and skipped for his room.

"Put your dirty clothing in the basket by the door!" Arville called after him.

He got to his room just in time. The girls had made up his bed and one of them had a hand on the box he'd brought that contained some of his equipment. "I can take care of that," he said from the door, startling them so that one jumped and the other squeaked.

"If you say so," said the one who had squeaked, while the other sniffed and flounced past him with her nose in the air. They looked very alike, with brown hair, brown eyes, and dusky skin. In fact, they looked like much younger versions of Mrs. Weaver.

He picked up his box and put it on the bed, keeping one hand on it, and staring at the remaining girl until she turned to leave.

"Keep your secrets then, little boy," she said over her shoulder. "You won't have anything in there I ain't seen before a hunderd times."

Perry almost laughed then, thinking about the things— some of them deadly—that he'd stowed in that case.

But it wouldn't do to break character with the peddler's son he was supposed to be. Let them think him a "little boy"; it did him no harm and might lead to them being free with their words around him.

Not that he thought Arville didn't have his finger on the pulse of Whithern. Arville might not be the most articulate fellow around, but he was a Herald, trained, seasoned, and with not only a Companion but also Ryu to help him.

But with the presence of two very nosy girls allowed to rummage unchecked through Arville's house as they cleaned, he decided it would not do to unpack the things in his special box, nor did he dare to leave it unlocked. So when he opened it, it was only to extract the key, which he hung on a strong, but slender, steel chain around his neck, then lock it again and shove it under the bed. Then he went through the piles of personal things and clothing he'd left against the wall last night and stowed it all away in the wardrobe and chest next to it, provided for the purpose. There was a second chest at the foot of the bed, but it was already full of linens and extra blankets.

When he finished putting everything away and wandered back to the main part of the house, neither Arville nor his father were anywhere about. After a moment, he decided to stroll into Whithern, which must be farther up the road. He could make use of his Gift among the animals in the village and see what he could learn.

It turned out that the village would have been within easy sight of Arville's home if a heavy growth of trees had not blocked the view.

The village was about the same size as dozens of nearly identical villages that they had already passed; that is, it was ridiculously small by his standards. The only difference between Whithern and all the other tiny villages they had gone through was that Whithern was guarded by a palisade of logs. There was no guard at the gate, however, and careful—if covert—examination of the ground at the foot of the open gate told him it hadn't been moved in quite a long time. So whatever was out there that the villagers had needed to guard against wasn't there anymore.

Or they didn't think it was.

The road did not go through the village. Instead, a lane broke off from the road, passed through the gate, and dead-ended in an open area with a well in the middle of the village. In a bigger place, he supposed this would have been a village square, but this village was too small to need one.

He went just inside the gate and leaned his back against the palisade, taking inventory. There were about two dozen cottages and one larger house. Around the well were the blacksmith, the baker (identified by the big ovens outside his house), and that one large building about half the size of Arville's house. This would probably be where the village leader lived, since the wealthiest man in the village was generally also the de facto leader.

:You have to respect Arville's delicacy in not moving into the village and building his home there,: observed Ryu.

Perry glanced down and to his side. While he had been looking over the village, Ryu had come up silently behind him.

:I can see where some people might have gotten offended,

and the rest might have wanted him to be the village leader,: Perry observed.

:Very good, exactly so. And, of course, he wanted neither. So he explained to everyone that the Heralds had asked him to build something big enough that he could serve as a sort of Guardhouse for the Guard patrol hereabouts, and he never let on that playing host to the Guard had been his *idea.:*

:Is there a tavern or inn here?: That was generally the best place to gather information.

:No. The baker sells beer and lets people gather in the main room of his house to drink it. That's the closest thing we have to a tavern.: Ryu made a laughing sound in the back of his throat at Perry's surprise. *:That's how things usually are in a village this small. Whoever brews the best beer ties a grain-sheaf over their door, which tells people that he also sells beer and lets people come inside to gather and drink it. In summer, folks usually gather outside to drink, though.:*

In fact, now that he was looking, Perry spotted two torch-holders and the remains of a couple of burned-out torches on either side of the baker's door.

:That is why no one thought anything about it when Arville said he was building a quasi-Guardhouse. People had been grumbling for some time that there was no Guardhouse nearer than two day's walk. I don't think there are more than three riding horses in this entire village. Most plowing is done by ox, and families go in together, three and four at a time, for a cart horse and cart.:

Perry pondered all this for a while, leaning against the gate. There wasn't a single person visible—but he could certainly hear people at work. *:I'm thinking I won't find out much about Arville's problem here.:*

:You would be correct,: Ryu agreed. *:No, what we are going to have to do is go out into the wilds.:*

Perry thought about that, and he grinned. Well, he had wanted to learn new things. This was going to be *very* new!

Of course, he couldn't just get Pog and go riding out into the wilderness on his own. First, that would be stupid. Second, his father would *murder* him for wandering off without warning, or a plan, or any idea of what he was doing. And third, that would be *incredibly* stupid. So instead, after a glance at Ryu, he strolled into the village just to have a further look around.

As luck would have it, the baker came out to check on his ovens at just that moment, and spotted him. It was pretty obvious he had to be the baker; aside from the fact he'd come out of what Perry had already figured was the baker's house, he was wrapped up in a huge white apron and had flour on his sleeves. "Ho, boy!" the man hailed him. "You're the trader's lad what's stayin' with our Arville, eh?"

"Yes, sir, I am," Perry replied, trying not to smile at "our Arville," as if the Herald were village property. "My name is Perry, sir, and my father is Mags."

"Well, good, the womenfolk have been looking forward to

seein' what you brought. And in the meantime, you can take Arville's order so I don't have to send my boy."

Seeing as he had been volunteered, Perry gave in with a good grace and waited while the baker checked his ovens. Then, when the man beckoned to him, he followed him inside the house—definitely a house, it was a little too big to be a cottage.

Once there, the baker loaded a grass basket with a meat pie and three fresh loaves and then topped the load off with a dozen seedcakes, each wrapped in a woven grass square. The basket was crudely made and probably wouldn't last past getting it back to Arville's house, but, then, that was all it was needed for. *If I'd known I was going to be dragooned into being a delivery boy, I'd have brought a bag or a box from the kitchen,* he thought with some amusement.

As he packed up the foodstuffs, the baker examined his own handiwork carefully. One of the seedcakes somehow was "defective" and the baker insisted Perry eat it. Two more were just as "defective" and were gulped down by Ryu. "Do I need to pay you, sir?" Perry asked, carefully picking up the packed basket and waiting for the answer.

"Our Arville pays by the moon," the baker said. "Off with you, that basket won't last forever."

So he trudged back to Arville's home, escorted by Ryu and trailing the aroma of fresh baked bread.

Missus Weaver was back in the kitchen when Ryu pulled the latchstring with his teeth and shouldered the door open so Perry didn't have to juggle the basket to get inside. She turned as he entered and smiled at him. "Put that basket in the pantry, there's a good lad. Is there a meat pie in there?"

"Yes'm," Perry replied, doing as he was told.

"Good, he got it in on the first baking. That'll be your supper, then, with the soup. Your pa'll be in the stable with our Arville." She went back to whatever it was she was chopping, and Perry took the hint, leaving the same way he'd come in.

Arville and his father were looking over the vanners, with Arville making some pretty intelligent conversation about the breed. "So how did you like Whithern?" Mags called, as Perry and Ryu came through the stable door.

"It's small." He had kept half his seedcake back, and he gave it to Dallen. "The baker is nice."

"There never was much trouble out of Whithern," Arville noted. "That's why I decided to move here. You're going to have to look farther away for the trouble. North and west."

Mags nodded. "Well, first we had better establish ourselves as genuine traders before we go off. I told Missus Weaver we'd be open for business tomorrow morning. So let's go get the trade goods out of storage and ready for display."

All of the trade goods were held in locked compartments under the caravan. Perry took the side of the wagon that was almost against the wall since he was the smallest.

Inside the compartments were paper-wrapped bundles of ribbons, woven trim, hanks of colored thread, and hanks of colored *chirra* wool spun finer than any village spinster could ever manage. Then there were the beads: hanks of thread on which tiny, glittering glass beads were strung, strings of larger glass beads, strings of copper, brass, and pewter beads, strings of semiprecious stone beads—so many different kinds it made his head spin. Last of all were two bolts of *chirra*-wool cloth and a few bolts of linen much more finely woven than any village loom could manage—the sort of thing to make a bridal veil or a fine shawl from. Over on the side that Arville and Perry's father were working on were the display tables for all these goods, ingenious things that could be taken apart and put back together again within a half a candlemark.

"Papa!" he called. "Should we just set everything out to-night?"

"No," came the answer from the other side of the caravan. "Just unload everything from the boxes into the caravan.

There are too many creatures around here that are attracted to shiny things. We'll set up in the morning."

The bead boxes were small but astonishingly heavy for their size. Perry put the bolts of fabric into his father's bed, along with the boxes of colored thread. Then the bead boxes went onto the bunks on either side of the caravan. He didn't drop the upper bunks down to use; he knew they could support a grown adult, but he didn't want to trust the weight of the beads to them.

His father came to help him with the last of the load, locking the door of the caravan behind them. "Tomorrow we'll find out just what sort of trade we can expect from a little village like this," he told Perry, as he made sure the lock was secure. "I have a notion of loading packs on the vanners and taking them out instead of packing up the entire caravan and sniffing for trouble. I think we might make a better target with just us and two horses."

"That's a good idea," Arville agreed. "That's a real good idea." He opened the door for them and sniffed. There was a rich aroma of gravy in the air. "I smell meat pie!" he said happily.

Perry exchanged a look with his father, and Perry tried not to chuckle.

———————

As soon as the sun was up, Mags rousted Perry out of his dreams, and with barely enough time to wolf down some eggs and buttered bread, he chivvied him out to the caravan to set everything up. "I'll set the prices at first," Mags told him as he carefully put each item in its proper place. "But I want you to listen and learn them as quickly as you can. If anyone brings anything to trade, though, I'm the only one that can make a deal."

"Yes, sir," Perry nodded. "Do you think anyone will trade?"

"Oh, they'll want to. Real coin is scarce out here; I fancy the only time they ever see it is when Arville pays for something, or the local Guard patrol comes through. The question is whether they have something a real trader would actually want."

"Because we can't act out of character from a real trader." Perry nodded. He furrowed his brow. "Are they actually going to have something we want?"

Mags shrugged. "Strange things come out of here. They might. Arville told me that traders don't come here that often, and when they do, they are generally traveling with no more than they can carry on a single mule."

No more than a sixth of their goods were on the tables, but that was because Mags only put out one of each item. The rest were still in the caravan. And their first customer was Missus Weaver. As soon as she finished her morning work, she came bustling out of the kitchen door with a bright and expectant expression on her face, and she clasped her hands with pleasure when she saw the colorful display.

"Oh—I had no idea you lads had all this in your wagon!" she exclaimed, and she bent over the table of colored threads and trim. "So many pretty things!" she added, looking at everything with a sort of hunger.

Mags chuckled and plucked a bright blue ribbon off the table. It was long enough for several purposes, if Perry was any judge. "My good lady, please take this with our compliments. You've been going to twice your usual work to feed us and tidy up after us; it's the least we can do," he said, presenting it to her stretched across his palms.

"Oh, my!" Her cheeks took on a pleased blush, and Perry realized that his father had managed to pull out a ribbon that matched her eyes. "Oh, I shouldn't—"

"I insist," Mags said, draping it around her neck. "You've earned it."

One hand caressed the ribbon as she smiled. "How did you know blue is my favorite color?"

"Trade secret," Mags replied. "Now, if you were planning

on doing any wool work, I can particularly recommend this—" He picked up a skein of the *chirra* thread. "It's much stronger than it looks, and it is extremely soft to the touch."

At this point, at least a dozen women and girls came around the strip of woodland that lay between Arville's house and the palisade of the village. They were all chattering away like sparrows, and when they saw Missus Weaver there ahead of them, one of them called out, "Now Mina! Don't you go snatching all the bargains before we can get to them!"

Then it was a very busy morning indeed. Everything had to be touched, examined, held up to the light, and set down again. Perry wasn't afraid that any of them would steal anything. For one thing, someone turning up in possession of a bauble or embroidering with thread everyone else knew she hadn't bought would be castigated. You just couldn't get away with stealing, not in a village this small, and definitely not with a Herald living next door. But he was afraid one of those hanks of tiny glass beads would have a thread break, sending the beads scattering everywhere. But evidently the thread they were strung on was sturdy stuff.

A few of the women, who already knew exactly what they wanted, had come prepared with real coined money. So two lengths of the fine linen, some bright linen embroidery thread, and a single hank of sparkling yellow glass beads were sold in short order.

But the rest had to look, and hear the prices, and ponder, and touch, and ponder, and ask whether "that price can't come down, after all?" and ponder some more. Mags treated them all with the same friendly courtesy and patience.

And "I'll be back!" they promised, one after another, and drifted back to the village. Perry could almost sense the thoughts buzzing in their heads like bees.

"They will be back," Mags said confidently. "Now they'll go see what they might have that I might want. That's where the real trading comes in." Then he laughed and sat down on a stool he'd brought out from the house. Perry sat on the ground beside him. "I'd have been damned good at this if I hadn't been Chosen."

"I know, I've watched you in the shop," Perry agreed. He was about to say more when a woman and a girl came into view. Perry had learned enough about the subtleties of clothing to know that the woman's gown was a step or two above that of the women who had been here earlier, while the girl's plainer outfit, and the fact that she was carrying a basket while the woman's hands were unburdened, marked her as the woman's servant.

This must be the wife of the man who owned the biggest house in the village, who was probably also the village headman. Villages this small rarely had a mayor; usually the wealthiest man or, more rarely, woman was appointed to speak for everyone.

:That is Una Miller. She is the miller's wife, and they have the big house in the village,: Ryu told him, confirming his thoughts. *:Don't worry, she is nice.:*

"Heyla, trader!" Una called as soon as she was within earshot. "You picked a fine morning to put out your wares!"

Mags bowed with a little flourish. "A fine morning it is, lady. I am Mags, and this young fellow is my son, Perry. What can we assist you with?"

Una dimpled at him; Perry judged she was several years older than his mother, and her general expression was of someone who regards those around her as friends. "Lady indeed! I'm just the miller's wife, you rascal. You won't get the better of me in a bargain with flattery!"

"I don't think I'd get the better of you in a bargain at all, dear lady," Mags replied, smiling.

She winked. "Well, as for what you can assist me with, I require the materials for two wedding veils, which should be equal in quality but unlike. I hope you have good ideas, Trader Mags."

Mags picked up the finer of the two bolts of linen. "To begin with, we'll have to have the fabric. This is called mist linen, I am told, and it is particularly well suited to veils."

Expertly, the woman ran her hand under the fabric and examined it. "Yes, this is perfect. Cut me two lengths of that—long enough to brush the floor behind, and fall to below the chin in the front—and let us go on to the materials for embellishing. I have two daughters, and as I said, I want them to have equal veils but not alike. Their coloring is like mine. What do you suggest?"

Mags stroked his chin with his thumb and forefinger. Perry was really curious at this point just how his father was going to address this. *He* certainly wouldn't know how to decorate a wedding veil!

"I would suggest these, for your older daughter." He pulled out three hanks of embroidery thread in shades of red; a deep red the color of wine, a dark rust, and a slightly lighter rust-color. "Embroider the veil's edge with flowers in these colors. Then use these yellow beads as the center of each flower." He plucked out a hank of the tiny glass beads in a deep gold and laid it on the thread in Una's hand. "The beads will sparkle in the light, and they'll weigh the edge of the veil down enough that it won't blow off her head. And for the younger daughter—" He pulled out three hanks of thread in three shades of green "—a scrolling of leaves and vines and these transparent green beads to represent buds."

Una stared up at him with amused astonishment. "Well, trader, I will say that you know your wares better than any fellow I have seen out here before! And that is a perfect suggestion. Have you enough of each dye lot for the entire veil?"

For answer, Mags whistled at Perry, who moved quickly and took the six hanks of thread. "Five of each, not counting the ones you have now," Mags ordered. Perry hopped into the back of the caravan and matched the thread with the ones in the storage and brought them all back out. While he'd been hunting, his father had cut two lengths of the mist linen to Una's satisfaction.

"Thirty skeins of thread, six hanks of beads, and two lengths of linen," said Mags, expertly folding the linen and packaging the thread and beads. It all made a surprisingly small bundle. "Now, shall we discuss price?"

Mags had seen his father at work in the shop before, so he knew the delicate dance going on here between merchant and customer—though in Mags' case, he never actually had to worry about making a profit, so his nonchalance didn't have to be feigned. His earlier bargaining with the women who had paid in cash had told him what the traffic out here would bear. Now he just had to strike a bargain where Una would be satisfied she wasn't being taken advantage of, and had gotten a sliver of an edge over him, but was not suspicious that she had gotten *too* good a bargain.

When it was all over with, and they had agreed on a price, Una fished in her belt purse and pulled out the requisite handful of coppers and a lone silver piece. And when she had picked up the package to hand to her servant girl, Mags pulled a ribbon the color of the dark red, another the color of the dark green, and a lovely dark blue and laid them over the top of the bundle, much to Una's surprise. "A little wedding gift from me, whenever the weddings may be," he said with a twinkle.

Una laughed, and thanked him. "Not until the veils are finished, at least," she added. "And the wedding gowns. That will keep them out of mischief. Thank you, Trader Mags. It was good bargaining with you."

"And with you, Una Miller," he replied easily. "I am also open to trade in small, portable objects, should you desire something for yourself."

"I'll consider that," she called over her shoulder and trailed by her servant, she made her way back to Whithern.

"Lydia taught me a lot about fabric and colors when I was roughly your age," Mags said, leaning against the caravan. "A couple of Dia's Handmaidens helped me out by teaching me how to estimate how much thread it takes to embroider something. And I'm good at memorizing, so I spent a couple of days with a merchant who sells this sort of thing down in Haven, learning what things should cost."

Perry nodded. His father continued. "The big thing will be trying to figure out even trades. You'd probably better leave that to me, unless something springs out at you as obvious."

Over the course of the morning, other women and girls turned up, looked, and said they would be back. They sold nothing but a few ribbons, some pins, and needles, and one string of blue glass beads suitable for a necklace. Mags seemed content, so Perry assumed this was exactly as he had planned for the day to go. Missus Weaver brought them something to eat at noon, and Arville wandered by and kept them company for a while.

Then, just before supper, the men began to turn up. As the first of them rounded the trees, Mags straightened up. "Ah, now things are going to get serious," he told Perry. "Watch."

And Perry did watch, carefully. Within moments, it was clear why the men of the village were here.

They were looking for presents for their wives. They were here to find out what, exactly, Mags was willing to trade for. And they were bound and determined this "slick trader" wasn't going to get the best of them.

The men gathered around Mags, and one by one, they made their cases. The first, who offered furs, got a rejection for "too bulky." Which was a relief to Perry, since he didn't look forward to potentially sharing a trip home with a caravan full of furs in the height of the summer. The second, however, held out his hand—

Mags picked something vaguely roundish off the man's palm and examined it closely. He then put it back down with a grin. "I'll take as many of those as you can bring me. Those are very good garnets."

The other men exchanged slightly startled, then pleased glances, and all but the one who had brought the garnets in the first place hurried off. The man remaining behind took a little sack off his belt and handed it, and the garnets in his hand, to Mags. "There's a lot of 'em that we bain't chipped free yet, Trader," he said, sounding a little worried.

"And I'll take as many as you fellows can bring me," Mags repeated. "At a fair price. You're lucky it was me that came here; I not only know stones, I know who to sell 'em to." Mags looked over the stones in the bag with a critical eye. "I think we can bargain for something pretty for your ladies, and you'll get some coin at the end as well."

They put their heads together over the display, with Mags asking lots of questions to draw the fellow out. Eventually, the man wended his way home looking completely satisfied, with a shawl's-worth of the fine wool, the *chirra*-wool yarn to embroider it with, several colors of embroidery thread, a string of agate beads and three strings of glass beads, a couple of hanks of the tiny glass beads, a full paper of pins, six needles, and two kinds of trim. And he still walked away with several small silver coins in his belt pouch.

"That's probably the most coined money he's ever had in his life," Mags observed, leaning back against the caravan. "We'll stay here for another candlemark or so in case someone else has a cache of garnets somewhere, but I expect they'll all have to go to wherever the field is and spend some time chipping stones loose. Or maybe send their younglings out to do it."

But no one else appeared, and at the end of the allotted time, they picked up the display tables, goods and all, and took them into the stable, where they left them in one of the loose-box Companion stalls. "Papa, what happens if they bring us too many stones?" Perry asked as they closed up the caravan and went back into Arville's house by the kitchen door.

"Well, I actually came well equipped for trading," Mags re-

plied, and he sniffed the air appreciatively. Arville ladled out
a thick soup into big bowls, and one of the fresh loaves and a
bowl of butter were on the table. "It takes time to chip a garnet
free of stone without breaking it. I don't think there will be too
many stones for us to trade or pay for, and this venture is
actually going to turn a very nice profit. I'll let the Jeweler's
Guild know about this place when we get back, and they can
send out a journeyman on a regular basis to buy."

"What are you buying?" Arville asked, cutting and butter-
ing the bread as they got settled.

"Rough garnets," Mags replied, helping himself to buttered
bread.

Arville blinked at him. "Those are worth something? The
littles just chip them out to play conkers with, there's a field
west of here where it's easy to find them."

"The ones I was offered are of good color and don't have
obvious flaws," Mags told him. "I know gemstones. These are
good. I was telling my son that I'm going to make sure the
Jeweler's Guild in Haven knows to send buyers out here from
now on. Your little town is about to become prosperous, so
before we go looking for your trouble, you need to sit down
with all the townsfolk, work out something that allows everyone to share in the prosperity, and get it on paper. I'll take it
back with me. Otherwise—"

"Oh, I know!" Arville replied, "When we were all on our
Training Circuit, one of the villages ended up with a gold mine.
Good thing Herald Elyn was in charge. She sat everyone down
and got everything in writing while they were all feeling too
dazzled to be greedy."

"You also don't want strangers rushing up here to claim the
land either," Mags cautioned him. "This isn't going to be like
a gold mine—garnets aren't *that* valuable. They'll be valuable
enough, though, to give everyone a nice, reliable source of
coin, which will come in handy if there is a crop failure."

He was about to say more when there was a timid tapping

at the door frame. They all looked up to see all the men of the village were back—including one who was rather floury. *The miller—who is also the headman, I guess,* Perry thought.

"We kind of overheard that last part, Arville," said the miller. "Ruvus here told us what you gave him for the garnets. Or, he told me, and I reckoned I'd better bring everyone here so we could get all this garnet business worked out while everybody is feeling friendly."

Mags looked at Arville in astonishment. Arville shrugged and mouthed *Luck* at him. Perry got what he meant immediately. This was Arville's Gift in action, for certain-sure. Arville wanted to live in a peaceful, friendly place where everyone got along . . . and his Luck was making sure it was and stayed that way. Suddenly, Perry understood why everything about this place that had seemed to be too good to be true actually wasn't. Wasn't too good to be true, that is. It was Arville's Luck.

"Well, all right, Jeffer. Bring the rest around to the front door. You all know where to go. Just let us finish our supper and we'll be right with you." Arville made it quite clear from his posture that he was perfectly all right with them invading his house—but he wasn't going to cut his supper short for anyone.

"We'll do that, Arville," said the miller, and the knot of men left the doorway and, presumably went around to the front of the house.

"Perry?" Arville said.

"Yessir!" Perry sat straight up.

"If you're done with your supper, would you go see if they need anything?" Arville asked.

Perry jumped up to do just that. It was easy enough to find where they were in the big house by the sound of voices. It turned out that at the front of the house was a single big room with three big tables put together in the shape of the letter "U" with chairs all around them. That's where the men were.

"Arville says to ask you if there's anything you need, sirs," he called over the murmur of voices, causing every head in the room to turn in his direction.

"Mugs, lad," the miller replied. "Baker's gone for a barrel of beer."

Perry took a quick head count, and fetched mugs until everyone had one. About that time the baker returned with a keg of beer in the back of a farm cart. Some of the men helped him carry it in and set it up. They settled in chairs around the table with full mugs; Perry lingered, wondering if there was anything else he should do.

"Making a good decision is thirsty work," said one of the men that Perry didn't know, and winked.

"Here we are!" Arville called from the door, carrying a roll of paper, with Mags behind him. He spread out the map on the middle table. "Trader Mags here says first we need to draw out where the garnet field is on this map so I can send it to Haven to claim it for Whithern." He looked up at all of them. "You do want to claim it in common, right?"

The men looked at each other, then back at Arville. "If that seems best. . . ." said Miller.

"It will be the easiest," Mags replied easily. "Right, Arville?"

"Aye. That's how we set up that gold mine in Bastion's Stone." Arville told him, while following the directions two of the others gave him to outline the garnet field on the map. "All right, then. There it is."

They all stood and looked at the map with varying expressions of contemplation on their faces, as if outlining the field on the map had suddenly made it more real for them.

"Now, the gold mine, we set up a system where we had a couple of men that were full-time miners and smelters," Arville continued. "They got paid a daily wage everyone agreed on from the beginning. That came out of what they got for the gold. And the rest got divided equally among everyone. Now, you can do that here, or you can work out some other deal."

After that, Perry quickly lost interest, as the men all pondered various schemes, slowly—ridiculously slowly, he thought—weighing the positives and negatives. When it became apparent that this would probably go on for candlemarks, he caught his father's eye with an imploring gaze, and Mags smiled and nodded at the door. Perry did not wait to be given a second invitation; he was out and into the main house in short order.

But he wasn't yet sleepy, and he wasn't nearly as much of a bookworm as his sister was, so he went outside. Ryu was lying down beside the kitchen door and looked up as he came out.

:They'll be at it all night,: Ryu told him. *:Really, you can't blame them. This is something that is going to affect everyone in Whithern for a long time to come. They want to get it right.:*

Perry was going to ask what was so hard about working out how to handle the garnets, then shut his mouth. Clearly Arville and his father knew things he didn't.

:They're Heralds. They have to know about how dynamics within a village work and can change. They especially have to think about the future, when Arville won't be here, his Luck won't be keeping the village peaceful, and there might be new people coming here, making it bigger, who will want some of that profit, too.:

Just hearing Ryu explain it all sounded far too complicated to think about. Another reason why he really didn't want to be a Herald, if that was how Heralds had to think! "I like my problems to have solutions," he said, sitting down next to Ryu and putting an arm over his neck.

:Well, I am not much good at pack dynamics either,: Ryu confessed. *:Oh, but that reminds me. We are about to have a visit from someone from my pack! A grand-nephew of sorts.:*

"We are?" He watched the fireflies floating above the yard between the stoop and the stable. "Why?"

:Because Larral is a neuter like me. He's looking for adven-

ture, and the pack thought I might provide it.: Ryu raised his head again, and snuffed Perry's free hand. *:I thought you and your father might like to have him along.:*

Well, Perry could certainly think of any number of ways in which a creature like a *kyree,* the size of one of Lady Dia's biggest mastiffs, could come in handy. Hadn't he just been wishing that they'd thought to ask for one of those mastiffs before they left? "Well, *I* would!" he agreed. "Will I be able to talk to him like I can talk to you?"

:I'd be surprised if you couldn't.:

The two of them sat there in comfortable silence for a long while, watching the fireflies and saying nothing. But Perry was thinking.

Mostly he was wondering about what this younger *kyree* was like—and whether, like Ryu, he was looking for a human to attach himself to.

Because if he was—well, Perry was more than willing to volunteer.

Mags' bed was positioned so that the morning sun struck him right on the face about a candlemark after sunrise if he didn't get up before then. This morning, it took having that reminder to get him out of bed.

Mags was still feeling sleepy and a bit muddle-headed after the long night of careful, deliberate negotiation and planning, but on the whole, he was content. And he had to wonder, as he ducked his head into a basin of water to wash up and wake himself up a bit more—would things have gone as smoothly without Arville's Luck driving everything? He didn't think so.

But the Luck had prevailed, aided by years of the people of Whithern mostly getting along and mostly on friendly terms with each other . . . and before everyone had gone to their beds, they got a solid plan locked down, in writing, and signed by all the men, with the agreement that all the women would come sign it today, so it would be on record that every adult in Whithern was behind this agreement. It should hold for decades, with no one objecting to it—except, perhaps, for someone new moving in here with the notion of exploiting the village or the garnet field. But any changes would be for the rotating Garnet Council to decide; a Council that, again, every adult in Whithern would serve on in turn. Eventually, of course, the system would run into someone determined to be greedy—

That's not likely to happen until Arville's gone. And by then, someone trustworthy from the Jeweler's Guild should be keeping an eye on things here.

"How late were you up?" Perry asked incredulously, as he came in for breakfast. It looked as if his father had been there long enough to eat two full servings of everything.

"Late enough. I wanted to make sure we got the job done while everyone was still feeling accommodating," Mags replied. "I think Arville's planning on sleeping in. He did most of the work, anyway. I just made some suggestions; he's the one who coaxed people around to the final agreement."

"So you got them all to agree?" his son replied, sounding surprised. Missus Weaver slid a plate of eggs, ham, and flatcakes onto the table in front of him, and he looked up to thank her.

"I surely didn't think it would take less than three days, but our Arville managed," Missus Weaver replied, with no little pride. "Berd told me all about it. It's a good arrangement. Everyone's a little bit unhappy, but mostly happy, which means no one's being taken advantage of."

Mags chuckled, while Perry looked a little confused. "Shouldn't everybody be completely happy?" his son asked.

"If everyone is completely happy, it means we must have overlooked something," Mags explained. Perry still looked confused, but he shrugged, willing to take his father's word for it.

The two ate in silence for a while longer, although Perry was just eating normally now, and not inhaling the food as fast as he could. Sometimes Mags wondered how he managed to not choke.

"Ryu says another *kyree* is coming to help us," Perry said, after a few moments of quiet that was very welcome after all of last night's babbling.

Now it was Mags' turn to look confused. "When did he say this?"

"Last night. Before I went to bed. It's like a grand-nephew or something. We're going to let him, right? Help us, that is," Perry demanded. "Think how useful Ryu was to Arville! And Ryu is too old to go running around with us, even if he would leave Arville, which he won't. I mean, we're not really supposed to be here, working out stuff for Whithern, we're supposed to be out there—" He waved his hand vaguely in the direction of the greater wilderness beyond Whithern. "We're supposed to be finding out if people are going missing, not trading for rocks or figuring out how to make sure everybody divides up the rocks so everyone gets a fair share!"

Mags sighed. Of course Perry didn't see all this negotiation and helping the village to deal with a sudden influx of wealth as being important. He could understand that. He probably thought this was something Arville should handle—negotiating agreements among villagers wasn't exactly what spies were supposed to do. And Mags had only gotten the villagers to agree to him "helping" Arville with this because of an invented-on-the-spot experience as a Master Trader who negotiated such things with his fellow traders all the time.

But Arville didn't have the cachet of being an impartial Herald here in Whithern. He had lived here too long and had too many contacts. Anything he would have suggested could have been challenged with the suggestion that he was being partial to his friends. But nobody could lay that charge on Mags.

He could also see Perry's side of things and why he was impatient to be *doing* something. At home, Perry would be attending the classes he enjoyed, having fun with his friends, or doing more special training with his father or Lord Jorthun.

Here . . . well, so far there hadn't even been much chance to use even the training he had, much less learn anything new.

Naturally he wanted some excitement—there was no excitement here. Truth be told, so far there hadn't been much for him to actually do, other than learn how to drive the team of horses. So he had latched onto the reason they were out here in the first place; to find out if Arville was right. The key phrase, of course, was *if* people were going missing, because at the moment they only had Arville's vague suppositions about it. Whereas right here, right now, they had a village to see to and a bargain to set up among the villagers that would last for generations.

The lad was bored. And there had never been any time for boredom in Perry's life so far. He wasn't in the least used to it.

Mags pinched the bridge of his nose between his thumb and forefinger and told himself to have patience.

"We'll get to that—" he promised. But Perry frowned. "But right now, we need to make sure there aren't going to be any problems with the agreement. This sort of thing can spin off feuds and bad feelings that last for generations."

"The longer we stay here, the more people are going to go missing!" Perry insisted, looking mulish. "And now we've got Larral coming—"

"Who?" Mags snapped, and then he reined his temper in.

"Larral. Ryu's grand-nephew. So we can leave Arville in charge of the garnet stuff. He can help us! He can—"

"Perry, I am very tired," he said, interrupting. "And this is something Arville can't do. I'll explain it all when I am not so tired. One more day or two isn't going to make a difference."

Perry subsided, but Mags distinctly heard him muttering under his breath, "—But what if it *does?*"

:*I have a thought. But you might not approve,*: said Dallen.

:*Let's hear it.*: Perry did not often show his temper, or sulk, but when he did, it could last for weeks—and Mags was essentially stuck with him and was not going to be able to escape his sour mood.

:Once this Larral arrives, we allow Perry to go out with him to do some preliminary scouting.:

:Absolutely not!: he snapped. He would have had no qualms if this had been a city—but Perry had no wilderness experience.

:Hear me out. Larral is a kyree. *His kind know their way around the wilderness. And Perry is a very clever boy. He can take one of the vanners and load it with camping supplies. It's summer, so it's not as if the weather is going to harm him. I think you should let him go. It will be good for him.:*

Mags groaned silently. If he went along with this and Amily ever found out about it, she would murder him.

I can't believe I am actually even considering this . . . Sure, he and Perry had "camped" with the caravan, but that meant Dallen outside, on watch, and the walls of the caravan between them and any potential large predators. And maybe Perry would give up after the first night—but Perry was stubborn, and maybe he wouldn't.

:Let's see what this Larral looks like,: he finally conceded. *:Then we'll make another assessment of your idea.:*

That seemed to satisfy Dallen, though Perry was still sulking. *When this* kyree *shows up, he'll probably be a giant puppy, and the whole thing will be moot,* Mags told himself. *Even Dallen won't dare to suggest this again.*

The signing was finally over. The last adult citizen of Whithern had just left, and Mags was carefully folding up the copy of the agreement that everyone had now signed, when Perry came running into the room in a high state of excitement, his bad temper forgotten. "Larral is almost here!" he cried excitedly. "Ryu says he's within smelling distance of us!"

Perry dashed out. Mags was in no great hurry. "Smelling distance" for a *kyree* could be leagues away, depending on the wind. He wanted to make sure he got the agreement tucked away safely, where it was unlikely to come to any harm.

So when he finally noticed the profound silence in the house and went looking for Perry and the rest, it was with a start of surprise that he discovered Arville, Perry, Ryu, Pelas, and Dallen in the yard between the stable and the house, all surrounding a massively muscled, exceedingly dignified, and fully adult *kyree*. The *kyree* looked up as he stood in the kitchen doorway and nodded at him.

"Rerow," the beast said, still with immense dignity.

"Ah, hello, Larral, it's good to meet you at last," Mags managed.

Larral nodded. "Ry Roose Rerry, Rags," came the next words from the *kyree's* mouth. It was impossible to take him with anything other than complete seriousness. Even if Mags hadn't a clue what he'd just said.

Ry Roose—what? For a moment, he couldn't make the words form any sensible sentence.

But then, the meaning, impossible as it was, hit him with the same impact as a bag of hammers. "You—what?" he gasped, staring from Larral to an excited and pink-cheeked Perry and back again. "You—ca—"

"It's not *exactly* like being Chosen by a Companion, Mags," Arville said, apologetically, scratching his head. "But it's sorta close. That's about the best way to put it, I guess. I don't think it would be a good idea to fight this—you know what I mean?"

Mags certainly did not know what Arville meant, but he did know that this wasn't just a boy's infatuation with a weird dog. That was obvious, not only from Arville and Ryu's decades-long partnership, but from the proprietary way in which boy and *kyree* looked at each other.

This wasn't something he *could* fight. All he could do now was hope that Amily wouldn't murder him. . . .

:She's not going to murder you,: Dallen said with no little irritation. *:You're overreacting. Your son just gained a protector and a best friend for life, with none of the complications being Chosen by a Companion brings to the one who is Chosen. And don't pretend that you don't know what I mean, Mags. Being Chosen is why most Heralds never marry or even have long-term relationships. You and Amily are the exception that proves the rule.:*

Mags bit his lip. Dallen was right. Being Chosen meant all sorts of things . . . and brought with it the burden of being a Herald with all that entailed.

:There, you see, not so bad after all, is it? And Perry can still go right on to become the King's agent. Look at it this way. It's a lot easier to fit a kyree *into a room than a Companion; a* kyree *can go wherever he does. And a* kyree *is a lot easier to hide than a Companion. Larral can always be explained away as being merely a dog, whereas Companions . . . we stand out like lilies in a coal mine. Not the best thing if you are a covert agent.:*

And that was certainly true, too.

: Now . . . about that suggestion of mine—:

"No," Mags said, firmly. He put a bite of supper in his mouth and chewed.

"But—" Perry began.

"No," Mags repeated. "I am absolutely, positively, not letting you and that overgrown furball go gallivanting all over the countryside alone. No matter what Dallen thinks."

He had spent most of the afternoon arguing with his Companion, who clearly had never been a parent. Perry must have thought he was going to get his way this time, because he had brought the subject up the moment that they'd gathered for supper.

"Peregrine, can you name me five occasions on which you have camped overnight in the wilderness alone?" he continued.

Perry, who'd had his mouth open to protest, blinked. And being a truthful boy, gulped, and answered "Uh . . . no."

"Four? Two? *One?*" Mags persisted. He already knew the answer, of course. "I would have no qualms about setting you loose in a city, or finding you a place on a large estate where you could work and observe. But I haven't given you the skills to live in the wilderness, and I can't give those to you overnight. Your *kyree* friend will be of very little help with that. If you were planning on an unorganized search, which right now is the only thing that you could do, given the scant information we have, have you any idea where to begin? And last of all, what exactly do you think you would be looking for out there?"

Perry subsided into a sulk. But knowing his son as he did, Mags was reasonably sure he was thinking all this over even though he was sulking. *I'm tolerably certain this is something every youngling goes through at this age. I'm also very sure I am going to get quite tired of that pouty face before he grows out of it.*

:*I'd call it 'rebellious' rather than 'pouty.':*

:*I'm the one looking at it, horse.:*

"Now, I'll tell you what I *will* do. I will let you look over the information on missing people. I'll let you have access to all the maps, give you permission to plot things on them with charcoal we can brush away, and you can see if you can find a pattern in the disappearances. You can question anyone here in Whithern that you like. And that includes Arville." He glanced over at the Herald, who nodded. "You can even take Larral and your horse and comb the countryside within a half day's ride of here. But if you are not back by sundown and the only reason is because you rode out farther than you should have, I'm revoking that privilege."

Some of the sulkiness dropped out of Perry's expression. "Yessir," he said.

"Now, as your spymaster, my suggestion to you would be to take the maps and Arville, and both of you go over them carefully after supper. And the same all day tomorrow. Then, if that seems like an endeavor that will bear fruit, start making inquiries in Whithern of people who have reason to know something. *Then* you should be able to determine the next direction to take your investigation."

More of the sulkiness drained. Now Perry looked a bit more like his normal self. "Yessir," he said.

"Meanwhile, Dallen and I are going to attempt to relay this agreement to Haven, so we can get someone out here who can ratify it. That's likely to take until bedtime." He had only tried relay by Mindspeech a couple of times, since most of his work was done in Haven. He'd been fairly successful at it, but his success this time was going to depend on how many Companions there were between him and Haven. And it was going to give him a splitting headache whether or not he succeeded.

"Yessir," Perry replied, and looked at Arville. "Is that all right with you, Herald Arville?"

"It's *great!*" Arville enthused. "I'm not all that good at organizing stuff, you know? If you're better than me, maybe we can discover something!"

"Not really good at organizing stuff" turned out to be an understatement. What Perry discovered was that Arville's notes consisted of rumors and queries from other people, nothing of his notes was even close to being in a coherent form, and none of his sources were even aware of other disappearances. So, slowly, carefully, with much cross-examining, Perry got Arville's information properly organized. By then, they were both yawning, and Perry was in no shape to look at maps by dim candlelight.

So in the morning, after a breakfast of bread and butter,

since Missus Weaver hadn't yet arrived to make the real breakfast, Perry took the maps Arville gave him to the big room where everyone had worked on the gemstone agreement, laid them out on the table, and began plotting each and every interrupted journey.

He was so involved in this project that Larral had to come and interrupt him for his proper breakfast.

And by suppertime, he had something that made Arville's instinctive reason for alarm look perfectly rational.

His father had recovered by then and was headache-free and willing to come look at his findings.

And his father's face got a very sober look when he did.

"Well," Mags said, looking at the map. "There's at least one good reason why all those people seem to have vanished from within this circle you've drawn. The only road through there goes right through the middle of your circle."

"Yes, but unless Arville's *only* collected the stories of disappearances from this area—"

"I didn't," Arville said immediately. "I rode all over this area, asking people about missing folks." He indicated a much bigger area, which had several roads through it.

"Well then," Mags replied to Perry's immense satisfaction. "Now we have something. I never doubted you, Arville, but looking at this, there's a pattern, and we need to figure out the cause." His father's face took on a deeply thoughtful cast. "We can't use the methods we do in the city. What other things have you noticed about the missing people, Perry?"

"There's never more than two of them, and if there are two, they're generally young," Perry said promptly. "Mostly, it's single people who don't have anyone that would ask after them seriously. Small peddlers with two horses or walking with a donkey. Casual laborers—there are a lot of those, and the stories Arville got were all from other casual laborers who asked if he'd heard from them or seen them. Some runaways.

Even some petty criminals who lit out once people started to look at them suspiciously."

"So, that sounds like it could either be an animal or animals that's attacking travelers on the road, or a single human bandit who is preying on them." Mags frowned. "Except, if it's a bandit, instead of taking richer targets, he's taking poorer ones. That doesn't make sense."

"I asked about strangers showing up with goods they didn't seem to know the value of," Arville put in. "With the missing small peddlers, you would think that it would be impossible for one thief to know what they were all carrying was worth. So if it's a bandit, he's keeping the loot all to himself."

"Which isn't logical." Mags frowned more deeply. "Huh. What are the odds it's an animal?"

:If it is, I can sniff it out,: said Larral.

"Larral says he can find any animal it might be," Perry relayed.

"Is there anything like a village in that area?" Mags pulled on the lobe of his ear as he studied the map. "Nothing's noted."

"Just an inn. Here." Arville tapped a spot on the road that had a little "x" mark on it. Looking more closely, Perry saw it wasn't an "x", it was a tiny crossed knife and fork. "I took a trip out there just to talk to the innkeeper, but I didn't learn anything new from him."

"And did you ask there about animal attacks?" Mags asked.

Arville nodded. "And all the missing people too." He scratched his head. "The innkeeper said he hadn't had any trouble with wild animals attacking his stock, that no one spending the night said anything about attacks, and that the missing people had never turned up on his doorstep." Now Arville frowned. "Now that I think about it, though, he was *awful* sure of that."

"Maybe a little too sure?" Mags replied, skeptically. "I find it hard to believe that an innkeeper, even one that doesn't get as much traffic as a really busy place, is going to remember every single customer that crosses his threshold."

Arville frowned harder. "Thinking back, aye."

"But what would an innkeeper—I mean, why would he be helping someone—" Perry looked from his father to Arville and back again. "He'd have no way of selling what he stole, would he? Even if the peddlers weren't carrying as much as we can, that's still five or six packloads of trading goods. I mean, people are going to question where an innkeeper out in the middle of nowhere got so much stuff. So why would he be disappearing people?" He didn't for a moment question his father's hunch about the innkeeper; it was Mags' job to be suspicious, after all. Well, it was his job, too.

"If that *is* what's happening, the reason isn't obvious." Mags pulled on his earlobe again and stared at the spot on the map where the inn was. "It isn't for what these people were carrying; it can't be, since most of them were not peddlers. A few personal belongings of relatively poor people aren't going to tempt anyone but the most desperate, and even if his inn hasn't got a lot of custom out here, it'll have enough to be profitable without doing away with his customers. It has to be for those people themselves. It isn't kidnapping, because none of them have anyone who would ransom them. . . ."

"Are you thinking what I'm thinking?" Arville blurted, looking horrified.

"You've got a rich field of garnets *here*," Mags pointed out, tapping the map where Whithern was. "This entire area is all the same kind of hilly territory, not unlike the mines where I was enslaved as a child. Where there are garnets, there are often more valuable stones. And if I needed slaves that were strong enough to work those mines but not so strong or clever that they would need more than a handful of guards . . . those sorts of people—casual laborers, peddlers used to walking long distances, and young people—are exactly the kind I would take."

"I've never heard of a mine there," Arville objected.

"And you wouldn't. This would be like that gold mine you and your friends discovered: a secret. *If* my guess is right, that is. If it's not—" Mags shrugged. "If it's not, I'd still bet the key to the disappearances is at that inn. This isn't part of Valdemar. There's no one keeping an eye on innkeepers and tavern keepers to make sure they stay honest."

He turned toward Perry, who looked up at his father expectantly.

"You and I are going to go out there," he said. "And Larral, of course. I'm going to need both of you."

Perry felt his heart leap. *He thinks I am good enough, ready enough, to go with him and help!*

Arville was frowning at the map. "I'm not sure you have legal standing to do that, Mags. Like you said, that's technically not in Valdemar. I mean, here's the border—and most of that part of the road is outside Valdemar."

"But the people who are missing *are* from Valdemar," Mags replied firmly. "And it might not be in Valdemar, but there's no other kingdom claiming it, either. I don't even think the Hawkbrothers are out there now."

Larral raised his head at that. "Res," he affirmed. His massive brow wrinkled, then he looked up at Perry. *:The Hawkbrothers left roughly a generation ago. There are humans claiming to be lords who have fortified dwellings and often villages, some of which depend on them, but the Hawkbrothers said the land you are looking at needed to be cleansed of inimical magic, and they withdrew to establish a new Vale.:*

Perry sympathized with his new friend. Given the limitations on Larral's speech, that would have taken a long time to say aloud, with them trying to puzzle out exactly what he was saying. "Larral says there are villages out there, and local lords, but the Hawkbrothers pulled out of the area about a generation ago."

"Your friend is proving to be a lot more useful than I would have thought," Mags replied. He looked down at the map. "All right, this will be the plan. We'll move slowly toward that inn, and Larral will be scouting for any signs of a predator large and bold enough to attack human beings. If we don't encounter anything, once we get to the area, we'll scout the inn carefully and determine only after we do whether we will be entering it."

Arville looked at him oddly. "Why would you do that?" he asked.

"Because I am very careful," Mags replied, as Perry nodded. "And I trust no one not in Whites."

It took them two days to get ready; Perry was surprised to discover that his father had actually made preparations for camping instead of using the caravan, and in one of the storage compartments on the roof of the caravan was everything they would need, from the canvas for a shelter to a hand ax. But he had to get it all down, make sure it was in good shape, then put together loads for the three horses they were taking. He wasn't going to ride Dallen; since they were still disguising themselves as traders, it wouldn't do to be riding a Companion. Maybe people would think Dallen was just a big white horse, but all it would take would be one person recognizing him for what he was, and their disguises would be over.

Dallen was coming along, of course, but covertly. And to do that, he couldn't carry a pack, as it would probably hang up on the underbrush.

Lily and Daisy would serve as his riding horse and packhorse, respectively, and of course Perry would be on Pog. Mags had to pack a smaller, lighter version of his trade goods, leaving out the bolts of material altogether as well as most of the beads.

And meanwhile, the women of Whithern were coming to

the caravan with garnets to trade, so he had to do this while also keeping up appearances. But Perry was finally of help here; he already knew how to weigh and appraise rough gemstones from working in the pawnshop, and he now knew the value by weight of the garnets here.

So unless a woman specifically asked for Mags, Perry waited on her. The elaborate and expensive trims were going very fast, and so was the fancy, soft wool and the woolen threads to embroider it with. One daring young woman bought enough of the mist linen to make a nightdress; when Perry told his father that, Mags laughed but said nothing.

He had a good idea why they were buying so much that could be considered "frivolous." For one thing, they were not yet relying on the garnets as part of their income; mentally, the stones were still the "worthless" rocks that the children chipped out to play with, and the fact that they could get anything for them made the ladies inclined to buy as much as they could. For another, women out here worked very hard and seldom saw pretty things they had not made themselves, and the men were at least vaguely aware of this. That meant that husbands, fathers, and suitors had motivation to go chip out a handful of stones after the work of the day was done, press them into their loved ones' hands, and say, "Go get yourself something nice." And, of course, there was nothing stopping any of the women from chipping out a handful themselves.

Finally, near sunset, what Perry thought was probably the last of the customers disappeared around the trees, going back to Whithern with her booty. And just when they were about to close everything up and get supper, Missus Weaver came out of the kitchen, a little leather pouch of her own dangling from her hand.

"I hope there's still some of that wool left," she said, before Mags could greet her.

"There is some—" Mags brought out what was left of the bolt. She measured out what was left, expertly.

"I'll take it all," she said, surprising them both. "I'm going to supply Berd with a fancy shirt. He hasn't a 'best' shirt at all anymore, and this one should be comfortable enough I'll actually be able to get him to wear it."

She consulted with Mags over the sort of trim that a plain and modest man would not be embarrassed to wear. Eventually they settled on black and gray; she went on her way with her parcel, and they went into the kitchen for supper.

Then, by the light of the setting sun, they packed up everything that they weren't taking with them and stored it all back in the locked compartments under the caravan.

"You can stay here, you know," Mags told Perry as they walked back to the house. "Camping isn't all that comfortable, even though this is the best season to be doing it."

Perry shook his head. "You won't be able to do half as much as if you have me and Larral along. And how would you hunt for dangerous beasts without Larral?" He tried to look as competent and prepared for anything as he could. "I'm not so soft that I can't sleep on the ground."

"Are you all packed?"

Perry nodded.

"All right, then. Get a good night's rest, because we'll be up early." Mags left his son at the entrance of the hall to the guest rooms and went farther into the house, probably to talk to Arville. Perry looked down at Larral.

:I'm glad we're getting out of here.:

:I am, as well. This does not seem the best use of our time, if there are people who are missing,: Larral agreed.

Perry grinned. It was nice to have someone who was in agreement with him.

He had thought he might be too excited about leaving to sleep, but instead, he found when he lay down, he wasn't excited at all. Instead, what he felt was more a sense of relief that they were finally going.

And it wasn't hard to drop off at all.

The next thing he knew, his father was shaking him awake. It was still dark outside, and he had to light a candle to see by. Since he could only take as much as Pog could carry, he was leaving quite a bit behind. Everything he wasn't taking with him was stored in the caravan now.

It was too early for Missus Weaver to be here, but she had left an egg pie for their breakfast. They made short work of most of it, and Arville, who had gotten up with them, inhaled what was left.

By the time the two of them set off, there was just a sliver of sun above the horizon. There had been no sign of Dallen as they loaded the horses and rode away from Arville's home, and for the life of him, Perry couldn't see the Companion anywhere. People had told him that out in the wilderness Companions could practically make themselves vanish if they cared to, but this was his first time seeing it for himself. How could something the size of a horse be moving around in the woods without a trace?

Larral stayed at Pog's heel until they got past Whithern; then, between one moment and the next, he disappeared as well, using his nose to hunt for dangerous beasts and his long legs to cover at least as much ground as Dallen could.

The entire first day was uneventful. Since Mags wanted to give Larral and Dallen plenty of time to search off the road for perils no one else had uncovered, their horses ambled, rather than moving briskly, and Mags used the time to drill Perry on geography.

Larral found them a good campsite, off the road but easy to get to, on top of a rise above a stream. They didn't have an actual tent, just a couple of pieces of waterproofed canvas that could be rigged into a rain shelter, and as pleasant as the evening was, they didn't even bother with that. They ate fish they caught in the stream, broiled over the coals on a fork of sticks, and watercress. Larral shared the fish. When they went to bed, Perry stretched his mind out as far as it could reach, but he didn't turn up anything. He was still trying when sleep overtook him.

The next two days were like the first except that at the second camp they ate rabbits caught by Larral, and at the third, Mags brought down a male duck that Perry could assure him was unmated.

By the time the fourth day dawned, Perry was certain that nothing was going to happen until they got to the inn.

He could not have been more wrong.

:Trouble!: Larral exclaimed, just as Perry heard it in his mind, weak and distant. A cry of distress. Frantic, acute distress. It might be weak, but the emotions of fear and panic were definitely there.

:Help!: It was distinct and clear, and in real words, not images, as articulate as Larral. But it was in the part of the Mindvoice where he expected to hear the nattering of birds, not something that sounded intelligent. *:Help! Help!:* And there was no doubt in his mind. He had to answer!

His head snapped around as he homed in on the mental voice, the fear the unknown projected impelling him. "Father, I have to go—someone's in trouble! Larral hears it too!" he gasped.

"What—" his father began, but he'd already wrenched Pog's head around, and without a second thought, he doubled back to a creek they had just crossed and set Pog dashing upstream, water flying in all directions. *Thank the gods this creek is sandy-bottomed and not rocks.* His heart raced; urgency flooded him as the Mindvoice got clearer and stronger the closer he got, and with it came the images of what was attacking . . . a mob of lightning-fast creatures that looked something like sooty weasels but were nearly the size of foxes. He got mere glimpses, though; whatever was holding them off, the originator of the call, was jumping around too much for him to figure out what sort of animal it was.

What if this is some kind of a trap?

:Larral—: he sent. But before he could voice his fear, Larral anticipated him.

:Not—a trap. Trust me.:

Pog somehow managed to catch up to Larral, and a heart-beat later Dallen plunged out of the undergrowth and down into the creek bed behind him. They raced in single file down the watercourse, sending up tails of spray. At a wider spot, Dallen slipped past Pog and took the lead behind Larral; Pog seemed to react to this with relief. He didn't slacken his pace, but he seemed more confident in his footing with Dallen in the lead.

Perry just leaned down over Pog's neck and concentrated on the cries for help. From the strength, they had to be getting close. He reached for the bow he had in a case at his knee—strung of course, because it would do no damn good at all if it wasn't already strung and he needed it.

He'd just gotten it out, and an arrow ready, when Larral made an abrupt left-hand turn, and they all crashed through the brush at the side of the creek, and came out under enormous trees. There was almost no growth under here; the canopy overhead was too thick to allow anything to grow. Larral lengthened his stride, a gray blur, with Dallen keeping pace beside him and Pog laboring to catch up. They were heading for a patch of sunlight—sunlight in which dark shapes were moving.

Larral howled and Dallen screamed a challenge. Then they were among those dark shapes, Dallen plunging and kicking, Larral's jaws snapping at them. This was well within Perry's bow-reach; he pulled Pog up, put an arrow to the string, sighted, and let fly.

He hit the thing he was aiming for, and with a shrill shriek, it flopped around wildly. Larral finally caught another one of the things in his enormous jaws, shook it violently, and tossed it away, limp. Dallen trampled the beast Perry had skewered, and Perry shot another.

:Come on!: Larral urged, and Perry stopped shooting to kick Pog into a gallop, following Larral through another scrim of undergrowth into a clearing.

The moment they came out into the light, Larral was momentarily swarmed by the evil creatures, whatever they were. But not for long. Dallen came to his rescue, kicking, biting, and trampling. The air was rank with the scent of blood, which seemed to madden the things further. Perry let off shot after shot, concentrating on the beasts trying to pull down Larral. Strangely . . . he couldn't touch their minds. Couldn't even sense them!

He felt Lily and Daisy as they plunged into the clearing, and soon more arrows were joining his in the air—just in time, because he reached for another in the saddle-bow quiver, and his hand closed on empty air.

And then, just as suddenly as it had begun, it was over. The only creatures left in the clearing were the dead and dying. The pack had finally realized they could not win this battle and had fled.

Perry raised his head to see what it was they had been defending—and looked into the eyes of half a dozen of the biggest ravens he had ever seen in his life. The size of a goshawk—or bigger. One of them shoved off from the ground and flapped wearily to land at Larral's feet.

:Thank you, friends,: he heard. *:The* slytha *pack nearly had us.:*

Why didn't they fly? he was thinking, and then a couple more of the ravens moved, and he saw why: the massive nest, on the ground, the branch that had held it up safe aloft broken, the four half-feathered fledglings huddled together in the middle of the mass of branches in mindless terror.

:You are welcome, friends,: he sent, causing all of the ravens to swivel their heads at once to stare at him.

"Would someone please explain to me what just happened?" his father said into the silence.

:Tell him these are Hawkbrother Bondbirds, and we rescued their young,: Larral said, shortly, as Perry slid down out of Pog's saddle, ground-tied him, and went to check Larral for injuries.

"These are Hawkbrother bondbirds," he repeated obediently, running his hands over Larral's back, sides, and legs. "Their nest ended up on the ground, and I guess these things swarmed it. Larral heard them call for help, then I did."

"All right, that makes sense. Are the babies hurt?" Mags dismounted and ground-tied Lily and Daisy, going to Dallen to check his wounds. Dallen's were obvious; from the knee down his legs were red from all the bleeding bites.

:My father wants to know if your babies are all right,: Perry relayed, finding to his relief that Larral's wounds were superficial and were already clotting.

:Frightened, but unhurt,: one of the ravens acknowledged. *:But the* slytha *will return.:*

:Then we'd better get that nest back up in the tree, hadn't we?: he replied, going to Pog for his coil of rope. "Father, I'm going to have to do some climbing. Can you make sure Larral and Pog are taken care of?"

"Climbing—" Mags blinked at him a moment, then took in the downed nest just past him. "Yes, absolutely. Will you be all right solo?"

Perry looked at the nearest tree; it was eminently climbable, with nice rough bark and knobby places everywhere where old branches had died back. He'd had to climb far worse. "No problem." He tilted his head back, peering up at the living branches. *:How far up would you like the new nest?:*

:Let us find a good place for it,: the raven he was talking to replied, and all the adults took to the air. He went over to see to the fledglings, soothing them with his mind, then, when they calmed and looked up at him trustingly, making sure they weren't injured.

They were probably the ugliest creatures he had ever seen, all over quills and bare skin. And already, with their fears eased, they were nudging him with hunger.

:Larral, are these things safe for the young to eat?:

Larral looked up from licking his small wounds. *:They tasted all right to me. Or as "all right" as weasels ever taste.:*

He dragged one of the dead things over to the nest, where the young birds, evidently old enough now to feed themselves, fell on it, tearing bits off, which they gulped down with enthusiasm. "How's Dallen, Papa?"

"Looks worse than it is; hazard of having a white coat." One of Dallen's legs was clean, Mags was working on the second with a bit of rag and his waterskin.

:Raven-friend!: He looked up at the summons, to see all of the adult birds sitting on a branch two massive trees to the left of where he was standing. *:Here is a good place!:*

Climbing the tree was even easier than it looked, although once he was perched astraddle on the branch the birds wanted him to use, he realized he was higher up than he had ever been before in his life. Rather than making him dizzy, he felt rather euphoric. It was pretty clear where they wanted the new nest built; this branch forked out into a "Y" shape not far from him. He could lash a third branch to make a triangular base on which to rebuild the nest. "Papa!" he called down, lowering his rope. "I need a branch as thick as my wrist and as long as Dallen is tall, and some cord!"

Once that branch was hauled up and lashed into place, the

ravens themselves brought him smaller branches to build the platform with; once the platform was in place, the ravens took over the rebuilding entirely. With six of them at work, there was soon a brand new nest in place, strong and deep. He gave the side of it an experimental shake; though it looked as if it were nothing more than a random pile of branches, it didn't even budge. He shook it harder; it still wasn't moving. Satisfied with their mutual handiwork, he had Mags send the babies up, one at a time, tied in one of his shirts as a sling. They settled happily into the new nest, and Perry left them there with another one of the dead creatures to eat as soon as they got hungry again.

Once down on the ground, it was obvious that the ravens were conferring up there. Perry left them to it and checked with Larral and his father.

"Well, that was exciting," Mags observed mildly. He had finished cleaning up Dallen's legs, and they were now white again, with pink lines all over them from the bites that were already healing. It never failed to amaze him how quickly Companions healed. Anything short of a major bone-break was half healed in a day.

"I thought you said the Hawkbrothers were gone from here," Perry said instead to Larral.

:They are. But there are always more of the Bondbird breeds than there are Hawkbrothers, particularly the crows and ravens.:

"All right, that makes sense," he acknowledged, and he looked up at the silent ravens, all sitting on the edge of the nest, facing inward, as if they were having a conference. Maybe they were.

"You should ask them whether they have heard anything about an animal that would carry humans off from the road," Mags observed, looking where he was looking. "Although those weasel-things might go after something as big as a human."

"The raven called them *slytha,*" Perry replied, frowning a little. "I dunno, Papa. They struck me as pretty cowardly; it might have seemed like we were fighting them for candle-marks, but it couldn't have been long."

:I have never heard of slytha *attacking even a lone human, unless he was injured,:* Larral confirmed.

Perry had already taken to looking for their spent arrows, and he relayed that. He collected the broken ones as well as the intact ones; after all, there was no point in leaving behind useful points, and they might be able to save the fletching feathers as well if they were careful. Each intact arrow was one more they wouldn't have to replace. Just as he picked up the last one by count, one of the ravens flew down to land heavily beside him. He squatted down, balancing on the balls of his feet, to keep himself at the raven's level, more or less.

:We are in your debt,: the bird said simply, tilting its head to look at him out of one very bright black eye. Again, he was astonished how clear the Mindvoice was and how close to human the thoughts were. It waited, then, and after a moment, he realized it was waiting for him to tell it what he wanted from them.

He almost asked it if it knew where it could steal some arrows for him to replace the broken ones but stopped himself just in time. Because these were ravens, after all, and they very likely did and would, and it might mean stealing them from someone who needed those arrows even more than he and his father did.

:Have you seen anything around here that would attack and kill a human being?: he asked instead.

The raven considered his question. *:Not on purpose,:* it said finally. *:Even in a mob the* slytha *do not attack anything bigger than they are. All the monstrous creatures are gone from here. Perhaps a bear, but I have not seen one in these woods.:*

It waited again, but he honestly did not know what to say to it. Finally it clacked its beak in frustration. *:You are not a*

Hawkbrother.: Actually, it didn't use that word. It didn't use any word; it used a concept that he instantly understood meant Hawkbrother but was a lot more complicated than that, probably reflecting the birds' complicated relationships with the Tayledras.

:No, I'm not,: he agreed.

:We will not bond to you,: it continued.

:I understand that,: he agreed again.

:If you need us, call, or send the kyree.: It waited to see if he was satisfied with that. At least, that was the impression he got.

:Thank you. That will be perfect,: he replied, and the raven heaved a great sigh of relief, ruffled up all its feathers, and then took off.

He glanced over at his father, to see Mags staring at him with a perplexed expression on his face. "Now I understand how other people feel when Dallen and I are having a long conversation," his father admitted. "I wanted to interrupt and demand to know what he was saying to you, but I knew how infuriating that would be."

Perry stood up and handed his father the quiver of intact arrows, rolling the pieces in the rag he used to rub Pog down with to keep the bits together until he could figure out what to do with them. "Larral said he's never heard of *slytha* attacking humans, that they never attack anything bigger than themselves, not even in a mob. Then the raven flew down to talk. It said the ravens were in my debt. Then we established that I have no right to make a Bondbird out of any of them, and they said to call or send Larral if we need them. Oh, and they haven't seen any animals attacking humans in their territory." He scratched his head. "Of course, that just means that a couple of leagues down the road, there could still be some animal or monster they haven't seen."

Mags nodded thoughtfully. "Interesting that they wanted you to acknowledge you hadn't a right to a raven Bondbird, though. Makes me wonder if they would have agreed to that if you had insisted on it."

Perry stowed the broken arrows in his pack and took the handful of intact ones his father gave him and put them in the saddle-bow quiver. They'd been really lucky. By his count, they hadn't lost any arrows, and no more than eight were broken. Considering how Dallen had been trampling the *slytha,* that was almost a miracle. "I wouldn't do that," he said firmly. "It'd be all right here, but what would happen when we went back to Haven? The ravens there wouldn't be Bondbirds. He'd be all alone, no one to talk to except me and Larral. That's not fair."

He mounted as his father did the same. "You're right, it's not fair. You did the right thing. We didn't put a price on our help, and it's not fair to demand one afterward." His father looked down at Larral. "I think we should find a camping spot early. Make a better job of tending wounds and get a good night's sleep."

"We could camp where we left the road; we'd have water there," Perry suggested. "And if there isn't anything right off the road, we might find something upstream, or there will still be plenty of time to travel on and find something better."

His father nodded, and with Larral leading the way, they left the clearing and the softly muttering ravens behind.

Perry hadn't realized how much ground they must have covered in their headlong dash to save the raven fledglings. Taking the route back slowly, allowing the cool water of the creek to sooth the bite wounds on Dallen's legs and on Larral's, occupied at least a couple of candlemarks. Now that they weren't moving at a breakneck pace, they saw plenty of signs that the watercourse had been sculpted in part by human hands. Or . . . *hands,* anyway. Why the Hawkbrothers would have wanted to do that, Perry hadn't a clue, but he supposed they must have had a good reason. Maybe flood control? The creek was broader than seemed quite natural, so the water ran quietly, with scarcely a ripple, and even when it was running with floodwaters, it looked like it would be easy enough to ford at the point where it crossed the road. The bed of the creek was smooth without being slippery, with a nice layer of sandy mud on the bottom.

Mags paused at that point, looking up and down the road, frowning. "I don't like this as a stopping point," he said, finally. "Larral, do you remember anything good on the back-trail?"

Larral shook his head.

"All right then, let's move on," Mags decreed. "We still have most of the afternoon ahead of us, and the odds are good we'll find a better site than here."

Perry didn't voice an objection, but he had to admit he was feeling the effects of the fight and the climbing, and if he was, surely Dallen and Larral were in no better shape. But they said nothing, so he kept his mouth shut.

But Mags proved to be right; it wasn't more than a candle-mark later, and likely much less, when Mags' head came up, and he said with satisfaction, "Dallen has a good spot for us."

A little farther off, there was a path running off at an angle to the road. Mags took it, and Perry and Larral followed; there was a bit of an uphill climb, and they found themselves on the top of a rock bluff, looking out over a little valley with another stream running through it. There was plenty of grazing, and Larral suddenly raised his head and bolted off down into the valley, saying only :Dinner!:

They built their fire, gathered armloads of grass to pad their sleeping rolls, and Perry took the horses to water while Mags tried his luck fishing. Then Perry staked the horses on the top of the bluff with enough line that they could eat their fill. He checked Dallen's legs again and salved the bites, but it seemed that *slytha* had remarkably clean mouths; the bites were all sealed shut, and there was no sign at all of infection. Perry lay down in the grass with the warm sun on him and let it bake his muscles. He came to the conclusion, mentally probing the mild aches, that it wasn't so much the climbing that had strained them as all the hauling up. He'd been the one bringing up all the big foundation branches that the ravens couldn't carry, and that wasn't something he did a lot of. He'd used muscles for that he just wasn't used to using.

So far this trip hasn't really been . . . dangerous. He wasn't sure how to feel about that. *The* slytha *weren't really going to do much besides nick us.* On the one hand, he probably should be relieved that things hadn't actually been dangerous. On the other hand . . . after all the build-up, he was a little disappointed that things had been so very quiet. He'd been expecting legendary monsters, and so far, all he'd gotten was a swarm of giant weasels.

He must have dozed off, because he came to with a start as Larral dropped two fat hares on his chest. *:One for your dinner and one for your breakfast,:* the *kyree* said. *:I am going to sleep so I can watch in the night.:*

Perry cleaned both hares, skinned one and spitted it over the fire, hanging the other in the tree they were camping under. Mags trudged up the slope with their leather bucket full of water in one hand and nothing in the other; evidently fishing hadn't gone well.

"Thanks, Larral," his father said, spotting the hare over the fire. Larral grunted, eyes closed, as Mags settled down to take over the cooking. Perry took the bucket of water from him to hang in the tree.

"Well, as you can expect, I would like to talk about the fight we just had. I have just one question," his father said, turning the spit slowly. "Did you go running off after the calls for help, or did Larral start, and you followed?"

"He started, I followed," Perry replied honestly. "But I

didn't think about it. I just ran off when he did, trusting he knew what he was doing."

"Potentially reckless, but I think you can be forgiven that much," Mags replied. "If someone's going to set a trap for humans using a Mindspeaking call for help, they're not going to do it in your range, they're going to do it in mine. I figured immediately that the very worst that would happen would be that some creature trying to lure other animals in for dinner was about to have the worst day of its life when you and Larral showed up."

Perry blinked a little, realizing that was true. "But I didn't know that, or think about it," he admitted.

"I did. Dallen and I might not have been able to stop Larral, but we could have stopped you easily. Fortunately, we didn't need to. Dallen concluded with Larral that the call was genuine." His father looked up from the hare and smiled. "You'll remember this for the next time."

Perry nodded soberly. He realized he had been so caught up in hearing the call for help and wanting desperately to answer it—and that he had trusted Larral's judgment so completely—that he hadn't thought about these things for himself.

But his father wasn't done. "Now, as I said, it was wildly unlikely anything that could really hurt us had used a call for help only someone with Animal Mindspeech could hear. Your Gift is ridiculously rare, Perry, and normally the people who have it are also Healers. Even if Dallen and I had not been there, you and Larral could have driven the *slytha* pack off. But the chance that such a call is a ruse is something you should take a moment to consider if something like this ever happens again." Mags turned the hare, then poked at it judiciously with his knife. "I think this is done."

Perry got a piece of wood that he'd split for the fire; his father used it as a crude platter and divided the hare between them. Then they sat on their bedrolls and enjoyed the peace and quiet until the sun set. Perry was about to wake Larral, when the *kyree* lifted his head, heaved himself to his feet, and shook himself all over.

:I shall take the night watch. I shall wake one of you if I tire,: the *kyree* said, then sat down on his haunches and stared out over the valley.

"I think that is my signal to sleep." Mags settled himself, pulled a blanket over himself, and was asleep in moments.

But Perry wasn't ready to sleep yet. There were too many questions in his mind.

:Larral, do Bondbirds usually stay behind when Hawk-brothers leave?:

:Hawks, falcons, eagles, and owls, no. The corvids, sometimes. Especially if the Vale has been crowded with them. A pair will stay behind or move off into unclaimed wilderness, raising enough young to form a mob, and only then go deeper into the Pelagirs in search of a Vale that has no, or few, corvids. It is much safer for the corvids to travel as a mob; they usually bond as a mob, and a pair is usually safe enough in the old Vale to remain until they have a mob.:

Well, that was a much more detailed answer than he had expected. *:Why don't the others do that?:*

:Because even the ravens are the smallest of the Bondbirds. Hawks, falcons, eagles, and owls are big enough, and have enough defenses, that they can confidently travel alone. They can migrate to a new Vale when their own Vale has too many of their bloodline, or just live out in the wilderness. You have not seen a Bondbird. They are . . . formidable. The smallest are quite large enough to make me think twice before attacking. The largest can easily kill a man.:

Suddenly he was overcome with the desire to see one. Or more! And their Hawkbrothers. And a Vale!

There was a note of amusement in Larral's Mindvoice. *:All in good time. For now, we need to pursue this mystery of missing humans wherever it takes us.:*

Perry nodded in the darkness. He had the sick feeling that

he wasn't going to like where this took them . . . but he would follow the clues anyway.

Larral woke Perry some time in the night so he could take over while Larral had a nap. He got out of his blankets, looked up at the stars for a reference, and reckoned it was four to six candlemarks till dawn. He could stay up for two or three, then wake his father.

Dallen dozed nearby, standing hipshot, which was a very good sign that his legs weren't hurting him. If they had been he would be lying down now.

There was no need to get up from where he sat and a very good reason not to—the less he moved, the less likely it was that anything out there would spot him. He collected the remains of the hare—all bones, they'd sucked every bit of meat from the carcass—and shoved them under the coals of the fire to incinerate. The moon was down, leaving nothing but the starry sky for illumination. It occurred to him that he had never seen a night this dark; even on the road with the caravan, there had always been lights left burning as a matter of caution. Back home in Haven, the Palace was always lit even late at night, and there were lights in the garden, the stables, and on the pathways. Here and now there was only the subdued glowing of the coals under a thickening coating of ash.

He didn't remember ever seeing so many stars.

And as he had noted before, the nighttime forest was scarcely quiet. From their vantage point atop the bluff, he heard the splash of animals drinking or crossing the river, the calls of owls and nightbirds, the song of insects. In a lot of ways, this was good; as long as that chorus kept up, there was very little chance of anything sneaking up on them without the night creatures seeing or hearing it, and the chorus would go silent. It was very peaceful—even if he knew that the peace was deceptive—and very beautiful.

But the fascination could only hold for so long. Eventually he felt his head bobbing, and he poked his father to take his turn. He lay down again and didn't wake until the smell of cooking hare tickled him awake.

"Maybe I should have asked to borrow one of those ravens for a little while," he admitted, as they saddled up for another day on the road. "It would be useful to have eyes in the sky."

"But you can use regular birds for that," his father reminded him. "No . . . I think you did the right thing. It's better for them to feel gracious about helping us, not grudging."

It was pretty obvious as they moved on toward the inn that was their goal that the landscape had become hillier—much hillier. Just for the sake of practice, whenever Perry caught sight of a bird soaring overhead, he made an effort to see through its eyes. Mostly, these were ordinary hawks and vultures, using the thermals to stay aloft with as little effort as possible. In the distance, he caught sight of what might have been buildings of tiny villages or small-holdings now and again, but there was nothing near the road. Which seemed . . . odd.

:Larral, why aren't people living near the road?: he asked.

:Because the road is where strangers are,: came the reply, with overtones of eating. Larral must have paused to catch something for a meal. He was a really big creature; he probably had to make a lot of small, rabbit-sized meals over the course of the day. *:Most people out here are suspicious of strangers except in the bigger villages. Otherwise, they will have a single person in the group, usually a large, strong man, who is designated to make contact with others.:*

He turned that over in his mind. *:Surely they need things after a while?:*

:Not as often as you might think. They often have their own small mills to grind their own flour, they make most of their clothing from leather, and when they do need something,

that single person will make a journey to a bigger village to trade for it. Or traders know where these small-holdings are and will come to them. If you were really traders, you would have gotten a more detailed map, showing where they were, and you would be off the road fairly often.:

It seemed a strange and very hard way to live. The food must be awfully monotonous!

:Tell your father I am looking for a camping site now,: Larral said, out of nowhere. *:I think it is going to rain, and heavily. Your little cloths won't keep that off; I will need to find a cave or enlarge a burrow.:*

"Father!" Perry called, but softly . . . something about the heavy silence, broken only by distant birdcalls, made him want to keep from attracting anything's attention. "Larral thinks it's going to rain badly. He's looking for a camping site, like a cave."

Mags looked over his shoulder and nodded. "I'll have Dallen help," he replied, and he held Lily back so he was riding side by side with Perry. "If it's going to rain, there are a lot of considerations when picking a site," he continued, in a low, conversational voice, as if he, like Perry, was reluctant to let his words carry past the road. "We don't want something under a tree at the top of a hill because of lightning strikes. We don't want something in the valley because of floods. It would be nice if we could find a big, dry cave large enough to fit us all, including the horses, but the horses won't melt if we can't get them into shelter. Larral and Dallen do have a reasonably good chance of finding something suitable, though, even if Larral has to enlarge a badger burrow, or something of the sort."

"That's what he said," Perry agreed.

"Look around us," Mags continued. "This is actually good territory to find a cave in." He gestured at an enormous rock outcropping they were passing by. "The only trick will be finding something that water won't be pouring into once the rain starts."

As the day drew on, Perry started feeling increasingly worried that they *weren't* going to find anything suitable. Could they beg shelter in someone's barn? Or would they be met with weapons and suspicion? But just as he was about to suggest that, Larral spoke up again.

:I have something perfect. It's big enough for all of us, and it should not get wet inside. Dallen is waiting by the road to guide you.:

"Dallen already told me," said his father, giving Lily a nudge with his heels to send her into a trot. "Just in good time, I think."

It was with great relief—because now clouds were gathering overhead—that he spotted Dallen a few more turns down the road. It was with even more relief that he heard Larral add *:And I caught you dinner.:*

:You're amazing!: he told Larral.

:Of course I am,: Larral replied. *:Tell your father to hurry up. I smell the rain.:*

"I'll get wood. You get fodder," said Mags as they shooed the horses into the cave and left Dallen to keep them there. Perry grabbed the little hand-scythe from where it was stored on the outside of his left-hand pack and ran out to the sound of distant, growling thunder. He began gathering and cutting the lush, waist-high meadow grass below the cave as fast as he could manage, bringing back as much as he could carry and dumping it in front of the horses before running back out again.

Now he could smell the rain, too. And the thunder was getting closer. Twice he passed Larral dragging a huge branch up to the cave; too bad Larral was of no help whatsoever with the fodder.

They had just about enough time to gather a fair amount of wood for a fire and a good, tall pile of grass for the horses to eat when the rain started. In fact, Perry was bringing in what he thought might be the last giant armload of grass when a bolt of lightning struck somewhere far too close, making him jump and shriek. Fortunately the barrage of thunder that pummeled them at the same time as the lightning strike masked his outburst, or he'd have felt horribly embarrassed by the girlish scream that had just emerged from his mouth.

But as if that lightning had literally split the clouds, the downpour began immediately, and he was soaked in moments as he scuttled the last few paces to safety and protection.

The good thing was that instead of sloping down into the cave, the cave floor sloped up into the cave, meaning it was unlikely they were going to get wet tonight. The bad thing was that the floor was stone, and besides sloping up, it was also tilted at a slight sideways angle. Perry could see it was going to be really hard to find a comfortable place to sleep tonight.

Oh, well. . . .

He dropped his last huge armload of grass on the pile the horses were already muzzle-deep into. His father had positioned the pile at the back of the cave so that their fire was going to be between the horses and the entrance to the cave. That, Mags had explained, was so they'd be unlikely to bolt out into the storm if they were spooked.

His father had already taken their tack off and piled it to one side, bringing the packs to the fire; Perry wiped the horses down with a handful of grass, checked to make sure they weren't thirsty, and joined his father at the fire.

Supper was apparently going to be hare again, though Mags had dug into their supplies to augment it with something else—what, Perry wasn't sure yet. Larral had been very busy; there were six fat hares piled up, and Mags was working on the seventh. "One good thing," his father observed, looking at the veritable waterfall cascading off the rocks overhead, down onto the stone at the mouth of the cave, and pouring down into the valley. "We don't have to go far for water."

Then he turned a crooked smile on Perry. "Beginning to regret coming out here?"

Perry shook his head. "We're dry—at least I will be in a

bit—and we have a dry place to sleep and food to eat. We're good. Could be lots worse."

"And it's not snowing," Mags chuckled. "The last cave I was stuck in, we were snowed into for a moon. We were lucky we had the caravan with us; if we hadn't, there might have been issues getting the horses and Companions fed."

"The same caravan we have now?" Perry asked.

"The same. I'll tell you about some of it tonight, if you like. Not all of it; there's a lot to tell."

Since Mags didn't often tell stories out of his past, Perry felt a surge of excitement. "That would be terrific!" he said with unfeigned enthusiasm.

"Be careful what you wish for," Mags cautioned with a chuckle. "It might be boring." Finally Perry saw what he was doing; making tea by dropping heated rocks into the leather bucket, which had a couple of mugs-worth of water and a bundle of dried herbs in it. *That'll be good about now,* he thought, shivering. He was drying off, but the wind that had brought the storm was cold, and the rock floor of the cave was pretty chilly too.

:The good thing about a storm like this, is that nothing is going to move in it,: said Larral, who was lying next to the fire, head on paws, nose twitching a little. *:We shall all be able to sleep tonight.:*

"You think this storm is going to last the night?" Perry asked aloud.

:And past sunrise,: Larral confirmed.

"Like it is now?" Perry asked in surprise, staring at the torrent of water outside. He could not imagine a storm raging all night *this* hard. Near-constant lightning did strange things to the cascade at the entrance, seeming to freeze the water in mid fall, and the thunder was an ever-present, low growl.

:Probably not. But enough that any creature that is not forced to be out in it probably will choose staying where it is.:

His father handed him the bucket after fishing out the little bundle of herbs. He took it, shivering a little, and drank the hot, minty liquid gratefully. He shivered as he began to warm up again. He passed the bucket back to his father, who drank the rest and picked out the stones to use again, then divided the now-cooked hare.

"Well," Mags said at last. "It was when we were still worried about the Sleepgivers who wanted me back in their hands, right after I escaped from them. I told you a little about them."

Perry nodded; his father had told him just enough to make him horribly curious. But he had understood instinctively that Mags really didn't want to talk about that particular passage in his life, so instead, he went to Lord Jorthun, who had sat him down with a hand-bound and handwritten book and the instructions that it was never to leave the library. Everything that anyone knew about the Sleepgivers was in there—all of it had been pried out of his father's skull by skilled Mindspeakers. And how those memories had gotten there in the first place. It had been very strange reading.

"Well, we were all still worried that they'd come after me again—turned out we were right, but that came later—so the Dean and your grandfather and Lord Jorthun hatched a plan to send me, and Herald Jakyr out on the sort of two-year mentorship that was the way they did things before there was a Herald's Collegium. And to make sure that my friends couldn't be used against me again, they sent Bear and Lena and Amily out ahead of me, with Bard Lita, in the caravan. Jakyr and I doubled back and met them on the road. I have to say that if we hadn't been so worried about the Sleepgivers, it would have been a lot of fun, and I was pretty happy to see the old caravan again."

"I can't see how six of you managed, especially over winter—" Perry shook his head. "How did you keep from clawing each other's throats out?"

Mags laughed at that. "We used Waystations most of the time, of course. Some of us in the caravan, the rest in the

Waystation. And when winter came, we were living in a cave complex that had once been used by bandits. The Guard stocked it for the winter before we got there, so supplies weren't a problem. But when we first went out, just after Harvest Fair, the weather was mostly good, and if it hadn't been for Jakyr and Lita sniping at each other, it would have been about the most perfect trip you could imagine."

"I dunno, I think *our* trip has been pretty perfect, and we don't have to share the caravan with four other people," Perry pointed out.

His father laughed and ruffled his hair, but he said nothing.

It was full dark by then; or, rather, it would have been, if there hadn't been so much lightning.

Perry watched the storm in fascination. Despite the fact that they were technically in shelter, he had never been so aware of the sheer power and ferocity of a storm. It was one thing to be inside a multistory stone building with weather raging outside. You could shut the window, pull the curtains closed, and retreat to the fire. It was quite another to have the storm mere arm-lengths from you, with no way to close it out.

Suddenly, Lily stirred. . . . and Perry knew why, immediately. "Oh, no you don't!" he exclaimed, jumped to his feet, and got her, and Daisy and Pog for good measure, led them to the rain-splattered opening of the cave, and backed them up to it.

Just in time. First Lily, and then as if she had triggered them, Pog and Daisy emptied themselves out. And the mess was immediately sluiced away by the "waterfall."

"Hmm." Mags eyed the horses, then the slanting floor, then the horses again. "I think we need to reconsider our stabling arrangements." He looked at Dallen. Dallen stared back for a while. "Dallen wants to know if you'll move the fodder. He'll show you where."

For an answer, Perry led the horses over to where Dallen moved, then brought the drying grass to them, armload by armload, until it was all piled up. This was at the side of the cave, at the lowest point of the side-to-side slant. So at least, if the horses let loose with another bout, it would all be over on *that* side, away from where they were sleeping.

Mags sighed. "Hazards of traveling with horses instead of Companions. Dallen says he'll keep them from wandering off if the rain stops while we're sleeping."

"Larral says it won't," Perry replied, looking to Larral for confirmation, only to see that Larral was sleeping heavily. He looped the lead ropes over each horse's back and left the long-suffering Dallen in charge of them. "I'm gonna see if there's anything in the back of this cave we can use under our blankets."

There wasn't anything. So he made a pillow out of his pack, folded his cloak under the blankets, and made himself as comfortable as he could. Eventually, with some wiggling, he found a sort of shallow depression that fit him tolerably well and finally fell asleep.

It didn't last nearly as long as he would have liked.

First, the arm under his pack fell asleep, and when a violent *boom* of thunder jarred him awake, he had to endure a passage of very uncomfortable pins-and-needles before he could fall asleep again. Then his hip began to hurt, so he turned over to his other side. Then the other hip began to hurt. In fact, he started to feel bruised all over. He rolled over onto his back, but that didn't work either. Rock was turning out to be awfully unforgiving to sleep on.

In fact, it wasn't until Larral took pity on him and curled around him for some extra support that he was actually able to find a comfortable position for the rest of the night.

At some point while he was asleep, the rain slacked off. The thunder that had troubled his dreams faded off into the distance, and the worst of the storm was over. When he woke at about dawn, unspeakably grateful for Larral's help overnight, the "waterfall" at the entrance to the cave had turned into something more like a delicate bead curtain.

He got up . . . a bit painfully . . . and walked over to the entrance. The stream that had been a mere trickle last night was a torrent now.

He examined the raging stream carefully. Or at least, as much of it as he could see from here. There was a spot almost immediately below where he was standing where the water welled up; he thought he remembered there being a massive tree trunk crossing what had then been a serene little brook. The water had flowed under it last night, so the fact that the stream had overtopped that log gave a pretty good measure of just how much was flowing now.

"As small as that stream was last night . . . I can hardly believe what it looks like. It could easily drown someone who fell into it now."

Perry looked up at his father, who was staring down at the stream himself. "Didn't you rescue Grandfather out of the river back home?" he asked.

"Yes, and a girl who . . . fell into it a year or so after that," Mags agreed.

By that moment of hesitation, Perry sensed that there was a lot his father wasn't telling him about that second incident, but he knew better than to ask about it. The King's Spy held a lot of secrets; not all of them were to do with protecting the Kingdom.

And not all of them are his to give away either. Not even to me.

"But that's the place I'd aim for, if I had to rescue someone again," Mags continued, pointing at the submerged log. "I'd catch her there, where the log can hold us both against the current, hold her head up out of the water, and wait for more help to pull us out."

Perry frowned a little, staring downslope at the place, picturing it in his mind.

Then, without warning, he was *there*, in the stream, tumbling helplessly in the current, struggling to breathe, struggling to get his head above the water long enough to get a breath, battered, bruised, and panicking. *:Mama!:* he cried. *:Mama!:*

And yet, it wasn't him—and he ran through the tall, wet grass, slipping and catching himself even as he felt his body tumbling in the stream. The log—he had to get to the log—

Then, as he was halfway down the slope to the log, he realized that it wasn't *him,* it was some young thing in the water upstream, fighting to stay alive. He snapped out of his running trance and focused on where he was, what he needed to do. The creature he had to rescue was close. Close enough for him to hear it cry in his mind. And like the ravens, this creature was not human, or he never would have heard it.

:Perry!: Larral barked in his mind. *:Here!:*

He glanced to the side to see that Larral was running beside him a coil of their rope in his mouth. They both skidded to a halt on the bank; he grabbed the dangling end of the rope and fastened it around his waist while Larral ran three times around a tree-trunk with the other end, then braced himself and nodded. Then Perry was slipping off the bank, into the icy water that hit him like a runaway cart. He didn't try to fight the current. Instead, he put his back to the tree trunk and inched carefully along it, getting the current to help him, with the water pinning him to the log, until he was in the middle of the stream. Waiting. And hearing those cries of *:Mama! Mama!:* growing nearer . . . and weaker.

The water was just about up to his throat, like a huge hand against his chest, shoving him against the smooth wood. A weaker current tugged at his legs. He knew he should have been terrified, but somehow he wasn't. Maybe that was only because he hadn't inhaled any water yet.

He vaguely made out sounds that might have been his father shouting from the bank, but even though Mags couldn't be more than a couple of arms'-lengths away, all Perry could really hear was the water rushing around him.

But the rope at his waist tightened up, and he knew by that

sign that his father had taken it over from Larral. It wasn't pulling at him, it was just a reminder that he had an anchor point.

The stream ran down a slight slope toward him, and at the edge of his vision, he caught sight of something, something tossing, cream-and-tan, on the surface of the flood. And with it, came a weak, mental . . . *Mama . . . :*

:Larral! It's coming! Here it comes!:

He shifted a little, gulped water as the flood smacked his face, snorted it out of his nose, and braced himself with his arms out.

The creature hit him. Briefly, he ducked under the water.

The breath got knocked out of him, and he had no idea how he kept the presence of mind to grab for the object before it tumbled over his head, over the log, and downstream out of reach. But catch it he did, and when he fought his way up to the surface again, got his legs under him, and got a breath, he saw he'd caught some sort of delicate fawn-creature, about half the size of Larral, both arms around the chest. Right-side up, thank the gods, or he wasn't sure how he'd have been able to get her turned round again. With a grunt and a wrench, he got a hand under her chin and forced her head above the water, hoping she was still breathing.

And . . . now what do I do?

Now he was trying to hold this heavy thing in his arms, he couldn't fight his way along the log without losing his balance, the creature, or both. But he couldn't stay there either; trying to hold against the flood, his arms were going to get tired, sooner rather than later, and he'd lose her anyway.

And worse still, there was plenty of current running *under* that log as well as over it. If he slipped and fell, he'd lose her *and* he'd get sucked under, maybe wedged under the log and die if there wasn't enough room for him to fit under there.

Now fear hit him. All he'd thought about was getting down here and rescuing this creature.

Bloody hell, he thought in dismay. *Now what do I do?*

:Larral!: he cried. *:Is there any way you can help me?:*

But it wasn't Larral that answered him.

:Hold fast a little longer, boy!: a Mindvoice thundered into his, sounding like a warrior in a play. *:We're coming!:*

: . . . Mama?: bleated the fawn in his arms, easing the fear he had that she was already gone.

:She's coming, Keep breathing. Help me keep your head up,: he ordered, and he felt the fawn straining her head and neck getting her nose a little higher above the roiling stream.

Then, down the slope they thundered, an entire herd of creatures, an avalanche of backs and horns and glimpses of bright black eyes. They poured into the path of the stream three and four and five deep, bracing against it, until they formed a wedge of flesh and bone that diverted enough of the torrent into the meadow that he was able, with his father keeping the rope around his waist tight, to scrape along the tree, and then heave the fawn up onto the bank, where she staggered a few paces and dropped to her knees.

Then Mags had him under the arms and pulled him up on the bank as well, and the living dam lurched ashore on the other side of the stream, and the tree trunk was engulfed again.

Oh, gods. Oh, gods.

Perry lay beside the fawn, coughing and panting. What he assumed was the fawn's mother pelted toward them from the herd, skidded to a halt on the wet grass next to him, and began licking and comforting her terrified and exhausted child. He began to shiver, until Larral nudged him into a sitting position and curled up around him. He collapsed against Larral's shoulder and hugged the *kyree,* in gratitude as well as for warmth.

Then the part of the herd that was still on this bank ambled over to join them. He was too tired to do more than fill his aching lungs over and over again with the blessed air, but after a while he began to feel warm again, and looked up . . .

His father and Dallen were standing practically nose-to-nose with one of these creatures, a really big one, whose head, unlike the fawn's, was crowned with a pair of spiraling, straight horns that ended in very wicked points.

He glanced back over at the fawn, who'd gotten shakily to her feet and was pressed into her mother's flank. *:Are you going to be all right, little one?:* he asked, gently.

She stared at him with big, still-frightened eyes. *:Ye-es?:* she said tentatively.

Her mother nuzzled her and then looked right at him. *:If it were not for you . . . :*

He felt something blow into his hair—a strong, hot breath that smelled pleasantly of hay. Startled, he craned his neck around to find himself eyes-to-muzzle with the big stag his father had been "talking" to.

:Well done, lad. If not for you, she wouldn't have lasted much longer. She slipped off the bank at a slippery spot, and we couldn't keep up with her.: Perry could not help but notice the sheer, controlled power of that Mindvoice. In fact . . . he was getting the impression that if this creature cared to, he could control all of them without a second thought.

And in immediate answer to that, the stag snorted the tiniest bit. *:Of course I could, lad. I am a King-Stag of the* dyheli. *I control the herd. I take it you have never seen us before.:*

:I've never been this far out of Haven before,: he replied eyes widening. *:Are you . . .:* And here he paused, because he had the feeling that if he said "like Bondbirds," this creature would be insulted.

:We are the allies of the Tayledras. Like the tervardi *and the* hertasi. *More like the* tervardi. *I cannot picture any of us serving as the* hertasi *do.:*

:Uh . . . me either.:

That seemed to amuse the *dyheli* no end.

"I see Roya has introduced himself to you," Mags said, interrupting the stag's amusement. "Perry, that was excellent thinking on your part. I'm very glad you went to the rescue; I'd have done the same if I'd been able to hear the fawn's cry for help."

:Then we must all be grateful that your son could,: Roya said, and there was an odd overtone to his Mindvoice that made Perry think he might be Mindspeaking at both the level where Perry could hear him and the level where Mindspeaking humans could hear him. . . .

. . . or was he actually strong enough that he could make even humans who weren't Mindspeakers hear him? Like Mags?

:Why yes, I am. That is why I am the King-Stag.:

———————

Mags stood at the mouth of the cave with Roya and Dallen at his side. It was still drizzling, but the *dyheli* didn't seem to care. Now that the fawn was back with the herd and her mother, all was right with their world, and they were feasting on the lush water-meadow grass. Behind him, Larral was curled up around Perry; Mags had made Perry some hot tea and he was wrapped in a blanket while his clothing dried over the fire.

There was a sea of cream-and-tan backs below the mouth of the cave. Among the cream-and-tan were three darker backs belonging to Lily, Daisy, and Pog. Roya had assured him that the horses would neither spook nor stray, and Mags saw no reason to disbelieve him.

The rescue had all happened too fast for him to feel any terror for his son until after it was all over. Now he could envisage everything that could have gone wrong; at the time all he had been able to do was to frantically get through each moment, and then the next, and then the next, with no room for fear.

Roya stood beside him, gazing down at his herd. *:We are in your debt, of course,:* the *dyheli* said, meditatively. *:But*

*since neither you nor we are likely to be here for much longer,
I am unsure how to repay you.:*

"I hope you mean that in the sense of both of us going on
our ways, rather than a portent of doom," he said aloud. Dallen snickered. Roya snorted.

*:We are not inclined to philosophy. We leave that to crea-
tures that need such things.:*

"I don't suppose you've heard anything about something
attacking lone travelers hereabouts?" he asked without much
hope. "A dangerous beast? Bandits of some sort?"

*:We have not been here in these parts long enough to have
heard anything . . . and our numbers would preclude any
creature or human of that nature attacking us,:* Roya pointed
out logically. *:Your offspring is asleep.:*

Mags looked over his shoulder. Perry was, indeed, asleep,
half curled up on the *kyree.*

*:He is a good and brave child. And with an odd Gift that
proved the salvation of my offspring.:*

"A bit impulsive about jumping in to help," Mags replied.
"This is the second time he's done that in the last few days."

:You do not approve?:

"I'm not sure what to think. Both times, it was warranted,
absolutely necessary in fact. I would have done the same.
Both times, everything turned out fine. . . ." He let his voice
trail off, sure that Roya would fill in what he had not said.

:But what if it hadn't?:

"Exactly." He sighed. "This trip of ours was supposed to be
a sort of testing time for him. Now I'm having second thoughts
about that. Is he exercising enough caution? I don't know."

*:Well . . . if it is any comfort, at least this time, he would
have had to be stronger than me to have resisted the call,:*
Roya said apologetically. *:I was summoning, trying to find
another herd downstream that could block the water and save
the fawn, or perhaps* hertasi *that could have jumped in to the
rescue. It was nonspecific, and I think he was caught in it.:*

For one very short moment, anger flared in him. But a moment later, he had tamped it down. Roya was a father, after all, just as he was. If it had been one of his children tumbling in those flood waters, what would *he* have done?

Set a wide net for help and not worry about who got caught in it. Just like he did.

"Being a parent isn't very easy," he said ruefully, voicing aloud a thing that had been festering in him since he first set his eyes on Perry, newborn. "No one gives you any instructions. They all just tell you 'you'll be fine,' as if it was something that was as instinctive as a bird flying south for the winter."

:Hmm.: For a brief second, he actually sensed Roya riffling effortlessly through his memories, quite as if he had absolutely no barriers in place. *:Yes, I can see, it would be particularly difficult for you, who have no memories of your sire and dam. But you balance your lack of a personal example by observing those around you and selecting what seems best. I believe, insofar as it is possible for me to judge, you are doing well. And if you doubt me, look to your son, who has twice saved others.:*

The sheer strength of the *dyheli's* mind would have terrified him if he let himself think about it. The only thing that tempered his reaction was Roya's attitude. The King-Stag really did not give a damn about what he found in a human's mind. He wasn't interested in using it, except as information in the moment. He didn't care about human secrets or human foibles—or human sins. It was the utter indifference, in the end, that made it all palatable.

Roya made a huffing sound. *:This strength of mind is the gift that was given to the King-Stags for the defense and prosperity of the herd. We were prey animals. We still would be if not for this. The King-Stag must be able to control the entire herd, to direct them against the things that would kill us, and do so with absolute surety. He must be able to use his mind as* *a weapon against our foes. And should the King-Stag fall, the Chief Doe must have the same strength of will and mind. But your thoughts and memories are of very little interest to me.:*

"I suppose not." He was more amused than insulted. "I probably seem pretty silly to you."

:Not at all, actually. I had heard of you Heralds. I doubted that you were half so altruistic as you were painted. I was wrong.: The *dyheli* gave him a penetrating look out of his near eye. *:I am glad our lands are neighbors.:*

Mags didn't know quite how to respond to that, so he remained silent, surrounded by the sound of the gentle rain and the steady tearing and munching of grass.

:I think,: said Roya, when they had both been contemplating the herd for quite some time, *:That we will remain here for a season. I was going to take us farther north and west, but it would be a shame not to make use of these water meadows, and we can easily share them with the deer here, as they seem few.:*

"That might be because of the pack of *slytha* that attacked the ravens," Mags observed.

:All the more reason to stay,: Roya replied, with a calm that made his next words seem all the more bloodthirsty. *:The sooner we can find them and trample them into compost, the better.:*

Mags gave the King-Stag a sideways look. Roya snorted. *:It is what we were created to do,:* he said, as if this were common knowledge.

He said it with such conviction that Mags was taken aback. He was as certain as if the god of the *dyheli,* whatever that was, had come down and declared it to him. Which was, again, disturbing. Was he dealing with a cult of sorts? A four-legged fanatic?

Roya began to make a wheezing sound. It took Mags a moment to realize the *dyheli* was laughing.

"What's so funny?" he asked testily.

:Your mistake. Our creator was not some god. Our creator was a human Mage. We know this. We carry the memory and share it with our descendants. We were created for war. As the gryphons were created for war. We make war on the lesser creatures of evil, the wyrsa, *the* slytha. *They make war on the greater. Although we are centuries from that time, we have never forgotten this.:*

Mags turned to stare at him. "You really *remember* that? How is that even possible?"

:You shared the memories of your father's people. How is that possible?:

Mags was left unable to retort. Because he still didn't understand how the Sleepgivers that had taken him captive had flooded him not with their personal memories but with what seemed to be memories going back hundreds of years. Those memories had been intended to turn him from what he was into a Sleepgiver like them. Thanks to Dallen, it hadn't worked.

Roya waited in silence for a while longer, then blew out his breath in a long snort. *:Since you are either exceedingly polite or unbelievably dense, what I am saying is that the herd and I will probably be here, if for some reason you need assistance with your mystery. You most likely will not, but you are far from home, assistance will be difficult to come by, we owe you more than empty gratitude, and we're not just a herd of silly cattle.:*

"Oh," Mags replied, taken off-guard by the offer. "Thank you! Actually, you're right on all counts. I'll feel better knowing you're out here, just in case."

:Good.: Roya appeared to accept that as a sort of deal. *:I am going to eat. I suggest you and the boy remain here overnight, to make sure he hasn't taken any harm from his adventure. In fact, you ought to take the time to make better, more comfortable beds and get some rest yourself.:*

Roya didn't wait for an answer; he trotted down into the field and soon was lost in it, visible only by the length of his horns.

:I know where there's a big patch of bracken, and some of it may actually be dry,: Dallen offered. *:Follow me, and we'll get enough that both of you can have a decent night tonight.:*

Mags got the little hand-scythe and some light rope and followed Dallen out and along the slope of the hill. Sure enough, well in under some trees, there was a nice big patch of bracken. And many of the fronds were young and tender enough to eat; he gathered plenty of those first. Then he cut plenty for two thick mats, bound it up with the light rope, and Dallen towed it back. He made up two beds, picked Perry up, and bundled him into the smaller one.

Larral stood up, shook himself, and looked Mags in the eye. "Ry run," he said with dignity, and padded out of the cave.

With Perry sound asleep, the entire *dyheli* herd between them and potential trouble, and Larral taking care of their food, there seemed no good reason not to follow Roya's advice. Last night had definitely not been an easy one for sleeping, and the warm fire, the sound of the rain, and the much softer bed lured him into the slumber that had eluded him him, and not even his worries about Perry kept him from it.

10

Mags and his son had scrambled up into the protective canopy of a tree to view their target from across the cleared area around it. Mags peered carefully through the foliage, being careful not to disturb it. Perry, however, was wedged in a crotch, eyes closed, concentrating.

So, here was the inn they'd be aiming for, and it looked perfectly ordinary. Not as big as The Weary Traveler, it was still impressive enough, since it was protected by a palisade of tree trunks with sharpened tops and had a stout gate. This place looked as if it could hold off pretty much anything short of a small army. Of course that was to be expected out here. Also to be expected would be that gate closing at sunset, because no one in his right mind went traipsing through thick woods like this after sunset, even if there was a road.

That it had a couple of guards outside the gate was a bit of a surprise. Mags wouldn't have thought that an inn this far out got enough custom to pay for the hire of two guards.

Then again, there was a certain family resemblance to

them; they might be a couple of sons or nephews rather than hired guards.

The forest had been cleared away from the inn for a couple of furlongs in every direction, leaving a sea of stumps, which would inevitably handicap a rush to storm the walls or the gate. This did make it a little harder to survey the place without being seen . . . but only a little, with Perry along.

They had left the horses hidden off the road with Larral watching them; Dallen was almost directly below them, somehow managing to be invisible despite the fact that he was a blinding white. If anything went amiss, Dallen could carry them both and run faster than any pursuer, even carrying double.

"Two guards inside the gates," Perry muttered. "But they're lounging about right outside the front door of the inn and drinking. There might be more inside the inn. There's a stable, too; I haven't looked in there yet."

Well, that sounded very like the guards were actually relatives.

"All right, inside the stable now. There's one very young man mending a halter; I think he's what passes for the chief stableman. There's five horses in the stable. Two of them are cart horses, the other three are riding horses. There's chickens and some goats. I'm looking for an animal inside the inn now."

A moment later, Perry spoke again. "I found a cat. There are three guests. They are all men that look very tough. There is one serving girl and a bartender. They look alike." He paused, presumably walking the cat around. "There is one cook and two more girls in the kitchen. Should I look upstairs?"

"Not right now. You can come back."

Perry opened his eyes immediately. "Well, what are we going to do?"

"Move closer, camp in the forest close enough that you can use the cat to eavesdrop on people tonight," Mags decided.

"I'd rather feel foolish for taking a lot of precautions we didn't need to than find ourselves in trouble."

"I'm sure Roya would approve," his son replied, smiling up at him.

"I hope so. I'd hate to have to explain to him that we needed the herd's help because we were stupidly overconfident." He glanced down at the ground beneath the tree. "Speaking of overconfidence . . . let's take no chances this close to the inn."

Perry nodded and followed his father as they traced their path back to where they had left the horses, never once putting foot on the ground. According to the information Mags had read, this was how the Hawkbrothers traveled too, moving from tree to tree, undetectable and mysterious to those on the ground. Well, a lifetime of wall-climbing and roof-walking had prepared him well enough to follow their example, and Perry, who had the twin advantages of not having been starved from infancy and having been trained to climb almost as soon as he began walking, was even better at it. Of course, it also helped that Perry was a third of Mags' weight, if that. Up here in the branches, Mags followed Perry's lead, rather than the other way around.

The farther they got from the inn, the better Mags felt. Of course, he could have used his own Gift of Mindspeech to skim over the thoughts of those within that palisade . . . but no. True, the odds were heavily against another Mindspeaker being in there, but with so many people missing and no burning time-candle counting down the marks to some calamity, well, he was going to err strongly on the side of caution.

It was measurably darker beneath the trees when they finally came down next to the horses and Larral. The *kyree* looked from one to the other of them. Mags shrugged and asked the obvious. "Perry, can you reach the inn animals from here?"

Instead of answering immediately, Perry sat right down on the ground so he could put all his concentration into his Gift.

Mags waited, patiently. It occurred to him that they had never yet tested the limits of Perry's ability when it came to distance. There would be a limit, of course. And that limit might depend on whether or not he had contacted a particular animal's mind before. *If we have to move close, we'll do it,* he told himself. *But I have to admit I'd be relieved—*

"I'd rather be lying down, but yes," Perry spoke up, just as he was thinking that. "The cat. I can reach the cat. I might be able to find a bat or an owl and fly it there, too."

"Good, that's excellent news. Let's find a secure place to camp, now." Their food needs were taken care of, thanks to all of them hunting and the humans doing some gathering along the way. Larral quickly found a perfect location: a grove of evergreens growing against a rocky outcrop. Their branches reached all the way down to the ground, which would make it hard for anything to force its way in toward them, there was just enough room for all of them once they worked their way along the rock face to a clearing, and there was just enough grass in the clearing to keep the horses satisfied.

Mags made a tiny fire, just big enough to roast their catches over the coals, while Perry piled long evergreen needles into a couple of beds. As the sky darkened, they quickly ate, and Perry settled into his bedroll while Mags stood guard. Birds began coming into what was probably their nightly roost here. Perry took a moment to reassure them, and they settled right in. Mags approved. They'd make a good sort of lookout; anything that tried to make its way in here would disturb them.

It was a little surreal . . . because the very few times as a child when he had felt even relative contentment had been on summer nights like this one. When he and the others had been released from the sluices, they'd been free to scavenge the forest around the mine for anything edible—and he'd generally found something, giving him the rare treat of a full stomach. And before he had to go back to the mine to the noisome pit where all the mine-slaveys slept, he'd scrape together a couch of pine needles and lie back, looking up through the boughs at the stars.

He could never have imagined his life now. If he'd been asked . . . he probably would have said he expected to be dead before he saw two decades.

Perry began to speak, quietly, and he shook off his mordant thoughts to listen.

It had been a lot easier to slip into the mind of the cat when he was lying down. And the cat, for her part, seemed to welcome him there. He found her in the kitchen, but she was quite willing to move into the common room when he asked her to. One hearth was as good as another to her, and she was less likely to be tripped over in the common room.

". . . bollocks," said one of the three men who had been in the common room the last time Perry had seen it through the eyes of the cat. "It'll be thin pickings until harvest, and if we get anything at all, I'll be gobsmacked." His expression was oddly melancholy, as if he had found himself in a life he didn't much like but didn't know how to change.

"Ye'd rather go back there for th' summer?" asked the second.

The first shook his head vehemently. "Bugger me, no!" He shivered.

"Me neither," said the third man. "I druther be on half pay here than full pay back there. I keep waitin' t'find *him* crawlin' around inside me skull, and wakin' up barmy."

"That makes two of us." The first man sipped carefully at his beer.

That was when Perry noticed something odd. These three men, who presumably, from their physiques and weapons, were fighters of some sort, were not acting like fighting men on their own in a tavern. They had finished eating what looked like a plain, though probably filling meal; the cat's sensitive nose picked up pease porridge flavored with bacon, and bread and butter. They had pushed their empty bowls aside, and were carefully nursing their tankards of beer, as if they anticipated having to make the single tankard last for the evening.

This was very different behavior from the two men he'd observed earlier in the yard just outside the inn. Those two had swilled beer as if there were no bottom to the barrel. They'd also seemed much more relaxed than these three.

Just to be sure, he walked the cat out the door to see if any of the four he'd noticed before were there now.

The gate was closed, and the two he'd seen drinking before were now pacing the wall. So . . . they were night guards. And yet, unless they had sobered up since the last time he'd watched them, they had to be tipsy. Night guards with no one around to hold them accountable. Which was not the behavior of the three men inside.

He murmured all this to his father; maybe Mags could make something of this. He was a little too busy negotiating with the cat to have time to think about what their behavior meant.

He sent the cat back inside, then padding up the stairs to what he suspected was the common sleeping room. Sure enough, there were the two gate guards from earlier, already sound asleep and smelling of more beer. The sleeping room was one big room, as was not uncommon in smaller, more remote, or cheaper inns, and in most cases guests were expected to supply their own sleeping rolls. There were seven sleeping places laid out with belongings here; two were occupied. Presumably the bartender, the cook, and the girls slept elsewhere—downstairs, perhaps. Maybe the four gate guards were related and actually were the ones supposed to be keeping an eye on the place, rather than the bartender being in charge. That would account for why they felt free to drink.

The girls probably slept in the kitchen, and the boy he had

seen earlier in the stable would sleep there, among the horses. And that accounted for all the people attached to the inn.

He sent the cat back downstairs. The three fighters were still having a desultory conversation. ". . . get out," the third man was saying. "Take my money, find a warm place down south. Do anything but this. Plenty of work bustin' heads in taverns." He hunched over, eyes glancing everywhere, and whispered hoarsely, "Don't tell me you ain't thinkin' the same."

"I ain't made enough to leave yet," the first admitted. "I don't mind telling you, I'm thinkin' about it, though. It'd have to be leave-taking from here. If we tried from there—"

"Aye." The man took a tiny sip of his beer. "Gives me the shivers, that place does."

They all subsided into morose silence. The cat lounged on the hearth, but not one word more did he hear out of them until the last of the beer was gone and they slumped up the stairs to bed. The cat yawned and asked him if there was anything else he wanted to see.

He had reported every word to his father, and after trotting the cat around to every place he could get it to go, there was no one else talking. With the exception of the night guards, everyone was asleep, the girls on the kitchen hearth, the boy in the hay in the stables, the cook and the bartender together in a little cubby off the kitchen. With disappointment, he left the cat to her own devices and came back to himself.

"Well, that was frustrating," his father said, softly. Perry got himself up on his elbows; his father was sitting on his own bedroll, the tiny fire between them and moonlight pouring down on them. The trees were full of sleepy birds; he heard them twittering and muttering to themselves.

"Aye," he said, sitting up slowly. "I wish they'd talked more. There was just enough there to sound interesting but not enough to sound like it's more than just being unhappy with whoever has hired them."

"I didn't want to do this," Mags said, slowly. "I think we'll have to play bait so I can get close enough to glean things from their unguarded thoughts. Or, I will, by myself. I don't think—"

"I'd make better bait if they're going after easy prey," Perry pointed out, suppressing alarm at the idea that his father was going to walk into danger alone.

"Under no circumstances are you going to go in there alone!" Mags snapped, reflexively, then seemed to catch himself. "Obviously, neither of us wants the other to go in alone, but if we go in together, we'll need to have every last possibility planned for. We can't chance any sort of slip, because if they catch one of us, they'll have both of us." He sat quietly for a moment. "We have to assume the entire inn is a trap, that everyone working there is in on whatever this is. So . . . we need witnesses, so they won't try to spring the trap on us while we're actually inside. Which means we need to wait until there is a party too big for them to take already there when we make ourselves known."

"That could take a while," Perry noted. "But that's what we're out here for, right?"

Mags patted his head. Perry decided that now was not the time to point out how that annoyed him. "It'll give us a chance to work out everything we need to do, including set up our escape route." It sounded as though he was prepared to start the planning right there and then, but Larral interrupted him with a huge yawn followed by a snort, and he laughed. "And it can all wait until morning."

"And I can keep listening in on them too, Father," Perry pointed out. "Every night. Maybe they'll drop something else and we won't have to do this."

"So that's two plans. One will almost certainly work out. Meanwhile, our first job in the morning should be to either find a better place than this for a camp, or make this into a better, more comfortable and secure camp." He sighed. "And I'm babbling. Get some sleep, Perry, and I'll do the same. We'll make real plans in the morning."

It took them no more than the next morning to turn the tiny clearing into a good place to work from. They took it in turns to go out with the hand-scythe and bring in horse-loads of fodder, which they shoved in under the trees. The horses approved of this, and it got potentially dangerous half-dry grass out of range of the fire—and cut drafts for good measure. Mags cut the turf away to make a fire-circle, which he ringed with stones, and rigged up a spit. They were tolerably comfortable, except for the minor inconvenience of having to take the horses to water. Unfortunately the three fighters were no more talkative than the first night, and the four guards seemed to spend their time drinking, working, and sleeping.

Three days later, Perry was finally able to tell his father that there was a trade caravan on the way. "Two wagons, two drivers, four guards," he reported, having caught sight of it through the eyes of a soaring buzzard. "It should get to the inn some time in the middle of the day. I don't think they'll dare to do anything in front of that many people."

"I think you're right," Mags agreed. "All right, do we need to go over the plan again?"

Perry shook his head, and hurriedly began making up the sort of pack a casual laborer would have. Just a single blanket rolled up, a frieze bag of the sort grain was stored in converted into a pack and stuffed with a grass mat he had woven, stuck all over with twigs and leaves. That last was to simulate meager belongings—and for use later. A sling and a pouch of stones on one side of his belt, and a well-worn knife in an equally worn sheath went on the other and a belt pouch with a few more things in it next to the knife. His father was similarly equipped. Both of them had cut walking staves out of downed and weathered branches. The horses were secured so they wouldn't wander out of the shelter. Larral was to guard the horses; with Dallen ghosting behind them, they headed out on the road. They would be traveling in the opposite direction from which the caravan was coming. Perry kept track of the caravan's progress through the eyes of the caravaners' horses and of birds overhead, timing their arrival at the inn to come about a candlemark after the caravan, once it was obvious that the guards and drivers intended to stay the night.

Perry couldn't tell by his father's unchanging expression of easy affability what he was picking up from the two guards on the front gate when they entered. He kept his own expression as dull as possible. A boy in his position, doing casual farm labor with his father, would be footsore, tired, probably not fed all that well, and as a consequence, uninterested in anything except his next meal. This would be just one more inn in a long succession of inns in his lifetime. Though inns would be far fewer than haystacks, barns, and open fields. There was no way they would be able to afford to stay overnight, but they would be hoping there was a meal cheap enough they could afford it, as a change from boiled oats, what they could glean by the wayside, and whatever they'd been able to kill with sling and stone.

Two of the tables inside were already occupied by the guards and the drivers. The girl had already served them with bread, beer, and stew, and she glanced at the two of them with an expression as dull as Perry's, before shuffling over to them. She was clean, but she obviously worked as hard as the cook and bartender could manage. Bruises on her arms suggested that if she was not actually beaten, she was often picked up off the ground and shaken until her teeth rattled. Perry took his mind off her; he couldn't rescue every ill-treated tavern wench in the world .

"Yew eatin'?" she asked. "Table's on'y for them as is eatin'."

"Wotcher got fer half penny?" Mags asked.

"Pease porridge," she replied. "An' water."

"Done." Mags nodded, and he and Perry sat down at a third table as she went to the kitchen and came back with two bowls of pease porridge almost thick enough to cut and two wooden mugs of water, slapping them down in front of the two of them and holding out her hand. Mags dropped a penny in it, and she shuffled back into the kitchen. No spoon was offered, but they were prepared for that, taking horn spoons out of their belt pouches, polishing them on the hems of their tunics, and digging in.

It wasn't bad, actually. In fact, it was rather good. Whatever else was going on here, the cook was the genuine article. Mags made small talk with the drivers, asking them about the road they had just traversed and whether there were any farms off it, establishing their personas and cementing in the minds of their listeners that the two of them were heading in the direction the caravan had just come from.

This was going to be important later.

Meanwhile, Mags was asking detailed questions about the couple of farms the drivers had passed. Were they planting or doing an early harvest? Both would mean possible work. Were they hedging or ditching? That meant the same. Perry was surprised and very impressed with his father; for all that Mags had been reluctant about this trip, given that he was, by and large, best in a large city, he'd worked out a persona that was coming across as genuine. All *he* had to do was keep quiet and look tired.

When they had finished eating, they licked their spoons clean, polished them again on their tunics, and stowed them carefully away. Then they drank the last of their water and stood up.

"Not stayin'?" called one of the caravan guards.

Mags shook his head ruefully. "Cain't. Ain't got the penny, an' even if we did, we needs t'get farther down the road toward work."

"I wouldn' chance the beasts," one driver opined.

Mags laughed. "We ain't carryin' food a beast'll smell, we never camp where we et if we killed somethin', an' most beasts in summer'll avoid a man if they can. Camp away from water, under bushes, yer gen'rally all right."

This elicited some sympathetic murmurs and advice on where to camp; Mags accepted these with every evidence of listening, then bade farewell to the men and left, with Perry following. They headed down the road in the "proper" direction until they were out of sight of the inn—and then quickly got off the road and took to the trees, getting themselves well under cover and adding to their concealment by enveloping themselves in their grass-and-leaf mats. From here they could see the road without being seen; more to the point, Mags could skim the surface thoughts of the men who were likely to pursue them, and, hopefully, they would learn a lot more than Perry had been able to.

For about a quarter candlemark, Perry was afraid their bait had not been taken. The road remained empty of everything but sunlight, dust, and the occasional falling leaf. And then, finally, the three men he had eavesdropped on appeared on horseback, their horses moving at a brisk enough walk to easily overtake a walking man and boy. They said nothing as they passed. They appeared bored; they were probably completely confident they'd soon have Mags and Perry in their grasp. Even if the two tried to run, they'd never escape three men on horseback.

Mags and Perry remained in the tree. About a quarter candlemark later, and the riders were back—and this time they looked considerably puzzled. "They couldn't have gotten that much ahead of us," said one.

"Maybe they went off the road?" asked another.

"Why would they do that?"

"How the hell should I know?" the first exploded. "I'm not a bloody Mindspeaker!"

They stopped their horses and quarreled for a bit, the first maintaining it was too much trouble to try to find their victims, the other two arguing in favor of a more thorough search.

The latter two won, and they headed back up the road in the direction they thought their victims had gone.

"We need the dogs," one said, before they got out of earshot. "This ain't the first time we've needed 'em."

Mags and Perry waited until they were long out of sight—and just when Perry was beginning to think he should see if he could find a bird to track them with, Dallen appeared under their tree. Still wrapped in their camouflage, they scrambled down, and Mags leaped on the Companion's back, pulling Perry up behind his saddle. Dallen took off like a shot. He sped deep into the woods, as they shed bits of grass and leaves behind them.

When Dallen finally slowed, there was nothing much left of their disguises but a few wisps of grass and one leaf stuck behind Mags' right ear. It was uncannily quiet beneath the trees; only as Dallen slowed to a walk did the sounds of birds and animals return. Perry hoped that the three men looking for them had not been watching for startled birds exploding out of the canopy; that would have been a dead giveaway. "Did we lose them?" Mags asked his son.

Perry sent his mind searching for birds with the three men in sight. He found a lazily circling buzzard for whom the antics of the three riders below him were enough to distract him from the hunt for food. The three of them had stopped in the middle of the road and were shouting angrily at each other. They were making threatening gestures at each other and back down the road, as if they couldn't agree on what to do next. "Yes," he said, pulling his mind back. "They're fairly well baffled."

Mags let out a huge sigh of relief. "That's good. Because it's pretty much what we were afraid of. This inn is a honey-trap. They're careful not to take anyone who will be missed, but no matter who it was that built it originally, kidnapping the unwary is the only reason it exists now. If we'd said we wanted to stay the night, they'd have given us a price we couldn't afford for the sleeping room, then when we hemmed and hawed, they'd have pretended to take pity on us and charged us a pittance for a place on the hearth in the common room. The cook would slip out, offer us some bread and butter and tea, as if she felt sorry for us, and to keep us from suspecting anything, she'd offer the same to the caravaners. The tea would have sleeping herbs in it. Once the caravaners went upstairs, and as soon as they and we had fallen asleep, they'd have trussed us up and carried us off."

Perry nodded solemnly. "And if the caravaners asked about us in the morning, they'd say we'd left at first light. They'd get a late start, 'cause of the tea."

"And they wouldn't think twice about it, since nothing would have happened to *them.* Well, since I made it obvious that we weren't going to stay, the mercenaries had to come after us." His voice turned grim. "All the mercenaries know is that their boss has a fortified place up north of here, and he needs a lot of labor. And it's not just labor they want, it's women, for 'breeding,' as well. The mercenaries haven't managed to get him more than one or two, but he paid them extra well when they brought one."

"Do you know why? I mean, why they want people? Is it a mine, like you thought?" Perry asked.

Mags shook his head. "They don't know. They only know that they deliver their prey to that walled enclave north of here and that all they ever see is other guards, never any of the people they delivered. It's a pretty unwelcoming place, more like a prison than anything else. And in the back of their minds was the thought that they've known men who asked too many questions, and those men mysteriously disappeared."

At this point, Dallen had brought them to their camp. They slipped off his back and squirmed their way into cover. "We should stay here until tomorrow, just in case they start hunting in this direction," his father continued. "Then in the morning we'll pack up and get out of here; with any luck we'll be home in six or ten days once we reach Whithern."

Perry, who had been expecting his father to begin concocting a plan to do something about this situation, sat down rather hard and stared at him. "But—why are we leaving?" he stammered. "We know they've kidnapped the people that are missing. We should be doing something about that!"

"Because this is not Valdemar, Perry," his father said, with heavy patience, as if he was forced to explain something to a toddler. "We can't just call in the Guard. Even the King can't do that. We're outside the Border; realistically speaking, and even though whoever is behind this is obviously kidnapping people, he may well be what passes for the authority here. Crossing the Border with the Guard would certainly trigger a local altercation and might well start a small war. And even though I technically have the power to notify the Guard that people are being kidnapped from this inn, I'd need a lot better reason than what we have now to get them involved."

"But some of those people that were taken were probably from Valdemar!" Perry exclaimed in dismay.

Mags shook his head. "It doesn't matter. We have to get to where I'm within range of relay Mindspeaking, report to the King, and get orders. And truth to tell, Perry, what he is probably going to do is order us to come home, and he'll close the road at the Border so no one from Valdemar is caught in this trap again."

Perry felt objections building up inside him until he wanted to explode with them. But one look at his father told him that nothing he said was going to make any difference. He subsided into sullen silence.

———

Perry had gone into the sulks again. Mags tried not to sigh visibly, but he was exasperated. *This is what I get for bringing a child along,* he thought, then suppressed the thought. Perry had been incredibly useful and had acted with much more maturity than a mere thirteen-year-old would normally show. The *kyree,* who never would have joined them if Perry hadn't been with him, had also been incredibly useful. And he could understand why Perry was angry—the boy was still young enough to think that it was their duty to rush in and rescue the people who'd been taken. And he had probably been plotting all sorts of clever ways that they could find out exactly what sort of forces they were up against, and how they could rescue the people being held.

Except that was exactly what they couldn't do, for all the reasons he'd told his son and many more. Technically, they were not even supposed to be here. The only reason they were not already in trouble was because they hadn't actually run into anyone or anything in official authority on this side of the Border.

:I doubt there is anything like a local lord here,: Dallen observed doubtfully.

:That just means that whoever this is could probably make the case that he is the authority here. And he could make up some law about conscripting people. And there is not a damn thing we could do about it except protest. Actually, the only way I could make a formal protest would be if I got my uniform and came back in my persona as a Herald.:

Dallen bobbed his head. *:True. And there are only the four of us. If we ventured anywhere near this place to investigate, we would almost certainly be discovered and possibly captured.:*

:I . . . have no good way of explaining this to Perry. He's still young enough to be idealistic. We are responsible for the safety of Valdemarans, of innocents. We can't just wash our hands of them and walk away. And yet, we have to. And all I can tell him is "Because I say so," which is not *how he was raised.:* He was as exasperated with himself as he was with Perry.

But Perry, although he was sulking, was at least making himself useful, cleaning up the horse-droppings with the crude shovel they'd made and taking them out to scatter randomly outside the grove. Perry might be sulking, but he wasn't stupid. He had Larral with him, and he was probably keeping an eye out for those mercenaries via the local wild birds as well as relying on Larral's keen senses. Mags waited until he was done, then asked, with meticulous politeness, "Perry, would you check the snares? You and Larral will be safer doing so than I will."

"Yes, Father," came the answer . . . still sullen, but perhaps with a note of conciliation that Mags had admitted there was something Perry could do that he could not.

I'll try again over supper, Mags decided. *Once he's cooled down a little. He's anything but stupid. I just have to get him to understand how complicated this situation is.*

Though how he was going to manage that . . . Mags had no idea.

:*You're going to try and find this prison, aren't you?*: Larral asked, matter-of-factly.

Perry finished gutting the rabbit he had found in the snare, then carefully wound up the snare. He strung the rabbit's hind feet on a willow switch with the first rabbit he'd found and moved on to the next snare before he answered. Was Larral actually on his side? Only one way to find out.

:*Yes, I am. We need to know what's going on. These people are right on our Border; they have a fortress, and they're kidnapping people and we don't know why! Even if we can't rescue them, we should at least find out why these dangerous people are doing this!*: This all seemed so *clear* to him, he couldn't understand why his father couldn't understand how important it was.

Larral didn't say anything until they got to the next snare—which was empty—and Perry had collected it. :*Actually, I agree with you,*: he said. :*There was nothing like this group of people when the Hawkbrothers were still here, or my pack would have known about them. They sound dangerous. I think you are right to want to find out what they are doing.:*

Now it was Perry's turn to be silent as they made their way to the last snare in the line, although now his anger with his father was tempered with excitement. Larral was on his side! Was it possible that Larral would help him convince his father? If the *kyree* would, there might be a chance he could at least make his father see reason!

Another rabbit dealt with, and they both paused. "We should make sure the mercenaries are nowhere about," he whispered, and Larral gave a brief nod and raised his nose to sniff the air.

Perry decided to check first with the inn cat; if the mercenaries had gone back to the inn, as he hoped, she would certainly be in a position to know. And as soon as he touched her mind, he knew he'd been right. She was crouched in the kitchen, ears flattened against her head, listening to the three mercenaries in the common room shout at each other. In her experience, people shouting meant things being thrown at *her,* eventually. He soothed her and pointed out a good place to hide; she dashed across the kitchen to tuck herself in behind a broom and bucket, then relaxed so he could listen.

At this point the shouting had devolved into recriminations as to which of them was the most to blame for their prey escaping. It sounded as if they were going to be at it for quite a while, unless the barkeeper had the authority to make them settle down.

He opened his eyes to see Larral regarding him steadily.

"The mercenaries are back at the inn," he said shortly.

:Good. And I have made up my mind that although your father seems to irrationally wish to avoid considering all options, you and I should not be so foolish. I want you to tell your father what you discovered the mercenaries have done. Eat dinner. Go to bed early and close your eyes, and you and I will discuss this further.:

He blinked in surprise. *:You mean—:*

:I mean I don't know yet. I think we need to discuss this, you and I, and I think your father is already set on the course he intends to pursue and is going to add nothing to this discussion.:

He swallowed hard. He . . . hadn't actually even considered going against his father's wishes . . . but maybe they should. *That might force his father's hand. What is it that Lord Jorthun says? "Sometimes it's better to make apologies than try to get permission."*

:All right,: he said, finally, and left it at that.

With no particular need for stealth, they hurried back to the grove by the quickest way and came on Mags bringing the horses back from watering them. "They're in the inn and yelling at each other, Father," Perry said, before Mags could ask anything. "It sounded as if they'd already decided we've slipped past them."

Mags nodded, and handed him Pog's reins. "We should still be careful. We can wait them out tomorrow, then leave the day after, when we are sure they have given up on finding us."

Perry said nothing, just led Pog around behind Daisy. Larral took Lily's reins in his mouth, lined up behind Pog, and they all squeezed in along the rock face in single file, leading the horses. Perry handed his father the string of rabbits and the snares and went to sit down on his bed. Mags got to work, spitting the bunnies and setting them up to roast over the coals.

It had been getting dark when he had reached the campsite, and by the time the rabbits were done, it was full night. There were just a few patches of starry sky visible through the tree branches overhead, and the only light came from their little fire. The pease porridge was a distant memory by now, and he was starving. When Mags handed him his share of the food, he devoured every shred of his bunny and gnawed the bones bare before tossing them on the coals to burn down. Then, without saying anything to his father, he rolled up in his blankets and put his back to the fire. His father probably thought he was still sulking. Fine. Let him. As long as he thought that, he wouldn't suspect that Perry and Larral were plotting.

:*All right,*: he said to Larral. :*What are we going to do?*:

Larral had lain down so that he could use the *kyree's* chest as a pillow; he felt Larral's breath puffing gently on the back of his neck before the *kyree* put his head down on his paws. :*First . . . I do not like that this is taking place this close to my pack. It is probably as close to my pack as it is to your Border, and this is a bad thing. It threatens both our peoples.*:

Perry sucked on his lower lip. :*See, that bothers me, but not as much as the fact that at least some of the people that were kidnapped were from Valdemar. We should be doing something to get them out!*:

Larral pondered this for a bit. :*If it were* kyree *I would feel the same. So there are two things. This is too near our territories, and they have already taken some of your pack. A show of force might free them.*:

:*Agreed. But Father won't get the Guard, and without the Guard there's just us, and that's not enough. He's right that we can't just find this place and order them to let our people go.*:

:*Even with the Guard there may not be enough force to accomplish the dual needs of freeing your people and putting these kidnappers on notice,*: Larral corrected. :*This is the difficulty. We don't know anything about them, really. All we know is that there is a fortified place, there are mercenaries, there are people being held against their will. That is not much information. There may actually be no real threat, and your father may be right; closing the Border may be enough to prevent further kidnappings and properly intimidate them. Or the leader behind all this may actually have a small army, and the threat is imminent. We must get information. The question is, how? I assume that if we find the place, you can gather information with any animals inside?*:

He thought about that very carefully. It was clear that Larral considered him to be perfectly capable of doing exactly what he said he could do. So he had better be careful not to say he could do more than he actually could.

:If there are animals in the right places, yes. But if this place is as big as a city . . . I could do a lot of looking and never actually find out much that is useful.:

Larral thought that over, taking images from his mind of Haven and the one or two smaller cities he had been to. *:That could present a problem.:*

He stifled a sigh. He'd actually thought about that—trying to find the place, lurk outside it, find an animal. And now that he was a little calmer, he was sure his father had thought of the same thing, and realized that if this place was too big, they could both lurk outside and use their Gifts and discover nothing of any worth. *:Aye. It could take a really long time.:*

They both pondered the problem . . . and that was when something occurred to him. *:When they were looking for us, one of the mercenaries said, "We need the dogs." Which has to mean that someone has trained dogs there. And I bet the trained dogs are wherever all the important stuff is going on.:* He felt his insides clench with excitement. *:If we can get where those dogs are . . . we'll be able to learn a lot, I bet!:*

:I hope you don't think I can simply walk in the front gate and—: Larral began.

Perry interrupted him. *:Both of us. I make out I'm a dog-boy. You're one of my dogs.:*

Larral caught on what he meant immediately, probably from his memories of Lady Dia's kennels.

:That . . . can work. You are small, nonthreatening. And dog-boys are valuable. But how do you prevent them from using you for some other purpose?::

:I just make out I'm addled. A lot of dog-boys and bee-boys are. And they won't turn a hair about my being addled, as long as I can do anything with their dogs—:

:Which you can.:

:—because the more addled a dog-boy is, the more he's supposed to be able to do with the dogs.:

Larral turned these things over in his mind. *:I like this plan. This can work. All right then. We will wait until your father is asleep. Then you will take only what you need and nothing that will give you away, and we will slip away. I can see in the dark well enough for both of us. We will go to the inn, and from there I will find the trail to this place. There will be one. The inn is getting its supplies from somewhere, and it is probably this fortified place. When we find it, we will present ourselves. And on the way, I can hunt for us and find shelter.:*

Perry felt his spirits rising again. Finally! They were going to do something about this! They might even be able to rescue the people who had been kidnapped! *:All right. Let me know when father is asleep.:*

He was nearly on fire with impatience. It seemed to take forever; the fire had burned down to coals buried in ash before Larral nosed the back of his neck. Moving as silently as he could, and finding his belongings by feel alone, he rolled up his bedroll and tied it, put on the belt with his knife and sling and other basic gear, and crept past the horses. *If father wakes up—he won't be able to see in the dark. He won't know I have my gear on. I'll say I need to relieve myself.* He was afraid for a moment that Dallen would wake too, which would have been a problem since Dallen *could* see in the dark, but the Companion slept as soundly as his Chosen. Without the need to set a watch thanks to the security of their hiding place, and neither of them suspecting he'd go off on his own, both of them slept as soundly as they would have at Arville's home in Whithern.

He and Larral eeled their way out, to find themselves in the moon-drenched forest. With one hand on Larral's back to guide him, and carefully trying to use Larral's keener vision to augment the little he could make out, they headed back in the direction of the inn.

The journey had a curiously dreamlike feeling about it. The air was sweet, cool, and still, scented mostly with evergreen. Thanks to seeing through Larral's eyes, he walked as surely as if it were daylight. There were very few active insects calling under the canopy, and the only birds were some distant owls. Whether it was Larral's formidable presence that kept predators away, he didn't know, but they might have been making their way through a forest in a tale, a woodland in which nothing threatening stirred. He felt tired and energized at the same time, jittery with excitement and yet strangely calm.

It took less than a candlemark to get to the inn, which was closed up behind its gates, the two guards walking the perimeter inside. Perry heard their footsteps in the near-silence as they paused in the forest just at the boundary of the cleared space. They sounded clumsy and heavy-footed. That reminded *him* to walk quietly.

:Let's look for that trail. I am sure there will be one.: Larral put his nose to the ground, and they wove through the trees as they slowly made their way around to the back of the palisade.

:I have it,: the *kyree* said, suddenly, his nose still firmly on the ground. *:Keep your hand on my back. The scent is strong: men and a team of horses, and there is no reason for any caravan stopping at the inn to have come back here. This has to be the pack train bringing them their supplies.:*

Into the darkness they went, with Larral pushing on, deeper and deeper into the forest, until Perry was too tired to walk anymore. Actually . . . he didn't say anything, because Larral was so intent on following the scent, but he began to stumble, regularly, and stifle yawns.

:You are weary,: Larral said, after the tenth stumble.

:I—: He didn't want to lie, but . . . he didn't think he could keep his eyes open anymore.

:You need sleep. I am sorry, I was concentrating too hard to

notice.: Larral brought his head up, and then he yawned, hugely. *:We both need sleep. Stay here. I will find a place to den up.:*

Then he was standing alone, in the dark.

He was afraid to sit down, even though his legs ached, because if he did, he was pretty sure he was going to fall asleep right there. He didn't sense anything dangerous out there, but that didn't mean this was a good time to let down his guard. So he stood there, in the dark, trying to stay alert, trying to listen for anything out in the darkness, leaving his mind open to the faint thoughts of all the nocturnal animals out there, looking for danger. And catching himself nodding off every few moments with a jerk.

At that point, Larral returned. *:Come along,:* he heard, just before Larral slid his head under Perry's hand.

It was not as far as he had feared. Larral had found them a good place to "den up" as he said; it was a hollow under a fallen tree, filled with dead leaves, as Perry discovered mostly by feel and partly by looking through Larral's eyes.

Perry took off his bedroll and shook out the blankets, putting one over the leaves and wrapping himself up in the others. Once he had made himself comfortable, Larral placed himself between Perry and the rest of the world. He took a sip of water from his waterskin, laid himself down, and was so tired he fell asleep without even thinking about what else he might be sharing that hollow with.

When he woke, it was full light, and Larral had brought something unexpected. Lying between the *kyree's* front paws was a mushroom the size of a small loaf of bread.

Perry sat up carefully to avoid hitting his head on the log, and he stared at it for a moment. "Is that safe to eat?" he asked, his mouth watering in spite of himself. He was very, very hungry, and he loved mushrooms, raw or cooked.

:Perfectly,: the *kyree* said with confidence. *:I've already had one.:*

Perry stared at him. "You eat mushrooms?"

:I eat many things besides raw rabbit. I am not a barbarian!:

Perry smothered a laugh and picked up the mushroom with both hands, biting into it. Even raw, it had a very satisfying, meaty flavor to it, and it was very filling. *:We call them meat mushrooms,:* Larral told him, as he reminded himself to eat slowly and carefully and not gobble. His stomach wasn't used to eating this much raw mushroom, and he didn't want it to get persnickity on him. *:So, I am told, do the Hawkbrothers.:*

He took a sip from his waterskin and another bite of mushroom. His stomach seemed happy. The only way this meal could be better would have been if he could have sliced this thing and fried the slices in butter. "I could probably eat these things for a week and not get tired of them."

:Well, they are not as nourishing as real meat, and I would not do that. But you will be all right for a day or two eating only those, if we have to. I do not think we will have to. I will certainly catch something by this evening.: Perry nodded, and he made sure to eat every crumb. Sadly, as he knew from experience, raw mushrooms did not keep well once cut, bitten, or broken into, so there was no point in trying to save any of it for later. He'd be more likely to find unappetizing slime than anything edible.

And once his stomach was full, they set off again, at a better pace now that he could see the ground with his own eyes. There was, in fact, a very faint trail to follow. If he had not had Larral's guidance, he might have taken it for a game trail.

And if he had not had Larral's guidance, he would never have known how near they were to their goal until he stumbled into one of the perimeter patrols, or they stumbled into him.

But Larral scented them long before they were a danger. *:Stop!:* he heard, and he froze. Larral's head was up and his ears flat. *:We need to move in under those bushes. There are two men approaching.:*

They both moved quickly, but as quietly as they could, and wormed their way into the middle of a thicket of bushes, in deep cover. They waited until the two men had passed and were well out of hearing distance before they moved again. From there, they wormed their way, still using the brush, closer and closer to their goal—which not only Larral, but Perry too, could smell by the faint scent of woodsmoke. They edged carefully through the brush on their bellies until they could see the fortress.

Like the inn, there was a wide area cleared of trees and brush between the edge of the forest and the palisade. And from where they were hiding, all he saw was the palisade of logs, not even a hint of whatever lay inside that barrier. The palisade stretched into the forest for as far as he could see from where he was, in either direction. This was much bigger than a mere "fortress," that much was clear. Bigger than Whithern, for sure. There was only one encouraging thing about it.

It was walled in by mere logs. If it had been built to withstand any serious attack by humans, it would have walls of stone. It wasn't as if there wasn't plenty of stone hereabouts, after all, and as big as this place was, they should have had plenty of labor to build stone walls.

:That may be why they are kidnapping people: for labor to build their holding into a real fortress.:

Perry took a deep breath. It was now or never. *:Any of those patrols around? We don't want to get stopped before we get to the gate.:*

Larral raised his head and took in several deep breaths. *:None that I can smell.:*

:All right, then. Do I look properly addled?:

Larral looked him up and down. *:Your clothing is smudged, there is dirt on your forehead and a leaf behind your ear.:*

:Good. Let's go.: He crawled out from under the bushes,

stood up, hunched his shoulders and put a blank look on his face, and started marching toward the gate.

By the time he got halfway there, he heard the buzz of voices, and looking out from under his hair to the top of the palisade, he saw the heads, shoulders, and arms of a few men up there. They were pointing at him, and gesticulating at each other, though they had not accosted him yet.

He was within a couple of horse-lengths of the gate when it swung slightly open. Two men came out, with crossbows pointing at him. He stopped but said nothing.

A third man, unarmed, emerged between the two. "Who are you?" he barked. "How did you find this place?"

"Dog-boy," Perry said, his hand on Larral's back.

"What do you want?" the man demanded.

"Dog-boy," Perry replied, and he wiped his nose on his sleeve. It took nerves of steel to feign that he was not nervous at all; inside he was shaking.

Now completely nonplussed, the man continued to shout questions at him, all of which Perry answered with "Dog-boy."

Finally one of the men with a crossbow muttered, "Sergeant . . . I think 'e's a real dog-boy. We could use 'im. Hellfire, we could more'n use 'im."

"Lookit the size of that thing 'es got with 'im!" the other exclaimed.

The sergeant sucked on his lower lip. "Dog-boy—show me what you can do," he said, finally, slowly and carefully enunciating his words.

Perry scratched his head and stared at him a moment, then looked down at Larral. *:Ready?:*

:Born ready.:

He made small, meaningless gestures with his right hand. Larral sat, lay down, got up again, turned right, then left, stood on his hind legs—which made him taller than all three of the guards—dropped back down and crawled on his belly, rolled onto his back, got up again, and as a finale, did a backflip.

When Perry looked back up at the three men, their jaws were hanging open.

"Dog-boy," he said.

The sergeant got his expression back under control. "You're hired."

Now Perry tried a few new words. "Food," he said, gesturing at himself and Larral.

"Done," the sergeant said instantly.

"Warm bed. Skins." He shook his tunic, which at this point had certainly seen better days.

"Done and done," the sergeant replied instantly. With a little hesitation, he held out his hand. "Bargain?"

Perry looked at his hand for a moment. Then he looked at his own, ostentatiously wiped it on the front of his tunic, and shook the sergeant's. "Your dog-boy," he said, breaking into a grin.

The two armed men smiled with relief and lowered their weapons. The sergeant motioned to him to go in through the opening in the gate. He did as he was told . . . and gaped at what he found inside.

He'd had a few ideas. . . . perhaps some wooden barracks, perhaps a village.

This was . . . a city. A city of two- and three-story-tall wooden buildings, old ones by the look of them, crowded so thickly together that the streets he could see from where he stood were barely wide enough for a single cart, and a cat would have had trouble getting between them.

He didn't have much time to stare, however, as the sergeant gestured to him to follow, and he realized although he was playing addled, he shouldn't play *stupid.* He followed, with Larral padding right at his side, sniffing.

:Most of these buildings are empty,: Larral observed.

:What? How can you tell?: He was already coming to the conclusion that this had been a bad idea. This place was a maze. There was no layout. It was as if people had simply built

things where there was space, and never mind what was logical. Where were the prisoners? How would he get out of here?

:*No cooking smells, no woodfire smells, no strong human
smells, and most of them smell of dust. I don't think whoever
is in charge here built this place. I think he found it and
moved in.*:

Right turn, left turn, left turn, right turn . . . he was already
lost.

:*Well, if they didn't build it, who did? And why did they
leave it empty?*:

:*There's nothing in my pack history,*: Larral admitted. :*Perhaps a plague?*:

He almost panicked, until he realized that if there was any
residue of a plague here, the mercenaries would have caught
it already. But he began to feel as if the buildings were all
staring at him, populated by a horde of lost spirits.

:*I cannot smell any spirits,*: Larral objected.

:*. . . Wait. You can smell spirits?*:

:*Of course I can. So can dogs and wolves and foxes. Cats
see them.*:

If he hadn't been playing a part, he would have stopped
dead in his tracks and stared at Larral. He couldn't do that, of
course . . . and the sergeant was hurrying through the eerily
silent streets, and he had to sprint to keep up.

The houses were all built in a single style, and it was one
he didn't recognize. The roofs were all made of slate and were
a peculiar, rounded shape, as if they were imitating the
mounded forms of thatch roofs. And there were two odd little
vents built into the street-facing sides of the roofs, vents that
looked uncannily like half-closed eyes. As if the houses had
faces, wearing a suspicious expression. It was extremely unsettling. The windows were very tall and narrow; the houses
themselves seemed narrow to him, too. It was as if they were
each a single room in width. Why would anyone do that, when
this town was in the middle of nowhere, and there was plenty

of space? The street between these houses was cold and damp, as if the sun never shone down here.

Perhaps the oddest thing was that although the wood was silvered with age, there was no sign of the buildings being in need of repair. It was as though there was something keeping them from damage, even by the passing of time.

All that, and the stillness . . . even if Larral swore these buildings weren't haunted, it felt as if the buildings themselves had a presence. A strange, not entirely friendly presence. As if the buildings were looking down on them and judging them.

No wonder the three mercenaries at the inn had been unnerved by this town.

Suddenly they turned a corner, and the street ended at a second barrier, a plank fence this time, made of the same wood as the houses. The fence was twice the height of a man, with a finished lintel at the top and a great, square gate. The sun finally penetrated down the street here, and the bronze hardware gleamed in the light. The sergeant shouted something, and the gate swung open in unnerving silence.

Perry and Larral squeezed through and found themselves in a large courtyard. There was one, single, enormous building in the center of it. Although it was built in the same style as the rest of the buildings in this strange city, it was four stories tall, as wide as thirty farm carts placed end to end, and had two rows of two dozen of those eyelike vents built into the roof. This building looked like a many-eyed giant glaring down into the courtyard with suspicion.

The courtyard was paved in slate that matched the roof. There was a staircase leading from the courtyard up to the second floor, with double doors at the top of it. *Probably the entrance,* Perry decided. Strange that there was no way into the first floor, though. The building, like the ones outside, was silvered wood and gray slate, cold, and intimidating.

The captain came in through the gate and waved it shut,

then made a shooing motion and hurried them around the side and to the back.

There, finally, were signs of life: single-story buildings with flatter gray slate roofs everywhere. Outbuildings with no obvious purpose, stables with horses, and people caring for them. Soldiers moving purposefully from building to building, and, finally, there were all sorts of smells, some pleasant, some not, but an overall scent of woodsmoke. And there was one particular building with a fenced yard, with barking coming from it. Now Perry acted as he thought a real dog-boy would, pushing past the sergeant and running to open the door into that building.

As soon as he did so, the din was deafening. And . . . the smell of urine and feces was overpowering. Someone was not doing his job. No wonder they needed a dog-boy.

:Lady Dia would have a right fit,: he told Larral.

:I do not know who Lady Dia is,: Larral replied, *:But I believe having a fit would be the appropriate response here.:*

So Perry looked around, spotted someone who was pretending to work, ran up to him, grabbed him by the front of his filthy tunic, and shook him until his teeth rattled.

"DOG-BOY": he screamed at the top of his lungs, at the same time issuing a mental shout of *:Shut UP!:* to every dog in the building.

In the silence that ensued, he let go of the man, who dropped to his knees, cowering.

"Now that's more like it," said the sergeant.

By suppertime, no one who had seen the previous state of things within these walls would have recognized the kennel. By dint of searching, Perry had located all four of the people who were supposed to be caring for the dogs. Two had been sleeping in the one clean corner, one had been pushing a broom around the yard, and one had been pretending to clean in the kennel. With Larral at his side, he quickly intimidated them, although to tell the truth, it wasn't all that difficult to do so. All four were men who seemed to have real mental deficiencies, and the scars on their skulls suggested reasons why. He discovered that the kennel was at least as well-appointed as Lady Dia's, with its own pump and a giant copper for heating water. He set all four of the attendants to a thorough scrubbing of the kennel itself with hot water and brown soap, while he put all the dogs—big, rangy mastiffs, all male—in the yard. Once they were all out there, milling around and whimpering with confusion at the sudden change in their lives, he confronted them.

They were already cowed by his initial mental command, and Larral's presence at his side ensured that they remained cowed. He looked the entire pack of twenty over, sternly, one at a time, until each one dropped to the ground in a submissive pose.

:Pack leader,: he told them—though actually it was not in words, but in the impression that he was their leader from now on. And it was in a mental tone that would accept no challenge. At this point, having never in their lives had a human's voice *in their heads,* they were not even thinking of challenging him. He got tail-thumping, submissive assent from all of them, immediately.

:Pack second,: he told them, projecting an image of Larral into their heads. And to confirm this, Larral went to each of them, took their necks briefly in his massive jaws, and gave each of them a quick shake.

He let them feel his approval, which got more tail-thumping, and a couple of the boldest came up to him to lick his hands. *:Play quiet,:* he told them, and he went back to supervise the cleaning of the kennel.

When the building was scrubbed so completely you could have eaten off the stone floor, he demanded fresh straw. What he got was heaps and heaps of long pine needles, which he frowned at, but was secretly pleased with. He hadn't actually expected straw—where would they have gotten it from?—but pine needles were a more than acceptable substitute, they'd repel fleas, and the dogs would appreciate the soft nests they could make in them. Each of the dogs had his own stall in the kennel, each equipped with a door so they could be locked in, but he had a notion that he could do with his Mindspeech what Lady Dia did with training. It had worked so far. Dogs, after all, were social; they did better when they could be with others.

When the kennel was clean, each stall had a heap of pine needles, and the water troughs were filled with good, clean water, he let the dogs in from the yard and sent his four helpers out to clean the yard as thoroughly as they had cleaned the kennel. Poor men. They might be as addled in reality as he was pretending to be, but at least once shown what they were supposed to do, they worked at it with a will.

The dogs surged into the building, and he stopped them with a gesture. *:No fight!:* he said sternly. *:No fight ever!:*

He got meek agreement from all of them. Next, he drummed into their heads that there was only one place they were allowed to use as a latrine, and that was the far right corner of the yard—thus, essentially housebreaking them. Only then did he let them sort themselves out according to their personalities.

As he had expected, the more dominant dogs did not take single stalls for themselves; instead they, and a friend, chose to bed down together. Sometimes two friends, which was all a stall could hold. It was the most submissive that bedded down alone, although he expected that to end soon enough, when they realized they didn't *have* to sleep alone. Dogs liked the company of each other; given a choice, every dog in here would have crowded together into a single nest. That wasn't possible, so they would sort themselves out as best they could . . . and be the better-tempered and easier to handle for not being stressed by loneliness.

He had toiled alongside his helpers, while Larral had kept an eye on the dogs in the yard to prevent play from turning into fighting, so he was just as soaked and filthy as the helpers were when a man who must be the captain by his weapons and dress opened the door into the courtyard, to check on his progress, accompanied by another mercenary.

"Down!" he shouted, as the dogs nearest the door started to rise from their beds, ready to bark, reinforcing the spoken command with a mental one. Every dog in the kennel flattened himself to the ground.

"Bloody hell, " said the captain, standing in the open doorway, his jaw hanging loose. The person with him looked just as dumbfounded. Perry raised his head proudly, his wet hair down in his eyes.

"Dog-boy," he announced.

"Damn." The captain shook his head. "Dog-boy, if every man around here was as good at his job as you . . ." He left the sentence unfinished. "Go with quartermaster. Food, warm bed, new skins."

"Food, warm bed, new skins," Perry repeated obediently and looked at the man who had been designated the quartermaster. He was of middling height, looked as though someone had roughed in all his features with a hand-ax, and clearly could, and probably did, double as a fighter. He didn't look all that friendly, but he was obviously impressed with what Perry had gotten done, because his jaw was just as slack with surprise as the captain's.

He clamped his jaw shut and nodded at Perry. "Come with me, Dog-boy," he said in a hoarse voice.

Perry followed him to yet another outbuilding, as Larral remained to keep order among the dogs. This was obviously a storehouse and contained everything a small army would need, including, he noted with interest, weapons. There he was heaped with several good blankets and even a canvas sheet to augment his own bedroll, as well as three sets of canvas tunics and trews, socks, and clouts. He was grateful no one had looked too closely at his boots, other than to check that he had footwear—they were rather too good for the persona he was assuming. "I'll send one of the lads over with your rations, Dog-boy," said the quartermaster.

Perry nodded vigorously. "Food soon."

"Aye. Food soon." The quartermaster seemed to take it for granted that Perry would be able to find his way back and ushered him as far as the door to the building. Perry took the hint and carried his loot back to the kennel. Once there he changed out of his filthy clothing into a set of the clean, and left the dirty stuff to soak in a pail of hot water, adding more pine needles to one of the stalls that the dogs didn't seem to want, making a double bed for himself and Larral there. This was where he put his few belongings and his spare clothing.

About a candlemark later, two men arrived with meat for the dogs in a pair of wheelbarrows, and a third person—a small, skinny, frightened-looking boy—followed them with a pail that he handed to Perry before he scuttled off. The pail smelled like stew, so Perry put it somewhere safe while he fed the dogs.

When the men had left with empty barrows, he turned his attention back to the pail—which had three nested pans in it, one on top of the other, holding hard army bread, stew, and something that on investigation proved to be a piece of sweet boiled pudding with berries in it. Certainly good food by anyone's standards.

:The meat is good too. Wild pig, if I am any judge.: Larral "felt" contented. *:Also . . . if I am any judge, that boy was one of the kidnapping victims.:*

Perry had been concentrating so hard on getting through all of this without slipping up, that he had momentarily forgotten their actual aim. *:Dammit!:* he replied ruefully. *:We need to get him aside somehow and find out where the others are!:*

:We also need to find out just how many fighters there are in this place,: Larral reminded him. *:And who is in charge. And what they want.:*

:And . . .: Perry gulped, suddenly realizing with a chill just what he had walked them both into. *:And how in hell we are going to get* out *of here once we find all that out.:*

Mags awoke in the darkness with a lurch and a sickening feeling in his stomach, knowing something was wrong. A split second later, as the sleep-fog cleared from his head, he knew exactly what it was.

Perry was gone. So was Larral. There was no sense of them anywhere in this grove.

He clamped down on his sudden surge of panic. They might just have left the grove because they needed to attend to nature . . .

But a methodical mental scan of the area quickly disabused him of that idea. He couldn't sense them anywhere, not even the wisp of a presence that Perry still had when he was shielding. They were gone; they had gotten far enough away that even he could not find their Mindvoices. That must have been what had awakened him—the absence of those familiar mental presences.

For the first time in decades, he felt a rush of pure panic, and he cursed himself for the complacence that had let him relax and sleep so deeply that Perry's escape hadn't even registered. *:Dallen!:* he cried, groping for Perry's bed, only to find nothing but pine needles.

All Perry's belongings were gone., which only confirmed the worst of his fears. There could be only one reason for that. Mags had refused try to find where the kidnapped victims were being held, so Perry had gone off to find out for himself.

That tore it. Now his panic overwhelmed him. He knew exactly what the fool boy was thinking—he thought his father was betraying his duty, and since Mags wouldn't listen to him, Perry had taken matters into his own hands. He must have slipped away with Larral as soon as he knew his father and Dallen were completely asleep. And now? He could be anywhere; Mags had no idea what direction he'd gone in, and without Larral to sniff out the trail, there was no hope of tracking him.

His panic ramped up and up until he was about to leap out of bed and go running out into the darkness in a wild search for his son—when he found himself stopped by Dallen imposing calm on him for a moment.

:Stop,: the Companion ordered. *:If we know nothing else, we know he's with Larral. You know what kind of fighter Larral can be. Short of a Companion, there's no other creature he would be safer with. If he were in trouble, we would know.:*

He took several slow, deep breaths.

:Better,: said Dallen. *:Now you can properly concentrate. I'll help you. Let's see if we can find him together. I know he is not a regular Mindspeaker that we can talk to at a great distance, but we can still use your Gift. There's no point in running off into the darkness when your Mindspeech will find him if he's anywhere between here and the inn.:*

He lay back down on his bed and slowly let the shields drop from his mind, stretching himself out as far as he could. He sensed the sleeping mercenaries, the cook and the bartender, the serving girl . . . he picked up the idle, half-drunken thoughts of the two patrolling guards. But either Perry was too far away, or the boy was shielding, or both; outside the inn there was nothing but emptiness.

:*He'd better be shielding,*: Dallen pointed out. :*You drilled that into him until it was second nature from the time his power began to manifest. These are the Pelagirs; this is no place to let your mind be accessible freely, even if all you have is Animal Mindspeech. The only reason he could sense the ravens and the* dyheli *is because his Gift is as strong as his shields.*:

But that jarred loose a realization. Wait—the *dyheli* owed them. So did the ravens, but he was not going to have any luck contacting the ravens, since he didn't have Animal Mindspeech. But he could easily Mindspeak with the King-Stag. The *dyheli* might even be awake, or at least merely dozing, and with Dallen boosting him, he might well be able to reach the stag from here.

:*That's a good idea. Let's give it a try, Chosen. The more allies we have to help find him, the better off we'll be.*:

He remembered very well what the King-Stag's mind had felt like, and with Dallen putting extra power behind him, as he did when Mags was Mindspeaking at great distances to other Heralds, he stretched himself to his limits. It seemed as though he was feeling around in the dark for a disturbingly long time, when suddenly, he sensed the mind he was looking for.

And it was awake!

:*Because you were making a great deal of noise, human. What ails you?*: The *dyheli* was definitely not in a good mood, but Mags plowed ahead anyway, describing what they had found, the argument he'd had with Perry, and that Perry and Larral had now gone off on their own. He was praying the King-Stag would understand, seeing as he was a father, too.

The *dyheli's* attitude grew—less grumpy—the more he spoke, which was encouraging. So he finished up with a plaint born of frustration as well as fear. :*And I don't understand why Larral, of all creatures, is helping him! I thought Larral was trustworthy!:*

The *dyheli* did not immediately reply. *:How old is your fawn?:*

Mags didn't see what that had to do with anything, but he answered anyway. *:Thirteen.:*

:That explains it.:

This was maddening. *:Explains what?:*

:The kyree *are fully adult at ten.:*

For a second, Mags wanted to murder the *dyheli* for being so obtuse—but then he got it. Larral had gone along with this insanity because, by his standards, Perry was an adult and could make reasoned and informed decisions, not emotional ones.

Which right now, did not help in the least. If anything, it made things worse, because Larral was going to assume Perry was capable of adult reasoning—

:Who is making emotional decisions now?: the King-Stag asked, rhetorically. *:Calm yourself. I will move the herd as soon as it is light and safe to do so and come to join you. Is there anything else? Something that might get us further aid in finding the pair?:*

:We encountered and helped some Bondbird ravens about a day or so on our backtrail . . . : He didn't know what else to say.

But he felt the King-Stag's satisfaction. *:Good, that will be useful. I will find them at dawn. There is absolutely no point in trying to wake a bird until it is light. I will let them know in no uncertain terms that if you helped them, they owe you. They will probably find you shortly after I speak with them. And I would be astonished if they cannot find your fawn in short order.:*

Somehow, that was all he needed to get his panic under control and be able to think again. *:Thank you,:* he replied, weak-kneed with gratitude.

:Oh, this is self-interest as well,: the stag told him frankly.

:And quite frankly, although the fawn acted impulsively, he is in the right and you are in the wrong. You should at the very least have decided to come consult me about this as soon as you had that much information. A group of armed men out here, where there was, to my knowledge, nothing but tiny villages, a few farms, and wilderness? These people could potentially move into our territory and prey on some of my herd before we were aware of them.:

Mags felt the King-Stag's weighty disapproval and winced.

:So I will help you, but be advised, I never do anything for only one reason.:

As that seemed to be that, Mags bid the stag a respectful farewell and broke the connection. He wiped his sweating forehead with his sleeve and tried to think of something, anything, that he could do besides wait for dawn. *:Do you think Arville and Ryu could help?:* he asked Dallen.

:They are both more fragile than they like to admit. They would try, but they could be injured and end up being a burden instead of a help,: Dallen replied. *:And at this point I recommend against using the Mindspeech relay to inform the King of anything except the existence of these people. Amily would certainly be informed of Perry's disappearance.:*

Dallen didn't add anything to that, but he didn't have to. Because Mags knew the rest. *Amily would murder me . . .*

––––––––

The ravens arrived at dawn. Four of them landed first in the trees around the little grove, then down on the ground next to Perry's deserted bed. They were young ones, if Mags was any judge. And this saddled him with a new problem. He didn't have Animal Mindspeech. So as they sat there in the little grove, staring at each other, he wracked his brain for some way to communicate with them.

"Dallen, can you talk to them?" he finally asked.

:Perhaps. I can try.:

Dallen looked down his long nose at the birds. They turned to face him—which was, Mags thought, an indicator of initial success at least.

And so he waited, patiently, as his Companion and the four birds stared at each other. Dallen did not move at all. The birds occasionally clacked their beaks or flipped their wing-feathers. He hardly dared breathe, terrified that if he disturbed them, they'd break whatever fragile strand of communication they had.

His muscles were aching with tension when Dallen finally raised his head, and the birds shook themselves and turned back to look at him.

:I think I made them understand what Perry has done and that it puts him in danger. First, they will go to the inn and see if Perry is there. If he is not, they are going to look for a place where there are many men gathered within a day's walk of that inn. And if they find such a place, they will look for Perry there first, then between there and the inn. They are fairly certain that wherever humans are there will be smoke from cookfires, which they can easily see.:

He let out his breath in a long sigh, then had an idea. "Can you ask them to wait a moment before they take off?"

Dallen turned his gaze back on the birds, and Mags fished in his pack for paper and thread. He got twigs and charred one end, and tied a scrap of paper and a twig to one leg of each of the four birds. They looked at their new burdens curiously, pecked at them a little, then looked at him and nodded.

He spread his hands wide. They took that as a sign to take off.

"Should we stay here or try to trace his tracks?" Mags asked his Companion.

:The ravens and the dyheli *know to look for us here,:* Dallen reminded him. *:And neither of us is much good at tracking in the wilderness. The best thing we can do now is collect food*

in case we don't have a chance to hunt for any once they find
Perry, so that we have some sort of supplies with us.:

Once they find Perry. . . . if they *could* find Perry. If he
wasn't already a slave, or worse. His anxiety started to ramp
up again. And his guilt.

This was all because he'd just shut his own child down
without listening to him. Sure, they might both be in danger
now, instead of just Perry—but at least they would be in danger together.

Perry had thought he was never going to get to sleep—sleeping
in a dog kennel, in the middle of the enemy, something he'd
never done before, should have been enough to keep him
awake. Add to that, he had no idea how he was going to get
himself out of this fortress-within-a-city, much less out of the
city, no idea how he could tell his father where he was, and no
plans whatsoever—it seemed a recipe for insomnia.

But he'd been working feverishly all day, and his nerves
had entirely masked how tired he was. Once he had a full belly,
Larral had lain down beside him, and the dogs had settled, the
next thing he knew, it was dawn and he was waking up.

The first thing he did was let the dogs out into the yard—
and only a handful of them started to relieve themselves in a
place other than the designated corner. A simple correction,
and they hurriedly went to join the pack. Well . . . that was
something, at least. His control over them seemed to be absolute. If he ran and they tried to set the dogs to find him, he
could have the pack running in circles while he escaped.

If I can find the way out.

The sun was just touching the horizon when the men with
the barrows arrived with the dogs' morning food. Perry examined it carefully and was satisfied—and grateful that Lady
Dia's Kennelmaster had taught him so much. It was a good

mix of all parts of the animals it had been cut from, with what looked like just a bit of crushed oats mixed in to give the dogs some roughage. Whoever had been making the food for these fellows knew enough about them to feed them right. As he had last night, he lined the dogs up and gave each of them a measured portion. There was some scuffling before he made it very clear to the more dominant dogs that he and Larral were not going to permit any stealing of another dog's food. Then the four helpers arrived, and he set them to cleaning up the mess in the corner of the yard. It was hard to tell since they showed no expression whatsoever except a constant bemusement, but he thought they seemed relieved that it was confined to one easy-to-clean space.

He cleaned himself up, turned the dogs loose in the yard, and considered what he should do for the rest of the day. But he hadn't gotten very far with that when the same boy as last night arrived with a new pail. The lad grabbed the old one from the night before and was about to flee when Perry seized his wrist.

The child froze, terrified.

"Are you one of the people these men kidnapped at the inn?" he whispered.

The boy's mouth dropped open, and he stared at Perry with eyes so wide he looked like a startled owl. He glanced from side to side, guiltily, to make sure there was no one else around, then gave a tiny nod.

"How many of you are there?" he asked.

"Dunno," the boy whispered back. "Me'n two boys does the fetchin'. There's some wimmen, but we never see 'em. They's for the Master. They's some men, does the choppin' an' diggin' an' stuff."

"You're not working in a mine?" Perry asked.

The boy shook his head vigorously. "What mine? Ain't seen nor heard of no mine. I gotta get back. I gotta get back, or I get beat."

Perry let him go. "Thank you," he said.

The boy ignored his thanks and sped off. Perry opened the pail to discover another piece of last night's boiled pudding and salted pease porridge. He ate quickly and left the pail outside the door to the kennel where the boy could get it without coming in.

If this had been Lady Dia's kennel, he'd have taken the dogs for a good long walk or a run; the more they worked, and the more he worked with them, the better it would be for him . . .

Well, he still could take them for a run, just not outside the compound. And it would demonstrate his control over them to everyone inside the compound.

He whistled to get their attention. When every head in the yard was looking in his direction, he let his eyes rake over the pack and ordered, *:Follow.:*

They followed, as obediently as baby ducks following their mother; he was literally chest-deep in dogs, his own head barely higher than theirs. He led them out of the kennel and straight to the fence around the compound. One circuit of the compound ought to be enough, he reckoned.

He had barely gotten the pack to the fence before he had an audience. Work near him ceased entirely. The mercenaries stared, goggling at him walking in the middle of his pack of enormous mastiffs; there was an air of uncertainty about the men, as if they were not quite sure what to think. He grinned, reinforced his command to the dogs to follow as they reached the fence, and broke into a run.

It wasn't much of a run so far as the dogs were concerned, but they enjoyed it, loping along beside and behind him. By now every man in the yard, it seemed, was watching them, either covertly as they worked or overtly. He heard murmurs that sounded astonished from those nearest. As the pack ran along the back fence of the compound, he wasn't just running with the dogs; his eyes were darting everywhere, and he was taking notes. This . . . was odd. There just didn't seem to be that many men here, given the size of the city. And Larral had said that the city itself was deserted. Was this it? Just a few handfuls of mercenaries and slaves occupying this vast mausoleum of a city?

He and the dogs raced up the far side the compound, past the side of the big building there, and turned to race across the front. The front part of the courtyard was still deserted, but he thought he sensed . . . something. As though there was someone watching from the huge building. Well, that was probably where this "Master" was, and where the Master was, there would be servants. So even if the Master wasn't interested in a mere dog-boy, the servants would be, which accounted for the sense of being watched.

:There are people in there,: Larral confirmed. *:I can smell them. Females as well as males. And some of them smell . . . very strange.:*

:How, strange?: he asked, but Larral couldn't seem to articulate it.

I hope that boy doesn't tell anyone I'm not as addled as I'm making out. He grimaced a little as he ran. Stopping the boy and making him talk had probably been a very stupid thing to do . . . but without Mindspeech, how would he have been able to find anything out from the youngling? He wished his father were here. *But if father were here, we'd be separated, and the gods only know what they'd be doing to him.*

When he and the pack rounded the last corner and moved into the back part of the courtyard again, everyone seemed to have gone back to their jobs. But he could tell, from the covert glances, that they were still watching, so he decided to give them a show.

He stopped halfway between the kennel and the fence, and the pack stopped with him. He made a twirling motion with his hand and gave them the mental image of what he wanted, and they ran around him in a tight circle at their top speed, first deosil, then widdershins. That accomplished two things: It proved his ability with them, and it wore them out a little. When they were starting to pant, he stopped them and had them all sit down at once. Then he ordered them to lie down, which they were very happy to do at that point.

Now he was definitely being stared at again. He cast a glance at the kennel door. It was wide open, as he had left it. He pointed at it dramatically and gave them the command to head back to what they considered to be "home" at a run.

They jumped to their feet and streamed toward the door, stopping for nothing. Meanwhile he took his time in a leisurely stroll to the door, entering and closing it behind him when he arrived.

The dogs were lapping up their fill of water and were perfectly willing to flop down all over the kennel after that exertion. He went outside to check on the progress his helpers had made in cleaning the yard.

That was when he heard the "quork" of ravens overhead.

And heard in his mind, *:Ravenfriend. Father seeks you.:*

He managed not to start.

:What we do?: the raven continued. *:Father sent us to find you, help you, then go back, show where you are.:*

:One of you land, in the yard, please,: he told the four of them. *:Just one. Peck around in the yard for a little, then come in the door. I will be just inside.:*

He sauntered back inside and waited. It seemed to take forever before a bold, bright-eyed raven with a piece of paper tied to one leg stalked in the doorway, spotted him, and hopped over to him as he squatted down to get on its level.

It held still politely as he untied the paper from its leg, and saw that there was a charred twig along with it. That was smart, but he had something better. The copper where the water was heated was black with soot, which would work just fine as a sort of ink.

The paper wasn't big, and he had to be careful not to smear

the things he was writing, but he managed to get a few words about what he was doing down and tied the paper around the raven's leg again.

Then something occurred to him. *:Do the rest of you have papers?:*

:Yessss,: the raven replied, eyeing some of the dogs' meat that had been left over.

:Eat your fill, then send another down, until I have all the papers,: he said—more as a suggestion than an order.

:I like you, Ravenfriend,: the youngster declared, then made two flaps to get himself to the pile of meat and began swallowing chunks of it. It wasn't long until he was satisfied, and he sauntered out the door and flapped off into the sky. A second raven stalked inside, and they repeated what he had done with the first. Perry kept his mind firmly on the task at hand and not on the questions without answers that were flooding through his mind right now. When he had finished with the last of the birds, he sent them all on their way . . . hoping no one had noticed them marching into and out of the kennel.

Then, once they were gone . . . he got up and staggered to his bed. Several of the dogs, sensing his distress and emotional turmoil, wandered over to him and licked his hands and face to try to comfort him. If he hadn't been so overwrought, he probably would have laughed; there is nothing quite like having your face licked by a tongue that is bigger than your hand.

But now that he had given his father the little information he had, he was all too conscious of what a hash he had made of this. He didn't know how to get away from this compound, nor out of the city. His father certainly couldn't break in here to rescue him. And even though he was right in the heart of this place, he didn't even know the most basic things about it—like how many mercenaries were here, or how many of the kidnap victims were still alive. In fact, the more he thought about what a mess he had made of the situation, the more he felt like bursting into tears.

:You are forgetting something,: Larral said, calmly.

He sniffed and wiped his eyes on his sleeve. *:What?:*

:Your father is an extremely powerful Mindspeaker. He can even Mindspeak with people who have no Gift at all. Once the ravens bring him here, he should be able to find a spot near enough to us that he can speak directly to you.: Larral nudged his way in among the dogs and laid himself down next to Perry. *:Let him concentrate on that while we concentrate on learning as much as we can.:*

He wanted to believe Larral. . . .

:I will count all the men in this courtyard, if that will make you feel any better. Once we know how many are here, we will have a better idea of how we can escape them.:

He sniffed again and smiled weakly. *:All right. But what if they—:*

:I will perform tricks for them and beg for food. And if they become aggressive with me, I will run back here. I very much doubt they will try to hurt me.:

:All right. But be careful.: When Larral went out into the yard, he went and washed his face, then picked up a shovel and went out into the fenced area to clean it with his helpers. And as he repeated the mechanical motions, he was watching through Larral's eyes.

The first group of men he spotted were sparring, so he didn't approach them. There were ten of them, in five pairs, with another ten waiting on the sidelines while an instructor corrected them. To Perry's eyes these men were good, very good. If this was the general caliber of the mercenaries this Master had hired, then they'd be more than a match for the Valdemaran Guard. This wasn't some unorganized bandit rabble. These were real, professional soldiers.

I wonder where they came from?

Surely not the Pelagir Hills. He couldn't imagine the Hawk-brothers allowing a group like this to set up housekeeping in their territory.

:There are many, many leagues of cleansed lands between the Pelagir Hills and the Dhorisha Plains past your Border along its southernmost western edge,: Larral told him. *:And while you Valdemarans may not know this, those lands are populated. There are all manner of minor lordlings. A mercenary company can easily find employment there.:*

Well, that was something that was never talked about in the lectures on Valdemar's neighbors . . .

:Probably one of those lordlings discovered this place, liked it better than his own keep, and moved in. Now he's trying to populate it.:

That . . . didn't sound likely. It didn't match what he'd seen so far. A lordling would have at least a village-worth of crafts-men, farmers, and servants. There just seemed to be a merce-nary company here, some servants, a few kidnapped people and this Master.

Though trying to repopulate this place seemed likely, this Master was going about it all wrong. Once people got wind of the fact that there was an entire empty city out here, he wouldn't have to kidnap anyone. Younger sons, people with pasts to escape, craftsmen looking for a new start would all flock here. You could empty out the poorer quarters of any big town just by letting people know there were houses free for the taking.

There was something altogether not making any sense.

:Then there must be a great deal we do not know and must learn,: Larral said thoughtfully, padding up to a group of mer-cenaries who were working on repairing and cleaning armor and weapons. And here Larral noticed something else peculiar.

:These men are afraid. Not greatly afraid, but definitely fearful of something and it is not me.: The yard was com-pletely clean, now, the urine washed away, the dung in a pile

outside the yard gate. Perry directed his helpers to sweep out the kennel. Really, there were actually too many helpers for the amount of work. He could only think that the kennel had gotten into the state he had found it because there had been no one supervising them. Left to themselves, he suspected they would clean the same patch of ground or floor, over and over, while urine and dung piled up next to them.

:What are they doing, besides smelling of fear and working?: he asked.

:Now and again they look up at that big building, as if they expect something unpleasant to come from it at any moment.:

So . . . whoever this Master was, he controlled these men by fear.

Could you even do that with mercenaries? Surely they could have chosen to leave at any time if there was only one Master.

This was becoming stranger and more alarming with every new thing he learned.

By the time Larral finished counting, he knew there were between fifty and sixty fighting men here in the compound. Some of the outbuildings were clearly meant to be stables, but the men had fitted them up as living quarters. A very good kitchen had been set up in one of them as well—Larral managed to beg meat scraps from the charmed cook. The little boy seemed to be the cook's errand-lad. The cook treated the boy with what could best be described as indifference, though others that passed through the area didn't hesitate to cuff or kick him if he was in the way. Clearly they knew nothing about how to handle children. As Perry knew personally, and had seen in his stint as a Palace page, there were better ways to get more work out of a youngling than hitting them whenever they put a foot wrong.

So there were as many as sixty men in the compound. Possibly another thirty or so out hunting and bringing in wood and other supplies they could get in the forest. Say twenty manning the gates and patrolling the wall. So . . . a hundred? Far too many for a standard detachment of Guards to take on.

Wait, there must be more guarding the prisoners to make sure they are working and not escaping.

As many as a hundred twenty, then.

Well, at least father was right about one thing. Something like this . . . the King would have to approve any sort of force. And I still don't know why all these men are so terrified of the Master.

When Larral returned, the kennel and the yard were spotless. Perry took pity on his feeble-minded helpers, made up four more crude beds with pine needles, and told them to sleep. Poor fellows. He wondered just how they had gotten those injuries, which seemed . . . very similar. Too similar to be coincidence.

Now that the dogs were completely tractable around him, Perry decided to inspect their ears for problems. Mastiffs, with their heavy, droopy ears, were prone to such things. He was working on the fourth one, when the captain turned up at the kennel door.

And this time the man looked . . . unnerved.

"Dog-boy!" he called, unable to see Perry from where he was standing.

Perry dismissed the dog he was working on, and stood up. "Dog-boy," he replied.

"Come here, Dog-boy," the captain ordered, and he looked him up and down. Now that the heavy work of cleaning the kennel and yard was complete, Perry had managed to keep the canvas trews and tunic reasonably clean, and the captain nodded a little. "The Master wants to see you, Dog-boy," he said.

Perry nodded.

"I'll take you to him. And your dog, too." The captain waited for a response. Perry whistled, and Larral padded up to stand beside him. "Now listen. Be very, very good," the captain told him, then bent close to his ear and whispered, urgently, *"And whatever you do, don't eat anything if he offers it to you."*

Perry tilted his head to the side, like a dog hearing a strange noise.

"No eat Master food," the captain amended.

Perry nodded. "Dog-boy," he said. "No eat."

"Good." The captain gestured to him to follow. "Let's go."

As Perry had suspected they would, they went around to the front of the big building, up the staircase to the second floor, and entered through the double doors. Once inside, the temperature dropped; it was dark, with very little light coming in those tall, narrow windows. And the strange, uneasy feeling of being watched only increased, until Perry felt as if there were a thousand pairs of eyes on him.

The first room they entered stretched along the entire width of the building and was absolutely empty, but as Perry's eyes adjusted he realized something. This room was built with exactly the same wood as the outside. And the color of the wooden walls of the buildings here was not silver with age; it was naturally silver-colored. He had never seen wood like that. This room's walls, floor, and ceiling were fashioned of that same silvery wood. It looked as though something had drained all the color out of the room.

But he wasn't supposed to be noticing things like that, he was supposed to be following the captain. And so he did, through more stark, empty, silver-colored rooms, until they came to an inner staircase and climbed it to the third floor. At the top of this stair two more of the mercenaries were posted as guards.

A long hallway ran down the middle of this floor, at the end of which on the right was another staircase. The hallway was lined with doors, some open, allowing light to penetrate into the hallway from those rooms. Now there were signs of people living here; some basic benches along the walls of the hallway, a faint smell of food, and more guards on the rooms with the closed doors. The captain led Perry and Larral to the left, past them, and all the way to the other end of the long hallway, where there was a set of double doors and four more guards.

The captain didn't say a word but gestured at the right-hand guard, who quickly opened the right-hand door for them. Perry followed the captain inside, keeping his eyes on the floor, and stopped when he stopped.

First, he glanced briefly to either side. This was another huge room, mostly empty. There were benches at intervals along the walls and not much else, not even curtains or shutters for the windows. Then he looked up through the curtain of his hair and realized that was clearly because all attention was intended to be on the throne directly opposite the door—and its occupant.

"Throne" was the only word that could possibly be used to describe the enormous, yet curiously square seat opposite them. It was at the top of three steps, on a dais, and it was exactly as broad as it was tall. It had armrests of a sort, and a pad not unlike a mattress was stretched over them and onto the seat—a brown velvet pad that looked like the color of dried blood to Perry. The throne itself was gold. Real gold. It was unlikely the throne was solid gold, but it certainly had a thick enough gold skin that no wood or stone grain was visible, just the burnished metal. So the Master certainly didn't lack for means.

And the . . . creature that occupied the throne was as odd as the throne itself.

He—Perry assumed it was a "he"—lounged indolently on the throne, leaning his weight on the arm to Perry's left. He towered over them, and his height had very little to do with the dais the throne was on. Perry estimated that, standing, the captain would barely come up to the middle of his chest, and the captain was not a small man.

He was bald. And his cranium was *enormous.* Just the upper part of his head, which bulged with blue veins. His eyes were the strangest color that Perry had ever seen in a human being. Yellow. Golden yellow, as gold as the color of the throne. His entire face narrowed down to a pointed, hairless chin just barely wider than his thumb. His body was thin and gangling, as if, to get his incredible height, someone had taken a normal sized man and pulled him vertically, stretching everything out unnaturally.

He wore a shapeless, sleeveless shirt of sorts, something that looked like random scarves sewn together, which only accentuated his strange proportions, and his lower limbs were enveloped in baggy trews of some soft fabric.

All this Perry took in at a single glance, right before Larral snapped at him, *:Shield!:*

Perry used the most effective and safest shield he had at his disposal; a false outer mind that only reflected the muddled "thoughts" of the addled dog-boy he was supposed to be. Memories of food, of dogs, of being beaten, and starved, in no particular order. Memories of his new dog-pack overlayed with satisfaction.

He dropped his eyes to stare at his feet.

"I have brought the new dog-boy as you ordered, Master," the captain said, in a subdued and subservient voice. "This is he, and the dog he brought with him."

"Look at me, dog-boy," the Master ordered.

Perry raised his eyes and let a memory of a wolf, and the

wolf's golden eyes, slide through the ones of dogs. He didn't have to feign fear. If Larral had ordered him to shield himself, then there was something to fear in this strange creature.

"What is your name?" Perry felt a rough mental "hand" running over his mind. Pretty certain that even the unGifted would be able to sense a touch like that, he allowed his surface thoughts to roil with confusion and apprehension. "Dog-boy," he said.

"Just that? Have you never had another name?" the Master persisted.

He let memories of living with dogs flood through his surface thoughts. "Dog-boy," he repeated.

That was when he felt himself seized in a remorseless mental grip, and it was all he could do to keep up the surface persona. He allowed his own terror to boil over and add to the very real pain, and he dropped to the floor clutching his head. "Dog-boy!" he screamed desperately. "Dog-boy!"

Larral growled and moved quickly to stand over him, still growling, but otherwise did nothing. A moment later, the terrible grip released him. He remained on the floor, whimpering, while Larral licked his face. When he finally sat up, he was unsurprised to find that his brain felt bruised, and it ached horribly.

So as soon as he sat up, he went down on his knees prostrating himself before the strange creature on the throne, leaving his surface thoughts full of pain and terror.

"There, there now, Dog-boy," the Master said in caressing tones. "We didn't mean to hurt you." And . . . a healing feeling, like warm honey, flooded over him, taking away some of the pain of his bruised mind. "You can stand up if you like."

Cautiously he sat up, then stood up. The Master clapped his hands, and a few moments later, a cowed and terrified man arrived with a tray on which was arrayed what looked like a half dozen cuts of meat cooked rare. It had a sweet, odd smell, something like pork.

"Are you hungry, Dog-boy?" the Master asked, in a silken smooth voice.

Remembering what the captain had told him, Perry shook his head and allowed nausea to wash over him. There was something very wrong about that meat, and he wouldn't have touched it if he had been starving. "Dog-boy," he said, weakly, making a motion as if he was gagging.

"All right. We're pleased with you, Dog-boy. We're pleased with what we have heard about you. You may continue to serve us." The creature turned his attention back to the captain. "You have done well, Captain. Our pack has a worthy caretaker now. Your gift and reward will be waiting in your quarters. You should be pleased with it."

"Whatever the Master deigns to gift me with, it will be more than I deserve," the captain said, quickly.

The Master laughed. "Of course it will be, you silly thing. That's why it's a *gift*. Enjoy it."

He waved a languid hand at them. "You may leave us now."

The captain bowed, and backed out of the room. Perry followed his example, and as for Larral, the *kyree* crawled backward on his belly until he was out of the room as well. The captain didn't breathe freely until they were well clear of the throne room and the doors were closed.

Perry saw then that he had been sweating profusely; Perry might have been doing the same, except that fear had chilled him rather than making him sweat. His guide stood there a moment, then passed his hand over his face, pausing to massage his temples. The two guards stared straight ahead, as if he and the captain weren't even there. Perry wondered if that was just discipline, or if the Master was controlling them. He hoped it was discipline.

The captain gestured for Perry to follow and broke into a trot. Perry was only too happy to follow suit; he personally felt that he couldn't get far enough away from that . . . thing in the throne room. If, at that moment, he'd been given an opening to flee this place, he would have, and never mind the consequences.

They moved quickly out of the building, down the stairs, taking them two at a time, and around to the back, and it was only when they were nearly to the kennel that the captain finally slowed down. The captain still had not spoken a single word by the time they reached the kennel.

Only when they stopped at the door of the kennel did he break his silence. "Go and lie down, Dog-boy," he said. "Your head will be all right after you lie down for a while." And with that, he left Perry at the kennel door and hurried back to his men.

Perry went inside the kennel, where he was greeted with enthusiastic joy by the dogs—so much so that he sat down among them and let them slobber all over him to their heart's content. Being licked by them felt a hundred times cleaner than having his mind manhandled by the Master.

In fact, the entire episode had left him feeling sick and filthy, as if something foul had been crawling through his mind.

:*I do not think I have ever seen so powerful a Mindspeaker,*: Larral said, subdued. :*We are very, very lucky you only have Animal Mindspeech and that he could not reach you directly as your father can. He could have killed you with a thought.*:

Perry shivered and fondled as many doggy heads as he could reach. :*We need to warn Father. If Father tries to Mindspeak me and runs into the Master before he finds me . . . .*: He quelled panic.

:*See if any of the ravens are overhead or in the forest.*: Larral suggested.

Even though his head ached more every time he used his Gift, he did as Larral requested and discovered that there were now eight ravens out there instead of the original four. Four of them were circling over the compound, while the rest perched in trees in the forest outside the city. He begged one to come but cautioned it to be very careful, giving it a mental image of what the Master had done to him.

He was unsurprised to sense the raven's contempt for anything the Master could do to *them,* and the bird did have a point. If the Master was unaware that such a thing as Bond-birds existed, they could operate right under his nose without him noticing.

Did he even realize I use Animal Mindspeech? he wondered. There had been nothing in his thoughts about the dogs to reveal that, after all. He had gotten the distinct impression that what the Master had done, mentally, to him, was what he did to every new man that came into the compound.

And that reminded him. . . . :*What was wrong with that meat?:* he asked Larral, knowing his friend's superior sense of smell would have pinpointed exactly what had caused the captain to warn him not to eat any of it. :*Was it poisoned? Drugged? It didn't smell at all right.:*

:*Oh. That,:* Larral replied, already looking out the door for the raven. :*Nothing like that. It was human.:*

Within a quarter candlemark, the raven was on his way off to Mags, a message bound to his leg—written with exquisite care on a piece of fine cloth that Perry had cut from his clout, and using the sharpest twig and the best ink out of soot mixed with water that Perry could manage to produce. Each word had been carefully chosen to convey the danger. Larral had even dictated some. And even when it was done, he was sick with fear that it wouldn't be urgent enough, that his father wouldn't understand it, or that he'd even dismiss some of it. But there was no other way to reach him and warn him; this would have to do, and he would pray to every god he'd ever heard of that it would be enough.

When the raven was gone, there was nothing left for him

to do but to act as if the interview with the Master had never happened, as if, like the poor weak-minded dog-boy he pretended to be, his memory was very short. His dinner arrived, but he set it aside; the pail would keep it warm enough, and right now, he was still nauseated.

He guided his helpers in another round of cleaning the kennel, he cleaned some more of the dogs' ears, he took the pack for another run of three circuits of the courtyard, fed them, finally had his own dinner, and saw everyone bedded down as soon as the sun started to set.

By that time, his head had finally stopped throbbing, and the ache in his brain had faded quite a bit.

Whatever the Master was doing at that moment, he surely could not be monitoring the very dull activities of the dog-boy. Perry allowed himself to relax a very little, and he spent a few moments just sitting quietly and not thinking about anything at all. His helpers filed out right at sunset, as they had the previous day. Evidently they had somewhere other than the kennel where they slept and ate. He was just as glad they were going away. With what he'd learned about the Master . . . he would not have been the least surprised to discover it had been the Master who'd half-brained them by way of amusement or some sadistic experiment.

And at that point, he became aware that he smelled distinctly doggy. *Ugh.*

There was one lamp in the kennel, and he lit it so he could see what he was doing. He gave himself a thorough wash in nice hot water from the copper once the hounds were completely settled. That soap was crude and harsh, but he didn't care. At least after he was done, it didn't feel as if his skin were trying to crawl off his body.

He opened the door into the yard so the dogs could wander out there to "go" if they needed to in the middle of the night. The dark sky overhead showed no moon, but it was spangled with stars, and a nice breeze wafted through, drying his naked skin. He washed his old clothing that had been soaking for two days, draped it over the stall walls to dry, changed to the second outfit he'd been given, and put the outfit he'd been wearing to soak in more hot, soapy water. He very much doubted that anyone would think twice about a boy who was addled being so cleanly; the addled got strange obsessions about things, and cleanliness would be one of the least offensive things to be obsessed with.

It had been a grueling day. He only realized how grueling it was when he finally lay down in his fragrant bed of pine needles, and the scent soothed his nerves and his head. He had actually fallen asleep and been asleep for some time when a soft touch on his dreams brought him awake in an instant.

:Perry.:

Papa! he thought, trying desperately to keep his thoughts "quiet." *You—*

:I got your message. I understand, and I am taking every possible precaution. The Master is sound asleep. And other than making sure of that, I am staying away from him.:

He couldn't help himself; he actually wept with relief. He hadn't been completely sure his message would convey an urgent enough warning—

:The King-Stag of the dyheli *managed to link me with the ravens, so I know where you are in that maze.:*

His heart leaped at that, but his father's next words sent it plummeting. *:Unfortunately. I have no idea how to get you out, not yet.:*

But we will figure out something, right? he thought, trying not to sound too desperate, even though he was certainly feeling that way.

There was silence in his head for a moment, as though his father was hesitating. *:The fact that this Master is such a powerful Mindspeaker that he has controlled over a hundred hardened fighting men is extremely disturbing. The King-Stag is actually quite agitated about this. I'd like you to stay there* *until we know what it is he can do, what his plans are, and whether he can be negotiated with.:*

Perry swallowed hard. Now that he was actually in touch with his father, he wasn't feeling nearly so . . . competent. In fact, if anything, he was feeling the exact opposite: lonely, scared, and very shaky. He didn't want to stay there and be a spy. What he wanted was to get out of there and home.

But it had turned out, after all, that he had been right about the need to investigate the kidnappings. And now . . . now his father was relying on him.

What's more, now that he had encountered the Master in person, he had the very strong feeling that the danger to Valdemar was greater than any of them could guess. One thing he was absolutely certain about was this: Whatever the Master's plans were, they didn't include negotiating with anyone.

I will, Father, he said, and added, *And I have a nice soft bed in a warm kennel, I'm not dodging sentries and patrols, and someone is feeding me cooked meals three times a day. I even have hot water. I'm better off than you are.*

:So you are,: Mags replied, and Perry sensed relief. Probably relief that he hadn't objected or pleaded with his father to be taken out of this place immediately. *It's a good thing he's no good at picking up emotions from that distance, or he'd know I'm lying.*

:Get rid of any evidence you've been writing,: Mags advised. *:If you need to write to me again, I'll have the raven carry you a feather you can cut a quill from, and he'll take it with him when he leaves.:*

Are you somewhere safe? Now worry about his father surfaced; there were patrols out there. For all Perry knew, there were lots of them.

:Quite. I've got as good or better a bed than you, and a fire. And I have a day-and-night dyheli *guard Now if I could just eat leaves, I'd be as comfortable as if I were in a fine inn.:*

As Mags had probably hoped, the image of his father eating leaves was comical enough to make Perry smile weakly.

:Now this is what I want you to do for me,: Mags continued. *:I want you to find out what sort of supplies these people have and how much. I want you to find out, if you can, what the Master wants. What he does with his captives—:*

I know some, Perry interrupted him. *He keeps women for breeding. I think maybe he also gives them for a night to people he wants to reward. And . . .*

He gulped, nauseated again at the memory.

. . . . he eats people. Larral told me the meat he was eating when he had me brought to him was human.

There was stunned, shocked silence from his father, silence Perry finally filled.

I dunno if they're his captives or one of his men that he killed, but like I said, he was eating human meat when I left him, and the captain said I shouldn't accept any food from him, so it's probably not the first time.

Mags was entirely silent for a very long time. So long, that Perry began to fear that something had happened to him. Then, finally, he replied. *:That's . . . very strange. Think of him so I can see what he looks like.:*

Perry obediently called up the image of the Master in his mind's eye, every detail he could remember. He sensed his father studying that image carefully, perhaps even burning it into his own memory.

:All right. Keep clear of him. Try to keep to people you think you can trust. You and I will work out some plans. The more you tell me, the less I think we know of the true situation. Right now none of this makes sense.:

That pretty much summed up *his* feelings on all of this.

:You're useful, and uninteresting. That combination should keep him completely uninterested in you, now that he's seen you with his own eyes. I think as long as you don't break character, you're as safe as anyone can be inside that com-

pound. For now, get some sleep. I'll talk to you tomorrow night. I'm both angry and proud of you, son. You know why I am angry.:

I— He faltered. Because of course he knew why Mags was angry. He'd run off like an idiot, confident in being able to stroll into enemy hands, get everything that would prove just how dangerous the Master was, and stroll back out again. Well, he was being paid for his stupid overconfidence. And for not doing the smart thing and persuading his father to at least look for the Master's stronghold.

And when he'd seen just how big that stronghold was, *he should have gone straight back to Mags.* There really was no excuse for recklessly marching down there and putting himself right squarely in the middle of things.

So yes . . . his father was dead right to be angry with him.

But his father's next words shocked him.

:We're both at fault. I've been training you for exactly this purpose since you were old enough to toddle. And you went off and did what you were trained to do. So I'm angry with you and with myself, and when this is over, we'll set up rules for both of us to follow from now on. But right now . . . my sense is that our Kingdom may be in danger, and our duty is here.:

Well, what could he say to that, except *Yes, sir.*

:Now sleep. And I love you.:

Larral curled up a little tighter around him, and he lay quietly staring up into the darkness. *:You're afraid,:* Larral said at last. *:So am I. We seem to have stumbled into something that is much, much bigger than we thought.:*

He chewed his lower lip. *:Papa thinks so too.:*

:Then you and I are the only ones in position to actually find anything out. I think this is important. The Master is more dangerous than we guess. I think he may be even more dangerous than your father guesses.:

:So what do we do?: he asked, then answered his own question. *:We treat him that way. We assume he can find out*

everything about us if we aren't crazy careful. So we'll be crazy careful. Using the ravens again . . . that's really dangerous unless there's no other choice.:

But Larral disagreed. *:I think he must be like your father, in that he cannot hear Animal Mindspeech. You talking to them should be all right. And using their eyes . . . :*

He felt a tiny stirring of hope. *:I can do that, and figure out the map of this place. Then at least we'll know how to get out if we have to run for it.:* He thought some more. *:Do you think he can't get past my shields?:*

:I think he has probably never seen anyone with shields before except for himself. I don't think he knows people without Mindspeech can raise them . . . : There was silence for a moment as Larral considered this. *:In fact, I am becoming more sure of this. He believes he has only to drop his own shields to know everything everyone around him is thinking. And if he wants anything, he believes he can easily force it out of them, as he tried with you.:*

:So that's something more we can guess about him.: It was something, anyway.

:That is a start,: Larral agreed. *:Now—:* he yawned. *:—dawn comes early.:*

Larral was right. And just that tiny sliver of a plan was enough to allow him to relax enough to sleep again.

"I can't keep calling you 'King-Stag,'" Mags said aloud, as he and the King-Stag stared at each other across Mags' tiny fire. The *dyheli's* eyes reflected the firelight in uncanny looking orbs of glowing green. Behind him, the back wall of the tiny cave they were in threw back the firelight, except where the *dyheli's* shadow stretched out along it.

:Well, you can, actually. It's what I am. But if you like, you can call me Roya, as I told you.:

Mags nodded. "Thank you. I appreciate that. While it's still fresh in my mind, Roya, I'd like you to look over this 'Master' and see if you can tell me anything about him." He did one more quick check on the Master, to make sure he was still sleeping deeply, then lowered every one of his shields so Roya could get the most information in the shortest possible time. It was a risk, lowering his shields like that . . . but right now, everything they did was a risk.

Roya was in and out of his mind in the time it took for three heartbeats. He shielded again. He blinked slowly two or three times as he purged the little hints of *dyheli* from his thoughts. Roya had chosen speed over finesse; that was fine with Mags, but it meant he left a little of himself behind. Stray thoughts, scents, even a taste of the sweet clover he had been eating this evening. Nothing disturbing, but it was all very foreign, and Mags needed to chase it away and make it evaporate.

Roya folded his legs underneath him and lay down on the sand floor of the cave, the better to ponder what he had learned.

One of the *dyheli* scouts had found this cave, which had no sign nor scent showing that the Master's mercenaries had been anywhere near it. It was close enough to the strange city that Mags could reach his son with his Gift, but not so near that there was any danger of patrols stumbling on it. It wasn't natural; it looked as if it had been made or carved out for someone or something—possibly as storage or shelter or both. But that was all to the good, because there was a firepit already here and a crack in the roof to let out the smoke. Mags had been able to cook a meal and warm some water to make pine-needle tea. There was something about a fire . . . it was comforting, even in the worst of circumstances.

:I can only assume the Master is a Change-Child.: Roya said at last. And before Mags could ask what that was, he added, *:There are pockets of twisted magic in the Pelagirs— the Hawkbrothers cleanse the land of these things, that is*

their ordained duty. But anything living that stumbles into one can be irrevocably altered. I think this Master or its mother must have done just that.:

Well, that would account for why it was such a strong Mindspeaker, he supposed. And why it looked the way it did.

"Does that give it any sort of special weaknesses?" he asked.

:Not that I know of. It probably has a weakness, but there are no specific ones common to all Change-Children.:

Mags rubbed his temples wearily with his right hand. *:Do I report to the King now, when I have so little information?:*

:Compromise,: Dallen said, interjecting himself into Mags' thoughts for the first time since they had secluded themselves in this cave. *:We'll tell Arville everything we know. And we'll have him take physical notes, so he forgets nothing. We'll contact him every evening once we are certain the Master is asleep, and we'll tell him that if he doesn't hear from us on a nightly basis, he's to contact the King.:*

That—was as close to perfect as they were going to get.

:I agree with that,: Roya put in. *:It is very wise to have someone far from here aware of what we are doing. That is why half my herd is with one of my sons, back where you found us, ready to retreat to Hawkbrother lands if he ceases to hear from me. You seek your herdmate. I will guard you from this Master while you do so.:*

Mags nodded. Arville would not have gone to bed yet. *:All right, Dallen, let's do this now, while Arville is still awake.:*

With Dallen's strength supporting him and Roya standing watch on the Master's mind, Mags made short work of finding his target.

He found the Herald sitting up by the fire, trying to read a book, and actually fretting over them. That made contact much easier. Arville was surprised, even a little shocked at being contacted mentally, but he quickly recovered and listened to Mags' plan. *:Let me go for a little, Mags,:* he replied, when he understood what was that Mags wanted. *:I can't—do this and walk around at the same time. And I need to get something to write with and something to write on.:*

:All right,: Mags agreed, and released the other Herald's mind. He lay looking up at the crack in the ceiling of the cave, watching the smoke getting sucked up into it, until he thought he'd given Arville more than enough time to get himself sorted out.

When he contacted the other's mind again, Arville was waiting, ready, sitting at the kitchen table with a good lamp in front of him and plenty of paper. It didn't take long to tell him everything Mags had gathered so far. Arville wrote it all down faithfully, and before Mags could say anything, he offered, *:So are you going to talk to me every night at this time? And if I don't hear from you, I send all this on right away?:*

:Yes,: Mags replied, and he sensed Arville frowning.

:I don't like this, Mags. I don't like that Perry is stuck where you can't rescue him. I don't like that you don't have anyone to back you up. You know Pelas and Ryu and I can't leave you out there alone,: he objected. *:If you don't contact me—:*

:If I don't contact you, it will be far more important to get this information to the King than it will be to come riding to our rescue,: Mags said sternly. *:I know what I'm doing, Arville. I've been doing this for decades.:*

Arville wasn't very good at shielding his thoughts. Mags clearly heard him thinking, *But that poor little youngling Perry hasn't. . . .*

And there was nothing to be said to counter that. Arville was right. Perry was in the middle of something far more dangerous than his father had any right to inflict on him.

But he'd inserted himself there, without Mags' permission. In fact, it had been expressly against Mags' wishes. And at the moment, Mags was unable to think of a good way to get him out that didn't also have an excellent chance of getting him killed.

:All right,: Arville sighed, after a long moment of "silence"—real silence on Mags' part, pretense of silence filled with anxiety on Arville's. *:I'll do it. I don't like it, but I'll do it. Can I at least try to get some Guards up here?:*

:I think you should, if only to protect Whithern,: Mags replied. *:If this Master gets impatient, he might start sending out squads to abduct people from their homes, rather than wait for appropriate victims to come to the inn.:*

:All right,: Arville repeated. *:I'll do that. You be careful, Mags!:*

What was there to say to that? *:I will,:* he replied, and he cut off the connection before Arville could sense anything from him other than confidence.

He opened his eyes. "Well," he said, not moving from where he was lying. "That's done. Now what?"

:Now we sleep,: Dallen said, firmly. *:That's always good advice when there is nothing else you can do.:*

Perry woke up with the sudden determination to wash all the dogs. Part of it may have been that despite their pine-needle beds, they were distinctly unfragrant, which was probably a consequence of their having been neglected for so long. But part of it was because it occurred to him that if the Master wanted to keep watch on him, he could use the four easily controlled creatures that arrived every morning at sunrise, and there was nothing Perry could do about it.

But if all the Master saw was a lot of wet, squirming dogs, well, he'd tire of that pretty quickly.

So as soon as the helpers cleared the latrine corner of the yard, he called them all together. With what looked like Larral herding but was actually Perry telling each dog what to do, he got four of them lined up by the water pump, each in the hands of a different helper. And then he set to work. Obviously the dogs did not like this; what dog ever likes being bathed? But Larral stood at the head of each as he came into Perry's hands for his bath, then stood aside when Perry let him run loose, and then herded another candidate into the helper's hands as Perry moved on to the next in line.

This was quite exciting and active enough for Perry and the poor, bewildered helpers. He felt sorry for the helpers; they'd probably never been told to bathe the dogs since they'd been hurt and assigned to kennel duty. But if the Master was watching, well, Perry had every hope he'd roll his eyes and find something else to do.

It went faster than he'd hoped, but then, mastiffs had very short hair. By the time the boy left the pail with his lunch just inside the kennel door, all the dogs were romping in the yard in every state from "still shaking themselves in disgust" to "completely dry."

The meal-boy was definitely avoiding him. Not that Perry blamed him. Not now, when he knew exactly what the boy was afraid of.

:*Something occurs to me,*: Larral said, as Perry ate his meal—and shared some with Larral. :*If the men are going to talk, they will do so at night, when the Master sleeps.*:

:*They'd have to know he's asleep,*: Perry pointed out. :*But I guess he would be, if all the lights are out in the Big House.*: He couldn't call it a Palace; it didn't look anything like the Palace in Haven.

:*Well, they like me. I can wander out there tonight, join them if they gather around a fire or something of the sort, and we'll see if they talk to each other.*:

After the bath, and in the heat of the day, all the dogs headed into the kennel for naps. Perry decided that he would take a stroll with Larral to see what he could see, with the things Mags wanted him to find out in mind.

This courtyard actually wasn't anything of the sort, he decided. If anything, it was more like the Palace complex back home. The courtyard itself was carpeted in dense grass; when the mercenaries had first arrived here, it must have been waist- or chest-high; now it was barely as tall as the first joint of his index finger.

I know what I would have done when I got here. If I had, or could make, sickles, I'd mow it down and dry it, and I'd have hay for the horses for months. It was pretty obvious what they were doing now; there were horses tethered out all over, keeping that grass short.

That big building obviously was something like the Palace at Haven, though it was considerably smaller. Then again, there were all those houses outside the wooden wall around the courtyard; important people in this city could easily have lived out there instead of in here. That building was more than large enough for a single ruling family and their servants.

He took a moment to walk around to the front; all he remembered was grass, but now that he was looking for it, there was a ghost of a driveway that went from the gate to the front steps. But the grass had completely overgrown it to the point that you had to look really closely to see it. *How long would that have taken? How long did this place lie empty before the Master and his mercenaries arrived?*

He went back to begin canvassing all the structures within this fence. Closest to the Big Building was the kennel, but there didn't seem to be a mews for birds of prey. Maybe whoever had built this place didn't use hawks and falcons for sport. Putting the kennel close to the living area was odd, too. Normally there would be things like storage buildings, a dairy, or a wash house here. Then again, normally there'd be gardens back here, and there wasn't a sign that there had ever been anything growing inside this fence but grass.

The more he looked at this place, the odder it got.

Well . . . maybe the dairy and the wash house were in the Big Building itself. And not everyone knew you could tame hawks . . . or maybe there was an even simpler reason why there was no mews. Maybe the people who had built this place knew all about the Tayledras and wanted nothing to do with them—and correctly assumed allowing any birds of prey onto the property was allowing a potential spy in their midst.

Well, just at the moment, he couldn't exactly snoop around inside the Big House—and it wasn't exactly urgent to find out where the ruddy dairy was.

So the nearest building was the kennel and yard. The grass in the yard had been pretty thoroughly killed by all the dog urine, so it was bare earth now.

Right after the kennel was the stable—or, rather, stables. There was more than one stable, but it looked as if these mercenaries didn't have many horses, so they were only using one for its original purpose. Empty wagons were parked against the walls.

The other three stable buildings had been set up as barracks; he'd seen that when Larral went exploring.

Which means there are no actual barracks buildings for guards or soldiers in here either. That's . . . very odd. Where did they put their guards? Or did they rely entirely on dogs as guards? If there had been a force of human guards outside the fence, and dogs and handlers only inside, he supposed that would work. Maybe that was the reason why the kennels were so big, and positioned right next to the Big House.

The two stable/barracks buildings on his left were empty, according to Larral, but they peeked in and saw cots and belongings in the stalls. But the two on the right—

:Careful,: Larral said, and they eased themselves inside.

It took a moment for his eyes to adjust, but he could already tell, just by listening to the snoring, that this was where the mercenaries on night guard were sleeping. Curiously, it was much cooler inside this building than it was outside. In fact, it was almost as cool as if the wood it was made of had the same insulating properties as thick stone. He hadn't noticed that about the kennel because he'd been keeping all the windows, and the door into the yard wide open to encourage a breeze to come through.

He pulled his attention back to the here and now. Because he'd based his estimate of the number of mercenaries here on the ones he and Larral had seen outside—and here were two whole buildings full of men he hadn't counted.

:How did you miss these men?: he asked Larral incredulously.

:Why are they sleeping in the daytime?: he asked back, just as incredulously.

They looked at each other. *:We both should be more mindful that you are a human and I am a* kyree,*:* Larral said, after a moment.

After a quick survey of the two tenanted stable buildings, it became obvious that there were at least twice as many mercenaries here as he had thought. Which begged the question: How many more had they missed on their first estimation? How many slaves?

:There may be more people hiding in plain sight,: he suggested to Larral *:We should amble on, and poke our noses everywhere.:*

:We should be looking for food. Boys are always hungry. So are dogs!:

The next lot of buildings were storehouses. Larral had paid very little attention to those, since nothing lived in them. But when Perry walked up to the first open door he saw and made an examination, he was . . . stunned at the amount of weaponry he found inside. Next to that storehouse was one for dry goods, mostly food. Next to that were other sorts of supplies. And when he added it all up, there were weapons, jarred and bagged and barreled and boxed foodstuffs, and other supplies enough for a small army. Hundreds of men and their support staff. More than was stored up on the Hill back home, that was certain. No wonder he was eating so well—the only thing these men needed to keep supplying for their rations was fresh meat, and not all that much of that—just enough to make broths and gravies.

Then there was the open space he had seen before, where the men practiced—and were indeed practicing now—under the watchful eye of their captain, who spotted Perry and gestured to him to join him.

Perry obliged, wondering what the captain wanted. Had the captain noticed he had been wandering about—or had it been reported to him that the dog-boy was putting his nose in places he hadn't ought to go?

He swallowed a little as he approached the captain, doing his best to conceal his trepidation . But the reason the captain wanted to see him turned out to be innocent enough. "Dog-boy, are you feeling well?" the captain asked. "After meeting the Master yesterday, are you all right?"

He seemed genuinely concerned, even a little paternal. Despite all of the horrible things that were going on here, Perry found himself liking the captain, who seemed to be a good man, and certainly seemed to be concerned about a lowly dog-boy. He looked at the captain from under his hair and finally nodded.

"Dog-boy," he said, making sure he sounded a little subdued.

"Would you like to take the dogs hunting tomorrow?" the captain asked. "Boar hunting?"

Perry straightened a little and allowed a more cheerful expression to pass over his face. "Dog-boy!" he agreed. "Hunt!"

The captain sighed with relief. "Good. Hunting will be a lot easier with your pack than without it." Perry got the feeling he was speaking more to himself than to Perry, since Perry couldn't be expected to understand too many words. Then he sniffed and took a good long look at Perry. "You were busy this morning?"

"Dogs clean," he said proudly. "Dog-boy clean."

The captain patted him on the head—not unlike a dog.

"Good dog-boy," he replied, then proceeded to ignore him in favor of supervising the fighting practice.

Perry stayed next to him for the next half a candlemark or so, watching the men train. It was a discouraging sight. They were very good, as good as any Guardsman Perry had ever seen. And if they were all that good . . . the King would need more than the usual company of bandit-chasing Guards to face them. In fact, it would be army facing off against army, in a siege situation, which was never ideal for the besiegers if the besieged had ample food and water available.

He remained there long enough to get a good sense for the skill level of all of the men currently practicing. Then Perry wandered away; the captain didn't stop him, which was at least a little encouraging, since that suggested the captain was comfortable with him going anywhere he chose.

There was only one more set of buildings. One was the kitchen that Larral had poked his nose into before. The cook, who turned out to be a very friendly man, was making a stew of beans and salt-pork, and he stopped long enough to give them both some slices of hard sausage before they even got around to begging. The cook oversaw four more men; three were normal enough, but one had similar head-scars to Perry's helpers and seemed just as feeble-minded.

There was definitely a pattern emerging here . . . but what did it mean?

One of the remaining buildings was a henhouse—built for a hundred hens or more, it looked like, and populated with fewer than twenty; they scratched among the litter of pine needles on the floor and clucked to themselves. Unlike the dogs, the hens didn't have a yard to go out into, but there were big, though barred, windows, which brought in plenty of light and air. And there were shutters here on the inside that could be closed to keep them safe and dark at night or to keep weather out.

These hens can't have been here when the army first ar-

rived. They must have brought the birds with them or gotten them later. Did mercenaries carry hens with them? He didn't know.

And the last building was something he'd been wondering about: one enormous, multiholed latrine. One, from the looks of it, and the relative lack of smell, with either a cavernous cesspit beneath it or actual tunnels to carry the sewage away somewhere else. This was actually the most impressive piece of work he'd seen here, especially if it did indeed have sewage drains.

He resolved to come here from now on, even though it was a long walk from the kennel. Using a bucket in the kennel was not much to his liking.

He made sure that his return trip to the kennel was just as aimless as the journey out; he and Larral investigated the buildings they had already looked into, and they even spent some time "talking" to a couple of the horses. By the time he got back to the kennel, the dogs were all waking up from their naps, relieving themselves, and looking for something to do.

:They're about to get into mischief,: Larral judged. *:They've been on good behavior until now because your arrival upset the regular order of things. But now they're used to you, and—:*

:And I'm going to nip that in the bud,: Perry said firmly. He stood in the doorway of the kennel and whistled shrilly.

Every head came up, including the helpers.

Ignoring the four humans, Perry summoned the dogs to him with a thought. When they were gathered around him, he made it clear to them that they were going to have a long run around the periphery of the courtyard, just like yesterday— but that this time they were to run full-out, with Larral in the lead, as if they were hunting. He caught their eagerness at this idea, and he got the sense that they had not had a full-out run since they had arrived here and their old dogmaster . . .

. . . he couldn't make out what had happened to their dog-master. It was as if he was gone yet still present.

And that made no sense whatsoever.

He chose a dog at random and went down on his knees beside it. He looked deeply into its eyes and told it to think of the dogmaster that was there-and-not-there.

He got a confusing image, as if two memories were warring with each other. Instead of letting the confusion continue, he forced one, one that felt like the newer of the two, to come to the surface. It did so only briefly, but as it slipped away again, he sat back on his heels in a state of cold shock.

It was one of his helpers.

When Mags awoke, Roya and Dallen were gone, and the cave was very quiet. His sleep had not been very restful; he'd been unable to put Perry's precarious situation out of his head. He remained lying quietly for a while. He wanted to think, without anyone else's Mindvoice interrupting him, and this was about the best chance he'd had to do that. He lay flat on his back and locked his hands together on his chest, then let whatever was seething in the back of his mind come to the fore.

Arville isn't happy about his orders. That was the thought that swam up out of his subconscious first, and no wonder. They were all in this situation because Perry hadn't been happy with *his* orders and had disobeyed them. And if Perry had disobeyed . . . what was Arville likely to do?

I don't think Arville is the kind to directly disobey . . . but if I don't give him something productive to do, he's likely the kind to find some loophole or other to wiggle through and make his way out here.

And that would only make things worse. Arville did just fine puttering around Whithern . . . but out here in the woods, Mags was less than confident.

All right then. What productive thing could Mags give the

old man that would keep him where he belonged but give him a sense he was providing direct help?

He didn't think too hard about it; he just lay there and waited for something else to swim to the surface. And what emerged was a fierce longing for something more in his hands than a simple belt knife. And while he was wishing, salt. And something better than the bare camping supplies he had. And . . . and . . . and . . . a list of things he needed or merely wanted piled up in his head, and then he had his answer.

This told him exactly what he could do to keep Arville out of trouble. One Companion, completely unburdened, could make it to Whithern in a few candlemarks. Two Companions, loaded with packs, even if one was old, could make it back by morning tomorrow.

:I heard that,: Dallen said. *:I like it. Roya can boost you just as easily as I can, so you can reach Arville with Mind-speech at the usual time. If I leave some time before noon, I can be there before sunset. When I get there, I can tell Pelas what we're doing; he'll tell Arville, and you can give me a list to give to them. Write out that list, and if you think of anything after I've left, you can add it when you contact him.:*

:It would be better if you had adequate weapons,: Roya agreed, butting in. *:There will probably be a need for them.:*

:Thank you, oh shining ray of sunshine,: Mags retorted. He sat up and reached for his shirt. *:I'll make the list before I do anything else.:*

Now he was grateful that he'd packed and repacked and re-repacked that damned caravan. He knew where everything was stored and could put his hand on what he wanted in the dark. And if for some reason Arville couldn't manage to find a few things, well, Arville's house *was* a sort of miniature Guard supply depot. Chances were, Arville had twenty of whatever he was going to ask for.

He was just grateful he'd thought to include paper and a

scribing stick when he was packing for this venture. He'd almost left them behind. If he hadn't had them. . . .

:*You'd have used the inner bark of a birch tree, you goose,*: Roya reminded him. :*And soot. Concentrate on your list.*:

Roya had found him a mushroom the size of a bread loaf and had brought it to him impaled on one of the *dyheli's* horns. That made a more than adequate breakfast while he was making out the list. He included Perry's weapons on it; if there was any chance he could get them to his son, he wanted to try.

When the list was done, he rolled it into a tight tube, tied it up, and tied the tube to Dallen's neck. Once the Companion was certain it was secure, he was off like an arrow, vanishing into the forest before he could blink.

Only then did Mags realize he'd been bent over so long, writing his list in the tiniest possible characters, that his back and shoulders were cramped and aching, and so were his hands.

:*Get a bath,*: Roya ordered, wrinkling his nose. :*You stink. And wash your clothing. It stinks too. If those mercenaries have noses, they'll find you by the stench alone. Follow me.*:

Roya led him away from the cave to a brook, went away and came back with a piece of soap-root held delicately between his teeth. It looked as if he must have dug it out of the ground with his hooves, as Mags had seen goats do to get at a particularly favorite root. He spat the soap-root out at Mags' feet and left again. That might have been to give Mags some privacy . . . but somehow Mags doubted it.

One of the *dyheli* does turned up some time after he was clean and redressed in his wet clothing—it was warm enough today he figured it might as well dry on his body—and timidly offered to guide him to food. He assumed she meant strictly vegetarian fare, but food was food, and he accepted gratefully. She paced her way delicately through the forest, pointing out mushrooms here, wild carrot there, herbs in the shadow of a bush whose buds could be eaten.

This was good for him. Slowly gathering foodstuffs, leaving as little sign of his depredations as possible, was occupying his mind, which badly needed occupation. He was stuck in one of those horrible situations where there was nothing he could possibly do that would make things any better, but not doing anything was going to drive him insane.

Of course, Arville was probably feeling that even more than he was.

He'd managed to gather enough roots, greens, and mushrooms for three or four meals, when Roya suddenly appeared out of nowhere, startling him and the doe he was with. She actually pronked straight up in the air before she recovered herself, and he was just glad his gleanings were tied up in a sack he'd made of a thin blanket, or he'd have been stuck with picking everything up again.

:We have an opportunity, but it is a short one,: Roya said without preamble. *:One of my stags has caught one of the men from the city out foraging alone and put him to sleep. You and I can pick his mind, leave him with some foraged food to make him think he simply lost track of time, and be gone without his Master knowing anything about it. We may not get much, but it will be more than we had.:* He looked at Mags and snorted. *:Much as it pains me . . . mount. If we go only as fast as your two feet, we shall take all afternoon.:*

Mags did his best to mount respectfully, and the *dyheli* shot off as fast as a Companion could move in this forest, where the footing was so uncertain.

It was the most uncomfortable ride he'd ever experienced.

Actually, uncomfortable was an understatement.

The *dyheli* had a very prominent spine . . . and Roya

bounced with every step, leaping through the undergrowth like a deer or a rabbit. Mags did his best to cushion the effect by gripping with his legs and trying to move *with* Roya, rather than counter to him. But there was only so much he could do, and he wished with all his heart for a saddle or at least some padding . . . and he blessed every god he'd ever heard of when the ride was less than a candlemark.

He was off Roya's back before the *dyheli* even came to a full stop.

The younger stag was standing over the prone body of a man dressed like the three in the inn, sleeping peacefully with a slight smile on his face. Wasting no time, Mags knelt in the bracken beside him, put one hand on his forehead to facilitate his Gift, and let his mind sink into the mercenary's.

How did you come here? That was the first thing he wanted to know—and not just because the answer would tell him if these people were native to the area or came from elsewhere, but because the images would very likely give him a good rough count of how many men there actually were, whether the mercenary himself knew or could count at all.

The images came to him, dreamlike, and he was looking out of this young man's eyes. He and his company—it was a full mercenary company—had marched up from the south, carefully skirting the Valdemar border because they had heard odd things about those Heralds. They had a contract, negotiated by one of the many minor lords here in the halfway lands between the really wild territory overseen by the mysterious Hawkbrothers and the border of Valdemar. Their new employer, Lord Fersson of Crag Keep, did not want his holding swallowed up by Valdemar and had bought their contract for the next ten years. There was some talk of gem mines; he himself knew nothing of this, he only knew that finally there would be an end to all the marching, and probably to most of the fighting, and that they'd be in one place and could put down some roots. This man was very happy at that moment.

He was very tired of fighting, of temporary camps, of tents in terrible weather. This new contract meant stability, real barracks, a chance to live like a normal human being.

But they were doomed never to get there.

He was too far back in the ranks to see what was happening, but the captain shouted, *"Halt,"* and halt they did. There was some talking. . . .

And then he was no longer in control of his own body. This was quite literal; he found himself marching again, tried to stop, and couldn't. He tried to shout with alarm, and couldn't. He couldn't even twitch a single finger. He panicked as he tried to struggle against this implacable, strange force that had made him a prisoner in his own body, but he got nowhere. He was completely under the control of someone else, and nothing he did could set him free.

And from the stiffly marching men all around him, this . . . power, whatever it was . . . had taken over all of them. Was it some hideous magic spell? Were they all under the control of an evil Mage?

Without really knowing how to fight this thing, he still tried to fight it, as he and all of his mates, the supply wagons, the dogs, the dogmaster and all were marched down a side road, then deep into a forest.

That was only the start of the nightmare. Although he could not control his body, he could feel everything. Feel when his legs started to burn from marching too long without a rest. Feel when his mouth grew parched, and so dry his tongue stuck to the roof of his mouth. Feel when his feet blistered, and the blisters broke and bled.

And still they marched, past sunset and into the night; they did not stop, not for a day and a night and a day again, although they were weeping and half mad with weariness and hunger. His head swam with delirium, and if he'd had control of his hand, he probably would have slashed his own throat to make it stop.

Then, just as the sun began to set, a strange, silvery city loomed up out of the forest. Mags noted there was no palisade around it at this point; there was just the forest, and then, with the trees pressed right up against it, the city.

They marched into it, wound their way through twisting, confusing streets, then in through a gate in a huge fence at the heart of the city. All they could see at that point was one enormous building in the middle of a sea of waist-high grass. And then they were released, just as suddenly as they had been controlled.

They all collapsed. He was sobbing with the pain of his feet and legs, and he wasn't the only one. Some of them were drinking from their waterskins and weeping at the same time.

Mags left that memory, and asked the sleeping man another question. *Who is the Master?*

But the man didn't know. He heard a great deal about the Master, and he knew that the Master could peer into your head and see all your thoughts. He knew the Master was the one who had controlled the entire company and brought them here. But he himself had never seen the Master. That dubious honor was reserved for the captain and the few mercenaries that the Master used as his personal guards.

What does the Master want?

The poor fellow didn't know that, either. But before Mags could ask another question, he got an answer to a question he had not asked. He was caught up in another memory, this time of the arrival of a caravan of wagons, all of them heavily laden with all manner of supplies. Mags understood from the memory that these wagons arrived regularly, with far more than was needed to take care of the needs of a single company of mercenaries. The Master was stockpiling supplies . . . and the young man understood that the Master paid for them in gold.

The reason for this particular memory emerging soon became clear. After the supplies were all unloaded, the young man approached the wagonmaster, and pleaded desperately to be allowed to come with them. He offered his entire life savings.

The wagonmaster laughed at him, and shoved him away. "Yer master give me 20 gold pieces fer every trip," he scoffed. "That's over'n'above the supplies. An' ye think I'm gonna risk that fer the likes o' you an' yer handful of siller?"

The memory receded, shoved away, actually, by a desperate need to think of happier things. Things like—well, it wasn't so bad, once they settled in. If you didn't somehow catch the Master's eye or break the rules, life was good. Decent food, easy work, a real cot in a real building to sleep on; and once they'd been there a while, each man had managed to contrive a pine-needle-stuffed mattress that wouldn't have been scorned in a real barracks. You just had to keep away from the Master. Never break a rule. Never try to run. It wasn't all that different from some of the other places he'd served, or so he told himself. Of course, they weren't getting paid, but they weren't actually fighting, either.

Sometimes three or four men took a supply wagon some-where and came back with it empty. And he had heard that more people—regular people, not fighters—were brought here from time to time. Certainly there were kids who ran errands that had turned up out of nowhere. He thought once or twice he'd heard a woman's voice coming from the captain's tent.

But those were things it was just better not to think about. And so he buried them deep in his memory again and reso-lutely thought of nothing.

Mags judged that was just about all he was going to get from the mercenary—which was far more than he had expected. He withdrew from the fellow's mind and slowly stood up.

:*Are you finished?*: Roya asked. He nodded.

"I'll leave some of this stuff with him, we can leave, and the stag can wake him up as soon as we're all safely away," Mags said, checking his bag and bringing out a couple of handfuls of roots, several bunches of watercress, and some lumps of sticky pine gum, which had a lot of uses.

He put that stuff down as if it had fallen out of the fellow's bag and started walking back the way they had come. Roya stepped in front of him. *:You'll take till sunset to get back on your own two feet,:* the *dyheli* said, amused. *:I promise I will be slower this time.:*

Mags hesitated for just a moment, then gingerly mounted. He hoped he wasn't going to regret this. . . .

He was very, very glad that part of his gleanings included willow bark, because he really needed it. And he made a note not to ever, ever ride a *dyheli* again, unless it was an absolute emergency. And even then, it would have to be with something between him and that hard, sharp backbone.

He comforted himself with the fact that Dallen would be back soon. By morning, in fact. So it should not become an issue.

I hope.

The willow bark helped. So did lying down. His injuries had settled to a mild ache when he sensed Dallen lurking in the back of his mind, waiting to be called. He decided to risk it; the bond between Herald and Companion was something that most Mindspeakers, no matter how powerful, had difficulty intruding on, or even sensing.

:Arville is collecting everything from your list,: Dallen said, as soon as he opened himself to the Companion. Mags could tell Dallen was tired but pleased with himself. *:I sense you learned something without talking to Perry yet?:*

:Quite a bit actually.: He detailed everything he had gleaned from the young mercenary. *:I have a horrible feeling that this Master is not going to be content to sit in his city with his own*

private army and abduct stray passersby. I think he's going to use that army, sooner or later.:

:That goes without saying,: Dallen agreed. *:The only question is what he intends to use it for. And who he intends to use it against.:*

:We are missing something here,: Mags mused. *:This all seems too . . . obvious.:*

:That creature Perry saw was not exactly subtle,: Dallen pointed out.

:But he wasn't stupid, either. No, this isn't a straightforward territory grab. Look, he's already got a bigger city than he has the population for! He's not going to repopulate it with a couple of kidnapped women! And we are discussing someone who can control an entire mercenary company with his mind, making them march through their own exhaustion. I don't know what he's planning, but it's not just a simple attack.: He brooded over the problem for a moment. *:You know, he isn't actually using the city as a city. He's using it as a base camp. He doesn't intend to stay there.:*

Dallen considered that for a moment. *:That seems a legitimate observation,:* the Companion said, finally. *:So I suppose we need to figure out where he intends to go and what he intends to do.:*

:And I am out of ideas,: Mags admitted.

:Is there anything more than you thought of that you want?: Dallen asked instead.

:Aside from all the Guard between here and Haven? Not really.:

:You wouldn't really want all the Guard between here and Haven,: Dallen pointed out quickly. *:This is someone who controlled an entire mercenary company with his mind. As soon as they got within his range, they wouldn't be our Guard anymore. They'd be his.:*

And that was possibly the most unsettling thing he'd heard in a very long time.

Perry got the dogs all settled for the night. They were much happier than they had been before his arrival; he could tell it by their relaxation and contentment. They really enjoyed being able to sleep together, rather than confined in separate stalls in the kennel. They'd truly relished their fake "hunt," following Larral around the courtyard until they were completely exhausted. The men had enjoyed it too; as soon as they had realized what was happening, they began placing bets on the various dogs and cheering them on.

But Perry had to wonder what the Master had thought of that little exhibition. Had he even cared? Had he assumed that Perry was merely doing the proper job of the dogmaster? Did he even know what the proper job of a dogmaster *was?*

There had been no sign from the Big House that the Master was watching, but who knew?

The dogs were mostly asleep when Perry finished his dinner; they were so used to his presence now that the bony lumps nestled together by twos and threes in the soft dark of their stalls didn't even move as he passed them with his lantern. He hung the lantern on a hook just outside the kennel door and went out into the courtyard to see what the men did at that time of the evening. If they were anything like the Guard, they'd be gathering in groups of friends, trading stories, telling jokes, taking care of little individual jobs like mending their clothing or equipment.

The courtyard was silent. The only men moving were those who were heading for the barracks, presumably having been relieved by the night watch. There was none of the talking and signs of camaraderie he'd been expecting.

I guess these fellows aren't like the Guard. Then again, the Guard doesn't have a Mindspeaking cannibal watching what they do.

He and Larral didn't act as if they found anything amiss.

255

They just ambled in the direction of one of the stable buildings that was showing a light, figuring that there would be someone awake in there.

And that was, indeed, where he actually found some of the mercenaries, including the captain, gathered, in what would have been the feed-and-tack room if this had been in use as a stable. They had a single lantern in the middle of the room, as if it were serving as a campfire, and the men sitting on barrels and boxes around it were busying their hands with various tasks. But there was not much talking going on.

Perry lingered at the door, just at the edge of the lamplight. Finally one of the men happened to see him. "Dog-boy," he said, sounding surprised. "Can't sleep, lad?"

The rest of the men turned to look at him as he nodded. The man who had spotted him gestured to him to come join them. He and Larral eased their way into the room; Larral took up a spot on the floor and lay down, while Perry used him as a backrest. No one else did much more than look at him. It was so quiet in here that his ears started to ring.

They all sat in silence for a very long time. So long that he feared they weren't going to talk at all. Finally, one of them cleared his throat and broke the quiet. "Dog-boy," he said, his voice full of unease, "did the Master give you food?"

"No eat!" he said with alarm, half starting up.

"It's all right, Dog-boy," the man said hastily. "As long as you didn't eat anything, you're *fine.*"

"No eat," he repeated, sitting back down again. He considered adding something but decided he wanted to keep Dog-boy as simple as possible.

But the men relaxed after that, and although they didn't speak very much, they did, at least, drop a word or two here and there. He learned that there was a regular supply caravan, one that brought twice as much in the way of supplies as they actually used. It had come in just before he arrived and was expected again in a fortnight. He learned that the captain paid the caravan master in gold that he got directly from the Master himself. He learned that the mercenaries themselves were paid in gold, too, but it was irregularly, and the intervals had increased with every moon they had spent here. They hadn't had a payday in three moons now. But instead of speaking of this angrily, they spoke of it sadly, in resignation.

Which made no sense. Why didn't they leave?

:Maybe they can't,: Larral suggested.

:Surely he can't control them all!: he objected.

:What if he can?:

That question brought all of his thoughts to an abrupt halt. What if that creature in the Big House could control an entire company of men with his mind?

That changed everything.

That meant there was no way they would dare bring the Guard against him. He could take over the minds of an equal number of *them,* and force them to turn against their own friends and fellows.

That would be an unmitigated disaster. Worse than an unmitigated disaster. It would be catastrophic.

What if that was what the Master wanted? What if that was his big plan? To keep kidnapping people until Valdemar took notice of it and sent up the Guard? The ones he didn't kill outright, he could capture, imprison, and, at his leisure, reduce their minds to nothing and make them his own. Then all he'd need to do would be to wait for more Guard . . . and more Guard . . . until he had an army.

:It could be done,: Larral admitted. *:There were Mindspeakers in the ancient days who were that powerful. The stories of the* kyree *say that they could also turn friends against each other, or break the mind so that you considered your old friends to be your foes.:*

He shuddered. This was horrible. He had to tell his father!

:I need to tell the kyree *too. This creature doesn't seem to realize we are intelligent, but if he ever does, I am sure he*

will want us as his complete slaves just as he enslaves hu-
mans.:

:Wait, if he could do that, why wouldn't he have done that
to the mercenaries here?: Perry couldn't help but think that
the only thing that was keeping the mercenaries here was fear
that they'd simply be marched back to the compound. So
maybe the Master couldn't change anyone's mind in that way.

Larral, who had been as tense as Perry, relaxed a little. *:You*
are right. But we know he can take over an entire company
and force them to do his bidding. So he can still do terrible
things to your Guard.:

How long before his father would speak to him? Surely it
was much too early. Mags would have to be absolutely certain
the Master was asleep before he tried. And if Perry went back
to the kennel to wait, all he would do would be pace the floor
or toss and turn on his bed.

So I might as well stay here.

They passed around a thin, sour wine in a leather wine
flask; the men all seemed to enjoy it, but when Perry tried it,
he made an elaborate face and waved it away, and they
laughed. That moment of humor seemed to make them relax
a little, and either that, the wine, or both loosened their
tongues. And they talked, as men will, about women they had
bedded, and epic drinking sessions, and embarrassing stories
about one another. Truth to tell, aside from the kidnapping
and captivity of innocent people—which most of these men
didn't participate in—they seemed perfectly ordinary.

:It is much easier to hate someone when you don't know
them,: Larral pointed out. *:Nevertheless . . . what do you think*
the captain's reward was? I think it was one of those captive
women. And I am sure he made use of her without a second
thought. So they may seem ordinary, but they are by no means
blameless, and it is a mistake to think of them as being any-
thing like your Guardsmen.:

Larral was right. He *knew* Larral was right. These men

were doing horrible things, and he had to keep that in mind, no matter how nice they were to him personally. But it was very hard when they seemed not much different than people he knew back home.

He didn't learn much else from them this time; some of them decided to play a dicing game, and others began whittling on carvings, mostly spoons. Finally Perry yawned hugely and got up. Avoiding the dice players, he padded out the door and into the night.

By the stars, he was pretty sure it still wasn't late enough for his father to contact him. It was extraordinary how slowly time passed when you didn't have something interesting to do! But, after all, that was why Lord Jorthun and his father always said, "The life of a spy is long spans of excruciating boredom punctuated by moments of sheer panic."

He decided to test something. He and Larral walked all the way to the entrance to the courtyard and the guards there. He looked at the gate and then at one of them.

The man shook his head, slowly and deliberately.

All right, then, there would be no getting out that way unless the Master allowed it. So now he knew.

They turned and made their way back. The extraordinary thing was how quiet it was. No sounds of night birds, no sounds of insects, just the occasional clop of a hoof as a horse shifted its weight somewhere in its stall, the sounds of the guards at the gate pacing back and forth, and the occasional footfalls of someone on his way to or from the privy.

On the way back to the kennel, he examined the Big House. There were lights in a few of the windows, but most of them were dark, especially on the top floor. Was the Master asleep yet?

Then, just as he reached the kennel, he felt it: a strange chill, the oppressive sense of being watched, and something he couldn't properly describe that made every hair on his body stand on end; it made him want to shrink down as small as he could and not breathe to avoid being seen.

It only lasted for a second, as it swept over him as if he were inconsequential, but he knew what it must be.

It had to be the Master, making a survey of his domain.

He held his breath, froze where he was, and concentrated on keeping his upper thoughts full of images of the dogs, but it didn't return. But he had broken out in a cold sweat, and he was still shaking when he got back to the kennel.

:When we leave on the hunting trip tomorrow, I will memorize the way in and out,: Larral said, unexpectedly, as they settled themselves for the night in Perry's bed.

:You can do that?:

Larral coughed. *:All right. Not "memorize" exactly. I am going to . . . scent mark it.:*

Perry thought about asking what that meant, then thought better of it, since Larral was obviously embarrassed by whatever it was. Though he had the shrewd notion it meant that Larral was going to dribble a little urine along the way, and if he stayed in the middle of the pack, no one would notice.

That wouldn't last past the next rain . . . but maybe they would be going out to hunt more frequently once they passed the initial test. Because this was a test, he was sure of it.

And at that moment, he heard his father's Mindvoice in his head—whispering, as though he too was afraid to attract the attention of the Master. Quickly, Perry told him what he had learned. And what he surmised.

:You are a step ahead of me,: Mags replied, sounding chagrined. *:But that makes it all the more urgent to deal with him somehow. And it is imperative we get this information back to the King quickly. Is there anything more that you can tell me?:*

:Only that I'm supposed to take the pack out to hunt tomorrow.:

:That's probably a test, to see if you try to make a run for it—and to see if you can truly command the pack. Not necessarily in that order.:

:That's what I figured. I'm going to be a good and obedient dog-boy.:

:If they start sending you out regularly, if Roya and I can figure out a way to hide you from the Master, that might be the time to get you out of there.:

But another idea had already occurred to him. *:But if they trust me and start letting me and some dogs go out on our own . . . that might be the way to get you* in *here.:*

I'd rather get you out and deal with the Master on ground of our choosing,: Mags replied firmly, and Perry could see his point. *:Be very careful, Perry. You're doing an amazing job.:*

And then the contact, the presence in his head, was gone.

Feeling lonelier than he ever had, he curled up with Larral and resolutely closed his eyes. He needed to make the best impression he could on the morrow.

Because . . . given the capriciousness of the Master, his life might depend on it.

────────────

The captain opened the kennel door to find himself facing Perry, with all the dogs behind him sitting quietly, all of them looking up at him expectantly. "So, you remembered we were going to hunt today!" the man said, looking pleased. "That's more than I—let's go. We have a long walk ahead of us."

Perry knew very well what the captain was going to say: *"That's more than I expected."* But that was fine, in fact, it was more than fine. It meant he was giving a sufficiently convincing performance of someone who was addled.

He whistled to the pack and led them out. The dogs had not been fed; he'd feed them double after the hunt. Feeding them before all that strenuous exercise would make them sick at least, and at the worst, it might even kill them.

The designated hunters of the day went in front; it was

pretty obvious from the fact that they were carrying boar spears, they intended to go after wild pig.

He could certainly see why they would want the mastiffs for that.

He and Larral walked in the middle of the pack; the hunters were not making any effort beyond a walk, and since *he* didn't know the way out, there was no point in getting ahead of them.

This early in the morning, the streets were shrouded in shadow, and it was damp down here, and chilly. The only scent his pitiful human nose could pick up was that of cold, damp stone from the slate roofs, but Larral's more sensitive one wasn't picking up much more than that. The early sunlight was just gilding the peaks of those strange roofs. He tried to sense if there was any sort of animal life in or around the houses lining the streets . . . he got nothing but a few birds, and those were just passing over the city on their way to somewhere else. It was as if this unwelcoming place actually repelled animal life too.

:That's probably because there is nothing to eat in those houses or their yards,: Larral pointed out. *:Why should mice or rats live there if there is no food nearby, and there hasn't been any for a long, long time? Why should birds nest here if they have to fly much too far to bring food back to their young?:*

It was truly a "dead city," then, and it gave Perry very uneasy feelings to be passing through it. He could tell that he wasn't alone in feeling that way. The hunters gave the empty houses uneasy glances when they thought no one was looking.

He was very glad when they got to the gates and out of the city. They swiftly trotted through the field of stumps, and once they were at the edge of the forest, the hunters stopped, and one of them made his way through the milling dogs to Perry.

"Dog-boy," he said, enunciating each word with great care, "we are hunting pig. Do you understand?"

He nodded, making his hair flop into his eyes. "Hunt," he said. "Pig."

And he crouched down among the dogs and made meaningless whistles at them, as if he were communicating with them in some sort of language only they and he understood. They gathered around him in "listening" attitudes, although, of course what they were listening to was all inside their heads.

Obviously, communicating with them in a way only they understood was exactly what he was doing, except he was speaking directly into their minds, showing them the quarry he wanted them to track and what he wanted done with it when they found it.

First, to find a herd of pigs, keeping them relatively close to the hunters while they ran the herd to exhaustion, then to pin them somewhere they couldn't escape from and give tongue when the pack had done its work. He stood up, made a sweeping gesture, and the dogs milled around for a bit, then moved off at a walk. The humans all followed, working deeper and deeper into the forest, until suddenly three of the dogs to the far right of the rest of the pack raised their heads and bellowed, then took off at a run, with the rest following.

The humans all followed at a trot, but they were soon outdistanced. The hunters didn't look concerned, probably because they trusted his control of the dogs, and Perry wasn't at all worried. The dogs had their orders, and they'd obey. For now, it was mostly a matter of keeping track of where they were.

The hunters moved off to his right, and Perry followed; they emerged on the top of a hill overlooking a meadow with a single, enormous tree spreading ancient branches above them. From there, it was much easier to track the pack as they belled in pursuit of their prey.

Perry stood there with his eyes closed, staying in touch with Larral and the former pack leader, cautioning them to slacken their pace when he could tell that the pigs were about to turn and stand at bay and helping them keep the herd together. And he was tracking the pigs mentally too, though it made him feel a little guilty, knowing he was basically herding them to their deaths.

The dogs had managed to crowd two separate herds together; one of females and their piglets and half-grown weanlings, and one of subadult males. There were probably as many as ten females and five males, and most of the females had litters. The cook was going to have his hands full preserving most of that meat, because even with a full company of men, they'd never eat it all before it went off.

The pigs would probably be running at full speed, except that the piglets couldn't keep up. The young subadult boars were still more used to following the matriarch of the herd than running off on their own, and in this stressful situation, they had defaulted to their piglet behavior. This was why Perry had to keep the dogs at a mere trot; that was the fastest pace the piglets could manage, running at what was for them full speed.

He kept his mind with the dogs as much as possible, but he couldn't help feeling sorry for the pigs. The only thing that kept him from abandoning this hunt altogether was that he could see signs already in this part of the forest that the pig population was much too high. They were destroying the undergrowth with their rooting and digging; he saw places where the meadow below them was dug up and ruined, and they had probably dug so many wallows near ponds and brooks that they were well on the way to ruining the water with muddying it. It was clear that there weren't enough predators in this part of the Pelagirs, and these pigs were very close to causing harm that would take years, if not decades, to repair. Wolves were the usual predators for wild pigs, and he hadn't heard any wolves since arriving here. Probably the mercenaries had trapped any wolves or run them off—and this was the result: a population of wild pigs that was now out of control.

He kept reminding himself while directing the dogs that this was something that had to be done.

:If these men weren't here, I'd bring in kyree *to hunt them until the wolves came back,:* Larral observed, and licked his chops at the thought of a suckling pig.

Finally even the adult pigs were exhausted. Larral had already located the perfect ambush point, a little cul-de-sac among some rocks. Now he took over the front of the pack as Perry ordered them to spread out to keep any of the pigs from escaping. About a candlemark later, the pigs were all milling frantically in the trap, and Larral bellowed the "at bay" bark, followed by the rest of the pack.

Perry didn't need to tell the hunters; they could recognize the change in the dog's barking for themselves. With a shout, they headed down the hill in the direction of the noise.

By now, of course, everything in this part of the forest that wasn't in hiding had fled to quieter realms, and there was very little chance of being attacked even by a bear, so the hunters were putting their best pace on without worrying about what might be in the way. Ordinarily this sort of reckless behavior on their part would be suicide—but not today.

They came out of the forest again to find themselves facing a field of enormous boulders, the smallest being at least twice the height of a man, the largest, two stories tall. These boulders formed a sort of crescent shape, and the pigs were now trapped in the bottom of the crescent.

With the dogs keeping the pigs pinned, the hunters strung their bows in a leisurely fashion and began picking off the piglets, one by one.

The air filled with the metallic scent of blood. The sows squealed as their piglets began to fall, five and six at a time. Perry closed his mind to the fear of the poor animals. This was a more efficient way to hunt, certainly—but it was terribly cruel. At least these men were good at what they did. They never had to use a second arrow, and the piglets died instantly.

But the smell of the blood drove the entire herd of swine frantic with terror.

All that skill with the bow doesn't bode well for the Guard if it comes to fighting them. . . .

"Dog-boy!" The leader of the hunters shouted over the din of the dogs when the last of the piglets lay unmoving on the ground. Perry trotted over to him.

Once again, the man spoke slowly, with careful, small words. "Can you get the dogs to let *one* pig at a time through to us?"

Perry stuck his finger in his mouth, gnawed on it, and pretended to think with a furrowed brow. The man was surprisingly patient; he didn't shout at Perry or repeat himself. He just waited until Perry allowed his face to brighten.

"One pig," he said, nodding, and turned toward the pack.

Again he made meaningless whistles as he told the pack to look up at him, and then he gave them their instructions, showing them what he wanted them to do. When he ws sure they had it all firmly in their heads, he shouted. *"Go!"*

Four of the dogs dashed in and startled a young boar at the far left edge of the herd. Seeing four dogs charging down on him, he squealed and ran instead of charging. The dogs opened up a corridor for him, and seeing a path to escape, he burst into a gallop—

Right onto the spears of two of the hunters.

As soon as he was dead, the dogs repeated the performance.

Two of the eight hunters left when there were only about three sows left, including the matriarch. At this point, Perry thought for a moment that they might let the remaining pigs go—after all, they had more than enough meat, and the cook and his helpers would probably be working day and night to get it all smoked for preservation.

But no.

When the last pig was dead, the hunters started butchering, gutting the piglets first. The leader called Perry over to him again.

"Dogs hungry?" he asked, gesturing at the growing piles of offal—which were perfectly good as dog food.

"Yes," he said, simply, and lined the dogs up in a row, giving each of them a careful portion of the bounty. Now it was all over, and at least he wasn't being bombarded by the terror of the pigs. Just the hunger of the dogs, who had been working long past their breakfast time, and were ravenous.

By the time they'd finished eating, the hunters that had left, returned. They had brought all the horses to pack the meat out with. The hunters were positively gleeful. Perry was feeling a little sick. It had, after all, been a slaughter, and an unfair one.

Since the dogs were still eyeing the meat, and he caught visions of stealing out of them, he rounded them all up and headed back toward the city, leaving the hunters still packing up the bounty. Larral led the way; he had to marvel how sure the *kyree* was of exactly where he was and where they needed to go.

But he realized, as he got away from the scene of the hunt, that he had learned a lot about these mercenaries by watching them. He knew now they had some expert marksmen. He knew they favored solid tactics and a well-thought-out approach to dealing with an enemy. He knew that they did not flinch, not even when a boar was charging straight for them.

That was more information his father should have.

And meanwhile—now Larral knew the way into and out of the compound. That was a definite plus.

And the guards might not let me *out . . . but I bet they'd let him go. He could make his way to the palisade, and see if there is another way in—or out.*

Things might not be as dire as he had thought. At least, not for the three of them.

And at least, not for right now.

Pelas had not done more than nap before leaving just after noon. Mags thanked him profusely for his help and begged him to stay until he was rested, but the Companion was clearly uneasy about being so far from his Chosen and wanted to go back immediately.

Mags felt one hell of a lot better with real weapons at hand. Not that they would do much good against someone who could control an entire company of mercenaries with his mind . . . but there were a lot of perfectly ordinary men in that place, and perfectly ordinary weapons worked against them just fine.

Even though at the beginning of this trek he had thought he was going into wilderness territory, he'd still packed up his roof-walking kit and all the things he used for climbing walls into the caravan with the rest of his gear. Now he was glad he had; it had occurred to him that if he knew the routes and timing of the patrols inside, he could get up and over the palisade and into the city itself without being caught. And he could get out the same way. If he could get Perry out of that inner court, he could get Perry out too; the only question would be how to extract Larral.

Dallen had eaten and immediately dozed off as soon as he was back, and Mags didn't blame him one bit. He must have put on every bit of speed he was capable of to get to Arville's house as fast as he had. He had put a good face on it, but it had been pretty clear he was exhausted, and needed a good, long rest to recover.

Now he had finished unpacking everything the two Companions had brought, and organized it, and he was left with . . . too much time on his hands before he could safely contact his son.

So he sat down on his bed and began methodically and minutely examining all of his equipment and weapons. He tested the strength of every thumblength of his climbing rope and the strength of his grappling hook. He made sure the braided wire of his coiled garrote was free of kinks. He made sure the all-black, skin-tight outfit he wore for night-prowling was still free of holes that might allow a bit of bare skin to betray him. Was the wooden cone he used to listen through doors and walls still in the kit? His lockpicks? His wafer-thin, latch-lifting knife?

And when he was certain that everything he could want or need was here and in good order . . . at least it was time to cook some supper.

After supper, he decided to take a walk until it was too dark to see. He set off alone, but it wasn't long before he was joined by Roya.

:Is this another form of pacing?: the *dyheli* asked, casually.

"I suppose it is," he replied aloud. "I want Perry out of there. But I need him in there. It feels as if I'm using him."

:Well, you are. And being what you are, you have to. You Heralds all know the time can always come for sacrifice and self-sacrifice.:

"That's just it. He's a child. And he's not a Herald. Not yet, anyway."

:Perhaps when you are both done with this place, not ever. Would that be a bad thing?:

"I try not to think about it," he confessed, as the *dyheli* paced gracefully at his side. "I've been trying very hard not to put *my* expectations on my children."

The King Stag snorted. *:That's not possible, and you know it. The best you can manage is to keep them from thinking you have any expectations for them.:*

Mags coughed. "I'd ask how you know that, but I already know the answer. How many times have you been a father?"

:I lost count at two hundred.:

Mags thought about that. "At least they feed themselves."

:A good point.:

They walked, side by side, through a forest that was slowly changing its face from day to night. It didn't become something entirely different . . . but it certainly was not the same "creature" it was by day. He put one hand on Roya's back, and they stopped at a little bluff that overlooked one of the many small watercourses that threaded their way through the forest. Moonlight streamed down through the break in the trees—and the silence was shattered by the scream of a rabbit.

Mags shivered.

:I think we should turn back now,: Roya observed dispassionately.

It was a distinct relief when Roya finally said, *:The Master sleeps.:* Mags practically turned himself inside out to get to his son's mind—to discover that his son had been waiting just as impatiently for him.

In fact, the instant Perry sensed Mags' touch on his mind, he began streaming thoughts, almost too fast for Mags to pick up on them.

. . . and Larral knows how to get out of the city to the wall now, was the last of them, and then there was nothing more distinct than the sort of circling repetition born of anxiety.

:You've done well,: he said, trying to project that he considered Perry to have done at least as well as a fully grown adult so far. *:And you're right. The King has to know about all of this, immediately. You are absolutely correct that sending companies of the Guard against this Master would be insane.:* As he spoke to Perry, he was getting a sinking feeling in the pit of his stomach, a feeling born of having known King Sedric so closely, and his father King Kyril before him.

:I think the King is going to order us to find a solution that won't involve the Guard,: he continued, being as honest as he could with the boy. *:And we* must *have a solution for him. We*

*can't simply allow an enemy like this to lurk on our Border
and wait for him to make the first move. That's suicidal.:*

Is there some sort of Gift that could . . . shut him off? Perry
asked.

:I've heard *that in the past, people have had their Gifts
burned out, but I'm not sure how,:* he replied, after a long moment of thought. *:I'll send that suggestion along. But, Perry, it's
possible, more than possible, that he's too strong to do that to.:*

*Maybe you should ask Roya. He's awfully strong. He can
control his whole herd.*

Mags wasn't sure about that; what Roya did was not so much
"control," as "direct," at least it seemed that way to him. But it
was worth asking. The problem was, Roya didn't have the same
urgency about getting rid of the Master that he and the King did.
Roya and his herd could just *leave,* but Valdemar couldn't exactly pick up its Border and migrate away from this danger.

*I sent Larral to make a run around the inside of the pali-
sade around the city,* Perry thought, evidently deciding his
father had been silent for too long. *He's going to see if there
are any other ways in or out of the city, or out of the courtyard. The guards didn't let me leave tonight, but they didn't
have any trouble letting Larral go for a run.*

Mags felt a surge of intense relief. *:I have my climbing kit.
I can go over the palisade and come to you if you need me,
once he finds a spot that's either unguarded, or is only lightly
patrolled.:*

He sensed his son's equal relief at hearing that. *All right.
I'll have everything Larral found out for you tomorrow night.*

*:We should probably say goodnight then, in case the Mas-
ter wakes,:* he said reluctantly.

*Goodnight, Father. I hope the King and the Heraldic Circle
have some good ideas for us.*

Mags let go of his son's mind and stared into the darkness
in the cave, just listening to Dallen and Roya breathe.

But all he could think was, *So do I, son. So do I.*

To Perry's surprise, Larral returned on his own, nosing the door to the kennel open and lapping up a prodigious amount of water before flopping down next to him.

:How did you get back in the compound?: Perry asked him.

:I scratched at the gate like a house dog and the guards let me in. They gave me the leftovers from their dinner too.: Faint memories of the delicious taste of suckling pig permeated the thought. *:I found a couple of good places for your father to get over the palisade, and I started on a hole under it. There's a spot where no one has* ever *been but me; it was full of dust and dead leaves, so no one has ever patrolled there on the inside.:*

Perry knew the outside didn't matter; it wasn't as if there were guards stationed outside the palisade within sight of each other all night. To post sentries like that would have required most of the company.

:What about the compound?:

:No one patrols the outside of the compound. The only

guards are stationed at the gate. He just needs to avoid being seen by people inside, and once everyone's asleep, either of the back corners would do for that.:

:But how—:

:Do I get out? The guards let me out here. I can either wait until the gate is open in the palisade and make a dash for the forest, or I can dig my way out under the palisade. The palisade isn't nearly as old as the city. I'm willing to bet that those logs are only sunk as deep has they have to be in order to support their own weight upright long enough for them to be pegged together. Three, perhaps four armlengths. As I said, I started on a hole already. It will take me two, perhaps three days to finish the digging job.: Larral paused to think. *:I should start a food cache out there.:*

:Better yet, when Father comes over the wall, I'll have him leave a food cache for you.:

:Excellent plan,: Larral approved. *:Now let's sleep. It has been a very long day.:*

———————————

It turned out to be a short night. The sky was still dark, and there were still a few bright stars in it when a commotion in the courtyard woke Perry and Larral; it immediately roused all the dogs and started them barking in alarm before he quieted them down. Something was certainly going on, but what?

With the dogs raising an alarm it would looks strange if I didn't stick my head out.

He got up and cautiously cracked the kennel door open. When nothing happened, he opened it fully and had a look around.

The captain, looking short of sleep and temper both, was mustering a group of heavily armed, equally sleepy men in the area between the kennel and the Big House. It was very clear from his manner and that of the men he must have booted out of a sound sleep that they were all both unhappy and afraid.

". . . and I want you to search every inch of forest between the city and a full league out!" he shouted.

"But cap'n . . ." ventured one of the men, carefully, "what are we looking for?"

"Damned if I know," the captain growled. "The Master says something's out there, but he don't say who or what. Just look for anything out of the ordinary!"

A couple of men looked askance at each other at that, but what could they do? The Master had given orders, however vague those orders were, and it was their job to figure out how to follow those orders or face the consequences.

"Dismissed!" the captain shouted. "Now get out there and find whatever it is!"

The men turned at a single barked order from their officer and headed for the gate at a trot. Perry ventured out and wandered toward the captain on a path that would intersect his.

When it did, the captain looked up and stared at him blankly for a moment, as if he didn't recognize the boy in front of him.

"Hunt?" said Perry.

That seemed to shake him out of his stupor. He smiled wanly. "No, Dog-boy. No hunting today. If we had a scent for your dogs to follow, it would be different, but at the moment we're chasing shadows." The last was said very bitterly.

Perry shook his head. "No hunt shadows," he objected.

"I know you can't." The captain patted his head roughly. "It's all right. If we find something, we'll have a use for you and the dogs."

Perry blinked at him, as if he only understood one word in ten. "Food?" he suggested, finally.

"Good idea. Come along." With Perry trotting at his side, the captain headed for the improvised kitchen.

There they found the cook just taking some loaves of bread

out of the oven. The kitchen was comfortably warm and smelled delightfully of bread and roasted pork. One of the helpers handed a loaf to the captain, who broke it in two, inhaling the fragrance with appreciation as it steamed into the cool morning air, and handed half to Perry. He mimed to Perry that he should pick the soft, hot bread out of the middle and eat it, to make a sort of bowl. Perry did that, and the helper took the two hollowed-out loaves from them and filled the hollow with cooked pork trimmings, bits of crisped skin and fat, and finished it with a half-ladle of broth. They stood there eating while the cook finished what he was doing, then turned to the captain.

"What the dark hell was all that about?" the cook asked, in a low voice, as though he was afraid to be overheard.

"Master sent one of his half-wits to drag me out of bed before dawn," the captain replied. "I got to listen to a candle-mark or more of hysterical ranting that *something* was in the forest, and I was ordered to find it."

"*Something?* How the hell are you—" The cook shook his head. "Never mind. Just tell me if I'm likely to find myself faced with having to cook . . ." He shuddered. "I'm tellin' you, Cap'n, I dunno if I can face that again—"

The captain shuddered too. "I don't think so. He's got his own half-wit to do that sort'a cooking now. And there's a better kitchen in his palace than what you got here. What *I* dunno is what'll happen if he decides to 'make a lesson' out of someone because we couldn't find whatever ghost he's chasing." The captain invoked the names of several gods that Perry didn't recognize. "The men cain't take much more of that. Someone's gonna snap, and I dunno how that'll play out."

Perry decided to take pity on them—because he'd had an idea. He tugged on the captain's sleeve, and before the other could reprimand him, said loudly, "Ghosts!" Then he flapped his free hand vaguely in the direction of the forest. "Ghosts!

Tree-ghosts!" He thumped his chest. "Dog-boy know! Dog-boy see!"

The captain stared at him a moment, as emotions passed over his face. First surprise, then anger, then the anger faded, and speculation took its place.

"What's the daft lad talkin' about, Cap'n?" the cook wanted to know.

The captain shook his head. "Not sure. But he did come out of the forest. Mebbe he saw somethin' there. Tree-ghosts?" he asked, turning Perry to face him. "What are tree-ghosts?"

"Ghosts. In trees." He made a *whooshing* noise with his mouth and moved his free hand through the air as if it were flying through the branches. "Up in trees! Dog-boy see!"

"When?" the captain persisted.

Perry scratched his head, as if the concept of "when" were a hard one for him. "Before here," he said, finally. "Suns and suns."

The cook and the captain exchanged a look. "Do you think—" said the cook.

"I think that if my men find nothing, I'm going to claim the forest is haunted and the Master himself woke up the ghosts," the captain said firmly. "I'm tired of losing men because the Master gets a burr up his ass."

The cook looked a little green. "It'll be worse if it ain't 'cause he got a burr up his ass—if it's 'cause he's pinin' for his favorite meal, an' he's makin' up an excuse t'get it."

Well, now I know where that . . . meat I was offered came from.

It seemed that the cook and the captain were very old friends and were willing to confide things to each other they'd never let out in front of the men. Perry feigned to have lost interest in the conversation now that he'd imparted his little bit of information; he ate bits of broth-soaked bread and crisp pork and looked at nothing but his improvised bowl. But the captain and the cook were filling in a lot of blank places in his understanding of this place and situation. It wasn't direct information, just a bit here, and a bit there, but Perry was able to put all the bits together into a coherent whole that made sense.

The Master, it seemed, had a habit of "making examples" out of men who—judged by some standard neither the cook nor the captain understood—exhibited "treacherous and suspicious behavior." They would be brought to the Big House and left there with the Master. Sometimes they came back days later, and if they did, they had terrible, half-healed head wounds and had only enough mind left to do the simplest of tasks. Mostly, they didn't come back. Perry surmised that the former dogmaster had been one of those who had come back. *Maybe he looked too tough to eat. . . .*

Perry learned that the Master always took the men two at a time, and they were always good friends, and he almost stopped eating as he realized exactly what must be going on.

The Master was surely forcing each pair of men—men who were friends—to fight to the death. Probably with some crude weapon like an ax. If one survived, he'd be a living, sickening example of why it was a bad idea to even consider rebelling . . . and a living example of why it was a bad idea to have friends here. And the ones that didn't survive, well . . . Perry already knew what became of them.

As he listened and filled in his information, he realized that the captain and the cook had already figured all of this out. If they had, probably so had all the other men. This certainly explained the lack of camaraderie, the curiously impersonal gathering in the tack room. If you'd had friends before you came here, it was better for both of you if you pretended that relationship had never existed. And if you hadn't, well, it wasn't a good idea to make friends. Not when you could be forced to try to kill each other on the Master's whim.

Much as Perry hated to admit it, this was a stroke of genius. You couldn't foment a rebellion if you didn't dare talk to each other. It didn't matter to the Master if the men were able to work together; he could control them all with his mind if he needed to. It didn't matter if they were loyal to each other. All that mattered was that they feared him. That would get him absolute obedience.

Brilliant. Diabolical, but brilliant.

And add to it that they all knew what became of their own fallen comrades. . . . that would evoke the sort of horror of the Master nothing else could do. Terror and horror would do more—so far as the Master was concerned—than loyalty and devotion.

But he realized something else. He was going to have to get a message to his father, and quickly, that the Master had noticed something out there in the forest, which probably meant that he had detected the *dyheli,* Dallen, or even Mags' Mindspeech.

He drifted away from the kitchen; the captain didn't stop him, so evidently he had no further use for the dog-boy at the moment. He and the cook were deep in a discussion of just what sort of "ghosts" could be out in the forest; evidently neither of them had ever heard of the Tayledras, because nothing they suggested sounded at all like a Hawkbrother. That seemed to confirm that these mercenaries had never heard of the Pelagir Hills before they arrived here. It seemed an odd omission. Everyone in Valdemar certainly knew about the uncanny reputation of the Pelagir Hills, and he was pretty sure the reputation persisted as far south as the Dhorisha Plains. *Maybe mercenaries just don't bother finding out about any place they don't plan to be working in.*

They were certainly coming up with all manner of spirits that might be haunting the hills, though, first and foremost being the former inhabitants of this city.

That was the last Perry heard as he drifted out of sight, and his desultory progress gave him plenty of leisure to set his own mind seeking the ravens. They were his best chance of getting a warning to his father undetected.

He found the entire flock of seven still waking up and thinking of breakfast. And that gave him an idea.

By the time the men arrived with the meat for the dogs' meal, he was sitting on a stool by the kennel door, playing with the ravens and feeding them tidbits from his own breakfast. He fed the dogs, turned them loose in their yard, set the helpers to cleaning the kennel, and returned to the ravens, now feeding them with the leftover dogs' meat.

Before long he had some of the men coming to watch him curiously for a moment. But the novelty soon wore off, when the ravens didn't do any tricks or anything clever. By lunchtime, he and his flock weren't attracting any attention at all. It seemed, as he had hoped, they were just chalking it all up to a daft dog-boy's extraordinary power of making friends with animals.

That was just what he needed. Now no one would pay any attention at all to the ravens' comings and goings. He could easily use them now to-carry messages whenever he needed to.

He went inside the kennel for a moment and got one of the ravens to follow, with Larral keeping watch to make sure no one had noticed. When the raven came back out, the flock took off together.

But one of them bore a message. And all of them were heading for Mags.

———————

A loud chorus of *quorks* called Mags out of the cave, and as soon as he emerged, a young raven dove down out of the branches of a tree and landed in front of him, holding out one leg expectantly.

His heart sank when he saw the paper tied to it.

With hands a lot steadier than they should have been, he freed the raven of his burden and hastily read the message.

Master senses something in forest. Sent mercs to hunt 1 leag. frm city.

His heart stopped pounding quite so hard, and with a sigh of relief, he went back into the cave and returned with dried rabbit and fish to reward the ravens with. The cave was more than a league from the city—even assuming this Master had any notion just how far a league was, or that the mercenaries were going to search that far. But it was possible that the Master had gotten some inkling of his presence, or that of the *dyheli* herd, and Roya needed to be warned.

So he sent out the merest thread of a thought to Roya and kept it to a single word. *:Come.:*

Then he sat down to wait.

He had actually waited for longer than he had expected when Roya finally ghosted his way out of the forest, appearing before him so quietly that he jumped a little, then recovered.

"I got a raven message from Perry," he said. "The Master has sensed something in the forest and is searching for whatever it is. For quite some distance out from the city, too—a full league, according to Perry."

:Hrmmm.: Roya not only made the sound in his mind, it rumbled in his throat. *:Thank you for summoning me at once. I did not anticipate this. I have had* dyheli *overwatching the city to keep an eye on these mercenaries, and I certainly do not want any of them harmed. Give me a moment.:*

Mags waited patiently. He had learned that patience was a requisite with Roya. The King-Stag did things in his own time, on his own schedule. He watched as the *dyheli's* long ears twitched, and his eyes darted rapidly behind his closed eyelids. It seemed to take a very long time; certainly the sun dappling the ground in front of the cave entrance had moved visibly when Roya's eyes opened again.

:There. They are withdrawing at a run. And they did, indeed, witness a group of men emerge from the city and begin what looked like a search. *They assumed it was a hunt for one of the Master's own men who had tried to flee.:*

"Do you think there's any chance the Master detected your scouts?" Mags asked, anxiously.

:I think it would be foolish to discount the idea. We really have no idea what he is and is not capable of.: Roya's chin worked as he chewed on what looked to be unpleasant thoughts as he chewed on his cud. *:I wonder if it is wise to contact your son as usual tonight. If the Master has detected any of our Mindspeech, he might be on the alert and searching for such a thing.:*

"Are you certain you can tell when the Master is asleep?" Mags asked . . . then something else occurred to him. "Once he is, can you lull him into a deeper sleep?"

:Hrmmm.: Roya considered this. *:Perhaps. It would make contacting your son less dangerous. And he is our only source of information at the moment.:*

"I thought about trying to read the surface thoughts of those mercenaries, but—"

:Risky. Very risky. But I think it is worth the attempt to send him into a deeper sleep once he is *asleep. If he starts to rouse, I am certain I can withdraw before he becomes aware I was there.:*

"In the meantime, can you ask the ravens to keep a watch on those searchers and come warn us if they venture too close?"

:Define "too close,": Roya retorted, with a touch of humor, *:I can run much faster than you.:* But then he nodded. *:Certainly I can. I can also assign my very best, and most stealthy,* dyheli *to trail them and come to us at the gallop should they venture in this direction.:*

Roya closed his eyes again, and Mags kept his mouth shut while the King-Stag was in silent communion with his own herd members and the ravens.

The wretched thing was, of course, that he was essentially helpless. While he had never tried to take over the mind of anyone, much less many people at once, the fact that the Master could do that almost certainly meant that he was an exponentially more powerful Mindspeaker than Mags. It was entirely possible that he had sensed Mags' Mindspeech with Roya, even at so great a distance.

Or worse; he had sensed Mags' Mindspeech with Arville. That shouldn't be possible, not with Companions protecting them, but if it was true. . . .

Somehow we'll have to neutralize him. He's too dangerous to be allowed so near to Valdemar.

―――――――――――

By noon there had been no further raven messages from Perry, and the mercenaries had retreated back into the city without venturing anywhere near Mags' cave and the area around it where the bulk of Roya's herd was. With the aid of a great deal of practice in acting as if everything were normal when it was, in fact, anything but, Mags checked his traplines and weirs, collected rabbits and fish, managed to shoot a couple of unwary young cock pheasants, and brought his catch back to the cave, where he selected what he was going to cook and eat immediately and prepared the rest for smoking and drying. He'd devoted a corner of the cave to a smoking fire and had racks made of green branches tented over his smoke source, with leafy boughs over that, holding the smoke in. He knew that he had to proceed as if he and Perry were going to need provisions; they could be left behind for the ravens if such things were never needed, but it would be a disaster if they needed food and didn't have it. It gave his hands something to do while his mind worried uselessly on the problem of how to get Perry out, and how to deal with the Master.

As soon as he thought Arville might be in a position to talk to him, he called his Companion and the King-Stag into the cave, sat himself down in a corner, braced against the wall, and had Dallen boost him and Roya guard him while he sent his mind streaming out to his fellow Herald.

Arville, it appeared, was more than ready for him.:*Mags!*: he exclaimed. :*I've been Mindspeaking all morning! The King wants more information—*:

Mags willingly told him everything he already knew, and the more he passed on, the deeper Arville's concern became. :*This is horrible!*: he exclaimed. :*We can't possibly send the Guard!*:

:*Obviously,*: Mags sighed. :*But that's not up to us. That's up to the King and the Council. The worst part of it is there is no way to find out exactly what else this Master can do. Listen, I want to know if there are any Heralds or Healers who know how to block or burn out Gifts. If we can do that, once his abilities are negated, we can just leave him alone. As soon as his mercenaries discover he's powerless to hurt them . . . well, it won't be pleasant for him, but that won't be our concern.*:

:*I'll pass all this on. Contact me again in two candlemarks.*: Arville broke the connection, and Mags could sense as he did how tired he was. This was probably more Mindspeaking than he'd done in a year or more, and all of it had been within a few days. For those who weren't strong Mindspeakers, it was exhausting.

Poor old man. . . . Here he thought he had gone to spend his last years in a safe and comfortable place, a place where he could be useful but where he could, fundamentally, rest. Now he was in the middle of a situation almost as dire as anything Herald-Mage Vanyel had faced. And Arville was well aware that he was no Vanyel.

Well, neither am I if it comes to that.

:*As far as I can tell, the Master was not aware of your conversation,*: Roya said soberly. :*I am taking great care that he not detect me, as well. He seems preoccupied with search-ing the city itself at the moment. I would say he was jumping at shadows—except, of course, we are not shadows.:*

:We certainly aren't. I wish I were a Herald-Mage rather than what I am,: he sighed. *:If I were, I could give him plenty of—:*

And then, it suddenly occurred to him.

:You have an idea.:

:Maybe. I'm outside the borders of Valdemar, so it might not work . . . have you ever heard of vrondi?:

:The Watchers? I don't know a great deal about them.:

:When Herald-Mage Vanyel realized that the Herald-Mages were being systematically assassinated, and that Valdemar was going to be helpless against true magic and the Mages that could wield it, he created a spell that summoned the vrondi *within Valdemar's borders to gather and aggressively watch any Mage who passed across the Border.:* He waited for Roya to assimilate all that.

Roya pawed the ground a little. *:Just . . . watch? Of course, that is what* vrondi *do, but . . .:* Then, all in a heartbeat, Mags saw understanding flood the King-Stag. *:Oh. Oh! By the horned moon . . . that would be maddening, wouldn't it?:*

:Literally,: he assured the *dyheli. :I watched it happen. A Mage from a land that is an enemy to us was part of a phony delegation when I was first at the Collegium. I saw him go slowly insane. In fact, there was more than one attempt in that time period, and they all went insane. Now . . . if I could somehow persuade the* vrondi *that he is of interest to them . . . :*

:It would certainly give him shadows to chase,: the King-Stag agreed. *:But I am no Mage, either. How would you per-suade the* vrondi *to do this?:*

Mags wished desperately that he had the Heartstone be-neath the Palace to talk to. Well, consult. It wasn't exactly alive. It was more like a sort of library of everything Herald

Vanyel had known and done and left in place to keep the Kingdom safe—

*:Bloody hell. Maybe Sedric can talk to it too. He's the King.
You'd think it would talk to the King. The only question is if
he'll be able to remember what it tells him long enough to tell
me.:* That was the rub. Vanyel had known, when he established the *vrondi* spell, that if anyone inside Valdemar began
to manifest the Mage Gift, he or she would quickly be driven
insane. So he had added a component that made it difficult, if
not impossible, for anyone inside the Border to think about
real magic, as opposed to Mind-magic—and, not so inciden-
tally, that was yet another safeguard against true magicians
operating inside Valdemar. The only time you could effectively
think about real magic in the here-and-now was when you
were in contact with the Heartstone.

:I think you are beginning to flail,: Roya observed. *:It's
perfectly understandable. This is a tense situation. But you
are grasping at twigs before you even know if a twig is there.:*

Anger flared, but he controlled it. Roya was right, damn
him! But that didn't mean he had to like it.

*:First, we find out what the King and Council have de-
cided,:* said Dallen, reasonably. *:Then we'll know what we're
expected to do. If we can't do what they want, we'll report
back—because there is absolutely no good going to come of
trying something, failing badly, and alerting the Master to the
fact we know of his presence. And we'll put it that way to
Haven, and wait for them to come up with a better plan.:*

That was sensible. That was absolutely sensible. He'd been
so blinded by his worry over Perry, and so certain that the
King would order them to eliminate the Master regardless of
the cost, that it had never occurred to him that trying and failing had worse consequences than not doing anything at all.

:That's why we're partners, Chosen,: Dallen reminded him.
:Two heads are better than one, as the saying goes.:

:Hrrm. I wonder if there is some other way we can mimic

spirits haunting the forest and drive him to barricade himself inside,: Roya observed. *:I wonder if there are* tervardi *about . . .:* Abruptly, he folded his legs under himself and settled onto the sand of the cave floor, as he did when he needed to concentrate. *:Let me know if you need me.:*

:How long has it been since I contacted Arville?: he asked Dallen.

:Not long enough. Go fiddle with your smoked meat. Go collect greens and mushrooms. And don't worry about Perry. Right at the moment, he's safer than we are.:

Right at the moment, I'm safer than Father is, Perry thought, soberly, as he watched the captain put together yet another group, this time to search building-to-building through the entire city.

Building- to-building—

:Did you—: he thought with alarm at Larral.

:I hid my hole under a big pile of dead leaves and other trash, and I wiped all my pawmarks clean except the ones I wanted them to see. I want them to think I took a turn patrolling the palisade. That might make them think they can scant on their own patrols.:

:Ooooo, clever!: Perry was suitably impressed. *:You make a great partner!:*

:So do you. And I have an idea. Let's see if they'll let us take the whole pack on a run around the inside of the palisade. That will really muddle my prints up.:

That was a great idea. Just . . . how to get daft dog-boy to convey that idea to the captain without making him suspicious that dog-boy might be smarter than he seemed?

Well, I'll think about this while taking the dogs on a run around the compound.

The dogs were more than ready for a run; in fact, he got

longing snatches of chasing the pigs and the delicious reward afterward that let him know they'd have been more than willing to go on another hunt if they'd been allowed.

They were disappointed when he let them into the courtyard and there were no hunters waiting, but they got over their disappointment when he directed them to go into a full run following Larral. The captain was still giving instructions to his men when the hounds took off, and he gave them a cursory glance, then went back to his men.

Then . . . stopped. And as his men stared, puzzled that he had broken off his harangue, he watched the dogs circle the compound under Larral's leadership.

Finally he looked for Perry and found him. *"Dog-boy!"* he shouted, and waved to Perry to indicate he should come. Perry obediently trotted over.

The captain looked around, searching, Perry suspected, for something to make a map of the city with. Finally he looked at his men, and ordered them to remain, and he pulled Perry over to the kennel. He got a half-burned stick from the fire under the copper and drew a circle on the wall with it. "Here," he said, stamping his foot, to indicate that this was where they were. Just to emphasize that, he did some little stick figures that might have been dogs just inside the circle, and looked at Perry with no real hope.

Perry gave the captain his best "thinking" face. Finally he repeated, "Here," and stamped his foot. Then he made a circling motion inside the circle on the wall. "Dogs," he said. "Run." And he waited with an expectant look on his face.

The captain just lit up. He made a bigger circle around the smaller one, vaguely sketched a lot of squares to fill it, made a big thick line where the gate to the compound was, then a bigger, thicker line where the gate to the city was, and sketched those same stick figures running just inside the palisade.

"Dogs run?" the captain asked, making the same circling

motion inside the palisade that he'd made inside the compound.

Perry grinned and bobbed his head. "Dogs run," he confirmed.

The captain was too dignified a man to whoop, but he looked extraordinarily pleased. "Bring dogs," he ordered Perry, and he went back to his men. Perry followed, pausing only for a moment outside the kennel to whistle shrilly and enforce that with the mental command to come to him.

". . . right," the captain was saying as he ambled up, and the dogs came streaming to him to line up and sit down, panting. "Dog-boy's beasts will run the edge of the palisade, and if there's anything that ain't a spook or a spirit out there, it'll likely be scared out of hiding. You'll be searching farther inside, looking for anything that gets flushed. That clear enough?"

The men all assented in one voice that sounded relieved. Perry didn't blame them. He wouldn't have been looking forward to a house-to-house search out there in that echoing, empty city.

"All right then, move out!" The men turned and followed their officer; the captain looked for Perry, but he and the dogs were already falling in behind them.

As they passed the compound gates, Larral glanced up at Perry. :*Should we head out on our own?*:

:*Better not,*: Perry advised. :*I'd rather they had no idea you know how to get to the front gates by yourself.*:

:*Good point.*: The men were moving at a military trot; it wasn't hard to keep up with them. When they got within sight of the gates, their officer halted them and gestured to Perry.

"Do you know what to do?" he asked anxiously.

Perry nodded and pointed at the gates. "Go there. Dogs run." He indicated with a swirling gesture that they'd be going deosil.

The officer's brow cleared. "Right. Off you go, then!" As

Perry and the pack trotted off, he shouted at his men. "All right then! Right face! Keep within earshot of the hounds! Look for anything that gets flushed out! Start the search!"

By that time the pack had arrived at the gates, and Perry started them off at an easy lope, instructing them to bay as if they were hunting, with Larral to lead them.

He stood there for a long moment, as the sounds of baying dwindled and died, and looked around. As usual, no one was paying attention to him.

He eyed one of the buildings nearest him. *I wonder if it's locked?*

He ambled up to the front door, which was flush with the street, and tried it. The door swung open, easily. He looked back at the guards at the gate, who still weren't paying any attention to him.

Well, all right, then, he thought, and went in.

Roya was still chewing his cud and thinking when Mags decided enough time had passed that he could reasonably try to contact Arville again. "Roya," he said, tentatively, "I'm—"

:Going to talk to the other human, yes, go ahead. The Master is still occupied with the city. Your foal is running the dog pack around the inside edge.: The *dyheli* made a sound in his throat that resembled a chuckle, and the sudden amusement in his thoughts suggested that was precisely what it was. *:Clever little fellow. It's almost as if he knew that we would be doing such things and is giving the Master something the Master believes will flush out anything hidden.:*

"Well, the Master probably ordered his mercenaries to search the city, and their leader got the idea that it would be less work if the dogs helped," Mags pointed out, then frowned. "That suggests we really ought to pursue this notion of giving the Master something to occupy and frighten him. First he sends men out to search the woods. Then he sends men out to search the city. Does that seem excessive to you?"

:Possibly, but I am not a human. Still . . . I have an idea or two. I am still pondering them. Meanwhile, see what your humans at home want to do.:

He got an instant response from Arville when he made contact. *:It's possible to burn out a Gift, but the Healer has to be touching the person he's affecting,:* Arville said immediately, without even exchanging any sort of greeting. *:Obviously—:*

:Yes, not practical. What else?:

:They want you and Perry to eliminate the Master,: Arville said unhappily. *:The exact words were, "at whatever cost." Mags, I—:*

:You are going to tell them that if we try and fail *we'll be putting Valdemar in worse danger than it is now,:* Mags interrupted him. *:The Master will then know about Heralds and Companions, and when he breaks either Perry or me, he'll know everything about them. Oh, and he'll know about* kyree *as well, so Ryu won't be safe either. Besides that, the Master will know we know about him, he'll know we are not even considering negotiating with him, and he'll have all the advantages. He can sit in his city and wait for us to make a move. Or he can sit at the back of his mercenary troops, lead them against Valdemar, and wait for Valdemar to give him more* troops. *And frankly, I don't see how Perry and I can succeed against him right now.:*

There was a very long moment of silence. Finally Arville replied. *:I never thought of that.:*

:I don't think they have yet, either,: Mags said. *:You relay that. I'll get more information from Perry tonight. Can you stay up long enough to get it from me after I speak with him?:*

There was dogged determination in Arville's reply. *:I'll do it if I have to hold my eyes open with my fingers,:* he promised. *:Talk to you then.:*

This time it was Arville who broke the contact, probably to get back to the relay and pass on what Mags had just told him.

Mags was just as glad. Contacting him while the Master was awake was risky, even with the Master preoccupied elsewhere.

He opened his eyes to find Roya still reclining on the sand, still chewing his cud. Roya opened one eye and gave him a jaundiced look.

:Go hunt mushrooms. Look for roots or herbs or check your fish traps. I am still thinking.:

The first floor of the house was two big rooms. The first looked like any of the rooms at the Big House: wood floor and walls, a single fireplace in the middle of the back wall, a door next to it. There was no paint, only polished woodwork, all of that same odd silvery-gray wood. The room smelled of nothing, not even dust. Which seemed odd. Perry would have thought that there would at least be dust settled everywhere in here . . . and surely the mercenaries hadn't actually cleaned this place had they?

Well, perhaps they had. Perhaps when they first arrived, they had set up "camp" in the houses nearest the gate, just to be safe.

He went through the door and found himself in a kitchen. There was an oven and a fireplace built into the wall he had just passed through, obviously sharing the chimney with the fireplace in the other room. There were pantries at either end and a long counter under the tall, narrow windows, with three big stone sinks with drainpipes leading into the floor, and a hand-pump on one of them. Which argued a very high level of sophistication—higher than Haven, in fact. There, only the homes of the wealthy had drains and sewers and their own indoor access to water. Here, it was a house right by the front gate, a house identical to every other house in the city, so far as he could tell at this point.

But all he had seen so far was a very small part of the city, and that was all along the way that led to the compound, however twisting and indirect that path might seem. Maybe there were poorer, less sophisticated neighborhoods away from the main thoroughfare.

There was a staircase leading up to the next floor along the left-hand pantry wall. It was the only way up to the second floor.

And that was odd, too. In Haven, anyone living in a house this size would have servants, and you'd never have servants sharing the same stairs as the masters of the house. You would also never see the masters using a staircase in the kitchen. Yet there was no sign that the single large room had been anything like a bedroom, which meant the bedroom—or rooms—had to be upstairs. Unless these people made public spaces out of their bedrooms? No, that wasn't possible. So either people here hadn't had servants, or they didn't care to waste space making two sets of access points to the upper stories when one would do.

He spared a moment to check with Larral. *:Where are you? I'm exploring an empty house.:*

:We aren't even a quarter way round,: the *kyree* reported. *:Do all the exploring you want.:*

Satisfied, he headed for the staircase.

The second floor also had fireplaces—four of them, this time, situated in the corners of the four rooms that the second floor was divided into, with their chimneys slanted to join the main one from the first floor. Each room led into the next; there were no hallways, so if these were bedrooms, it meant that people had to traipse through other peoples' rooms to get to their own . . .

Then again, there were parts of the Palace like that. The masters would sleep in the farthest rooms, and the ones you went through to get to the bedrooms were sitting rooms and solars. And certainly the rooms he shared with his family there were just as odd.

There was no furniture and no sign of what these rooms had been used for—but once again, there was a single staircase leading up to the third floor at the far end of the building. He climbed it, to find himself on a floor identical to the one below it. It included a staircase leading to what must be the attic, with those peculiar, eyelike windows in the slate roof.

Once again he climbed the stairs. There were no fireplaces here and no dividing walls, just the slanted roof, and the chimney coming up through the floor and into the ceiling.

And there was no dust here either.

The attic was entirely empty. And it might not have been used for storage, either. It might have been where the servants all slept, all the beds lined up like so many sleeping spaces in an inn, since many people felt that servants didn't need privacy of any sort. But he did discover one thing. The heavy parchment-like substance that had once kept the wind and cold out of this room was torn out of several of the windows. Only the fact that the slate roof overhung them so deeply had kept weather out as well. There were some faint signs of bird droppings on the sills, but evidently even birds had been discouraged from nesting here.

By what, though? That was the real question. Was it just that the single big room intimidated them? That didn't make any sense. He'd seen birds nest in haylofts, in attics like this, all the time. He double-checked the ceiling, and there were plenty of places among the rafters where birds could have tucked nests. Could it just be that there were *so* many places to nest here that the birds just hadn't gotten to this house? That didn't make sense either. This house was the closest to the forest on this side of the city. And there was a food source of sorts in the guards, who certainly must drop the occasional crumb or piece of meat.

I should ask the ravens to look into one of these houses and tell me if they feel something wrong. The ravens had much keener senses for some things than a human did.

Or . . . maybe these houses actually are haunted. Larral had said not . . . but . . . well, how did he know for certain?

He shook his head, mentally chiding himself. This was getting him nowhere, and it certainly wasn't helping in figuring out how to handle the Master. *I should really be concentrating on finding out what his weakness is. Besides being seriously insane, that is.*

Then again, insanity by itself wasn't always a weakness. It could be a strength.

He trotted down the stairs and took a second look around the rooms on the third and second floors, trying to spot if there were marks on the floor or the walls that might show where furniture had been. But there was nothing. This house might as well have been brand new, with no one ever living here at all.

Since Larral and the pack weren't back yet, he took the time to check three other houses along this street, though he didn't go farther than the second floors. All were identical to the first in every way. To be honest, it was beginning to make him feel a bit spooked. What kind of people could possibly have lived here? Had it all been one gigantic semicommunal enterprise, with all goods held in common, as a few settlements on the southern border did things? Was that why every building was the same, so no one could boast of having more or suffer from having less than anyone else did?

And where had they gone? Why had they stripped out every possession before they left? To be honest, he was more disturbed by these mysterious, long-vanished people than he was by the Master. The Master was just a powerfully Gifted lunatic with a taste for human flesh. Not being able to categorize these people bothered him at a fundamental level.

But he didn't get too much more time to dwell on it all. As he came out of the fourth house he'd explored, he heard the dogs baying in the near distance, so he made his way back to the gate to wait for them.

"Find what you were looking for in there, Dog-boy?" one of the guards at the gate asked.

Perry stuck his finger in his mouth and chewed on it for a moment. Then he shook his head.

"Well, that'd be because there's nothing in there to see, eh?" a second guard said, in a slightly more kindly tone of voice. "Dunno where the Master gets 'is gold, but it ain't from these empty 'ouses."

Fortunately the arrival of the pack, now tired enough that they were moving at a lope rather than a run, put an end to any need to interact with the guards. Perry gathered the pack around himself and waited for the arrival of the men that he'd come with. Meanwhile, one of the guards worked a pump to fill a water trough that was right at the gate; Perry had seen it, but he'd thought it was nonfunctional. When it became apparent that it worked, he wove his way through the dogs to take over the job so they could drink.

By the time they had their fill, the men had finally returned, and it was their turn at the pump. They drank from their hands and put their heads under the spout while he worked away at it.

"Did you turn up anything?" one of the gate guards asked.

"Not a damned thing," the officer replied. "Nothing but echoes, and them dogs did a damn fine job for us. If there'd been even a sparrow, they'd've routed it out."

The men all exchanged weary looks, as if they would have liked to say something but knew they dared not. Perry just kept his upper mind full of the dogs. If the Master was bothering to look at him, he'd be bored stiff.

Finally the officer mustered his men, and they all headed back to the compound, with Perry and the pack bringing up the rear. The dogs were thinking of food and sleep, in that order. They'd gotten a good run today, and it would be quiet tonight in the kennel.

His dinner and the dogs' were waiting when they got back

to the compound. Perry sent two of the helpers back to wherever they stayed when they weren't helping him and kept the other two to speed up the feeding. The dogs ate quickly and were obviously thinking with longing of their soft beds as they ate. They didn't even try to steal choice bits from each other.

As he had hoped, by the time the sun started to set, they were down and sleeping. He thought about trying to contact the ravens but thought better of it. Having found nothing in the city, the Master might be in a foul mood and looking for something or someone to take his ire out on. Better not draw attention to himself.

He and Larral took a last walk around the compound (and visited the privies) and saw that the men were all evidently thinking the same thing. There were no gatherings in the tack rooms. They were getting their food from the cook and taking it to their allotted spaces to eat, then busying themselves with a chore or going straight to sleep. They even avoided looking at each other.

In fact . . . he could only think of one name for the mood that seemed to be on them. Dread.

But however annoyed the Master was, he didn't turn his attention to the men tonight. The compound remained silent, with nothing but the occasional neigh or whicker of a horse to interrupt the silence as Perry walked back to the kennel with Larral faithfully at his side. Following the example of the men, he settled down in his own bed with Larral serving as a pillow, keeping his upper mind, still, full of dogs, with occasional glimpses of ravens.

He wondered what his father had learned. He hoped all the *dyheli* had gotten out of range of the hunting mercenaries. He wondered what it was that the Master had detected—or thought he had detected.

And most of all, he dreaded to hear what the King and his Council had decided. Because he didn't think there was any chance at all that he and his father could handle the Master alone, much less the Master guarded by all his mercenaries. And he wasn't at all sure what his father would do given those orders.

How bad would it be if I asked Roya to knock him unconscious and keep him pinned down until Larral and I can escape on our own and drag him home?

At least he was pretty sure that Dallen would be on his side.

He must have dozed a little, waiting in the darkness, but he woke up immediately at the touch of his father's mind on his, the faint scent of the pine needles of his bed in his nose.

And he woke up with the knowledge that he had to make the most of his time, in case the Master woke up and began nosing about. Before Mags could say anything, he unloaded every single detail that he and Larral had learned, even the things he had seen in his fruitless exploration of the empty buildings. When he finished, there was silence—but not the silence of "absence," because he knew his father was still there. It was more like the silence of someone who was fitting a lot of information into what he already knew. He knew that was what it was. He wanted to scream with impatience, but he restrained himself. It wouldn't do any good and might somehow alert the Master.

Finally his father spoke. *:I'm going to tell you something, but don't overreact to it, Perry. I'm not going to follow orders I was given by the King because the odds of failure are high, and the consequences of failure are even higher. The fact is, we've been ordered to eliminate the Master regardless of cost, and I am not sure what the consequences are going to be of disobeying those orders. I've registered my objections, and I'm waiting now to see what the Council says. I think they will agree with me, but I'm not certain.:*

Perry had been tense, waiting for just that, and now he relaxed.

:I wouldn't allow it anyway,: he heard Roya say, faintly, in the same part of his head that he heard Animal Mindspeech in.

Now, this was interesting. When his father "spoke," using Mindspeech that was so powerful that he could make even people who had no Gifts at all hear him, it felt as if the thoughts were his own, except they were somehow in his father's voice, coming from somewhere near the top of his head.

When he Mindspoke with intelligent animals like Larral and Roya, the words came in other, very distinct voices, did not feel as if they were his own, and came from somewhere right between his ears.

He'd had the feeling for some time now that Mags could not hear what Roya and Larral were saying when they Mindspoke this way, and this pretty much confirmed his guess. Evidently Roya did not want Mags to know this particular fact, so he replied the same way. *:Why not?:*

:Nothing to gain, everything to lose,: came the terse response. *:If you get taken, this Master will find out about my herd.:*

Well, that's good, he said, where his father could "hear" him. *It means I won't have to figure out a way to escape on my own so I can hit you in the head, tie you to Dallen, and get out of here.*

He sensed his father actually chuckling at that. *:We are trying to think of a way to make the Master believe there is something besides us out here. I thought of trying to invoke the* vrondi *to watch him, but there's no telling if the Heartstone under the Palace will talk to the King, and I don't know any real magic except the Truth Spell.:*

He blinked up at the ceiling. *Well, you can get in here at any time, I think. Larral can get you in under the palisade, you can get over the fence around the compound, drop me a rope, and the two of us and Larral can get out the same way you came in. But that will tell the Master that you're here.*

:So we save that for an emergency. If you think you are in danger, we'll act and then retreat back to the Valdemar Border.:

Then something occurred to him. *Can Roya find some Hawkbrothers? I would think they'd have something to say about this Master.*

There was a pause. *:He says he has already sent his son with half of the herd to do so.:*

Then I think maybe we ought to wait until we know whether or not they are going to come down here and do something about him. He didn't know a lot about the Tayledras, only what was written in some of the histories about Herald Vanyel, but they certainly seemed formidable enough . . . and the Master probably threatened them as much as he did Valdemar. So maybe Roya could get some Hawkbrothers to intervene, even though this was no longer their territory.

You and Roya should tell them about the city too, if you can get their attention. They might be willing to come down to look at it as well as deal with the Master.

:You're sure you are in no immediate danger?:

He considered this; he felt that as long as the Master thought he was daft, he was safe. *I'm probably still safer than you. The captain seems to like me, the men aren't bullying me because of the dogs, and the Master thinks I'm daft and not worth bothering about.*

:All right then. Let me know the moment that changes. Send a raven if you have to. I will contact you again tomorrow.:

And then—there was the absence that meant his father was "gone."

:All right. Now we can talk,: Roya said, still faint and far, but audible. *:I will knock your father out if he changes his mind and tries to attack the Master alone. If that's what you want.:*

:It is *what I want. Please!:*

He sensed Roya chuckling. *:I have Dallen's assent. While I understand your King's reasoning, that it is better for a few to fall for the good of the herd, I sense that the Master knows more of Valdemar than you think he does. And if he got his hands on your father, Dallen, or both, he would learn still more. Meanwhile I have something I wish you to do. The next time you and the pack go off to hunt, I want you to go* here.:

Roya planted a very clear path in his head of how to get from the gate to where "here" was.

:There is a firebird and its mate and young there. If you can speak to them and they will listen to you . . . we will have a distraction for the Master. Something he is not expecting.:

Perry's eyes widened. He knew exactly what Roya meant. A firebird could, literally, start fires. And if they wanted a distraction . . . Perry could show the firebird where to start carefully situated fires. In fact, working with the ravens, the lot of them could create "campfires" out in the forest that could be spotted from the city, fires that would have no one around them when mercenaries came running to attack whatever had built them. That would give the impression that the city was being watched by something the Master could not detect.

:Why haven't you gone?: he asked.

:Because it is too near the city and the Master for my comfort. I do not want him to discover there are any of my kind here either. Particularly if he does not already know about us.:

:They'll run out of meat again soon enough. Will the birds stay near the nesting site for a while?:

:They should. There is a huge thicket of a sort of berry they like and lots of insects. I don't think they will leave for at least two fortnights.:

He felt a rush of elation, because it wouldn't be more than a day or two before he was sent out to hunt again. *:That's plenty of time. I'll tell you how it goes. You're brilliant, Roya!:*

:I know. Sleep well, clever foal.:

Mags broke off his conversation with his son to contact Arville. He had a headache beginning between his eyebrows, and he was sure that Arville, who was not in the least used to doing this much Mindspeaking, was feeling even worse.

He was right; he could tell just from the tenor of Arville's thoughts that the man was in pain. *:Mags, the Heartstone, whatever that is, won't talk to the King without you there. And they sure didn't like it when I told them what you told me, about it being too risky to take on the Master with just the four of you, but they agreed that you're right. So they are going to try and make a better plan.:*

He felt the tension in his chest and neck ebb a little. *:That's good. All right, this is what Perry learned. You can pass it on to them, and then that will be all for tonight. And for most of tomorrow, I think.:* He quickly passed everything on to Arville and to Pelas, knowing that the Companion would remember what Arville did not. *:You might ask the Chronicler to see if he can find any references to a city like that. It's like nothing I've ever heard of. Perry is right, the composition of the buildings he was in makes no sense, unless they are meant to house units of a communal society, and . . . I've never yet heard of a communal society that held together long enough to construct a city like that.:*

He felt Arville's sigh. *:I don't understand a half of what you just said, but I'll let them know,:* the old man said wearily. *:Is that all?:*

:That's all. You're a lifesaver, Arville. Get some rest as soon as you can.:

The assent was wordless, rather than concrete thoughts, and they both broke the connection at the same time.

:I know of a society that is communal that would hold together long enough to build a city,: Roya said suddenly. *:In fact,* hertasi *could and would build anything they chose to.*

But those buildings were made for humans. I've never known hertasi *to serve anything other than Tayledras, and Tayledras have never lived in cities like that. They only live in Vales with a Heartstone. Not only that, but I cannot imagine how those buildings would be in such good shape after being clearly abandoned unless there was magic involved in the creation and preservation of them.:*

"Why would anyone waste magic on making buildings?" he wondered aloud.

But thinking of real magic got his mind going in an entirely different direction. Suddenly a very horrible thought occurred to Mags. "What if the Master is not merely the most powerful Mindspeaker I've ever seen?" he asked, looking across his little fire into Roya's dark eyes. "What if he's also a magician? What if *the magic* is what's making his Mindspeech so strong?"

Roya's chin stopped working, and he stared back at Mags. *:You've seen this before, haven't you? Magic working with Mindgifts, I mean.:*

He nodded. "When I was just a Trainee. And if I were anywhere near where I could get a fast messenger to my cousin, I would ask him for advice. But I have seen exactly that, and I wonder if this is the secret to his power. It's entirely possible that he is using blood magic to increase his Mindmagic powers."

:That might explain why he is eating human flesh,: Roya observed.

"It does? But—"

:He may not be formally trained. He may be blundering his way. If he honestly does not know it is merely the act of slaying someone that allows a Mage to siphon off their magic power, and thinks he must actually consume their flesh to gain the power, that would explain his cannibalism.: Roya went back to chewing his cud.

Mags shuddered. Just when he thought he had seen the

depths to which a human could go . . . someone else came along that proved he hadn't. "Is there any way we can use this against him? If he is merely blundering his way around using magic?"

:I suggest that the less we have to do with him directly, the better. I am working on a way to distract him from you, me, and the herd for the moment. And quite frankly, he's insane. I am not even going to attempt to predict most of his behavior.:

"Oh, gods." Mags pinched the bridge of his nose between his thumb and forefinger. "I am never going to be able to sleep tonight."

Roya cocked his head to the side. *:Oh, well, if that is all you are worried about at the moment—:*

And it was not until morning that he awoke.

———————

Perry startled up out of sleep with an inarticulate exclamation as Larral shoved a cold nose into his ear. But a moment later, all the dogs began barking as the captain shoved the door to the kennel open. Perry hushed them as the captain peered inside, his figure silhouetted against the early morning sky. "Dog-boy?" he said. "Are you awake?"

As if anyone could have slept through all the dogs going off like that.

"Dog-boy," Perry affirmed.

"Can you and the dogs hunt today?" the captain asked.

"Yus," Perry replied shortly, and he held back his glee.

"Can you and the dogs hunt men?" the captain asked, which took him aback for a moment. But he quickly recovered, pulled himself up out of his pine-needle bed, and walked over to the door.

"Got smell?" he asked, matter-of-factly, crossing his fingers and hoping that question didn't betray too much intelligence.

"Not one of our men," the captain amended.

He scratched his head, dislodged a pine needle, pulled it out of his hair and chewed on it for a long while. "Long hunt," he said, tentatively. "Slow hunt."

"That's all right," the captain said with relief. "It's even all right if you don't find anything."

"Go now?" Perry asked.

"Yes, now." The captain turned to go out into the courtyard, and Perry and the dogs followed him.

There were only four men out there today, which made sense, considering that Perry was fairly certain the Master had decided on this harebrained scheme, and the captain didn't expect to find anything. However, the captain had the sense to not put dogs that were starving out in the field; the helpers turned up candlemarks early with the usual barrows, and the dogs were allowed a half-ration breakfast, while Perry was given a half a loaf of bread stuffed with cress and cooked pork, which he ate while the dogs were fed.

Then they all headed out, through the city and straight out through the gate. Which was perfect, since that matched Roya's instructions.

When they reached the forest, the lead man of the four mercenaries gave Perry a sideways look, but Perry ignored him. He crouched down among the dogs and gave them their orders. Obediently they spread out along the forest edge, noses to the ground, diligently hunting, then disappeared into the underbrush. Perry looked back at the four men.

"Will they call if they find something?" the leader asked.

Perry nodded and disappeared into the forest, following them.

Of course, he knew they weren't going to find anything. And the mercenaries probably knew they weren't going to find anything as well—after all, *they* had been hunting all over these woods since the Master got that burr up his butt. Perry was pretty sure they were going to go just far enough into the forest to find a good spot to lounge in and make themselves comfortable for the rest of the day—or however long it took the pack to make a circuit of the city.

Well, this was just going to give him the best chance possible to find those firebirds without any interference.

Once deep enough inside the forest, he gave the pack their orders to spread out and search in a big circle around the city, but join him when he called them. Obviously he did not want a pack of dogs startling the firebirds and getting themselves—and possibly him!—hurt. Once they were well on their way, he and Larral made sure they were on the right path and then began a slow and careful approach.

He remembered Arville's story about his encounter—or rather, encounters—with firebirds. The male had been stealing small, fireproof, shiny or bright-colored objects from a village on Arville's Circuit, and the villagers had accused a servant girl of taking them. It had been Arville and Ryu who had traced the odd scent from the site of one of the thefts to the firebird's "bower," where he courted his female. Arville had shown the villagers what was going on, and the villagers had proudly protected the bower, collecting the occasional brilliant, fiery feathers the male dropped and making sure to put out plenty of bright, fireproof, worthless things for him to take to build his bower with. Every couple of years, Arville had taken the opportunity to check on the village, and for at least twenty years the firebird had nested there faithfully, and they had protected the pair.

To be sure, firebird feathers were incredibly rare and worth a small fortune, so it had certainly been in the villagers' interest to protect and nurture them. But nevertheless, it was still a good thing for them to have done.

So Perry had a pretty good idea what he was going to encounter. And he knew he would have to somehow contact the birds before they saw him and reacted to him and Larral—though they would probably ignore Larral if they had ever seen *kyree* before. Then he would have to see if they were intelligent enough to work with.

Then would come the last, and easiest, part: trade them shiny things in return for working with the ravens to start small, controlled fires to keep the Master and his mercenaries busy chasing shadows.

And just when he was wondering if the firebirds had moved on, despite Roya's assurances that they weren't going to for at least a fortnight—he encountered six curious and very . . . fiery . . . minds.

And to his shock, the two biggest and brightest sensed *him,* too!

:Who/what/where?: came the startled response. *:What want? Show self!:*

He exchanged a look with Larral, both of them equally shocked. *:What do you think?:* he asked the *kyree.*

:I think we'd better,: Larral replied. *:Before they come hunting for us. . . .:*

18

He and Larral moved cautiously toward the spot where—if Roya's instructions were correct—they would find the fire-birds' current territory. It wasn't easy. Those berry bushes Roya had mentioned were brambles—which Roya had not bothered to mention, but which explained why the mercenar-iess hadn't spotted the firebirds. There was a way through them, but . . .

:We're coming as fast as we can,: he called to the two adults. At least, he assumed it was the two adults. *:There are a lot of thorns.:*

Rather than words, he got concepts. *We know* and *this is how we like it,* or at least, he thought that would be the right sense for what he was picking up. And as they made their careful way through the brambles, he had an idea. If he was going to prove he was trustworthy, it wouldn't be a bad thing to have not only Larral but another former Tayledras ally along.

He sent his mind looking for the ravens and soon found

them, and he asked if one or more could join him. They, of course, wanted to know why—and what was in it for them, of course.

:I'm meeting the firebirds, and I don't want to be turned into a human torch.:

He got a sense of *oh, those conceited bastards. . . .* and they were definitely laughing at him.

But two of them also agreed to join him, and before he and Larral had managed to struggle into the clearing, they were following along, hopping from branch to branch of the brambles over his head.

Arville hadn't gone into a very long description of the firebirds, only that they were "really pretty," so he hadn't been sure of what to expect. But when he got into the open space and looked up at them, where the six of them perched in their nesting tree, they took his breath away.

The male, of course, was the most splendid. He was about the size of an eagle, though he had a straight beak rather than a hooked one. The first thing you noticed about him, though, was the literal fire aura that surrounded him. He literally looked as if he were on fire. Only after you took that fact in did you notice he had a long, sweeping tail of about eight lobe-ended feathers, that his colors shaded from blue on his head to purple on his shoulders and rump, to red on his wings and tail, to yellow on his primaries. His eyes glittered at them.

The female and the four youngsters were slightly duller versions of the male and had shorter tails.

:You bring the troublemakers.: The male eyed the ravens, who looked right back at him with amusement.

:They're my friends,: he said, not entirely sure they were going to back him up—

:We are! We are!: they affirmed, with laughter in their Mindvoices.

:You come from evil place,: the firebird continued.

He took a deep breath. *:I am with Roya and his herd,:* he

countered, projecting an image of the King-Stag. *:We want to rid the place of evil. Then you and your family could live here without fear of arrows and evil men.:*

The bird looked at him, first with one eye and then the other, as though he was not quite sure what to make of this peculiar human who could Mindspeak and proposed getting rid of other humans.

:We help how?: the answer finally came, and he could breathe again.

The firebirds flew down out of their tree and stood on the ground in a small group, a little apart from the ravens, while he demonstrated what he wanted from them. The ravens and the firebirds were gratifyingly quick at picking up exactly what he wanted them to do—and were just as keen as he was to *not* burn down the whole forest. He showed the ravens how to clear a fire ring down to bare earth, then how to build a starter fire, the kind with kindling at the heart and a cone-shaped starter fire of heavier wood around the kindling.

The ravens proved very clever about finding sticks that were exactly heavy enough, then hammering at weak points with their massive beaks so they broke off to the right length. Then the firebirds practiced snapping off just enough flame to light it without sending the entire construction up at once. The youngsters proved better at this than their parents, perhaps because they weren't able to muster much fire yet. When he was certain they could do exactly what was wanted, he called a halt to the practicing.

:Can you see in the dark?: he asked the male.

He got the equivalent of a snort. *:Easily.:*

:Then wait until after dark to light these.: He turned to the ravens. *:Put the fires where they can be seen from the city. Lighting one or two a night, always in different places, will be best.:*

The ravens were absolutely entranced with this idea. *:Look for us,:* the one that seemed to be serving as the de facto leader said to the male firebird. *:That's where the stick piles will be. We'll be nearby. We want to see the fun when the men come running out of the evil place!:*

:Because of course,: the female firebird said, but she didn't seem put out, *;you are troublemakers.:* However, she also didn't see the point, and she turned to Perry. *:This makes evil go how?:*

:It makes evil look for where we are not,: he replied. *:We need the evil to be confused because he is very strong.:*

:Oh!: exclaimed the female in sudden understanding, although she didn't elaborate. *:So evil thinks enemies in forest.:*

:Right, enemies he can't find or catch.:

The male appeared to be pondering this. *:Crazy, makes him.:* the male cautioned. *:Dangerous maybe.:*

:We'll have to take that chance,: Perry said. *:He's already dangerous.:*

The firebirds all nodded, heads bobbing in perfect synchronization. *:Do this, we will,:* the male agreed.

:This'll be fun!: The ravens were very enthusiastic about the plan. *:Want to see them come running!:*

Larral decided to put his two coppers worth in, finally. *:We have sent to find Tayledras, but we need to keep the evil confused and looking for things that are not us until the Tayledras come.:*

The female tilted her head, and to Perry's mind she looked skeptical. *:If they come,:* she corrected. *:Tayledras not here in long . . . long . . . :*

:If they don't come, we will find a way to remove the evil,: Perry said, with a confidence he in no way felt.

The male and female firebirds put their heads close together for a moment, and Perry understood they were talking to each other in private. The male turned back to him. *:Wood burns,:* he said, flatly. *:City is wood. City burns, evil burns.:*

Oh, great, now the birds wanted to burn down the entire city! :*Probably, but let's not risk that yet. You could set fire to the whole forest, and then where would you be?*:

:*Forest not burn,*: the male said with complete confidence. :*We not let forest burn.*:

Perry just blinked. So they thought they could control an entire burning city? He didn't want to test that. :*Let's just make him think there are enemies he can't find. That may make him tired, fighting shadows. Tired is weak, and weak is easier to kill.*: For a moment, but only a moment, he was appalled at himself for thinking that last. But then he reminded himself that the Master had already murdered many people, had enslaved or effectively enslaved those he'd left alive, and had done worse than enslave the women he'd kidnapped.

The birds—and Larral—certainly didn't seem to have any problem with the idea of killing the Master.

:*Agreed,*: Larral replied.

:*Agreed. For now.*: The birds were a tougher nut to crack than Larral, but at least everyone was satisfied with the current plan.

Now that everything had been sorted out, Perry stood up to go. :*Thank you, friends,*: he said, steeling himself for the difficult task of getting out of the bramble thicket. :*Thank you very much.*:

:*Do not scratch out eyes on way out,*: the male firebird said sardonically—which actually made him laugh a little.

:*I won't,*: he promised, hoping getting out was going to be easier than getting in.

When he was a reasonable distance from the brambles, he sought for and found the dogs. All they had found was a lone sow and her piglets, and since he hadn't said anything about not hunting, they'd surrounded her, killed her themselves, and had a second breakfast. Now they were eager to get back to the kennel and nap, and about a quarter candlemark later, they had caught up with him.

Meanwhile Larral had found where the four men who were supposed to be hunting interlopers were actually lounging about, waiting for the dogs to find something. In another candlemark, Perry and the pack had made their way there.

They all got up when the pack made its appearance, and the one in charge turned immediately to Perry. "Nothing?" he asked.

Perry nodded. "No smell," he said. "No track."

"I thought this was a fool's errand," the man in charge muttered, then raised his voice. "All right, you lot. The Master might argue with us, but even he can't tell a dog that there must be a scent where there isn't one. Back to the compound."

"About time, I'm starving," complained one. "This idea was as daft as Dog-boy. If you ask me, the Master's jumping at shadows."

The one in charge gave him a sharp look.

"Watch your complaining," he warned. "No telling whose eyes the Master is looking out of. "

The man blanched. "Didn't mean no harm," he said uneasily. "Just that we've been out here all day."

The one in charge nodded and motioned for them all to move out. Perry and the dogs brought up the rear this time.

No telling whose eyes the Master is looking out of? That's something more to tell Father. Mags could do that himself, of course, and Perry and his mother could both see the world through the eyes of any creature whose mind they could contact. His mother called it "mind riding," though Perry had never really liked that name, but he had never been able to think of a better one. He wished now that he hadn't taken on the persona of the daft dog-boy; he couldn't ask questions now without betraying himself. So he just led the pack along behind the rest as they made their way back to the city and the compound.

But the moment he set foot in the city again, he noticed a change. Before, it had seemed as if there were a presence, or presences, behind all those blind windows, watching.

Now it seemed as if something had roused those presences. And they were not at all happy about the interlopers in their midst. If he had looked up and seen angry people glaring at him, he would not have been at all surprised.

And he wasn't the only one to feel that way. The men at the gate were uneasy and kept glancing back into the city, and as soon as they set foot on the main street, the four men with him took on the same air of unease, peering up at the buildings or down intersecting side streets.

:I don't feel anything,: Larral said, in answer to his unspoken question. *:But I'm not human, am I? I think this is aimed at humans, people who don't belong here.:*

Certainly the dogs weren't at all disturbed, trotting along calmly, giving no indication that *they* sensed anything at all, much less something wrong.

The sensation of being watched by something hostile only grew with every step they took deeper into the city. *What happened? It wasn't like this when we left this morning!* Could the Master have done something to trigger this effect?

The men, who had been walking quite slowly until now, began to speed up, until by the time the entire group reached the gate to the compound, they were all moving at a brisk trot. Perry was as relieved as the rest of them when the gate slammed shut behind them, and the strange sensation of being watched by hostile eyes slowly faded. Whatever was going on out there in the city, it wasn't affecting anyone in here. *Or at least . . . it's not affecting ordinary people.*

Since no one said anything to him, he ran the dogs over to the kennel, and since it wasn't time for their evening meal—and they'd already helped themselves to wild pig anyway—he turned them out in the yard. They hadn't been running the way they had during the real hunt, so they still had plenty of energy to lope around the yard and play.

He was thinking about what he should do next, when the captain appeared at the door of the kennel, and on seeing him, called to him. "Dog-boy, we need to go to the Big House and the Master. The Master wants to see us now."

Oh, bloody hell! His heart raced in panic. That was the very last thing he wanted to do! What if his outer mind slipped? What if the Master pressed him again.

What if the Master suspected *him* of being the cause of whatever-it-was he had sensed out in the city and out in the forest?

He couldn't, did not dare, allow the Master to get close to him again. And he didn't have to fake feeling terrified.

He stiffened and shook his head wildly. "No! No! Master hurt Dog-boy!" He backed up into a corner and braced himself there, his heart pounding like a drum at a village dance. "No Big House!"

"The Master won't hurt Dog-boy again," the captain said impatiently. "Come on! We must go to the Big House now!"

"Nooooooo!" he wailed, and he projected his fear into the pack until all the dogs came running in from the yard and stood between him and the captain, growling.

The captain took a step back at that and looked from the pack to Perry and back again. Clearly he had no idea what to do next. Obviously the Master had ordered him to bring Perry. Just as obviously he wasn't willing to brave the angry and defensive dogs. And he couldn't order the pack shot—the men needed them too much.

Perry had no intention of going anywhere near the Master, and he'd do whatever he needed to do to keep it that way. Once was enough. Never again! *If he gets inside my head again, I'm dead!* His mouth was dry, and his palms sweating, and the dogs were getting more agitated with every passing moment.

The captain finally swore and stalked off, and Perry slid down the wall and sat on the floor with his arms wrapped around Larral, sweating all over now so his clothing was sodden with fear sweat. That's where he sat until the helpers came with the dogs' dinner.

That was when he noticed there was one less helper.

After darkness fell, he had a good wash to get all the stinking fear sweat off himself. Then once he was clean and in clean clothing again, he crept out of the kennel and went in search of the captain. As he had expected, he found the captain with some of the men, in the tack room where he had been before.

". . . and he's on some kind of a tear," the captain was saying. "I haven't seen him like this since he kidnapped us all and brought us here." Perry made a slight sound, and everyone looked up and straight at him, in various postures of alarm, until they saw who it was.

"Dog-boy bad," he whimpered, as the captain stared at him. "Bad Dog-boy."

As he had hoped, the captain softened. "Nah, it's all right, Dog-boy," he said. "You were right to be afraid. Come here."

Perry crept over to the captain and sat at his feet, like a dog himself. "There, now, see? We're all friends again," the captain said soothingly. "You tell your dogs we're friends."

"Friends," Perry repeated obediently. He actually thought about licking the captain's hand like a dog, but he decided that would be overplaying his hand.

"So what'd he say?" one of the men interrupted.

"Well, he didn't like it when I told him the dogs found nothing out there. And he kept ranting about there being enemies in the city. I finally told him what Dog-boy said about there being spirits out there, and he just . . . stopped. Just froze for so long I thought he was god-struck."

"Cap'n, have you been out there lately?" one of the men asked. "I dunno about spirits, but there's *something* in the city, and it don't much care for us. It's like thousands and thousands of eyes just. . . . staring. Angry. This place wants us *gone.*"

"Well, when he snapped out of his fit, he started rantin'. Said that the *White Riders* were responsible for all this. That we had to get our hands on one, and his horse too. I told him, I'd never heard of no White Riders, and the boys stationed down at the inn hadn't told me about no White Riders, and he said he was gonna start sending us east, patrols of us, until we found one and brought it to him."

Perry stiffened at that, but the captain didn't notice. "Did he say why?" the man that had spoken up asked.

"Said that the White Riders were the key to everything, that once he got hold of one, he'd be able to do anything he wanted to." The captain shook his head. "I dunno what he could do that he can't do now. Truth is, I'm scared to find out."

"That's dafter than Dog-boy," the man replied. "What the Master said, not you bein' scared, cap'n."

He might have said more, but at that moment they all heard the sound of running feet coming toward this building out of the darkness, then another of the mercenaries slammed into the doorpost, panting. "Cap'n! There's watchfires in the forest!"

"What!" The captain leaped to his feet, sending Perry tumbling. "Arm yourselves! On the double!"

Perry scampered out of the way, then slipped out of the building in the confusion and ran to the kennel, just in case the captain might decide to use the dogs. But evidently that didn't occur to the man—or maybe he didn't want the pack running around on the loose in the dark—because he and the now-armed men charged right past the stable, making for the gate on the double.

They still hadn't returned when Perry felt his father's touch on his mind, and he quickly unburdened himself of everything that had happened. *What's going on with the city?* he asked. *Is that something you or Roya did?*

:It's not us,: Mags replied. *:I don't know what it is, but, Perry, I want you out of there now. I don't like what you just told me about the Master, not at all, and you're right, you don't dare get into his hands a second time. Things are cascading out of control. If they take you out for a hunt—run. If they don't, I'll come for you. But I want you out of there before three more days pass.:*

Not half as much as I want to be out! Perry replied, trying not to sound as frantic as he felt. *But, Father, he knows about Heralds, even if he doesn't know about them by name—*

:I've already warned the ones on Circuit in this area. They're all taking shelter at Guard posts.:

Perry hesitated. *Father, if he can see through the eyes of his men—and if he was powerful enough to take over the entire company when they were three days' march away from here—I'm not sure even being with the Guard is going to be safe.*

:Neither am I. But one problem at a time. Stay away from him, Perry. And keep those shields up. I love you, and I'll get you out of there.:

And then his father was gone.

The captain and his men returned before Perry was able to get to sleep. He heard the men trudging back to their improvised barracks, though not one of them spoke. He peeked out of the kennel, and their posture was that of exhaustion. He went back to his bed; he must have drifted off, because the next thing he knew, Larral was nudging him awake. It was still dark, but he could tell by the sudden draft that the kennel door was open, and there was a light at the door. "Dog-boy?" the captain said, holding the lantern over his head and peering around.

"Dog-boy," he replied, standing up so the captain could see him.

The captain moved over to his stall and sat down on the stool Perry kept there. Perry sat down on his bed. "Dog-boy, you said there were spirits in the forest?"

Perry nodded, warily.

"Have they come into the city?"

Now that was a question he hadn't been prepared for. He shivered, and stuck his finger in his mouth. *Now how the hell do I say "I don't know" without looking less daft than I want to?*

Fortunately the captain solved his problem for him. "So there is something in the city? But it might not be the same thing as in the forest?"

He nodded. The captain sucked on his lower lip. "All right, thank you, Dog-boy." Perry expected him to get up and leave, but he didn't. Instead, he remained sitting there, and after a moment, he began speaking again. "The Master's in a rare taking. We found watchfires out in the forest and not a sight nor sign of who made them. And he keeps insisting there's something in the city, and all we can find is dust. Your dogs routed out nothing, but I can feel it, and so can most of the men. And now you. . . ." He sighed and shook his head. "The Master's up to no good. That is, he's not been up to any sort of good ever, but . . ." He paused for a moment. "There's daft, and there's evil. And there's daft *and* evil. I'm thinking he's both, and he's about to crack, and I dunno what he's going to do when he does."

There was a long silence then as Perry sucked on his finger and looked up into the captain's face. And he knew this man had gone along with the kidnapping and worse of perfectly innocent people . . . but it was hard not to feel sorry for him. And maybe he and his men had just been picked up and swept along by this terrible force that was the Master, and they were no more to blame than a log swept up in a flood is to blame if it hits someone and kills him.

The captain sighed again and patted Perry's head. "And you can no more understand what I'm saying than one of your dogs, can you, lad. But there's some comfort in saying things out loud, and at least I know the Master ain't spying on me through your eyes."

"Master bad," Perry said, tentatively.

The captain patted Perry's head again. "Master very, very bad. Master is the worst person I've ever encountered. And that's saying something."

They sat there together in complete silence for a very long time. The captain brooded, his face in shadows, inscrutable. Perry would have liked to have gone to sleep—and probably could have and the captain wouldn't have thought twice about it—but he felt that he didn't want to leave the man alone with thoughts that were surely dark ones.

But he couldn't help it—he kept yawning hugely. After the third time, the captain roused himself from his thoughts, patted him on the head again, and stood up, taking the lantern with him. "You're a good lad, Dog-boy. Better than many men I've known. Get some sleep, and let's hope the Master doesn't break out in some new outrage in the morning."

He left as abruptly as he had arrived, and at this point, despite the fact that his nerves were stretched to the breaking point, Perry was so tired he fell asleep.

He woke when the helpers arrived.

Two of them.

He didn't say anything, but the missing one today was the one who had been the dogmaster. The dogs noticed and made circuits of the yard and the kennel, looking for him, until he finally gathered them all together and managed to convey that the former dogmaster was dead.

Dogs understand death, though usually only if they see that death in front of them. Normally they only understand inexplicable—to them—absence. But Perry made it clear enough to them this time, and they understood it enough to all sit down at once, point their noses to the sky, and howl out their grief.

That thoroughly unnerved the other poor helpers, who went out into the yard to nervously clean up the latrine corner and fill the big water troughs out there.

It also brought one of the mercenaries running. He looked around in bewilderment at the howling dogs, at Perry with his arms around Larral, and the expression on his face turned from alarm to baffled confusion.

But he didn't get a chance to say anything to Perry, because at that exact moment, there was another commotion from the Big House, and he turned to see what it was.

Perry hushed the dogs in their grief, trying his best to reassure them, as he went to the door to see what it was. And felt as if he had suddenly been dropped into an icy river.

The Master had come out of the Big House.

He was carried in a sedan chair on the shoulders of four stony-faced men, who may or may not have also been mercenaries. They might have been some of the men who had been kidnapped; the only thing that Perry was sure of was that they were certainly under his mental control, for they showed absolutely nothing: no fatigue, no interest in what was going on around them, no resentment at being forced to carry the Master as if they were slaves—nothing.

The captain came running as the Master waited in the yard with an air of impatience. And something it took Perry a while to identify, and when he did, he was struck dumb with surprise.

It was fear.

The Master, who could take over an entire mercenary company with his mind from three days' march away, was terrified.

The captain ran past the kennel, panting, and stopped just short of the Master's chair. "Sir!" he said, snapping to attention. "At your command, Master."

When the Master spoke, instead of the menacing purr his voice had held the last time Perry had seen him, he was shrill, and his voice shook with anger and terror. "I want every man here! Inside these walls! I want the gate locked and barred! Nothing comes in! No one leaves! *Now!*"

"Yes, *sir!*" the captain snapped, and turned to his men, who stood there in a kind of disbelieving paralysis. "You, you, and you! Down to the gate, bring the men back on the double! You and you—get ready to slam the inner gate shut and slide the bar as soon as they are inside. *Move!"*

The five men he had singled out broke into a run. The Master watched them for a moment, then the men carrying his sedan chair turned it and marched back to the Big House.

The captain stood where the Master left him, staring after the man. Finally he shook his head. "So it's a state of siege against invisible enemies now, is it?" he said to the empty air. And he turned and headed back toward the barracks and the kitchen, presumably to consult with the cook about rationing.

:*Well . . . this is interesting,*: Larral said. :*I will need to find a place where I can dig under the fence.*:

:*Is it possible to find a spot that's hidden in here?*: Perry asked skeptically.

:*I think so. I'll just have to be extremely careful about—*:

Whatever Larral had been about to say, Perry would never hear it. Because at that moment, that sensation of being watched by thousands of hostile eyes came back, except now it was here, inside the compound. And he wasn't the only one to feel it;all around him he could see the men looking startled, or glancing around in a panic, or just holding very, very still, as if by doing so they could escape the wrath of whatever it was that was glaring at them.

:*Well . . . this is different,*: Larral said, calmly. :*I feel it too.*:
:*You do?*:

:*But not as if it's directed at* me. *I just sense a general hostility. Indulge me a moment and try something.*:

Perry turned his head slowly to look at the *kyree.* :*Try what?*:

:*Talk to it.*:

Was Larral insane? :*With the Master awake and paying attention? Have you lost your mind?*:

:*The Master can't read Animal Mindspeech. Use that. Talk*

to it like you'd speak to the dogs, in feelings and pictures. Tell it you're not a part of any of this. That you're here against your will.: Larral's tail swayed a little, encouragingly. *:The worst that will happen, after all, is nothing.:*

:All right,: Perry said, with extreme skepticism, and he tried to broadcast those extremely complex concepts in the simple forms of emotions and images.

Finally he closed his eyes to concentrate better. After a while, as sweat began to prickle his scalp, he felt whatever it was slowly turning to focus all of its attention on *him.*

And then . . . as he repeated his images and feelings over and over, including memories of the Master trying to turn his brain inside out, suddenly, it was as if someone had completely cut off a stream of water. He opened his eyes, a lightness coming over him as he realized that he was no longer the target of that terrible regard.

He could still sense it, but as an observer, perhaps the same way Larral sensed it. He looked down to see Larral looking up at him expectantly.

:It worked!: he exclaimed.

:I thought it might,: Larral replied. *:I don't know what this thing is . . . I suppose it is something like the 'soul' of the city, or maybe a sort of* vrondi *. . . but the longer the Master has been here, the more it has been rousing. And now the Master has done something to awaken its wrath.:*

:Blood magic?: Perry asked.

:Some particularly bad blood magic,: Larral confirmed. *:And if this felt uncomfortable for us . . . I do not think I would care to be the Master right now.:*

The oppressive tension continued to build over the compound; the mercenaries huddled together in uncertain groups, as if afraid to face the unrelenting pressure of the presence alone. The helpers got the dogs' evening meal as usual, then, instead of staying to clean, headed for the Big House and disappeared into it, as if they had been ordered there. Perry retreated back into the kennel and closed the door as the last of the men that had been recalled from the main gate and from patrolling the wall closed and barred the gate into the compound.

His helpers did not reappear, and he had the sinking suspicion he was never going to see them again. Gazing at the Big House through the cracked door, he thought he knew what had finally awakened the presence and aroused its ire. The Master might be insane, but he wasn't stupid; if you are going to use blood magic to raise a lot of power in a hurry, it isn't your servants who are going to be sacrificed or your soldiers, it's those who are the most expendable. People you can do

without. Prisoners, in fact, and those who won't be missed.
The cripples. The kidnap victims, who might rebel, are certainly expendable.

And I haven't seen that boy in the last couple of days.

He closed the door, but closing it did nothing about the
images moving through his mind. It made him physically ill to
think that all of this could be his fault. If he hadn't decided on
his own to find out what was going on . . . the Master wouldn't
have gotten it into his head that there was something spying
on him. Things would still be the same for the people who had
been here; maybe life was horrible for some, but at least they
were still living. If he'd just obeyed orders, they might still be
alive now.

He'd thought that working in Haven's poorer quarters had
inured him to a lot, but the thought that the Master must
surely have slaughtered all of his kidnapping victims by now,
and that he might be to blame for that, had him rattled.

He was just glad the presence had decided to leave him and
Larral alone. If he'd had to cope with that feeling of guilt *and*
the smoldering anger of the presence, he wasn't sure he'd
have stayed sane.

But if it was my fault—would that thing have sensed that?
Surely it would have. Surely it wouldn't have decided to leave
me alone. He wanted to believe that, but could he? It made
him want to open himself up to the thing out there again and
confront it, ask it if *he* was to blame . . . and yet at the same
time, he knew he couldn't, wouldn't do that, because he
couldn't handle the answer if it was "yes."

He sensed the terrible regard of the being out there press-
ing down on everyone in the compound except for himself and
Larral. He knew the mercenaries were close to snapping, and
he didn't want to be visible if one or more of the men broke
under the strain. True, he could not possibly be blamed by
anyone for this unknown *thing* out there, pounding everyone
with its anger, but—under that onslaught of anger, people

were not going to act rationally. He was not one of them, he was a stranger, and alien, even inferior—and he was smaller and weaker than any of them—and that made him a potential target regardless of logic.

As the sun dropped, the tension rose. And he wasn't immune to it. Although he was no Empath, nor a human Mindspeaker, the emotions of fear and dread were so prevalent out there that even the dogs sensed them; they milled unhappily around the yard, clearly not wanting to go out for their usual run, too restless to stay put and too upset to work off their energy in play.

Finally darkness drove the dogs inside the kennel, where they lay down in small panting groups, unable to sleep, Outside the kennel walls, flickering torchlight blossomed, visible over the top of the walls around the yard. He paced inside the walls of the kennel, as restless as the dogs, until he couldn't bear it any longer. He had to look and see what was happening out there in the courtyard.

What he saw sent ice up his spine.

The men—all of them, as far as he could tell—stood in motionless, scattered groups around the compound, holding lit torches. He shaded his eyes with his hand so that he could look closer. The faces of the nearest were utterly blank, but their eyes—their eyes held helpless terror.

There was only one thing that could mean. The Master had taken control of them. Probably the only reason Perry had been spared was because the Master needed the dogs—and to have the dogs, he needed Perry, needed him free and able to act normally. The dogs wouldn't obey commands if he didn't act normally.

Somewhere near the front of the compound, he heard shouting. It was too far away, with the Big House between him and the shouter, and the voice was too uncontrolled, for him to make out words, but it was clearly the Master, shrieking incoherently at someone.

No, not someone. Some*thing*. The Master shouted at the presence, probably daring it to do more than just glare at them.

:*Something is about to break.*: Larral came up alongside him, ears pointed at the noise. :*I think the Master might have been goaded into action. Be ready. This might be our only chance.*:

He nodded. Larral was right. The only question was—chance for *what?* To escape? Or a chance to eliminate the Master? Was it even possible to get near someone who could control an entire mob of people when he chose?

Even as he wondered that, the Master's voice rose an octave, and his words became clear.

"*Go!*" he screamed. "*Burn it! Burn it* all!"

And now the men moved.

And as the two men nearest it unbarred the gate, and the rest began a stumbling run out into the night-shrouded city, the Master's voice broke in the laughter of the mad.

Roya's watchers had come running that afternoon with the news that the Master's fighters had abandoned their posts at the gate of the city and left those gates standing wide open. Mags, Dallen and Roya had raced to a spot where they could overlook that part of the city where the gates were, and now that they were here, it was clear that something very strange was going on.

Mags felt a very real, and very powerful presence looming above him, one not unlike the presence that inhabited the Haven Heartstone in the basement of the Palace. Except this presence was much more . . . awake than that one was. And where the entity in the Heartstone was unemotional, this one was nothing but emotion, and that emotion was rage.

And even as he wondered if his mere existence out here

had somehow called up a sort of *vrondi* in response to his wishing he could do so, Roya's words in his mind told him he had guessed wrong.

:It's the spirit of the City,: Roya said, *:I have heard of such things, but I have never seen them. It has been roused by something, and what roused it has enraged it.:*

The entity's attention was concentrated inward, not outward, so at least it wasn't them it was angry with. *:Something the Master did?:* he hazarded.

:Likely,: Roya said shortly. *:It is . . . letting its anger be known, concentrating its rage on them. I would not wish to be standing in the Master's place right now. Or that of his men, to be honest.:*

He tried to imagine what it must be like, having that white-hot glare of anger concentrated on you, unable to escape it, and the first thing that came to his mind was that his son was out there, under it. *Perry . . .* he thought, with alarm. Immediately, and trying not to panic, he sent his thoughts flying in the direction of his son, in flagrant disregard of the fact that the Master might detect him. But Dallen and Roya had already anticipated that was what he would do, and they shielded him until he touched Perry's mind, found him unhurt, though unsettled, and knew he was all right.

He removed himself without contacting Perry, withdrew behind the shelter of his shields as well theirs, and looked soberly at Roya. "What have we done?" he asked, not at all rhetorically. Because he was pretty certain that this had been their doing, even though he wasn't sure how.

:Goaded the Master into something he would have done anyway,: Roya replied, sounding very sure of himself. He glanced at Dallen, who nodded. *:We did nothing to rouse this creature; it awoke because of something the Master did. I think we can both guess what that was. Blood magic requires blood and death, after all. I suspect the thing was already awakening the first time the Master murdered someone for his*

power; now the Master has killed not one but several victims, and the entity is fully awake and outraged.:

:All we did was hasten what the Master was going to do anyway,: Dallen confirmed.

Roya bobbed his head. *:We are now in the unfortunate position of having to react, rather than act. Tempered by the fact that the Master will not be acting on us; he'll be acting against the entity, so whatever* he *does, he won't be ready for what* we *do.:*

"I just want to get Perry out of there!" he said desperately.

:And this will give us a chance to do that,: Roya stated. *:But we will need to be ready to move as soon as that chance presents itself.:*

For the first time in a very, very long time he felt absolutely helpless. *I don't know anything about magic, I don't know this place, I don't know what the hell is in that city and . . . I've never gone up against someone who is a stronger Mind-speaker than I am.* Nothing in his own training, nor in those borrowed memories of the Sleepgivers, seemed to apply here. To be honest, he was terrified, and completely out of his depth, and for a moment he felt himself flailing.

Then he steadied himself. The Master wasn't ready for them, and there were three of them to his one. Dallen and Roya were powerful in their own right. *We'll improvise,* he reminded himself. *I'm good at that.* But to do that, he needed to see what was going on.

"I think we should move into the city," he said, finally. "We can't do or see anything from here."

Roya considered that, his tail switching restlessly. Finally he nodded, though with obvious reluctance. *:I think you are right, but I don't like the idea of being pinned in by all those walls.:*

"I don't blame you," Mags replied, mounting Dallen. They had been in such a hurry he hadn't bothered to tack Dallen up at all. Dallen wasn't wearing a saddle, but that had never mattered that much. And it wasn't as if a Companion ever needed a bridle. Really, saddle and bridle were for the convenience of the Herald, not the Companion.

:We should go slowly and carefully,: Dallen cautioned. *:They might be waiting in ambush just past the gate. If you probe for thoughts only a little ahead of us, you should be able to find anyone lying in wait without alerting the Master.:*

He nodded. "Right. Sprint across the empty space, we'll take cover just inside the gate, and I'll look ahead." He hunkered down on Dallen's back, and the Companion leaped into a gallop, with Roya barely a nose behind.

Once inside the gates, Roya shied off to the right, while Dallen jumped left, both of them ending up peeking around the corners of the buildings that stood just inside the entrance. But there was no one in sight, or within a limited range of his Mindspeaking, and briefly, peering through the growing shadows as the sun sank lower to the horizon, he had the dizzying impression that he was looking into one of those places where mirrors were set up to reflect each other into infinity. Every building looked exactly like every other building. This wasn't illusion caused by shadows; the buildings shimmered with a dim silver light of their own, the last of the sunlight reflecting off their walls. He made out each identical building clearly. It was disorienting; it looked nothing like any city he had ever been in before.

Artificial. Where are the shops? Where are the inns? That should be the first thing a visitor sees to a city. This looks like a city that was built by someone or something that had never seen a real city before, someone who only knows a city is made up of buildings.

Well, that was going to make sneaking through it more challenging . . . he dismounted. *:Follow me,:* he said to Roya and Dallen. *:This could get interesting.:*

Sneaking with a Companion and a *dyheli* was definitely a challenge. His initial thought was to take to the area behind the houses and tiptoe along the alleys—only to discover there wasn't any such area. There was nothing like a yard immediately behind the building, only a bare width of ground about as wide as a man was tall, and the space that separated the buildings side-to-side was even smaller. There was no back door and no alley. Which gave him the impression that whoever had built the city had also never seen a house before. This . . . this was like a child's dollhouse in a toy city, never meant for use. This place *looked* like a city, and the buildings *looked* like houses, but neither were suitable to actually live in.

Or maybe what had lived in them was nothing like a human.

That doesn't matter. All that matters is figuring out how to use this as cover.

He considered their options. All the while acutely aware of that . . . entity. If he closed his eyes, he could picture it, a great, shadowy, amorphous thing with a strange, blank mask for a face, looming over the city and staring down at the center of it with hatred hot enough to set the buildings on fire.

More than anger, now. Hatred had been added to the anger, a righteous, burning hatred that must sear the soul of anything sensitive enough to feel it.

The image persisted after he opened his eyes; he glanced up, half-expecting to see the looming shadow over his head. Nothing was there. No hint of darkness against the cloudless sky.

Nothing for it then; he followed the path that Roya—who had an excellent nose—sniffed out for them, slipping from building to building and pausing frequently to check the vicinity for the minds of anything human.

They didn't reach the site of the inner compound until dusk, where they were confronted by the closed and barred gates. So far as he could tell, without alerting the Master, all the mercenaries had taken shelter within the compound, frightened out of their wits. Or perhaps the Master had called them back, to protect him against the siege of something that wasn't using conventional weapons. The three of them looked at each other, then both Roya and Dallen wordlessly looked to Mags for an answer.

:We fall back a little,: he decided. *:Just to where we can still see the gates. And we wait to see what happens next.:*

It wasn't a *good* strategy, but it was the best they could do.

And so they waited, aware mostly of how silent it all was, aware of the looming, ominous presence that seemed unaware of them, as the sky darkened and the night came on. And all too close was the mind of the Master, burning with rage, convulsed with fear. Although Mags did not try to read him directly, he sensed that the Master had tried and failed to grapple mentally with the entity, and that it had flowed away from him like so much water. The Master had never encountered such a thing before. It terrified him even as it infuriated him.

It terrifies me! Mags thought. *What* is *this thing? And if it's so angry with the Master, why doesn't it do something besides glare at him?* Not that the glaring wasn't effective, in its way—

—and the vrondi *back in Valdemar can drive a Mage insane just by staring at him.*

:I suspect the empathic projection of anger is *how this thing attacks,:* Roya suggested. *:It's not physical in any sense we recognize—it can't attack directly. This might be all it has. But I cannot imagine trying to weather this for an entire evening, much less days or weeks.:*

Already Mags felt impelled to run out into the middle of the road and shout impotently at the thing, and he wasn't the focus of its power. And the entity certainly showed no signs of tiring. It might be able to do just that: continue the barrage of anger and hatred for days, even sennights, at a time. Could the Master withstand it that long? Could his men?

Can Perry get out somehow while they're occupied with each other?

The sound of a voice screaming broke into his thoughts. Though muffled by the fence, the words were clear enough.

"Come out, you coward! Fight me! Show yourself!" followed by a string of profanity. *"Stop hiding, you motherless bastard! Meet me face to face!"*

Though Mags had never heard this voice before it was clear who it was: the Master himself. It held equal amounts of anger, fear, and arrogance.

:I don't know what he expects,: Roya said dispassionately. *:The thing doesn't have a body, at least not as we understand the idea. How does he expect it to fight him directly?:*

:I don't think he understands that,: Dallen observed. *:If our surmises are correct, and he literally believes he is consuming someone's mage-power by consuming their flesh, he might not understand that something can exist independent of a physical body.:*

"All right, then! I'll show you! I'll burn you out!" the Master shrieked. *"Burn it! Burn it all!"*

And a tremor passed through the shadowy presence, and the anger abated, just a little.

:Or,: Dallen added, *:the Master has discovered that the creature* is *the city. And now the creature knows that he knows this.:*

The bar on the other side of the gate scraped in its holders, and the gate swung open. A half dozen torch-bearing men trotted through the portal, with more coming from behind. Mags, Dallen and Roya shrank back into the shadows, but they needn't have bothered; one look at the mens' faces showed they were staring blankly ahead, completely under the Master's control and oblivious to anything but his commands.

———

It took Perry a moment to realize that the Master meant that literally, that he meant to burn the entire city down around their ears. He ducked back inside the kennel and gathered the restless and anxious dogs around him, then drove images and commands into their heads. Images of the city in flames, a wildfire, which every animal instinctively fears. And images of them running, escaping the city for the forest, and waiting there for him. He repeated those images over and over, as the hounds whimpered with fear and distress, until he was sure they would all obey him. Then he flung the kennel door open and let them loose with a single spoken "Go!" Then he sent the same images into the minds of the horses, maddening them until they broke their tethers and broke down the doors of their stalls and, one by one, raced out the open gates.

The dogs streamed out of the kennel, raced past the Big House, passed the torch-bearing mercenaries, and out the open gates, as the first of the houses just outside the gates blossomed into flame.

The smoke blew in through the open gate as the Master laughed. Firelight cast flailing shadows on the open gates as more houses went up. The wood must have been as dry as tinder. . . .

"There! How do you like that?" the Master crowed. *"Threaten me, will you? I will bring you to your knees!"*

:He's more likely to burn us all to a crisp!: Larral exclaimed. *:The fire's spreading by itself now!:*

Sure enough, there were flames showing about the fence from places where surely the men hadn't reached yet, and sparks being carried aloft by the wind that the fires themselves had created. Heat radiated from outside the fence—warm, and getting hotter by the moment.

:We've got to get out of here ourselves,: Perry replied, grimly. *:But without drawing his attention!:* He looked about, a little wildly, as if some sort of disguise would present itself to him obligingly—

And one did. One of the mercenaries still within the compound stumbled toward him blindly, torch in hand.

Perry tackled him at the knees, bringing him down. The torch rolled away, still burning. The mercenary got to his feet, oblivious, and stumbled on, but Perry had gotten what he wanted.

The torch.

:Run for it, like the dogs,: he told Larral, and setting a blank look on his face, he trotted off clumsily, holding the torch aloft as the others were.

Gusts of heat came at him from the direction of the gate, and now there were flames dancing above the fence halfway around the compound. He passed the Big House and fancied he smelled blood and rotting flesh, and he wondered if it was his imagination. And there was the Master, a torch in his own hand, staring defiantly upward and raving at something. Something that wasn't there except in his own imagination? Perry doubted that. He could feel the edges of the anger, now mixed with something else, that poured down on the Master. *:Don't see me,:* he half ordered, half prayed. *:Don't see me.:*

He passed the Master as Larral dashed out of the gate. Elation blossomed.

And was crushed, as he felt the Master suddenly turn his attention toward him and freeze him where he stood.

"*You!*" the Master shouted. "The dog-boy! *This began with you!*"

And the pain crashed down around him, felling him to the ground, the torch falling from his nerveless hand as he screamed in sudden agony, every nerve on fire with pain.

———

The dogs, and then horses, poured out of the gates as fires sprang up in every building within sight. The pack streamed past the corner where Mags, Roya, and Dallen hid—but one of the blank-faced mercenaries trotted into their building, and they realized that in a moment their hiding place was going to be one more component in the growing inferno.

And Perry was still in there. . . .

Mags swung up onto Dallen's back, and with no further thought for hiding, the three of them galloped up the street between buildings whose windows were sprouting leaves and tongues of flame and in through the open gates. There they paused for a moment, trying to make out anything among all the dancing shadows cast by the flames showing over the walls.

A wordless cry of pain rent Mags' heart, and instinctively he guided Dallen toward it. He barely registered his son, curled in fetal position on the ground. He had eyes only for Perry's attacker, and he flung himself from Dallen's back with his hands outstretched for the bastard's neck.

But the Master saw him coming and evaded him, twisting out of the way like a half-spirit himself, and as he eeled out of range, Mags turned his fall into a controlled tumble, somersaulting twice before leaping to his feet and—

—freezing, as the Master took control of his body.

Only to see a white shape charging the Master and lashing out at him with hooves that would have been lethal had they struck their intended target.

But they struck a good length away, as if Dallen's eyes had tricked him. Dallen screamed with fury, dancing in place, raging, until—

—:*Join me!*: Mags heard, and he joined with Roya, and pulled Dallen into the meld, and the three of them pitted the full force of their combined minds against the Master's.

Fire roared all around them. Heat poured down on them. Sweat poured down his back and face and plastered his hair to his head. They stared into the Master's mad, red eyes, and he stared back at them, seeming to take strength from the inferno around them. They were locked in a mutual, deadly embrace. Mags knew that he and the others dared not turn their attention to escape, or the Master would take control of them one at a time and force them to fling themselves into the flames. They could *see* that in his mind. But the Master dared not try to escape either, or they'd crush him, and bind him, mind and body, and drag him off to face justice.

Deadlock.

Literally.

The longer the fires raged outside that fence, the likelier it was the flames would jump to the compound, and they would all die together.

Mags spared only a heartbeat to look for Perry and saw that he was not where he'd fallen. And that was enough for him. Perry was smart, and he and Larral must have run out the gate, racing ahead of the flames.

Larral would get him back to Arville. Arville would get him home again.

And meanwhile, the deadly peril to Valdemar in the wilderness would be finished; he, Roya, and Dallen would see to that.

He allowed himself a moment of agony at the thought of never seeing Amily, Abi, and Tory again, pain that sent tears of regret burning down his cheeks. *I'm sorry*—he thought.

—and suddenly he was free, as a shriek of pain ended in a horrific gurgling noise.

He stumbled and fell to his hands and knees, and he looked up to see his son, fists clenched at his sides, standing over the writhing, dying body of the Master. There was a knife in the Master's stomach, a gaping hole where his throat had been, and blood on Larral's muzzle.

———————

Perry ran to his father's side, grabbed his shoulder, and tried to tug him to his feet. "Father!" he shouted over the howl of the fire. "Father, we have to go!" Mags looked stunned, or disbelieving, or both maybe, but a moment later, he shook his head and scrambled to his feet. Perry tugged him to where Dallen stood, swaying drunkenly, and shoved him at the Companion, then ran to Roya, who stood with all four legs locked, blinking owlishly.

:ROYA!: he "shouted" into the *dyheli's* mind, which seemed to snap the King-Stag out of his daze. "Roya, we've got to go! We've got to go now!"

Roya shook his head until his ears flapped, danced in place for a moment, and seemed to be his old self again. :*On my back,*: he ordered. :*You'll never make it out on your own two feet.*: Since Mags had already mounted Dallen, this seemed a smart choice to Perry. He jumped up on Roya's back, settled himself with his legs over Roya's forequarters, just behind where the neck met the spine, and grabbed a double-handful of the ridge of hair that formed Roya's "mane."

They ran for the gate.

And stopped.

The twisting street ahead of them was completely engulfed in a solid wall of flames.

And even as they stood there staring, the winds of the fire lofted one burning brand over the wall, then another, and another until there was a virtual rain of fire coming down on the nearest part of the compound—several burning chunks of wood landed against the side of the Big House—and fire began to lick up the walls.

Perry looked wildly around the compound, pummeling his memory. He wouldn't believe there was no way out! There had to be a way to escape! There had to be *someplace* safe in there, someplace they could wait out the—

:*Hey! Not dead, you!*:

A new voice in his head, but one he knew.

Instinctively, he looked up.

It hadn't all been fire*brands* that had lofted over the now-burning fence. Six of the burning objects had been fire*birds!*

:*Want out, you?*:

He gulped, mouth gone dry. :*We can't!*: he replied in despair. :*We're not like you! We can't go through the fire!*:

The male danced his contempt in midair. *:Not stupid, we! With us, no burn, you!:*

"The firebirds say if we follow them, they'll keep us safe!" he gasped to the others.

His father looked up at the hovering firebirds, then at Roya. "Is that true?" he asked, doubtfully, and yet with a voice full of rising hope.

:I don't know. But do we have a choice?: Roya replied.

:Thank you! Thank you!: Perry shouted to the birds. *:Please, get us out of here!:*

:Like the wind, run!: the male cried, and lofted ahead of them, straight toward the flames.

With no prompting, Dallen followed, with Roya close enough to have eaten Dallen's tail, and Larral alongside Roya.

As they passed through the now-burning gate, the flames fanned to either side, and the burning air cooled, just a little. With the male flying just ahead of Dallen's nose, the female just behind Roya's tail, and the four fledglings in formation above their heads, they galloped through a clear place in an inferno like the heart of a furnace, protected by a sort of moving bubble of safety. How the firebirds could even see, Perry had no idea. All *they* could do was follow where the male led, singing as he flew.

It was still hot enough that his nose and mouth were parched in moments and his skin quickly grew hot and tender. And it was a good thing that it could not have taken them more than a dozen heartbeats to gallop free of the worst of the fires, because he didn't think any of them could have gone much farther than that.

Once they were clear and the way ahead of them was nothing more than empty buildings just now showing the first flickers of flame, the firebirds left them, flying up, then curving back, blinding red and yellow against the night sky, to go back to dance among the fires. They kept running, though not at the breakneck speed they'd put on to get clear.

Larral took the lead now, following the scent-trail laid down by the hounds, down the twisting, winding street.

:Fire keep we from forest!: Perry heard the male firebird call in his mind. *:Keep you run!:*

They didn't need to be told twice. They pounded down the street, aware now that the fire had a voice; it thundered and bellowed behind them, demanding more to devour. They were running into a wind, as the fire pulled everything toward itself, including the very air. And when the outer gate came into sight, Perry nearly sobbed with relief.

They rushed through it, across the field of stumps, now brightly illuminated by the inferno behind them, pushing against the wind the fire created and into the darkness and cool shelter of the trees. And there they stopped. The fire had a life of its own now, sucking in air, fire vortexes dancing above the flames, and the wind this generated roared in the tree branches above them. Perry only hoped that the firebirds were right, that they were powerful enough to keep it from jumping into the forest.

Dallen and Roya's flanks heaved with exhaustion as Perry and his father slid off their backs and turned to stare at the burning city.

"Is—*it* still there?" Perry wondered aloud.

His father squinted into the fires. "I think so. It's hard to tell; it stopped pushing out all the rage and hate when the Master died."

:I don't sense an absence,: Roya managed.

Before Perry could ask, or say, anything else, he was suddenly set upon by dogs, swarming him from every direction, knocking him to his knees, and covering him with slobbering kisses. It was just as well; they provided all the cover he could have asked for, hiding the fact that he had just broken into a torrent of silent sobs, tears streaming down his face that they licked away with their loving tongues.

20

There was nothing left of the city but a few blackened timbers sticking up out of a sea of ash. Smoke still hung in the air, hovering in skeins over the top of the ruins, and the stench of smoke permeated everything. Here and there parts of the ruins still smoldered, sending up threads of more smoke to join the rest.

Perry closed his eyes, concentrated, and searched for the presence, his heart in his mouth. When his father had told him last night what Roya had said the entity actually was, he had nearly felt crushed with guilt. It was bad enough that he might actually be the cause of all the death and destruction that had occurred. Difficult as it was to face, he knew he might have triggered it when he ran away against his father's orders, so sure he was doing the right thing. But it would be so much worse if he'd been the cause of the "death" of a strange and wonderful creature that had lived and died without any of them aware it had even been there until it was too late. He was terrified that he would search for the entity now, and find nothing.

What he finally felt was so unlike the concentrated rage he'd sensed before that he almost missed it.

There was still a presence there, but it wasn't looming over the ruins in rage, not even in muted anger. Instead, he felt something entirely different from the entity hovering there.

Soft, silent grief. The entity no longer loomed with menace; it hunched over the ruins in a posture of mourning.

"It's still there!" he called out to Roya, and he jumped on the King-Stag's back. "It's still alive!" He sneezed from the smoke and ashes in the air, but he felt impelled to draw nearer to the creature.

He expected Roya to gallop down to the ring of ashes and stubs that represented the palisade, but the *dyheli* took his time, pacing gravely toward the ruins at a slow walk, head bobbing with each step. *:Talk to it,:* the King-Stag urged. *:Get its attention. See if you can get it to talk to you again.:*

"It didn't exactly talk to me the last time," Perry objected, but he did as the *dyheli* asked, anyway, projecting images and emotions at the invisible presence as hard as he could, a combination of *thank you,* and *we're still here,* and *how can I help?* It was so strange—now that he sensed it again, the presence was so strong he expected to see it when he opened his eyes and looked up, but there was nothing there but the sky and the smoke.

It wasn't until they reached where the gates had once stood that he seemed to get the entity's attention. He sensed it coming out of grief, sensed it turning toward him, sensed it bending its full regard—thankfully, minus the hate and rage—on him. He closed his eyes again, and "saw" it against the dark on the inside of his eyelids, still amorphous, with a masklike "face"—but now the eyes of the mask dripped tears of grief so profound he felt his own eyes sting.

How can I help you? he cried to it again, unable to bear the thought that this creature was so lost in sorrow.

He sensed it reaching out blindly to him, only half-aware of his presence but seeking some sort of comfort from him.

And then he was caught up in memory that was not his own, as the creature mourned for what was lost and for what might have been. Quickly, Perry brought Roya into this melding of minds with him, and Roya did not resist. *If I need to break free, two are better than one, and Roya has the strongest mind I know,* he reasoned. *And if I don't need to break free—I want a witness.*

The creature did not know what it was, or what spark of life had brought it into being. It did not know how long it had been here, bound to this piece of land and unable to go beyond it. It only knew that one day, it became aware that there was more to life than the passing of the seasons and the slow procession of the years. One day it became aware of itself, and in that awareness, knew that it was *lonely.* It began to search, sifting through all the thoughts that came to it, for more of its own kind. And finding none, year after turning year, it looked for something, anything else, that could keep it company.

The simpler birds and animals were not enough. But dim with distance, it heard the thoughts of other creatures, things that called themselves *people,* and *humans,* and it tried to call to them.

But they could not hear it, not in any meaningful way; they did not return its salutations and were not drawn to it, and for a time it lapsed into apathy and depression, isolated and miserable. It feared that it would be alone forever. It thought that all it would ever be able to do was observe, never interacting, never *speaking* and never being answered.

But one day, seeing a far-off woman lure a wild cat into her home with the promise of food and a warm hearth, it had an idea.

What if it could lure humans to it with a similar promise? The thought became a plan, and the plan became a deed, and it began to grow a sort of "shell" for itself, a shell made of vague, partly understood glimpses of human dwellings and intuitions about what a sustained population would need.

Perry watched in awe and wonder as in the creature's memory a building—the one he had called "The Big House"—literally rose from the soil, emerging as if it were being grown. First, the slatelike roof. Then the wooden supports and walls of the upper story. Then the stair and the second story—all created organically by some mysterious alchemy at the direction of this strange being. Like a root system, it grew sewers beneath the ground to carry away waste and wells and plumbing to bring water in. Like lungs, it grew fireplaces and chimneys. And when the building was complete, so far as it could tell, it moved on to more. The outbuildings came next, as the presence consulted those distant minds as to what was needed. Then the tall fence to protect whoever would come to live there.

Perry could not tell how long this had taken, for the creature had little grasp of time beyond the passing of the seasons. And the entity had paused and rested often, for this was no easy thing to do.

It rested for a longer time when the inner compound was done, and waited, sending out a vague message of welcome, but then, partly to keep itself busy and partly for the pleasure of the building, it began to create more and more. Building by building, organically, the twisting streets formed, lined by more constructions on either side, until at last there was an entire city outside of the compound.

And at last, at long last, a human came.

It was a strange human, with an odd, sharp, fiery mind, and it was accompanied by others whose minds were foggy and shadow-shrouded. But it saw what the entity had created and it was pleased; it was more than pleased, and it settled into the Big House and within the turn of another season had brought more humans to live in the compound with it.

And now the entity settled into a kind of weary dream state, no longer alone and content to rest until these humans, these people, filled the compound and the streets and "houses" with more of their kind. It had thought that all was good; it would watch them, and help them when it could, and soon, it was sure, they would become aware of it and greet it as a friend and equal.

Until the one in the Big House began the killing.

Now . . . the entity was no stranger to death. It knew humans died from time to time, that they were not immortal, and illness, age, and accident snuffed out their bright lives without warning.

So it did not think at all about it when the first deaths happened. But then . . . then there were more, and more, and suddenly it woke up and realized that it was the first creature, the one that had originally settled in the Big House, that was causing all this death and that it was doing so for the sake of the power that flowed from death. And that made the entity angry.

But what sent it into a rage was when this person snuffed out the three smallest of the human life-sparks and then the lives of the two life-bringers. There was no reason to do this. It was wanton. It was mad. The entity realized then that the first human it had brought here was diseased. And the entity erupted with impotent wrath, for it could not directly do anything, not even to stop the dying.

And for that, it mourned. For that, it sorrowed, a sorrow overlaid with guilt. For if it had not brought that first human here, every one of those dead would still be alive. So it mourned the deaths of the humans it had sought as companions without realizing it had harbored a viper, and it sorrowed for the loss of the beautiful thing it had built that now was nothing but ashes. And it wept that it was alone again, and would always be alone, for how could it lure more humans again, unable to tell if it was giving shelter to yet another evil?

:So make a place for me and my herd,: Roya suggested calmly, intruding on the entity's grief.

? The entity bent its regard again, this time not on Perry but on his companions.

Companions plural, for Larral, two of the ravens, and the firebird family had all come to join him, drawn by curiosity at seeing him standing so still for so long.

:Are we not as good or better than humans?: Roya declared. *:We do not slaughter one another. We eat grass and leaves and would rather avoid those things that wish to kill us than kill them in turn. We will keep you company. Grow again, but grow for us.:*

:And us! Us! Us!: the ravens agreed.

:And we!: the firebirds chorused.

The entity pondered them for a very long time, and a tendril of thought reached out to Perry. Without words, it said, *I trust you* and *I know you* and *Is this a good thing?*

:It would be a very good thing,: he said, reassuring it as he would have reassured the dogs. *:It would be a wonderful thing. The* dyheli, *the Bondbirds, and the firebirds will be grateful to you and care for you.:*

It sent a questioning brush of thought to Roya, who seemed to understand that it was asking *And where do I begin?*

:With a meadow,: Roya replied, simply, and in Roya's mind an idyllic meadow blossomed, the most perfect of dream meadows, watered by clear springs, rich with lush grasses and healing herbs and flowers, with tall trees to offer shade in the heat of the sun, and dust wallows to kill the insects that plagued them, and a warm, sheltered place for the herd to huddle when winter winds blew.

Perry kept his skepticism to himself, but it seemed to him that Roya was asking rather too much of the creature. After all, as far as he could tell, it had taken the entity decades, even centuries, to grow the city.

So his yelp of surprise was completely natural when the

ground in front of them heaved and churned, and suddenly a wave of grass and flowers erupted at their feet and rippled across what had been a sea of ash and burned timbers.

The last lingering taint of smoke was gone, replaced by the scents of flowers, fresh grass, and clean water. Perry stayed with Roya and the others for the rest of the day, making suggestions when Roya ran out of ideas, as Roya's herd slowly gathered around him. His father left him alone once he had come down and satisfied himself that the entity was benign and Perry really was needed. Instead, Mags circled the perimeter of the new meadow, marveling at trees growing up before his very eyes, at berry bushes appearing out of nothing, at a spacious winter shelter not unlike a huge, meadow-topped stable, creating itself out of rock and sod. He might well marvel, since this was, for all intents and purposes, the purest of magic at work. And finally, just at dusk, Perry suggested the final touch, called up by the memory of the glade where the firebird family lived. A barrier of foot-long thorns, as broad as a house and as tall as the three-story buildings had once been, sprang up where the palisade had been.

"Nothing will get in through those," Perry said with satisfaction. "And nothing will want to. They should cut the wind too, which will help in the winter."

The entity agreed and showed Roya how it could open and close a path through the thorns in the space of a few moments. The creature made it clear it could and would do that whenever any of the herd wished to come or go. :*I think we're done,*: Perry thought at the presence. Then something occurred to him :*What do we call you?*: he asked. :*Creatures like us need names. We can't keep calling you "It"—it's rude.*:

What do I do? came the question, as always, not in words, but in concepts. *Call me by what I do.*

Perry thought about that. *:I think you—guard. You're Guardian.:*

Yes.

And then, as if the building of this little *dyheli* paradise had been occupying all of its mind, the entity suddenly *looked,* with all its attention, on what it had built. Looked at the *dyheli,* who had already taken possession of it, at the foals pronking and dashing around their mothers, at the yearlings scampering to explore every finger-length, at the does and young stags looking about and realizing with incredulity that here, at last, they were *safe.* . . .

Guardian looked at all this with wonder and amazement, as if it could not believe it had done all this—sensed the thoughts of its new companions, then opened up to those thoughts and encompassed them. And suddenly, it exploded in an overwhelming burst of pure, blinding joy.

It was like being hit with a brilliant white light for a moment, but a light that held only brightness and wonder and elation with no room for grief, for guilt, or for sorrow. It wiped away all thought. And when Perry came back to himself he found he was grinning and crying all at the same time.

Mags watched his sleeping son by the light of the last fire he would ever light in this little cave, and wondered, *what now?* Obviously nothing was going to be the same. Perry had gone through too much, and the shadow of adulthood lay over his sleeping face as he lay cuddled up with Larral. He'd hoped to help Perry grow up a bit on this journey—but he hadn't intended it to be so fast or at such a cost.

:We never intend that, but it happens anyway,: Dallen reminded him.

He sighed. *:He's never going to be a Herald, is he?:*

:No, he won't. Not that he hasn't got a good heart, but he's

too pragmatic to be a Herald,: Dallen replied. *:That's partly what you see now, all that pragmatism coming to the fore, shaped by what he's gone through. He'll do things you wouldn't and sleep soundly afterward. Not,:* the Companion added, *:that you need to worry about him becoming anything other than another Lord Jorthun.:*

Mags bit his lower lip. There was something to be said for that. Perry would not hesitate—just as he had not hesitated to run away and do what Mags was not willing to do. And Mags had the feeling that if it had been Perry who had gotten the orders that he and Mags were to get rid of the Master no matter the cost, if Perry—or at least an adult version of Perry—had determined there was no other way, Perry would not have hesitated as Mags had.

Actually, an adult version of Perry would have done what the boy had done—he'd just have been smarter about it, and he'd have made certain that he convinced Mags to go along with it too. And if he'd done that? Things probably would have turned out differently. Maybe better.

:Well, we just have to get him there, then,: he replied. *:Make sure he gets the experience and knowledge he needs so he doesn't make stupid decisions. And then, turn him loose as the King's Spymaster.:*

:That won't be for a good long while yet,: Dallen assured him. *:Meanwhile . . . don't forget to give him time to be just Perry.:*

Mags smiled a little and settled into his bedroll. *:I'm sure you'll be there to remind me, horse.:*

His only answer was a snort.

In the morning they set off for the inn—just the two of them, the dog pack, and Larral, for the dyheli and the birds were settling into their new paradise, and Guardian was brooding happily over them all like a mother hen with new chicks. "I don't know how we're going to feed the pack," Perry fretted, for the fifth or sixth time.

"We're close to the inn, and we know what they were doing now," his father said, with his jaw set. "I'll be very surprised if we can't take whatever provisions we want, backed up by the dogs. And they'll count themselves damned lucky if that's all we do."

But Larral, scouting ahead, reported that there was no one there; they picked up their pace, and discovered it was, as Larral reported, utterly deserted.

"Huh." Mags dismounted, as did Perry; Mags went inside to examine the rooms, and Perry and Larral scouted around the outside. There were signs that the five horses had been there, and a wagon and the goats, but all of them were gone now. There didn't seem to be as many hens as Perry remembered, and the ones that were there were scratching around in a disconsolate fashion, with not so much as a grain in sight. Perry went to the stable and got a generous helping of oats to scatter for them, feeling they ought to have one good last meal. He found nests in the stables and collected four eggs, then went to join his father inside the inn.

:I smell ten people,: Larral said finally, when they gathered at a table in the common room.

"I found all the belongings stripped from the room upstairs and the cook's room," Mags reported. "And it looks like they loaded up their wagon with that and enough supplies to get them to a town. I think that at least some of the mercenaries escaped the fire, and fled through here to tell the fellows that were kidnapping travelers what had happened. Maybe they caught some of the horses, too."

Perry hoped one of them had been the captain. He might have participated in some terrible things . . . but he hadn't done so willingly, and he'd been kind to Perry. "Well, it looks like they made a meal of the hens before they left," he offered.

"I guess there wasn't room in the wagon to take much but their things and the goats."

"Let's make a good meal ourselves and get a decent night's sleep," Mags continued. "Then we'll load up the dogs with packs of food. They can each take their own rations. I think there's enough miscellaneous cloth to make basic packs."

Perry brightened at that idea. "They'll abide it and not try and eat what they're carrying if I tell them not to," he assured his father. He'd been worried about how they were going to transport enough to feed each dog, but this, clearly was the way. The mastiffs could carry quite a bit if they weren't having to run.

The remaining hens met their fate. He, his father, and Larral made a good meal of it with a stew made of one of the hens and the fresh vegetables they'd found still hanging in the larder. The rest of the hens fed the dogs that evening. Then he and Mags made up beds on the floor of what had been the common room, next to the fire. Mags fell asleep right away, but Perry stayed awake, brooding into the coals.

Finally thoughts that had only been vague before began to solidify as he examined them. *:Are you awake?:* he asked Larral.

The *kyree* yawned. *:I am. Your head has been very busy.:*

:I was feeling horrible because I thought I was the one that woke up Guardian and made the Master start killing people.:

:Yes, you were. And you know that still might have been the case,: Larral pointed out. *:There is nothing that Guardian showed you to contradict that.:*

:But Guardian was feeling guilty, because he gave the Master the city, and he thought if he hadn't done that, all those people would still be alive.:

:That's true as well.: Larral wasn't offering any advice. And Perry didn't really want any. What he wanted was to articulate something, then see what Larral thought of it.

:And we're both right. And we're both wrong. Because the

one that's really to blame is the Master. Guardian just offered a home. All I did was . . . show up. The Master is the one who decided to kill people.: He frowned. :But am I trying to give excuses for myself? I'd do it all over again. The Master had to be stopped.:

:That is also true. And I would have made the same decision to go with you. But it's also true we could have done better with your father's help.: Larral sighed. :We did what we could with the information we had, but in hindsight, it would have been much wiser not to go alone.:

:Which means . . . next time, we get more information. Next time, we fight for what we think is right and don't just run. We take the time we didn't take before. If we'd done that, maybe we'd have been able to help more people.: He felt more at ease now. Better able to sleep.

The next day, they gathered up everything of use that the dogs could carry. There was old canvas, some bedding, and curtains to cut up and make into crude dog packs, and a bit more human food as well that was worth packing up and taking. There was plenty of dried meat and fish to supply the dogs for a few days, and Larral had assured them both that he could make up the rest by leading them out to hunt once the group stopped for the night.

The handful of days it took to get to Whithern passed quickly; Perry was very glad that Arville knew they were coming, because that meant there would be a hot meal, plenty of food for the dogs, and clean beds waiting for them. They rode into the village of Whithern surrounded by the dog pack, with Larral at their head.

It occurred to Perry that it must look as if they were arriving at Whithern straight from a hunt, much to the astonishment of the village. Perry kept his mouth shut; Mags made up a sufficiently vague story about finding the pack with their dead dogmaster and being adopted by them.

Arville knew the truth, of course—and it was Arville that

had the best idea of what to do with them. The dogs were very happy to eat and bed down in the stables as soon as they arrived; traveling all day was more tiring for them than hunting. Arville made his proposal over an excellent meal of chicken and dumplings.

"These are mastiffs," he pointed out. "I bet a third or a half of the houses in the village'd like to have one. Protection for the house, protection for the littles, and a hunting pack come fall. Let me go around tomorrow and find out who wants one."

He was as good as his word. He left as soon as they'd all eaten breakfast. Before Mags and Perry had gotten the caravan half packed, he was back with a list of seven families who each wanted a dog, and the village headman wanted two.

So after dinner, Perry went off to the village with the entire pack, and one at a time, he managed to find dogs that suited families, and families that suited dogs. Then he made quite sure that each dog that was to remain had a very clear idea of his duties and knew that he was to be a very good boy to his new family. The dogs not only understood this, but when they realized they were each to be the only dog for a family with several children who were already impatient to play with them, they were overjoyed. As for the headman's two . . . they were siblings, and would have been unhappy separated. So when they drove off again the next day, it was with nine fewer dogs.

And as they moved back through Valdemar toward Haven, they left behind dogs, one here, another there, with innkeepers and farmers, herders and hunters. Until by the time they rode up the Hill to the gates of the Palace, there were just four—the best of the pack, in Perry's opinion—left.

———————

Mags had never been happier to see the roofs of Haven in the distance or the gates of the Palace as they came up the Hill. At the point when they'd cut down the pack to just a few dogs, the dogs had been able to ride in the caravan, saving their energy and allowing them all to move faster. Thanks to Rolan, Amily would know to the moment when they were going to ride in through the gates of the Palace, and so would all their friends. So Mags wasn't at all surprised when the whole family was there at the gate to meet them. What did surprise him was that Lady Dia, Queen Lydia, and the four royal children were all there as well.

Of course, no one mattered to him as much as Amily. He didn't actually remember dismounting from Dallen; it seemed as if one moment he was coming through the gates and seeing her, and the next she was in his arms. He found he was shaking with emotion; he half dreaded what she was going to say to him about what he had allowed Perry to endure. But she said nothing, just held him as tightly as he held her, and finally he relaxed and simply reveled in being together again. And it was some time before he broke off the embrace to discover that Perry had already taken control of the greetings himself—mostly by distributing presents.

Very large and impressive presents. . . .

". . . and I'll be right here to make sure they know their job," Perry was saying earnestly to the Queen, as all four royal children flung themselves all over two of the mastiffs. "They'll be better than having a Guard in the room." And then he dropped down on one knee next to baby Kee, who had wrapped both arms around a patient mastiff's foreleg. "And now you don't ever need to be afraid of anything again, Kee. This fellow is as brave as gryphon and fierce as a thunderstorm. I picked him out especially for you. What are you going to call him?"

"Gryphon," Kee said decidedly, looking up into the mastiff's face. The dog gravely bent and plastered Kee's entire face with his enormous tongue, making Kee burst into giggles. Mags would have given a lot to see into the dog's mind just now, because the tail was drumming a fast beat on the ground.

It appeared that this was love at first sight for both the little prince and the enormous dog.

Perry smiled and left his friends to argue over what the name of the other mastiff should be, and he turned to Lady Dia as Mags and Amily watched. Mags was . . . astonished, in a very pleased way. He'd had no idea this was what Perry had had in mind when he'd insisted on keeping these four dogs. He'd more than half suspected that Perry expected to keep them himself, and he'd been trying to work out how much trouble they'd be in the suite.

"And these two are for you, Lady Dia," Perry said gravely. "I can never repay you and Lord Jorthun for all the training you've given me—and are going to keep on giving me—but at least this is a start."

"They're *beautiful,* Perry!" Dia replied, stunned. She dropped to her knees next to the dogs, heedless of her fine gown. "Oh, aren't you *magnificent,* my very good boys!"

Good boy were words both dogs understood very well, and they immediately wagged their tails with enthusiasm. And when everything in Dia's posture suggested she was not at all averse to being sniffed and examined—which they had probably wanted to very much, given that not even her perfume would ever cover up the scent of her other dogs to sensitive canine noses—that was what they did. Her response, scratching behind their ears and under their chins, cooing about *what good boys* they were, cemented it. They were hers for life.

Oh, Perry was helping with that, Amily thought at him, amused.

:I'd have been surprised if he weren't,: Mags replied.

But Perry had turned to his siblings. "Open your hands and shut your eyes," he commanded. "I'm going to give you a big surprise."

For once, perhaps seeing the gifts he'd given the others, they did it at once without considering any trickery.

Which was just as well, since there wasn't any trickery.

Mags blinked to see what Perry pulled out of his pack. He was as surprised as the children were going to be. How had Perry kept that secret for this entire trip? How had he kept his father from catching so much as a glimpse?

Because Perry is going to be a very, very good spy, he decided.

When Abi and Tory felt a faint tickle on their palms, they closed their hands quickly and opened their eyes.

Abi's eyes went huge and round, to match Tory's mouth. She couldn't manage to get out a word. Tory could only manage "Oh!" In their hands were one brightly glowing feather, each—glowing with enough light to be visible even in the bright sunlight. Abi had what looked like a male's scarlet and yellow primary. Tory had one of the shorter, purple tail-coverts.

"Those are firebird feathers," Perry said with great satisfaction. "Abi, that wing feather is bright enough at night to read by, and you can use it as a bookmark if you want to sleep."

"Perry!" Amily laughed. "Don't encourage her! She reads too much at night as it is!"

"And Tory, your feather is just bright enough at night to use as a nightlight. So you won't stub your toes in the dark anymore." Mags was astonished all over again at Perry's newfound sensitivity. Or had he been that sensitive all along and his father had never noticed it? Because Tory suffered from nightmares and had wanted a nightlight, but everything Mags and Amily had tried had been too bright or burned out too quickly. He had thought that the other two children were blissfully unaware of Tory's problem, and certainly Tory had begged them to say nothing about it.

Tory just cradled the feather in his hand and gazed at it in grateful wonder.

"Hey." Perry poked his brother playfully. "You *told* me to bring you something shiny. So I did."

"You *did!*" Tory finally managed. "You're—a champion!"

Perry beamed. "Does this mean I get first pick of the pocket pies now?" he asked.

Tory closed his hand carefully around his feather. Abi was already halfway back to the Palace with hers. "Maaaaybe," he said warily.

"Back to our rooms, all of you," Amily said, in a firm voice, as stablehands came to take care of Dallen and the horses and caravan. "It will be supper time soon, and I want you to be clean in time for it." Tory ran off after his sister. Perry lingered.

"On that note, I am going to take my leave before these handsome fellows get restless," Dia said. "And Perry, we'll expect you at the manor some time in the next three days to continue your lessons."

"Yes, Lady Dia," Perry said immediately, looking pleased. Dia departed for her manor with her dogs trotting precisely at her side.

"And we should be doing the same," Lydia agreed. "We'll have to make arrangements for feeding, sleeping, and so on for Gryphon and Drake."

"They're housebroken," Perry said helpfully. "I'll come with you and show them where you want them to go and how to get there." Queen Lydia and her children headed back to the Palace with Kee actually riding on Gryphon—and the mastiff allowing it, Perry walking alongside with Larral, chattering about what the mastiffs needed. Amily and Mags took their time sauntering back to their quarters.

"I'm not angry," Amily said, as soon as there was no one to overhear them. "I was, but then I realized that Perry was going to get his way once he got his mind made up, and nothing short of tying him up and gagging him was going to stop him."

Mags sighed with relief. "We raised a headstrong child."

"We raised a child with strong ideas of right and wrong and the drive to correct the wrongs," Amily corrected.

I don't think that's it, exactly, Mags thought, but he kept his thoughts to himself.

"Rolan tells me, however, that he is not . . . quite right to be a Herald," she continued calmly. "I had had my suspicions, but this trip confirmed them."

"I don't think he actually wants to be one, either. And he's got Larral," Mags pointed out, at which Amily broke into laughter.

"Larral! I looked up *kyree* when Rolan told me about him, but I didn't think they were as big as a mastiff!" She shook her head. "At least he should have the sense to stay out from underfoot."

"He's an adult by their reckoning. He's more likely to join in our conversations whether we want him to or not. Oh, and you'll be able to hear him; he Mindspeaks. He also attempts human speech, though I expect you and Perry will have to interpret until we get used to it." He had to smirk a little at her look of surprise. "Things are going to be interesting for a while."

She stopped just as they reached the entrance. "I'm not at all unhappy about this," she said quietly. "In fact, I don't care if *none* of them become Heralds. I just want them to discover something they can do that makes them contented and feeling as if they are doing something worth doing."

He pulled her closer for a moment. "That sounds like very good sense."

"Of course it does," she replied. "I said it."

"Yes, dear," he replied, with faint mockery. "Of course, dear. Whatever you say."

"Beast," she replied without rancor. "Let's go feed the starving mob. With a side trip to organize something for the monster *kyree*."

He let her go, and slipped his arm around her waist. "It's good to be back home," he told her, opening the door for her.

"It's better to have you," she replied. "I hope you never have to do something that takes you away from us again."

"From your mouth to the gods' ears," he told her. *If only.* . . .